# All the Moments of Forever

## A Time Equation Novel

# E. S. Martell

All The Moments in Forever

Copyright © 2017 by Eric S. Martell

Second Initiative Press

Printed in the USA
ISBN: 978-0-9989805-0-8
All rights reserved.

No portion of this book may be reproduced in any form without written permission from the publisher or author, except as permitted by U.S. copyright law.

*Vox audita perit littera scripta manet.*

This is a work of fiction. All the characters and events portrayed in this book are fictional, and any resemblance to real people or incidents is purely coincidental.

<u>Dedication</u>

This book is dedicated to my readers who asked for a follow-up to my first time-travel novel: Heart of Fire Time of Ice.

Thanks for reading and enjoying!

# With All the Time in Forever, Will She Have Enough?

Kathleen's quantum physics research allowed her to develop a mathematical formula that gave her control of time-travel. At least one shadowy group besides her government wants her secret. After having escaped a deadly attack by inadvertently jumping into the Pleistocene, Kathleen found a way to break her self-imposed barriers and not only survive but thrive with the aid of a handsome Clovis culture hunter.

Now the two have been driven out of their refuge in the inter-glacial Sangamon period by hostile pre-humans. Forced to return to modern times for medical assistance, they find that the same antagonistic forces are still at work.

The government wants time-travel for unspecified strategic reasons and has developed a method based on another time-traveler's experiences. Unfortunately, this method has proven to be unreliable, stranding the initial traveler in the distant past. Now they want Kathleen's information even more than before and will stop at nothing to get it.

Cadeyrin is captured and held hostage until she surrenders her formula. Will he be set free if she cooperates? And what about the mysterious other group that wants the secret?

Once again, Kathleen Whitby meets a seemingly insurmountable set of challenges. Will her intelligence and natural creativity allow her to overcome the complex mixture of enemies and problems she now faces?

# Contents

# <u>Acknowledgments</u>

I rely on my wife, Sally, for critique and feedback. She also makes sure I eat while I'm writing, which is helpful and convenient. Without her help, my stories would never find their way out of my head.

I'd also like to give thanks to Fred Alan Wolf, Ph.D. whose ideas on time-travel greatly influenced the story.

I owe thanks to the American Museum of Natural History for stimulating my childhood interest in prehistoric fauna.

My special thanks to Aleksandra Klepacka for her wonderful cover and back page art. She is talented and exceptionally good at understanding what the story demands in terms of cover art. Her cover illustration compliments the story quite nicely.

Grateful thanks to Adriana D'Apolito and 3P Editing for her many invaluable suggestions. Her careful work greatly increased the readability of the manuscript.

Thanks for the overall cover design and typesetting go to Kelley York of SleepyFoxStudio.

# From the Author

This story is a sequel to Heart of Fire Time of Ice. I had originally intended that to be a stand-alone novel, and it works well by itself. It introduced Kathleen and Cadeyrin, and two other characters: Reed and Geoff Jarpe (Kathleen's attorney). I loved writing about Kathleen. Her character showed a tremendous amount of growth throughout the book. This personal transition continues into the present story.

Writing Heart of Fire Time of Ice required me to invest so much energy in researching time-travel and the past that I wasn't ready to give up on the idea.

As a result, I wrote Paradox: On the Sharp Edge of the Blade. This is the story of Logan Walker and Serensaa. Professor Wolf makes an appearance near the end of Paradox and his role continues in the present story.

Readers will be able to enjoy All of the Moments in Forever without having read either of the other two books. Still, since the books are woven together in a loose trilogy, there are inescapable cross-references. I've tried to keep these to a minimum, and I have made an effort to explain them when they occur.

Not all readers appreciate prequels, and so I didn't write one for this current story. Instead, my approach required blending bits of the characters' individual histories into the story to give the reader a better insight into their motivations.

I recommend you read the three novels in sequence to ensure a better understanding of the present story. Then, if you are still interested, you can follow up with the two additional books in the series.

Finally, I want you to know that I greatly appreciate your reading this story. I promise that I will do my best to ensure that you won't feel that you've wasted your time.

I sincerely hope you enjoy the story.

*Namaste,*

*Eric Martell*

# Chapter One

# A Threat

Kathleen paused and looked around in sudden alarm. Something was wrong. She didn't know what she'd sensed, but there was an indefinable feeling of presence. There was something in the dense evergreens, something that might represent danger. Ulfsa had stopped a few feet ahead of her, his ears flat and his back fur ridged. His lips were drawn back in a silent snarl displaying all of the threat he could muster. The wolf's tail was clamped tightly against his haunches. Whatever it was, it frightened him. She shrugged the sling of her rifle off her shoulder and cradled the weapon in both hands, ready for action.

The mid-Sangamon interglacial period was not without its normal dangers. The North American mega-fauna was threat enough for any human, regardless of how well they were armed.

Kathleen and Cadeyrin had set their home in the middle of a howling wilderness almost exactly one-hundred-thousand years BCE. The animals held no surprises for Cadeyrin. He'd lived all of his life hunting them. The thing that he continually marveled over was their number.

Here in pre-human North America, the animals thronged. In Cadeyrin's home time, the last part of the Pleistocene during the final glaciation period, there had been far fewer animals. Their sparsity was more due to the harsh climate than the actions of humans, although humans did their share of killing.

Fire drives often resulted in far more dead animals than the hunters of that time could use. This waste was thought to be a necessary part of hunting, but Cadeyrin's people generally were conservation-oriented, killing only what they needed. They usually did not engage in fire drives. Those were the provenance of the first tribes, the ones who had migrated from Siberia.

For her part, Kathleen sometimes thought it was amazing that humans had survived long enough to form modern civilization. Her origin in the twenty-first century hadn't prepared her for such a life. At first, she'd had a difficult time adapting. Had it not been for Cadeyrin, she would have been killed many times over. Now, despite her initial handicap, she had become a seasoned huntress. She was proud that he no longer worried about her going out alone.

Cadeyrin was a Clovis culture hunter. His ancestors had come from Europe, following seals along the edge of the sea ice. Kathleen had been lucky to encounter him; he'd saved her from becoming the prey of a Smilodon, a saber-tooth tiger during their initial meeting. She'd been thankful every day since. The two had fallen deeply in love, and after some cultural and personal missteps, they had bonded irrevocably. The twenty-first-century physicist and the ice-age hunter were mated, and neither could imagine life without the other.

Now she felt a heightened tension in the air as if whatever it was had decided to attack. The sense of presence grew imperceptibly. There was a sensation of threat. She raised her carbine, a hard-hitting thirty caliber, and prepared to empty the magazine. She'd purchased thirty-round magazines and had never regretted it. Better to have too much fire-power than not enough.

Ulfsa shifted nervously. He'd arrived just a few minutes earlier. When she and Cadeyrin had started their hunt, Ulfsa had gone with the man. Their intent was to jump a deer. If Cadeyrin couldn't shoot it immediately, Ulfsa would trail the animal.

Most deer would eventually circle, coming back to familiar ground. The wolf would continue to follow, guided by his exquisite sense of smell, until the deer circled. On its way back, there was a good chance that it would pass within range of either Kathleen or Cadeyrin.

Kathleen had been looking for an open area in the heavy spruces. While a deer would travel quickly through the trees, it was more likely to run through an open area when tired. When Ulfsa came up, she realized that he'd lost the trail or, as it now appeared, something more serious had arisen.

The wind shifted, eddying around the spruces, carrying the scent of resin, and something strange. She sniffed. It was like…somewhat like a heavy, musky body odor. Her mind flashed back to a day at the Minneapolis Zoo. It had been hot. When she'd walked by the gorilla enclosure, one of the male gorillas had been near her location. The current scent reminded her of his strong body odor.

No gorillas here, she thought. It must be something else. I hope it's not a bear.

She turned slightly. The presence had moved to a thicker clump of fir trees. She couldn't actually see anything. She'd somehow sensed its movement. She glanced quickly down at the wolf. He was looking fixedly at the same clump. She lifted her rifle, aimed, and squeezed the trigger. The bullet ripped through the fir branches as the sound of the shot rang through the air. She waited.

Nothing happened. She gradually became aware that the tension had dissipated. Whatever it was had retreated when she shot. Ulfsa had lifted his ears, and his tail had returned to its normal position.

There was a sound in the brush behind her. She didn't turn, recognizing the oncoming steps as those of Cadeyrin. He was running at full speed.

He stopped beside her, panting. He held his rifle at the ready also. After a moment, he sniffed the breeze, then lowered his firearm.

"Gone," he said. "Let's move forward a little so I can check the area."

Kathleen felt a sense of relief at his presence. She could rely on his keen senses to detect things that she would miss. Her heart beat faster as he brushed past her. She amazed herself. They'd been mated for several months, and she still quivered with anticipation when he touched her. She'd never get tired of his body and his incredibly quick mind. His English was now almost flawless.

They walked forward silently, paced by their wolf partner.

There was a scuffed mark in the forest floor on the far side of the fir trees. Cadeyrin bent down, inspected it, then walked on. He abruptly stopped, pointing at a soft patch of earth. A large footprint indented the ground.

Kathleen's first thought was that it was a large bear, but then she saw that the conformation of the track was wrong. It looked more human than bear-like.

Cadeyrin grunted, then explained, "Forest Giant, I think."

Kathleen jerked in surprise and looked to see if he were serious. She shook her head negatively, then said, "We're too early for there to be any men here. When we moved back from your time to now, I was careful to move us far enough back that no humans would have come to this part of the world. There are humans right now across the seas, but my people have never found any remains from this time here on this land. The soonest any humans will arrive on this continent will be fifty-thousand years from now."

He smiled, obviously liking what he saw as he gazed into her eyes. "Yet, there is the track. It does not tell an untruth," he said.

She looked at the print again. It did look human, but it was quite wide and much longer than her own foot. She glanced at Cadeyrin's moccasin-shod feet. The print in the soft earth dwarfed them. If foot size was indicative of the creature's height, it would be huge.

"How large is this thing, anyway?" she asked.

Cadeyrin thought for a moment, then answered. "I've never seen one. They were very rare in my time. Perhaps there are more now. I've heard that they may be somewhat taller than me, but not much." He held his hand a good foot over his head, leading Kathleen to understand that his idea of not much and hers differed considerably.

He added, "They are also supposed to be heavier than all but the largest man. Look at the track, see how deep it is? Now watch this."

He stepped down in the soft earth, his foot leaving a print beside the larger one. It was only about half as deep. Kathleen knew that Cadeyrin was at least two hundred pounds, probably more. He had very little fat and was quite heavily muscled, something that she found incredibly attractive. She shook her head, trying to clear her thoughts of his body. That meant the unseen creature weighed over four hundred pounds. It must be quite bulky.

She asked, "How strong are they?"

Cadeyrin shrugged. "I don't know. It was said that they are much stronger than men. They are dangerous, but they only carry sticks, not pointed weapons."

He paused again. "If they are here, they know we are here also. They may become a problem for us. The old stories say they are enemies to men. I want you to always carry a weapon. If you don't have your rifle, at least carry a pistol. I don't want one of them catching you by yourself and unarmed. The stories say they will kidnap human women."

Kathleen shuddered. She'd been threatened by enemy tribesmen in the past and didn't want to relive that experience. She looked up at her mate and said, "I promise. I'll be careful."

He turned and led her back the way they'd come. After a few hundred paces, he said, "Let's go out to the forest edge. Perhaps we can find some prey there. It's getting late, and the deer will be coming out to feed."

———— ◆ ————

Kathleen mulled the afternoon's discovery over in her mind. The idea that there was an indigenous population of possibly hostile hominins made her quite nervous. She didn't like the thought of having to constantly watch for intelligent enemies in addition to the ever-present large predators.

If they couldn't live safely in the here and now, then she'd have to figure out another time for them. She briefly thought of bringing Cadeyrin back to the twenty-first century. She imagined him in modern clothes walking across the university campus. Every time he went out in public, he'd probably be attacked by lustful women. He was, she thought, very desirable. That led her to another topic.

Cadeyrin was sitting at the table of their travel trailer, his back to her. He was working on cleaning their weapons. He had a natural ability for mechanical work. She attributed it to his mastery of flint-knapping, but wherever it came from, he had quickly learned to clean the firearms. He could field strip and reassemble them like a trained soldier.

She moved over behind him, bending to nuzzle his neck. He placed the mechanism he was cleaning on the table and caught her arms, turning his head so that their lips met. One thing quickly led to another, with the result that it was dark before they'd fixed their evening meal.

During the night, she lay awake thinking. In addition to possible competition for Cadeyrin's affections, moving back to her time also had another drawback. It was highly likely that the government agency that had tried to co-opt her method of time-travel would try to force her to disclose it. They thought it would be useful for military and espionage work. She didn't think those people would give up easily.

The possible use of time-travel for espionage undoubtedly represented a true prize for the government. It would provide a significant advantage for the side that owned it. That was something she didn't want to see. She was afraid that it would almost instantly destabilize the global political structure.

The time-travel method was her discovery, and since she was the only one who understood it, she felt that it was her property. To have a bunch of bureaucrats trying to force her to pass the information on was not something she wanted. Yet, if it wasn't safe for them here in the Sangamon, they'd have to go somewhere or somewhen else. She wasn't sure how to answer the question of where.

Well, when you don't know what to do, the best thing is to gather more information about the choices. Either you'll discover something that helps you make up your mind, or the situation will change while you're waiting.

She decided to shelve the problem for a while. Perhaps the answer would be obvious tomorrow.

# Chapter Two

# Attack

A loud thump on the side of the trailer woke them. Cadeyrin was out of bed and by the door with a rifle in his hands before Kathleen got her feet on the floor. He motioned for her to get her weapon and join him.

She groped in the dark, shaking with alarm, and then caught up her rifle, slotted a full magazine in place by touch, and allowed the bolt to slam home. Cadeyrin hissed at her in response to the noise.

There was another thump near the front of the trailer, then a horrible crash as something large hit near the door. The wall bulged inward, and a piece of the interior paneling split off.

Cadeyrin swung the door wide, looked out, then loosed a series of shots at something. There was a scream of mixed rage and pain from the darkness outside, then something crashed against the door frame, struck Cadeyrin in the side in passing, and impacted loudly against a cabinet.

Cadeyrin had dropped to his knees. Kathleen jumped behind him and looked out the door. There was something large and black charging at the opening. She jerked her rifle up and shot again and again. The thing dropped only to be replaced by another oncoming mass. She fired four more shots at its middle. It bent over and moved off to the side, groaning as it went.

That was all. Things became very silent, save for Cadeyrin's labored breathing. Kathleen located one of the combat flashlights and scanned the area outside. There was nothing. Either the two creatures she'd shot had been wounded and had left, or their friends had dragged them away. She could see a smear of bright red blood on the grass, so there had been something there. It hadn't been some horrible nightmare.

She turned to Cadeyrin. His face was white, and he was having difficulty breathing. Sudden concern suddenly flooded over Kathleen. She'd thought he was just startled. "What's wrong? Where are you hurt?" she asked.

Cadeyrin's voice was weak and hoarse. "It hit my left side. I think it broke some ribs." He paused, gasping for breath. "It feels like I can't breathe."

The flashlight revealed a large stone that had smashed in the cabinet on the wall. It had struck with such force that it bent the door jamb out of shape. It was lucky that the jamb had absorbed some of the energy. If it had hit Cadeyrin directly, it was large enough to have smashed his chest totally.

She knelt and felt his side. He gasped with the pain as she touched the rapidly spreading bruise. She looked up at his face. It was pale and drawn with pain, but he tried to smile reassuringly at her. "I'll be alright. I've broken ribs before. It will be painful to move for two or three hands of days, but I'll get over it," he whispered, then coughed, wincing.

Kathleen suppressed a gasp of alarm. Blood was now running from his lips. He wiped at his mouth, his hand coming away covered with blood. He looked at her, opened his mouth to speak, but then lay down with a groan.

Kathleen said, "The broken bones have punctured your lung. We need help for this. We'll have to go to my time."

He shook his head in weak denial. She'd traveled back and forth repeatedly, bringing needed supplies back with each trip, but he had refused to go with her.

She'd been trying to teach him to travel through the years, using her formula, paired with an altered state of consciousness. She knew he could achieve the altered state needed, but somehow he had never mastered the trick of blending it with the visualization of the relationship between the mathematics of time and his physical energy field.

He'd told her that he worried about somehow becoming separated from her in time. She'd always found him before, but perhaps if he were moving temporally, she'd be unable to locate him. He couldn't bear the thought of never seeing her again.

Cadeyrin coughed again, drawing her back to the present. More blood was leaking from his lips. She realized that his injury was serious.

A sudden whine from the door ripped her attention from his face. She whirled with the rifle at the ready. It was Ulfsa. Their wolf was struggling to get inside, but his right foreleg wasn't cooperating. They'd hurt him as well. Kathleen grabbed his left leg and pulled, helping the big wolf inside. He made no attempt to bite, although the movement must have hurt his damaged leg.

At that point, there was another crash from the rear of the trailer. The attackers had hurled another stone at the flimsy structure. Kathleen dropped her rifle, grabbed the wolf with one hand and Cadeyrin's wrist with the other. She closed her eyes, concentrating on her formula, as she tried to get her mind in the right state. If only she weren't shaking so badly.

There was a growl from the door. Kathleen involuntarily opened her eyes. An ugly, human-like face was looking at her. She closed her eyes again and concentrated more intently.

⸺◆⸺

The large, hairy hominid squeezed through the small opening. The creatures that had invaded what the dominant male considered the group's home territory were no longer inside. The strange space was full of exotic scents and odd items. He pulled at some of them, easily ripping things off the walls. Frustrated, he slammed his fists wildly around, wrecking the interior of the trailer.

He kicked something that moved. He squatted a little and then seized the thing. It looked like a shiny stick. He fumbled with it, then took hold with both huge hands and wrenched. There was a crack as the wood broke.

The other part swung towards him as the rifle broke in half. The now exposed trigger struck a broken piece of paneling, and the gun exploded with a boom. The bullet hit the creature, and it dropped, partially blocking the door.

Outside, others of his kind looked on. They made calling noises, but the big one, their leader, moved no longer. They backed away in fear.

They had set out to drive the unwanted small ones away. Now the invaders were gone, but so was their leader. They murmured together as they moved back into the dark. They wouldn't come back to this site. It was dangerous. Perhaps the small ones had left some powerful curse.

They would move on to another part of their territory and not return.

———◆◇◆———

It was bright daylight. Kathleen opened her eyes, shading them from the glare. They were in the middle of an asphalt road, the country road that she always took to go back to Minneapolis.

Her present-day house was just a few yards away. She hurried to the garage for the Land Rover, regretting that she'd never brought Cadeyrin to this time. It took a couple of tries before the engine started. It had been a few months since she had been here.

———◆◇◆———

Life in the Sangamon was pleasant. The climate was pleasant, and she had reached the point where she wasn't worried about the occasional challenges posed by predators. She'd made sure they were well-armed, and no animal of the Pleistocene was a threat to a human armed with a modern firearm of sufficient caliber.

The thought of facing giant bison, mammoths, and mastodons had bothered her at first, but Cadeyrin had calmly pointed out that such beasts were almost never a problem unless disturbed by humans. That helped some. She resolved never to confront one of them.

Her worry completely dissipated when she'd learned the precise position of elephants' braincases. The large pad of muscles on top of the head necessitated by the trunk tends to make inexperienced hunters think the brain is much higher than it is. A well-placed shot, on the level of the eyes, even from one of the lighter rifles, was capable of penetrating the brain of both mammoth and mastodon. As for the giant bison, their migratory pattern kept them mostly out of the territory that Kathleen and Cadeyrin had staked out for their own.

So, she hadn't been to the house for three, no closer to four months. She was reluctant to leave Cadeyrin's side. Their initial love had blossomed into something that Kathleen could never have conceived of in her former life.

Thinking back on it, she felt as if she hadn't been born until she'd been forced to escape into the Pleistocene and met Cadeyrin. The partly crippling scars around her waist and hips had somehow kept her tied to a huge lump of self-pity. She'd never been able to deal with the awful feeling of rejection surrounding her birth. So what if her mother hadn't wanted her and had tried to abort her? She was here now, and she'd proven herself by discovering the formula for time-travel. And even more, she'd found a love that somehow seemed to span time once she'd come to grips with her feelings towards Cadeyrin.

As for him, although he was unfailingly kind, and gentle with her, he lived up to her expectations of a man of the ice age when he was hunting or defending their territory. He was capable, strong, cunning, and fierce. He was also quite intelligent. His English had become almost as good as her own, and with her tutelage, he had learned to read and now devoured books rapidly. His vocabulary had increased rapidly.

She pulled the four-wheel-drive vehicle up beside him. He was partly reclining in the roadside ditch, breathing raggedly, a trace of blood on his lips.

She couldn't lift him by herself. He was far larger than she, and his massive muscles made him bulky.

"Can you stand?"

"Yes, if I can get my feet under me. You'll have to help me, though. I'm feeling dizzy." The glazed look in his eyes and the wheeze in his breath reinforced his words.

She braced herself, pulled on his good arm, and supported him up the shallow embankment to the open passenger door. He worked his way in and then lay back, his chest heaving as he gasped for air.

She yanked the rear door open, and half boosted, half lifted Ulfsa into the back seat. He whimpered in pain and lay down, licking his injured foot.

# Chapter Three

# Help

THE Land Rover shot down the narrow, two-lane road, ran the stop sign, and headed towards Minneapolis. Kathleen used the car's phone system to call 911. The operator directed her to exit the highway and drive to a nearby fire station.

She pulled up in front of the building just as the EMTs were coming out of the opened door. They'd already started the ambulance and had the gurney ready. They hoisted Cadeyrin out, got him on the gurney, and did a quick check that resulted in an oxygen mask on his face.

His eyes were wide as he sought Kathleen's face. She nodded, trying to keep a smile on her face.

"The mask will help you breathe," she said.

Cadeyrin nodded weakly and lay back with his eyes closed.

The lead EMT said, "We've got to transport him now, Ma'am. His lung is filling with blood and needs immediate attention. Do you want to ride with us?"

She placed her hand on Cadeyrin's shoulder. His eyes opened a little, and she leaned close to say, "These men will take care of you. They're going to take you to a hospital for emergency treatment. They can deal with wounds like yours. I'd like to come with you in their truck, but I'd better bring ours, so we won't have to depend on anyone else for a ride."

His lips moved, and he wheezed, "Yes. You follow."

The drive to the hospital was a blur to Kathleen. She concentrated on following the flashing lights of the ambulance and tried not to think about Cadeyrin's condition. Still, she found her mind focusing on aspects of their life together. Her thoughts kept drifting, and then she'd think of something he'd done or said. From that, she'd invariably move on to what she'd do if he didn't recover. The prospect was grim. She couldn't conceive of ever wanting to live without him.

Ulfsa was quiet in the back. She looked back to meet his steady gaze. He was lying on the seat, his paw extended in front of him. He was naturally stoic about pain and might have been feeling a considerable amount, but he didn't show it.

It seemed like forever before they reached the Emergency Room. She slammed the Rover into a parking spot, cracked the rear window a bit, and cautioned Ulfsa to stay.

He didn't move as she locked the vehicle and sprinted for the sliding doors. She arrived just as the two techs were wheeling Cadeyrin inside.

His eyes were open, his pupils wide, but he seemed to calm and breath more easily when she took his hand.

The next few minutes were a whirlwind of activity that ended with her sitting outside an operating suite. Cadeyrin's lung required immediate surgery.

Kathleen tried to look through one of the tatty magazines in the room but soon discarded it to sit and clasp her hands. She wasn't much at praying. Cadeyrin was intensely spiritual, but Kathleen hadn't ever been able to generate a similar belief. Now she wrung her hands, unconsciously trying to send him energy to get through the surgery.

She didn't know how much time had passed, but the door swung open, and the attending physician came in with a smile on his face.

"It was a bit of a mess. Your man had four ribs broken, and two of them splintered. That's what punctured his lung. We removed the pieces, patched and drained the lung. We cleaned up the breaks, stitched everything up, and moved him into the critical care ward.

"Will he be okay? I – I mean, how long will it take for him to recover?"

The doctor smiled at her, "He's your husband? Right?"

Kathleen nodded, "Yes. We're..." She paused. They weren't formally married, but that didn't make any difference to her. "Yes, he's my husband."

"Well, he should recover well. I've never seen a man in quite as good a physical condition as him. Is he an athlete of some sort?"

She smiled back. "Not really. I mean not any formal sports. Cadeyrin's just...I guess you could call him an outdoor enthusiast. He hunts a lot."

He looked puzzled a moment, then shrugged. "We'll have some paperwork for you to go through. We rushed him in here quickly, but you'll have to fill out the forms, of course."

He patted her on the shoulder, then said, "We'll need to keep him for a few days. He's in a lot of pain, and we'll need to keep tabs on his lung. We've got to make sure that it doesn't fill up again. Overall, if things develop the way I think and based on his physical condition, we should let him out in five or six days. He'll be unable to do much for several weeks, though. It takes weeks for broken bones to knit completely, so he'll have to take it easy. Who's his primary care physician?"

Kathleen thought, then said, "No one here locally. Perhaps you could help us locate someone. We've got a house here, but we usually live elsewhere."

He glanced at her with a cocked eyebrow, then said, "I'll see about recommending someone. Will you be staying nearby?"

She smiled, "Yes. I'll be in the nearest hotel when I'm not by Cadeyrin's side."

The doctor looked her over. Her sweatshirt and pants were clean but worn. She didn't seem to exude the usual feeling of desperation that many of his low-income patients had, but still..."

"That could be expensive? Are you sure you're going to be okay?"

Kathleen nearly laughed, "Oh, well, money is no problem. I've got plenty."

She paused, thinking of her attorney, Geoff Jarpe. She'd have to check with him about the investment fund. She had a little over a million in the bank, but the fund should be somewhere north of three hundred million at this point. Even if it were not, if it was entirely gone, she wasn't worried. She could still go back a few days and buy the winning lotto ticket, then return and collect. That was simple.

"When can I see him?" she asked.

"He should be regaining consciousness now. I'll have the nurse come out and get you shortly." He disappeared through the door.

Kathleen walked to the window and ran her fingers through her tangled hair, watching her reflection in the glass.

She'd have to go out and take care of Ulfsa soon. She'd check on Cadeyrin first. He'd undoubtedly want to know about their wolf and then would insist that she get care for his injured foot.

There was a shuffle behind her. An administrative worker had brought in a clipboard that was practically overflowing with paperwork for her. She sighed and sat down to puzzle her way through it.

❖

She had nearly completed the forms when a nurse appeared to guide her back to the ICU. She scribbled her name one last time and then followed the nurse through some doors.

❖

Cadeyrin was suffering, but he mustered the strength to smile at her. Kathleen subconsciously noticed that the two attending nurses were hanging around acting as if they were infatuated. She smiled to herself. He was a hunk. He'd kept himself clean while living in the Pleistocene, but once he had access to warm water and the plumbing in their camper, he had cleaned up to modern standards. Now, with his long hair and close-cropped beard, he looked like a model for a romance novel. His injury-induced paleness slightly marred his overall appearance, but the muscles showing on his arms and chest provided an irresistible distraction to the nurses.

She moved closer and took his free hand. Someone had started an IV and placed an oxygen tube over his head. He grimaced weakly and asked, "What are all these things? No one has said anything to me about what they are."

He wheezed. His lung was still partially filled with fluid. He shook his head slightly, then commented, "Is there a shaman here? Will he do magic of some sort?'

Kathleen leaned forward and kissed his forehead. "Yes. There is a kind of shaman. Here they call them doctors. They've already fixed your ribs and lung. You just have to recover now. I'll be here with you, so don't worry."

"I'm glad you're here. Everything is strange. Our trailer is familiar, but this...This place is far more than I could ever imagine."

She smiled, "I know it's overwhelming, but you'll get used to it. There are many more people alive now than in the past. They live peacefully with each other. You're safe here in the hospital. It is a place of healing."

He responded, "It stinks of death to me. Besides, I don't feel like they fixed my ribs. They hurt, and I can barely breathe."

She squeezed his hand. "Your ribs are bound tightly to keep them from moving. They cleaned up the broken bones, patched the hole in your lung, and then bandaged you. It will take weeks for your bones to knit."

"I've had broken bones before." He sniffed. "I know how many moons it takes for them to heal."

Kathleen raised her head to see the two nurses staring at him with amazement on their faces.

"He's from another culture," she said. She didn't want him to become some odd carnival attraction for the staff. "He grew up without the benefit of modern medicine, and it's strange to him."

That was a weak response, but it was the best she could come up with at the moment. It was becoming clear that she hadn't thought the possible problems completely through. Saving Cadeyrin's life had been Kathleen's primary focus. Now that he was out of immediate danger, she'd better think through the repercussions of bringing him to this time. It would be better to take him back as quickly as she could.

The nurses looked at each other, then back at her. The brunette said, "If it takes living in another culture to have muscles like his, I want a man from there for me."

The other nurse added, "The surgeon said he'd never seen anything like this guy's condition. Is he a professional athlete or something? He's loaded with muscles."

"No, he's just the product of outdoor living." Kathleen mentally dismissed them and returned her focus to Cadeyrin. He moved a little and said, "My ribs hurt."

One of the nurses moved forward to lift a cable with a button on it. "Just press this button when you feel too much pain. It will give you something that will make you feel better."

Without waiting for him to answer, she pushed the button.

Cadeyrin looked at Kathleen with an alarmed expression on his face, then the lines on his face relaxed as the drug took hold again. He smiled a little, then closed his eyes.

Kathleen brushed his hair back and said, "I've got to take care of Ulfsa."

He roused a little and whispered, "Get him help. I'll be okay until you get back. This button thing is amazing. I hardly feel any pain now. You go help him."

His eyes closed.

Kathleen looked up at the two nurses. "Which of you is on duty now?"

The blonde replied, "I am. I'll keep a close eye on him. We should be moving him from recovery to a room in an hour or so. We just need to make sure there isn't any additional bleeding."

Kathleen said, "I've got to go take care of our wo – uhnn, dog. He was injured too. Will you make sure the nursing staff has my phone number?

Cadeyrin is very intelligent, but he's also not used to our culture, and he's perhaps far stronger than you would think. If you need to, call me, and put him on the line. He'll listen to me."

The nurses looked a little alarmed at the implication, but then both nodded. The blonde added, "It'll be no problem giving him a little extra attention. In fact..." she giggled a little, "It'll be a pleasure."

Kathleen grinned. "You're too late. He's all mine." Then she turned and walked out. Ulfsa needed attention.

———◆———

There was a police car parked by her vehicle. She trotted over just as the cop was starting to pull his service pistol.

"Hey, what are you doing?" she snapped.

"Step back, lady. I'm going to shoot this animal. It tried to attack me."

"No, you're not. That's my car, and he's my pet. If he growled at you, it's because you tried to open the door. He's under full control."

She moved between the man and the door.

He frowned. "You can't just go off and leave a dog or – what is that? A wolf? Anyway, you can't leave it in a closed vehicle. It might die of heatstroke."

Kathleen shook her head. "Are you kidding? It's probably only about fifty degrees right now. There's no danger he's going to have heat stroke. Like I said, he's guarding the car. Now I've got to get him to the vet. He's got an injured foot. Please step away so that I can get in."

He said, "Look, lady, you can't get in there. That animal is immense, and he's obviously dangerous!"

Kathleen ripped the door open and jumped in before he could grab her. Ulfsa wagged his tail and immediately lay down in the back seat.

"See? He's fine, except that his paw is injured, and I have to get to a veterinarian."

The policeman relaxed, shook his head in amazement, and said, "I was sure he'd eat you. Are you sure you're okay with him?"

He sounded more relaxed. Perhaps he'd just been concerned. Kathleen smiled and answered, "I'm fine. He's been mine since he was a little puppy. Now, may I go?"

The cop nodded. "Yeah, go get your wolf-dog treated, but don't leave him alone in a car again."

She started the engine and pulled out. She'd located a convenient veterinarian on her phone's browser. The clinic was just a few blocks away.

# Chapter Four

# Grid

The alarm went off. The loud clanging continued despite Grid's attempt to slap the damned thing. He couldn't open his eyes. They seemed to be stuck shut. He wiped at them, then dropped his arm dispiritedly. His hand struck something smooth and hard. He fumbled for it. It was the vodka bottle, but it was no good. It was empty. He sat partway up, ignoring the pounding in his head, and slammed the bottle on the clock. Both broke. Shards of glass flew, and the clock pieces scattered among them.

He lay back down, but the sunlight was coming in through the blinds. He was awake now and might as well get up. Maybe a hot shower would help with his headache.

He had a happy thought. Maybe the oxycodone prescription from his injury was still in the nightstand drawer. He looked. It was. The little pills promised release from the hammering pain, but then he remembered that he'd sworn off the things after the first bottle. This bottle, a refill, had never been opened. He wasn't going to take them now, regardless of the excuse. If he did, he might take all of them at once.

He hadn't prepared himself mentally for the bathroom. Annie's cosmetics were arranged neatly on her side of the sink. He groaned. The memory of her silky skin rasped against his mind. He'd never feel her touch again.

He staggered over and turned the shower on, then waited for it to get hot. Maybe today wouldn't be so bad. It was going to be hard, though. He had to see Annie's mother. He'd missed the funeral, having just arrived last night. Sarah would blame him again, as usual, but it wasn't his fault. He'd been out on patrol when the police had found Annie's body in a public park. The news hadn't reached him for several hours, and then he still had to return to base before he found out anything.

They'd sent him home on leave, of course. The 75th Rangers would just have to get along without his particular skills for a while. Maybe he'd simply disappear. He didn't feel like living at the moment. The thought of the pills in the other room passed through his mind. All he'd have to do was take them all and go to sleep. But he might be better off back in the sandbox. At least he had a good chance of helping his friends over there.

He had to go through Europe to get back, and by the time he arrived in North Carolina, Annie was already buried. There had been a closed casket service, something that his military experience had trained him to see as normal. It wasn't much different from a combat death, really, except that Annie had been the center of his world since their marriage last year.

He choked down some cold cereal and then headed for Sarah's house. Annie's father had been dead for several years, and Sarah lived alone. The house was in need of maintenance. Even he could see that. Sarah wasn't coping well with her widowhood, and now, having lost her only daughter, she probably was in complete collapse.

He knocked, then opened the door and went in. His mother-in-law was sitting in front of the TV. It wasn't turned on, but she was staring at it as if it were playing the world's most interesting program.

"Sarah? It's me," he ventured.

She turned slowly to him. "Jason Gridley! You're late! Why in the hell did you have to leave her alone? Senator Rasmussen came to her funeral, but you? Her husband? A no-show! If you'd been here, maybe she wouldn't have committed suicide."

"Look, it wasn't my fault. I couldn't get here in time. You know I had no choice. I had to go back. Orders."

"Well, why did you marry her? Maybe if you hadn't, she'd still be alive."

Sarah was irrational as always. First, she accused him of not being here when Annie needed him; then, she said that he should have never come into Annie's life.

A sudden thought struck him. "Sarah, I haven't seen the police report. What do you know about how Annie died?"

"She killed herself. She went to that park in the middle of the night and shot herself in the head." She sobbed, then said, "I can't believe I'm even talking to you!"

He shook his head in denial. That couldn't be correct. He'd been sure that someone must have murdered her. "No. No. That's not right. First, Annie wouldn't kill herself. I know that with all of my being. Second, she had a morbid fear of guns. She wouldn't even let me have one in the house. Where did she get the weapon?"

Sarah's eyes widened. "But...but I thought it was yours. Aren't you the great soldier? Don't you have to have guns around?"

He shrugged. "I don't mind guns. I use them daily when I'm deployed, but for Annie's peace of mind, I don't have any here. I had one, but I got rid of it when we got married."

She shrugged, trying to pass off his protestations as non-material to the discussion,

Grid continued his line of thought. "You know that Annie was afraid of guns. We were joking once, and she said that she could understand people overdosing on drugs but not shooting themselves. She felt it was the difference between going out messily and an easy death."

Sarah interrupted, "What difference does it make now?"

He said, "When I was recovering from my back injury last summer, the doc gave me a script of Oxy. It's still in the nightstand drawer. Untouched. There's not a pill missing from the bottle. Annie knew it was there. If she'd wanted to kill herself, she'd have used the pills. She didn't do it."

Sarah asked, "Well, if she didn't, someone did. Who was it and why?"

He said, "I'm going to try and find out. Has Senator Rasmussen said anything? I assume he's already appointed a new personal aide."

"Oh, he sent a card and said some things at her funeral, but he didn't seem like he was too upset. He had a new woman who was managing his schedule. She sat by him at the service. I guess the foreign relations committee business requires the constant presence of an aide." She paused, then added, "I didn't like her."

He couldn't take much more. He'd been sure that someone had murdered Annie, that it was not her doing that took her out of his life. That explanation hurt but helped him in another way. He no longer felt the sense of anger that he'd been feeling. The thought of her killing herself made him feel totally rejected. He could understand killing. He'd lost many friends to enemy action. It was bad, but sometimes it couldn't be helped.

Back at their house, he called the police department, identified himself, and asked for the name of the detective who was handling the case. The upshot was that the detective told him it was a clear-cut suicide, and there was no reason to investigate. Annie was just another closed file.

His next call was to the coroner. He got a little more information there. The coroner was willing to let him read the report.

---

The circumstances of death seemed odd to Gridley. A jogger had found Annie at six in the morning. She'd apparently shot herself in the right occipital part of her skull with a pistol. The weapon was nearby, but there were no discernible fingerprints on it. She'd have had to hold it almost directly behind her head to cause such a wound.

The coroner said that it was possible, and he had no reason to doubt that statement, but he felt like it was a difficult place to shoot yourself. Most people opted for either the temple or the mouth. There was something off about the situation.

He went home and sat at the kitchen table, his head in his hands. After a while, he opened the cabinet. There was a half bottle of tequila there. Without pausing, he pulled the cork and took a gulp.

Thirty minutes later, he was passed out on the kitchen floor.

---

The doorbell was ringing. No, it was the phone. It was dark outside, and the clock on the range said nine. It must be late. Gridley had started drinking in mid-afternoon, so he'd been lying there for nearly six hours. He struggled to his feet and staggered to the counter.

It was Lt. Rance calling. He had to be on base in the morning to pick up his new orders. They were urgent and, although it was regretful, he was reassigned and had been ordered to report in as quickly as possible.

# Chapter Five

# Sent into Hell

Grid showed up on base and reported to Lt. Rance.

"Okay. Here's your new assignment," Rance said, handing him a packet.

He opened the envelope and removed the materials for a brief glance. They had temporarily assigned him to a special group outside of Mclean, Virginia. He was to report ASAP.

Gridley looked at Rance and asked, "You know anything about this, Sir?"

The lieutenant had the grace to flush a little. "Not really. Your record apparently qualified you for some special mission. Colonel Franklin asked for you specifically."

Gridley sighed, "Wasn't there anyone else, Sir? My mind just isn't in it right now."

"I can understand that, but it was something about your rep in the field. The Colonel was kind of worked up about a request from some senator acting on behalf of some special-ops group. They want someone who is expert at infiltration, both in urban settings and wilderness. Your name came up in conjunction with Death Valley."

Jason sighed, then said, "Crap, Sir! Won't that ever go away?" He wiped his forehead, brushing at the perspiration. It wasn't too warm outside, but the humidity was higher than what he was used to in the desert.

"Look, you go and slip through the toughest training course in Ranger school without getting captured or killed. You got the drop on two of your instructors. You earned the rep there, then your work in the field added a lot to your reputation. I can't help it that he asked for you specifically. Now follow your orders."

Rance half grinned, showing that he was sympathetic but unwilling to discuss the issue further.

———◇———

The tall, muscular sergeant snapped a salute, then turned and strode out of the office, his stride betraying the extent of his disgruntlement.

At ten hundred the next day, Gridley was sitting in a briefing where everyone seemed to know what was going on but him. Everyone except him was a civilian. They were excitedly talking over each other. Eventually, chaos turned into order when a man in a black suit came in and sat at the head of the table.

"Welcome, and a special welcome to Sargent Jason Gridley. He's been loaned to us by the 75th Rangers and is an expert at infiltration in all sorts of environments. We will brief him on what he's supposed to do later, but, based on his record, he will have no difficulty accomplishing our first mission."

There was an excited buzz of conversation as all eyes turned to Grid. He made an aborted half-bow from his chair, then sat back trying to evaluate the people. Based on their rather eccentric clothing, it looked like most of them were scientists. Black-suit was obviously the one in direct charge but probably reported to someone higher up who controlled the purse strings.

An older man was speaking. "We've got the kinks in the VR display worked out, and the sequencing of images has now been complete. According to our calculations, they are optimal for March of 1981."

Black-suit interjected, "I hope you can be more specific than that! We need March 30, 1981, at 2 p.m."

The older man paused, then continued, "Well, yes. We're set for 2 p.m. or at least as close as we can get. You understand that we can't be quite that precise. We're trying for a period between noon and two. The subject will then have plenty of time to act. The actual event occurs at 2:27 p.m. If he arrives a few minutes before that point, the sergeant should be able to act decisively."

Black-suit glanced at another man and asked, "Is your side of the process ready, Dr. Mckinnon?"

"Yes. We believe we've perfected the formula. It's fast, short-acting, and leaves no residual effect on the subject. We've loaded a standard epi-pen with the return dose. The sergeant will have to take it within thirty seconds of initiating the VR feed for the return, or it may not work. Timing is critical for this."

Black-suit looked at Gridley. "I believe you've probably got some questions, but hold them, please. You'll be fully briefed. We've got a video for you to watch that will give you all you need to know about the mission. However, since you're undoubtedly burning with curiosity, I'll summarize it for you. It isn't a secret." He waved his hand inclusively around the table. "Our entire group knows the mission objective. You, Sergeant Gridley, are going to travel back to March 30, 1981, and at 2:26 in the afternoon, you are going to shoot President Ronald Reagan with a pistol loaded with blanks. The resulting confusion will cause John Hinckley to fail to hit Reagan in his assassination attempt. He will be there, of course, and will pull his pistol. The secret service agents will arrest him, and that will be that. Reagan is spared an operation, and time in the hospital, Hinckley will get what he deserves, and you'll return to the present."

Gridley's eyes narrowed. "I'm assuming that you have this time-travel thing worked out. This whole thing is too elaborate to be a hoax." He looked around as if to determine whether he was being set up as the butt of an elaborate prank.

Several of the men laughed, and the older man who had been speaking before said, "No. No hoax, young man. We're going to send you back alright."

Black-suit said, "It will be up to you to duck back into the hotel, enter a small room near the main desk, and initiate your return. You'll need about a minute for that, so you'll have to avoid the secret service for that length of time. It might be a little tricky, but we've got video and a mock-up of the lobby for your training. Your superiors have assured me that you can do it."

---

By ten that night, Grid was fairly sure he had the moves down. He'd watched the video of the assassination attempt repeatedly and knew where every agent was at each phase of the action. He'd also walked through the mock-up of the hotel lobby over and over until he was sure he could reach the room within five seconds.

He was tired and tense. This project was crazy. The idea that he could travel in time was hard to grasp, but he had immediately thought of the possibility that he could use the technology to go back and save Annie. That intensified Grid's interest to the point of obsession. He would learn as much about this as he could, and then he'd see if he could change his personal past. He wanted her back.

---

The mission launching room was a disappointment. It was simply an office. They'd taken him to Washington, near the Hilton Hotel. There was an office building there, he didn't pay much attention to the name, and they led him into a suite on the ground floor.

Black-suit was there to direct things.

"Gridley, once you're back there, this office is going to be empty. We've had it rented as a front for over forty years. Most of the time, it's not used. We checked the records, and it wasn't used for the first six months of 1981, so you won't meet anyone in here. Exit the office, go directly across the street, don't draw attention to yourself, and be prepared to improvise if necessary. We want you to use this pistol to shoot at Reagan."

Here he handed Gridley a small revolver.

"It's loaded with blanks. They don't look like blanks, though. The bullets are a lightweight composite that will ablate when it begins to move. The gun will fire normally, but nothing will strike the President. Don't worry about him. Try to stand just behind Hinckley, shoot before he's ready, then trip him as you get away. The protective detail will grab him, find his gun, and things will work out as they already have, except you'll have saved a president from a nasty wound. The press will mention that there was a second shooter, but there will be no sign of you. We're tracking the newspapers, so when the description of the event changes, we'll know you were successful."

It seemed clear, but there was something about the situation that made him feel uneasy. He was confident that he could get clear after the shooting. Whether or not the return equipment would work correctly didn't bother him. If he ended up stuck in 1981, he'd be in his sixties now. He'd make sure that he was tracking Annie on the night she was scheduled to commit suicide, and he'd prevent her death. He might not be her husband then, but he knew he would still love her.

The chance that he could save her in that way almost was enough to make him not use the return equipment, but if he demonstrated the viability of the system, and cooperated on other missions, they'd owe him. He'd find a way to ensure that they let him save her.

He took the little revolver and nodded. He checked the cylinders. They were all loaded with .22 caliber cartridges.

Black-suit said, "Hinckley had his revolver loaded with explosive Devastator rounds. The rounds in yours look superficially like them but, as I said, behave entirely differently. Now, let's get you ready to go."

⎯⎯◄O►⎯⎯

He was going to wear a customized virtual reality headset to make the jump. It was linked to a small tablet that he would carry in his breast pocket. Once in the destination time, he'd remove the headset, fold it flat and tuck it into his pocket for use during the return phase. They gave him a pen injector device. He was to inject the drug directly into his carotid artery to initiate his return. After that, he'd have only a few seconds of rational thought to don the headset and start the video program. He had been cautioned that waiting too long could throw everything off.

He sat on the floor. There was no furniture in the office in 1981, and they didn't want him falling, possibly breaking the equipment. The headset was light – just plastic and the tablet was small. The mission launch was nothing. Black-suit said, "Go!"

Someone injected him in the neck. He thumbed the start icon on the app, and images started flowing around him, appearing to be three-dimensional in the headset.

At first, they were intelligible. Grid made out pictures of street scenes. The cars were different. He recognized them as old autos of the period. People were dressed a little differently, but overall, the scenes were familiar. The video sped up gradually until it became a blur. The effect made him dizzy. He felt like he was falling. His perception became intently focused, and he was unable to think. For a moment, his breath seemed to catch.

The video stopped, and he gasped. His heart was racing. Shakily, he removed the headset. The office was empty. He rose and checked the revolver. Just to make sure, he removed one of the cartridges. The bullet felt solid. It should be easy to break, but it was solid. He looked at it carefully. It was an explosive Devastator brand cartridge. They had loaded the revolver with the same bullets Hinckley had used. If he, with his marksman's skills, shot the President in the chest, Reagan would not be injured. He'd be killed. He'd been set up. Totally set up. They meant for him to kill Reagan.

He looked around, thinking. The blank walls gave no answer. If he interfered with the assassination attempt, he'd change history. He hadn't thought of it before. That might have some adverse effects.

After a bit, he decided that his best course of action would be to let events play out as they had. Reagan would recover. It was bad that Brady ended up paralyzed, but that was what had happened.

He considered. His initial impulse was to return and shoot Black-suit with the little explosive cartridges. They'd involved him in something evil. Of course, if he did that, Annie would never be saved. On the other hand, he could muffle the revolver and shoot it to convince them he'd fired at Reagan, but since the actual history wouldn't change, they'd be suspicious. Maybe they'd just assume that the scheme hadn't worked. He'd still have learned how to time travel. It'd be up to him to figure out how to steal the equipment and drugs to be able to save Annie. It was a dubious chance, but that was what had to happen.

He searched the office and found a painter's dropcloth. The thick canvas could be folded enough times that it would stop the .22 bullets, especially if he backstopped the pad with the concrete floor.

He carefully muffled the pistol and fired. The aluminum and lead azide bullet exploded as it hit the concrete, but the dropcloth kept the blast at a minimum. No fragments came back through.

He moved the pistol slightly to another part of the dropcloth and pulled the trigger again. In a minute, he'd shot all six rounds. He'd tell them he'd fired all six within about a second. Hinckley, amateur that he was, had fired all six in about 1.7 seconds.

Grid sat down, arranged himself, donned the headset, pricked his neck with the pen injector, and thumbed the start icon. The video started.

All went as before, except the images were different. They moved so quickly that Grid couldn't make them out, although he thought he saw ferns and pine trees. That was strange. There were few such plants in the section of DC that was his destination. It was all city, not wilderness as this appeared to be. When the video stopped, he gasped for breath. The air was dry, arid. He felt like he was in the desert again.

He ripped the headset off. He was somewhere or somewhen else. There were rocks and conifer-like trees around him. On the other side of a ridge, something was making a honking noise, but there were no people in sight. The sun was in the wrong place too.

He cautiously stood and looked around. The return hadn't worked correctly, whether by intent or by accident, he didn't know.

# Chapter Six

# Problems

The Vet was a petite, middle-aged woman. She paused uncertainly at the door to the examining room, staring at Ulfsa.

"That's a wolf! That's not a dog. Do you expect me to treat him?" She seemed puzzled but not unduly alarmed.

Kathleen sighed. It might have been better if they had left Ulfsa in the Sangamon. Here, he would frighten anyone who saw him.

"Yes. His paw is injured. Don't worry about him. He's been with me since he was a puppy. He doesn't know anything about wolves."

That was an outright lie. Ulfsa often spent time with the local pack near their trailer. The pack had seemingly accepted him as a provisional member, and as far as she was aware, there had been no fights. Of course, Ulfsa was larger than the average wolf. He ate well, and Cadeyrin didn't short him on his share of any kills.

"Yes, but he's still a wolf."

This wasn't going to be easy. The Vet still hesitated.

Kathleen grabbed Ulfsa's injured leg and lifted it. He whimpered a little and cocked his head to look at her face. She bent within an inch of his jaws and carefully felt his foot. It seemed like there was a toe, no two toes out of line. Ulfsa had somehow broken them.

The vet moved in, encouraged by Kathleen's nonchalance.

She gingerly reached for the foot but paused when Ulfsa looked at her.

Apparently, he recognized that she was there to help. He'd never been around friendly humans other than Cadeyrin and Kathleen, but somehow he knew that the small woman meant no harm. In a most un-wolf-like manner, he licked her face.

The Vet recoiled, then laughed shakily. "Here, let me look," she said.

———◦———

It turned out that three of his toes were broken. The Vet splinted them.

"That will hold them relatively immobile. The toes bear most of his weight, so he won't like to use the foot and may be on three legs for a while. Bring him back in every week for me to check. Try to keep the splint dry. When the bones knit, maybe in seven or eight weeks, we'll remove the splint, and he'll be as good as new. He might try to pull it off, though. Discourage him from that, if you can."

Kathleen asked, "Could you board Ulfsa for a day or two? I'm stuck here, my husband is in the hospital, and I really don't have the time to watch him."

The Vet shook her head negatively, but then she noticed the expression on Kathleen's face. She said, "I'm not set up to board animals, especially one of his size, but if he behaves, I could keep him in an examining room for maybe a day or so. Will he let me leash him so I can take him out?"

Kathleen nodded. She and Cadeyrin had tied Ulfsa at times when they didn't want him involved with a hunt. They had done this when they were after dangerous animals and didn't want him possibly getting injured. He'd never exhibited any anger or resentment over the treatment.

"I'll put the leash and collar on him. We can hook him to the examining table, and he'll most likely just sleep. I'll check in with you every couple of hours to make sure he isn't causing a problem. Don't worry; I'll pay you well for the help."

"I'm not worried about payment. The idea of caring for a wolf is something that I think is exciting. I just don't want to have to tell you he's killed someone or some animal or run away. Besides, you look like you can use the help."

Kathleen laughed shakily. She could use the help, and it had looked for a moment as if the woman was going to turn her down.

"Yes, it'll take a load off my mind. I'm worried about my husband. He has some broken ribs and a punctured lung."

"Oh. I hope he's not in danger." The woman smiled sympathetically.

Kathleen said, "No. He's been in the ICU, but they're going to move him to a room shortly. Here's my phone number, if you need to call me." She took a prescription pad off the counter and wrote on it.

"Now, I need to check on my husband."

⸎

Once on the road back to the hospital, Kathleen made a phone call to her attorney. She only had to wait a few seconds before Geoff picked up.

He didn't spend any time with social amenities. "Hi, Kathleen. I'm glad you called. We've got a bit of a problem. It came up two days ago. I've been hoping that you'd call. I've left several messages, but I don't think you check your phone often."

She had never told him about her time-traveling. As far as he knew, she simply traveled around the country or the world and was often out of touch.

"Yes, well, I'm here now. What's the problem?" He had aroused her curiosity.

"The government, the IRS to be specific, has flagged a couple of your accounts and frozen them. They say they're suspicious that the money comes from something illegal, possibly the drug trade."

She drew in her breath. "Is that normal for them to do? You know I don't have anything to do with drugs."

He laughed dryly. "Yes. I know your money came from lottery winnings, and I've overseen each investment we've made. I can say with complete confidence that no drugs, other than an investment into one of the big pharmaceutical companies, are involved. Your investments have been doing well. If we consider the total before the IRS' action, you've almost doubled your money. The accounts they froze had just north of twenty million dollars in them. They must have been watching the balances for some time since they waited until I'd used them to hold an unexpected profit before reinvesting it. They caught us at precisely the right time when the accounts held an all-time high amount of funds."

She said, "I've been a little afraid of something like this. I think I need to come in and talk to you."

He paused, then said, "Well, uh, maybe coming in isn't exactly the best strategy. They're probably watching my office that is if they actually think you're involved in something highly illegal. They can smell money like vultures smell roadkill. We'd better meet somewhere else, but where?"

She said, "I've got an idea about where we should meet."

At that moment, something strange happened. Geoff laughed and said, "That's what you told me you'd tell me. Say no more. I know you're on it."

◆○◆

Kathleen hung up and thought hard. At the exact moment he'd laughed, she'd decided to go back in time a week and meet with him. He'd immediately made it clear that she'd already communicated with him. She had apparently jumped back and done that. It was still confusing to her. The ability to proactively impact events in her past required careful planning, if for no other reason than she could not afford to be at the same place at the same time.

She'd done that once for a fraction of a second and had suffered almost complete amnesia about much of her recent past as a result. Somehow the energy wave patterns of dual temporal existence interfered with each other wiping out parts of her memory.

She wasn't about to attempt to solve the problem by changing the past without extensive planning. She could go back in time before the IRS had acted and move the funds, but maybe it would be better to let them think they had her over a barrel. Let them freeze the accounts. It was only a fraction of her wealth, and she could always get more.

Still, she needed to talk to Geoff. She decided that he had the need to know about her ability. He'd proven his reliability in a powerful way. She'd given him complete control over around two-hundred million dollars, and not only had he taken care of it, he had also almost doubled it. His accounting reports were scrupulously straightforward. He did charge a premium, but he had never attempted to short-change her.

If he had to help her face the IRS, he'd need to know a bit more about her abilities. Besides, perhaps he could help her strategize.

◆

She pulled into the hospital parking garage, parked, and looked around. There was no one nearby. She got out and moved into the shelter of a support beam. No car could get close to the spot, so she didn't worry about any possible conflict. She closed her eyes for a moment, then opened them. Her SUV wasn't there. She dialed Geoff's number.

When he answered, she said, "Geoff, this is Kathleen. The next time I call you, meet me in thirty minutes in front of the Tate Physics Lab on the university campus. Don't ask questions. A situation is developing where we'll need to meet outside your office with no observers. Bye."

She hung up, closed her eyes, then walked out of the shadow of the support beam, paused by her SUV, then headed to the ICU. The nurse there gave her a room number, and she went up the elevator to the third floor.

The room was empty. The bed was messed up, and it appeared as if someone had just left. While Kathleen was looking at the room in puzzlement, a nurse came up behind her.

"They came and got him a few minutes ago. He got a phone call, and then some guys came in, flashed some badges, and took him out somewhere."

"W–what badges? Who came and got him? Do you mean my husband, Cadeyrin? The big, blond man with the broken ribs?"

Kathleen's vision faded momentarily. It was like looking through a dark tube. There was blackness around the edges. She became aware that she was shaking and tried to stop but couldn't even when she gripped the back of a chair. She took several deep breaths and managed to recover a little.

"Yes. You're Kathleen Whitby, right?"

"That's me. Who got my husband?" Kathleen looked at her hands. They were still shaking, and now she felt dizzy.

"I think they said they were Homeland Security. Don't worry. They took him off in a wheelchair, and they know that he's seriously injured," the nurse added.

Kathleen said, "That's what I'm afraid of. They might hurt him more, especially if he's injured. He isn't so easy to hurt when he's healthy."

The nurse laughed, "I can believe it. I've never seen such a hunk...uh, I mean– "

Kathleen said, "He is pretty amazing. Where did they say they were taking him?"

"They mentioned that they were going downtown. I think there's an office somewhere there." She paused, obviously considering, then asked, "What did he do? Are you two in some trouble?"

Kathleen shook her head negatively. "I don't know why they'd want him." She whirled, staggered, caught herself, and started off at a fast pace.

In fact, she suspected that was a lie. They evidently were still after her. She'd escaped before without disclosing the secret of time-travel. She didn't trust the government or any organized group with that information. It would be too easy to abuse, and it would inevitably lead to a total loss of freedom for everyone. An all-seeing police state that could send agents back to intercept or kill anyone who attempted to go against it wasn't her ideal vision of the future of the world.

Just as she pushed the elevator call button, the nurse caught up with her. She'd apparently decided that Kathleen was telling the truth and now had a more sympathetic expression.

She said, "I'm sorry. It's just that those men looked so threatening. They had a doctor's order to release him. There was nothing I could do. I don't want to see him hurt. They took him out in a wheelchair through the emergency entrance. They had a large black SUV waiting there."

The nurse had been concerned enough to trail behind the men and had just given her some useful information.

Kathleen nodded. "I know you don't want him hurt. It was good of you to follow them. I don't know what's going on, but I want you to know that Cadeyrin and I are not criminals. I've got to go now."

She wasn't quite sure how she got to the campus. Driving had seemed like a blur. Now, she was standing in front of the Tate Physics Lab, looking at the window of what used to be her beloved mentor's office. She heard footsteps and turned to see Geoff approaching.

"I'm glad you're here. I had a little trouble getting out of the office. A man was watching my car, so I walked a couple of blocks and took a cab." He seemed amused that he'd been involved in some cloak and dagger stuff.

"Let's go sit on that bench. This is going to take a while to explain," she said.

⸺◆⸺

Thirty minutes later, Geoff sighed and said, "This changes everything. I'm not sure how to work what you've told me into my view of the world. It may take some time." He paused, then added, "So you can travel in time at will. And that's how you won the lottery. It's almost like cheating, not that I mind. I still think the lottery is a sin tax on stupidity."

Kathleen answered, "Well, I felt guilty about possibly taking the money from someone else, so I chose a period where there was no winner. Best I could do. I needed money, and I didn't have much time."

Geoff snorted, "It looks like you've got all of the time forever if you need it."

She smiled, "Yes, but all the moments in forever can make an incredibly complex puzzle. I rarely try to change things. It's much safer if I live life as normally as I can."

He said, "I can sort of see how that might be. You wouldn't want to go back and do something that would eventually keep you from being born."

"Yes, but it's more complex than that. A change in the past results in the world diverging onto two separate paths. One would be the main path if no changes were made. The other is a secondary path that is the result of the change. The good thing is that the time flow is far more robust than most people can imagine. It has a strong tendency to heal itself. That is, the two worlds merge back into one as soon as events can accommodate the merge. The main thing I have to watch out for is meeting myself. There are dangerous repercussions from that."

Geoff shook himself, "Well, I'll ignore that. I don't understand it anyway. We'll probably need more money. You're a multi-millionaire, but it might take more to buy your way out of this. Can you figure out a way to generate more funds? I mean without winning the lotto again. I don't want you to draw attention to yourself. They'd probably refuse the payout this time."

She thought about it for a moment, then answered, "Yes. I'm sure there are several ways to get more. Right now, do I have access to enough money to get a hotel near your office? I don't want to go home until I've gotten this straightened out."

She'd been managing well until this moment. Now her breath caught, and she choked back a sob. Geoff looked concerned and reached for her hand. At his touch, she began to cry softly.

"All I want is for people to leave us alone. It's just that I can't give the government or whoever the other group is the secret. They'd destroy the world with it. They wouldn't mean to, maybe, but the temptation to temporally rearrange things is so powerful that they would."

Geoff asked, "Why don't you just go back and not bring him to this hospital?"

She wiped her eyes. "That wouldn't work. Cadeyrin needed immediate care. He had a punctured lung, and it was filling with blood. I had to get him to someone who would help. I can't just go back and tell myself not to do something. It doesn't work that way. I can go back and change things as long as I don't occupy the same time as my future self. Anyway, I'm afraid to meddle too much. The time stream is robust. It heals itself like I said, but there could be a point at which too many changes make it diverge permanently, and the results might be disastrous. They could be terrible. I just don't know."

He sighed, "I don't understand all of the ramifications. It'll take getting used to. Meanwhile, I don't think you can just go into any hotel downtown. They're undoubtedly looking for you too. You'd better find a hiding place. Let me work on this for now."

She said, "I don't know where to go...uh, cancel that. I do have somewhere I can go. Somewhere they'll never find me. How...how much additional money do you suggest I raise?"

He shrugged. "I'm not sure. It may take a lot or none at all. What are the chances that they'll leave you alone if you give them the formula?"

She grimaced. "I don't think they'll let me go. I might tell someone else, or some other organization might get me. They wouldn't want any competition. Oh! If they know about you, you might be in danger too."

"I'm pretty sure they don't exactly know that it's me who is responsible for managing your funds. They can trace the structure I set up to an overseas firm, but they will find it difficult to get beyond that point. I control everything, of course, but I've concealed my name almost as well as yours. Now go. Get more funds and call me on this number for updates." He handed her a card with a phone number written on the back.

He added, "I've purchased one of those prepaid phones. They don't know the number yet. You should buy one too. Don't use your regular cell phone. Here's four thousand in cash. Consider it a loan. I'll charge you that extra next billing cycle. Now, get!"

⸺◆⸺

Funds were no problem. Kathleen had a debit card at her house that accessed one of her accounts that the IRS had not yet frozen. She had about two million there that she could draw on. She'd just have to slip in and get it when no one was watching. She smiled to herself. She wasn't used to thinking in such terms.

There was no sense returning to the hospital. That would only give whomever it was an opportunity to pick her up also. The same with her house. Geoff had set up a series of corporations to hold title to it, but now she had no confidence that the government hadn't traced all of her assets. With that in mind, she started the SUV and headed back in the general direction of the hospital. She needed to get Ulfsa before he became a victim of the situation.

⸺ ◦ ⸺

The Vet was surprised to see her but acted relieved when she explained that she'd found an alternative place for the wolf.

"I've got him in the examining room where we were. I was afraid to move him, and I've been nervous about checking on him also," The Vet said, looking over her shoulder at the door down the hallway.

Kathleen strode down, opened the door to be greeted by Ulfsa. He had heard her coming and was standing, wagging his tail, expectantly.

⸺ ◦ ⸺

Once she had him in the Land Rover, she headed in the general direction of the Mississippi River. There was a park there, which had been there since the late 1980s. She made a slight detour on the way to visit the University library. There she used a public computer for some research, printed out a few pages, and left. Next, she stopped at a coin shop and purchased some silver dollars. She selected relatively inexpensive Morgans and Peace dollars of low grade. They weren't very collectible, but she only wanted them for their bullion value. She bought as many as she could. It was lucky that the shop was large, and the owner had an extensive inventory of silver. The two hundred coins took every cent that Geoff had given her, even after she'd made the best bargain that she could. What was worse, from her standpoint, was that the bundle of silver weighed nearly thirteen pounds. She went out to the SUV and got a small backpack from the rear hatch. That would suffice to carry the coins easily.

# Chapter Seven

# Temporary Refuge

After twenty minutes of driving in heavy traffic, she pulled into the parking lot at Boom Island. The park was adjacent to the Mississippi and had been created in 1988. That was before her birth, so she was safe from meeting herself.

She shut off the Land Rover and got out, then swung the pack over her shoulder. Just as she was clipping the leash on Ulfsa, three black SUVs turned into the lot at high speed, their tires screeching as they blocked her vehicle in place.

Kathleen put one hand on Ulfsa, who was growling, and waved cheerfully with her other hand at the men who were jumping out of the vehicles. They were armed and apparently prepared for a difficult time arresting her.

They had just started to raise their weapons when they abruptly realized that there was no one to shoot. The woman and the big dog had disappeared.

—◦—

The weather was colder and overcast with a thin drizzle. Kathleen looked around, orienting herself. The land was undeveloped. The park wasn't yet in existence. Across the river, the Minneapolis skyline had shrunk and changed somewhat. It wasn't as grand as it was going to become. She sighed and started to walk back towards the nearest road. She could hear traffic in the near distance. She'd taken a step and was pulling on the leash when Ulfsa whined. She turned and looked again. An old man was sitting disconsolately on a log close to the river. She led Ulfsa in that direction.

When she got close, she could see the moisture on his face. He was wearing a ball cap, but it didn't seem to offer much protection from the mist. He glanced at her, then returned to studying the currents in the river.

Kathleen had no specific destination go in mind. She'd escaped and now needed to find some type of sanctuary. Her main goal was to get Cadeyrin released from his captivity. She could probably use her time-travel ability to get him out. Meanwhile, she was here and could use her recently researched knowledge to generate additional funds.

First, though, she needed somewhere to place Ulfsa. As far as she could predict, he'd simply be a problem. He didn't fit into a modern city where people were alarmed by his feral appearance.

After a moment, the old man raised his eyes to hers. She smiled and said, "Hello."

He looked at her face, bypassing the scars along her jaw and looking directly into her eyes. Then he glanced at Ulfsa before he responded, "Hello, yourself, young lady. Where did you get the wolf?"

She moved close to him. "How did you know he's a wolf?"

He snorted. "He isn't a dog, that's for sure. He seems attached to you. Did you raise him?"

Kathleen sat down on the other end of the bench.

"Yes. I found him. He was an orphaned puppy."

The man looked away, then back. "There aren't any wolves around here. Maybe up in the north part of the state near the boundary waters. Not many people would take the time to raise a wild animal like that. Do you have any problems with him?"

As he spoke, the entire situation came crashing back on Kathleen. She was improvising and had no definite plan, just a vague hope that she could figure out a way to get Cadeyrin and escape the grasp of the government and anyone else that wanted her secret.

Her despair must have shown on her face. She wasn't very good at hiding her emotions. The old man turned towards her with concern in his eyes.

"You're in trouble, aren't you, Honey? Maybe I can help. It's not like I have much else to do these days."

She wiped at her face. "No, I...uh, well maybe you could help. Why are you out here in the rain?" The thought that he might help aroused her curiosity, and she wanted to explore the situation,

It was his turn to look distressed. He turned towards the river, then said, "My wife died a couple of weeks ago. My only child, my daughter, is somewhere in California, but we haven't spoken for years. I'm sitting here because I don't like to be in the house. It reminds me of Marybeth."

They were quiet for a time. Kathleen was trying madly to figure out a way to enlist his aid.

He broke the silence first. "Maybe you'd like to come to my place. I'm safe. Too old to be a threat to you, especially with that wolf as a bodyguard. It's too wet and cold out here for you."

She smiled and said, "And, it's not too wet for you?"

He shook his head negatively, then seemed to consider, sighing deeply. "Honestly, I don't know why I'm telling you this, but I was considering going for a swim."

She blurted out, "But that would be suicide! The water's too cold right now..." She trailed off as she realized that was what he had in mind. "Oh! But, but surely you have someone who would miss you, some reason to – to live."

He started walking toward the road. "Not that I know. I'm retired, no real skills other than work. I don't even like to read much. No. Not much to live for now that Mary is gone. I guess I was just surviving, trying to take care of her. She had breast cancer. She fought it, but it won in the end. Now, I don't know what to do."

Kathleen's personal problems had overwhelmed her ability to cope, and now at his story, she began to sob silently in sympathy.

He put his arm around her shoulders, ignoring Ulfsa, who was sitting, watching the two.

"Now, Honey, just take it easy. You don't have to cry for me. My time is pretty much done. It was good, but now I'm tired, and it's nearing the end. You've got problems of your own. I know. I saw it in your face earlier. Maybe I can help a little. I'm not much use, but I'll help if I can."

It was almost a mile to his house, a long walk to a small two-bedroom in a row of similar homes. He ushered her and Ulfsa into the living room, telling her not to worry about getting water on the floor. Both she and the wolf were dripping wet.

He brought towels and then fixed coffee. When Kathleen had dried herself and Ulfsa as best she could, then warmed up with coffee, they began to talk.

Kathleen said, "My problem is complicated. Can I trust you?"

He leaned back, sipped his coffee, then said, "The only way to know for sure if someone is trustworthy is to trust them and see if they live up to it. I can tell you that I have no intention of harming you in any way."

She took too large a sip of her coffee and burned her tongue.

"Ow! Too hot!"

Ulfsa sat up and looked at her with concern.

She recovered for a moment, then decided.

"Okay. I need someone to watch my wolf for a time. I'm not sure how long, but not more than a few days. Would you do that?"

He smiled, "I'd be happy for the companionship if he'd be willing to stay with me. Would he be difficult?"

"No, he's quite well trained. I think you could control him easily if I told him to stay with you."

"That's easy," he said. "Is there anything else?"

She swallowed. This was it. She'd either have to trust him completely or lie convincingly, and she'd never been good at that.

She blurted, "I need some additional money, as much as I can get. Also, I need a safe place to stay on and off."

He shook his head. "I can't help with the money. All I got is social security, and they want Marybeth's last check back since she died before the end of the month. I'm going to be on a very tight budget with my own retirement." He paused, then continued. "You can stay here when you need to. I've got a spare bedroom. That's no problem. Oh, I guess you might want to know my name. I'm George Schwartz. You didn't tell me your name either."

"Oh, Kathleen Whitby. I'm pleased to meet you, George," she said formally.

George's eyes had continuously strayed to the scars on her jawline. He had ignored them before, but now that she had introduced herself, he apparently felt that it was appropriate to ask about them.

"Kathleen, what caused those scars? They look painful."

She shook her head, "I'd rather not talk about them. It's painful. But, so you'll know, I was aborted. I mean, my mother had me aborted, but I lived. I've got those scars and others you can't see."

He looked grim and was silent as he thought about it. Then he said, "Life can be really tough. I'm sorry. I hope you don't hold it against me for asking. Sometimes my curiosity is a problem."

She said, "Well, I'm going to give you more to be curious about."

She opened the backpack and removed the coins, letting them spill out on the coffee table.

He reached out and examined one.

"Those are all silver, aren't they?" he asked.

"Yes. All silver dollars. There are two hundred of them. In a few days, they're going to be worth about forty-nine dollars apiece."

"Yes," he said. "I've heard about those Hunt brothers from Texas. Seems like they've bought almost all of the silver right now. People are kind of mad about it."

"On January 15, silver will hit a peak of a little over forty-nine dollars an ounce. I'd like you to sell these for me at that time."

He frowned, "You didn't steal these, did you? And, how do you know silver will hit that price?"

She drew a deep breath and let it out. "So, here's the truth. I bought those dollars in the time I came from. That's 2016. I know silver will hit that price point because that's its all-time high. I also know who will win the Super Bowl for the next several years. Can you bet on it for me?"

He leaned back, his eyes wide, then laughed loudly. "Young lady, I don't know why, but I believe you. But that isn't really betting. It's more like shooting fish in a barrel. It's a sure thing."

She smiled, relieved. This was going to work out.

"Let me get in my backpack. I've got the information about the football games there." She pulled out a printout. The next seven Super Bowl winners and scores were listed. She handed it to him.

He looked at the information, his hand shaking a little.

"I can't believe it. I just can't believe it."

"What? That I come from the future?" she asked.

"No. No, that the Steelers will win this year. I was sure they'd lose to the Cowboys. Man! It will be a pleasure to place some bets for you. This is going to be fun."

He rocked back and forth gleefully. "What else can I do to make you some money?" he asked.

"I need you to take the money and make bets for the next few years. You can see you'll win. Then in 1986, I want you to take everything you've made and buy Microsoft stock. It'll be very inexpensive. Around eleven cents per share."

He said, "I own a few shares of stock, but I'd never buy anything that cheap. It must be some penny stock and probably won't do anything. What is Microsoft anyway?" Then the realization hit him. "Oh. Wait. How high will it go?"

She smiled, "In my time, it will be selling at around sixty dollars a share."

George smiled slowly. "I just hope that I live that long. I'd love to see an investment like that. But, don't worry, Honey. I'll leave the stock to you in my will, so when I go, you'll still get it."

The three of them sat silently for a while, contemplating mortality and infinity. The only sound in the house was the ticking of the wall clock. Eventually, George heaved himself up and asked, "How about some supper? I got some hamburger for the wolf, and you and me can have soup and maybe a cheese sandwich."

They ate and then spent the remainder of the evening finalizing plans and making sure George knew the critical dates. At ten, Kathleen retired to the spare bedroom. Ulfsa sat up with George for a while. It seemed like he'd taken to the old man, but he eventually came in, sighed, and went to sleep by the foot of the bed.

# Chapter Eight

# An Ultimatum

Somehow Kathleen managed to sleep. George had the unfortunate habit of snoring. It was steady throughout the night. Sometimes soft, once in a while loud. It was so constant that she finally found it reassuring and relaxed.

The next day, she told Ulfsa to mind his behavior, then transferred back to 2016. George watched as she left. She intended to ask him later what it had looked like when she disappeared. She was curious about the effect on observers.

◄◊►

She walked to the bus line and headed for Geoff's office. As she was waiting in the lobby for Geoff, a man in an all-black suit walked in with a rather nasty grin on his face. She looked up as he came to a halt in front of her.

"Kathleen Whitby! I've been waiting for you to show up here."

She started in alarm, her mouth open, but sat back when he said, "No. Don't worry. I'm not going to try to arrest you. Nothing so simple as that. If I wanted to hurt you, I'd have shot you the moment I came through the door before you could travel to another time."

She started to speak, and once again, he interrupted. "Yes, I know about your time-travel. It makes you difficult to locate, but I'm pretty sure it doesn't make you invulnerable. Bullets move faster than people can react."

Kathleen had recovered herself by then. "Who are you? And more importantly, what do you want with me?"

He sat down opposite her in a relaxed position as if he knew he had the entire situation under control.

"You can call me Agent Jones. You've got something I want, or rather your government wants, and we've got someone you want. How about a trade? We can keep this as civilized as can be, provided you cooperate."

She saw Geoff start into the room. He saw the man and changed direction to confront him.

"What are you doing with Ms. Whitby?" he asked.

Agent Jones looked him over, then said, "I assume you're her lawyer? You know we could have you disbarred for aiding a traitor. Ms. Whitby has refused to help her government, and I suspect that you've been helping her avoid us."

Geoff replied, "I don't think she should be speaking to you at this point. Bring in a warrant for her or a subpoena. Then we'll sit down and discuss this issue."

The agent stood, straightened his tie, and said, "It's a lot simpler than that. We are holding an illegal alien. We may decide to deport him or possibly keep him in Gitmo as a spy. He's fine right now, injured but healing. However, if he's locked up as a spy, he might not receive the quality of care we're giving him. Who knows? He might get worse quite rapidly."

All the while he was speaking, he was watching Kathleen's expression. She could feel the blood rush out of her face when he implied that Cadeyrin might be deliberately injured.

The agent snickered. "Ms. Whitby, you're really not cut out for this. I can tell by your expression that you're genuinely concerned about the man. He is rather an attractive specimen. I can see why you think highly of him. Is he from the past somewhere? We don't have him in our database."

She looked at Geoff. He seemed a little taken aback at the brazen threat. She addressed the black-clad man.

"Agent Jones, you are holding my husband. I want him released now. As for the time-travel equation, I don't think it should be exploited. There's too much potential for harm."

Jones shrugged. "That's not for me to decide. We've got scientists working on the concept. Your knowledge is a matter of national security. If I could hold you, I'd arrest you, but I'm sure you could escape. Mr. Cadeyrin cannot, ergo we hold him in your stead. If you want him back, you'll help us. It's as simple as that."

He turned to Geoff. "Don't think that any court can free him. You can get a writ of Habeas Corpus, but we'll just transfer him out of the country. You know the NDDA gives the president the ability to hold anyone indefinitely, even citizens, which this man certainly is not."

Kathleen's shoulders slumped. She looked at Geoff and said, "I'm going to go talk to these people. Don't worry about me. It'll be okay."

Geoff replied, "I don't think you should go. If you give them the information they want, they could simply shoot you. It's not in their best interest to have you running around, possibly telling other people the secret of time-travel."

The agent smiled. "No. That's not the case. If she cooperates, we'll set both of them free. They can go back in time and be perfectly safe. We have no interest in her. We only want her secret. By the way, we know about all of her accounts. You did a good job hiding them, but we've found them now. I can have the funds frozen or tell IRS to free up the money they already have started to confiscate. It's your choice."

Kathleen turned and walked toward the door, leaving Geoff standing. She turned back to him at the door. "Geoff, I'll call you in a couple of hours."

The agent added, "That's fine. I've got a car waiting outside. Ms. Whitby, please come with me."

⸻◆⸻

They ended up in an office on the other side of the river, in St. Paul. Kathleen didn't expect Cadeyrin to be there, and he wasn't. Instead, there were two other agents and two men who introduced themselves as physicists.

"Ms. Whitby," one of the physicists said, "May I call you Kathleen?"

She shrugged, "Whatever you want."

He continued, "I admire what you've done. We haven't figured out exactly how you did it, but your solution is obviously more elegant than our current research."

Kathleen's attention sharpened. "What do you mean? Do you have time-travel?" she asked.

"Well, of a sort. I don't suppose you know about Logan Walker, do you?" he asked.

"No. Who is he? A physicist somewhere? I've never heard the name," she said.

"No. Walker's a college student. An archaeologist, I think. However, he can travel in time somehow. He disappeared, then suddenly showed up again with some odd effects that caused a professor at his school to vanish. From the description, it was due to a temporal paradox that resulted from touching a knife to a copy of itself that had traveled in time. Professor Wolf has made a thorough study of the effect, and we've based our theorizing on his findings."

Kathleen said, "I've heard of Professor Wolf. He's in Florida, isn't he?"

The man answered, "Yes. Unfortunately, Walker and a girl, whom I believe he brought back from the past have disappeared, so we can't get any additional information from him, but Wolf swears that he would be of no further help. He just doesn't know enough. His temporal journeys were apparently the result of drug usage, and he doesn't have the ability to duplicate them consistently."

She thought, then asked, "So if you have time-travel, what do you need with me?"

He said, "Here's the thing. We've got the ability to move people in time, but it seems to be random, and the one subject that we've sent back has not returned. We don't know if he's still alive. We need to find out how you control the effect."

Kathleen snapped, "And if you knew, you'd only use it to kill other people. There's too much power there, too much chance of destroying things. The universe can take a small amount of fooling around in time. It tends to heal itself, but if a person were set on changing things, it is easily possible. You could destroy our country or even the world. The wrong action could change everything."

Jones laughed then. "No, relax. We haven't got anything so radical in mind. All we want to do is to make a few tweaks. Perhaps some of our enemies fail to develop the atomic bomb, for instance. Would that be so bad? It'd make us a lot safer."

She stopped with her mouth open. Jones couldn't actually be that naive.

"Yes, it could be very bad. We don't know what long-term result that will have. There are far too many variables to ensure control. Maybe one of the men you interfere with is going to go on and create a damping field that stops nuclear reactions. Maybe he'd create some new form of radiology medicine that cures cancer. Maybe a lot of things. The point is, you can't afford to take those chances."

Jones shrugged. "Listen, all I know is that we'll use it to defend ourselves. If some possible invention is delayed, then someone else somewhere will invent it. How can you know? What I can assure you is the ability to travel accurately in time will be used for our good. For the good of our nation, to protect everyone."

They had convinced themselves that they were right, of course. Kathleen could see that there would be no arguing with them on the desirability of time-travel. She remembered the man they'd somehow sent off and decided to try to divert them from the main issue.

"What about the lost man? Where did you send him?" she asked.

The physicist replied, "Gridley was supposed to go back and stop a relatively recent event that made the newspapers. We could monitor it by watching for changes from recorded history."

She was speechless for a moment. How did they think they'd know when their very knowledge would change? After a moment, she got back to her question, "What happened to the man, this Gridley? Where do you think he is?"

"That's just it. We don't know. Would your formula help determine what happened to him? Would you work on it with us?" he asked.

She replied, "I'd like to help him. Surviving in the past is hard. I'm lucky to be alive. Will you release Cadeyrin if I help find your man?"

Jones replied, "No. Only if you give us your formula. We'll be grateful if you get our man back, but the formula is the thing we want. He can live out his life in the past or die. It's not important. He was just a soldier. He knew his duty, unlike some people in this room."

"I'll have to talk to my attorney first. You understand if I say that I don't trust you at this point. I'll give you my answer tomorrow. Will that be acceptable?" she asked.

Jones said, "Don't take too long. Time's flying. Your husband might have a relapse."

Kathleen snorted again. "Time always flies, but I've got all of the time there is. Don't you do anything to him. I'll be in touch."

⸻ ❖ ⸻

Once on the street, she caught a passing cab and returned to Geoff's office.

# Chapter Nine

# Not Birds

Gridley brushed his hand over his face. Where was he? Or, better yet, when was he? For lack of any better plan, he headed for the ridge. The honking noise had ceased, but whatever had made it might still be there. He moved quietly, taking advantage of the vegetation, a mixture of evergreens and deciduous trees that did not look familiar. It certainly wasn't the northern Virginia area. He felt like it was dryer, less humidity, too.

The other side of the hill was covered with dense conifers. There was no sign of the honker. Grid moved carefully down the ridge, keeping his eye on a single spot that attracted his attention. There was something on the branches of a tree. It looked like a stain, probably nothing, but it was all there was.

Once he got closer, he could smell blood and entrails. The odor was unmistakable. He'd smelled it often enough in battle to have it burned into his olfactory memory. He immediately slowed and moved deeper into cover. After holding still for a few minutes, he became convinced that there was no danger in the vicinity.

He moved close. The stain was blood splattered over the needles of the conifer. Under the shield of the lower branches was a body. It looked like some kind of bird thing to Grid. He dragged it out. The head was missing. That accounted for the blood. The body was maybe as big as that of a large dog, but the tail was long. It was almost twice the length of the body. The whole corpse was covered with short feathers that were a combination of green, blue, and red. The pattern was colorful, but Gridley could see that it would work as camouflage if the creature's habits included hiding in the undergrowth.

The one remaining arm was wing-like. It was broader than that of a mammal, and the feathers were longer than those on the rest of the body, but not long enough for the creature to fly. He straightened the arm. There were fingers at the joint. Fingers with sharp claws.

He glanced at the legs. They were partly feathered, but the lower leg was skin-covered. It reminded him of a bird of prey. The foot was taloned. The inside toe had a huge curved claw. In death, the claw was drawn up. He fingered it. It was sharply curved, about five or six inches long, and obviously deadly. What was this creature, anyway?

His study was interrupted by a slight noise on the other side of the tree. He ducked and crawled under the branches. Looking out from under the overhanging needles, he saw a crude nest on the ground between a large fallen tree and another conifer. He moved closer.

There were three unbroken eggs in the nest. There had been more, but they and one side of the nest had been crushed. Something had stepped on it; something that was quite large. Grid couldn't make out the footprint. The ground was too hard, but from the width across the damaged part of the nest, the creature had to be larger than an elephant.

The noise repeated, and one of the eggs rocked back and forth. It was starting to hatch. Grid squatted down to watch.

⸻ ❖ ⸻

It had been almost an hour. The egg had broken, and the chick or whatever it was had stuck various portions of its anatomy through a hole it had made, but it hadn't come out as yet. Gridley was growing tired of waiting.

He carefully picked up the egg and broke little chunks of shell off to enlarge the hole. He was just reaching for another piece that was partly loose when a small creature popped its head out and cheeped cheerfully at him.

It was wet and not attractive, but it looked for all the world like a baby bird until it opened its mouth. Its muzzle, for that was what it was, not a beak, was full of small, pointed teeth.

He rubbed his finger over its head. The feathers were already drying. They were like down and felt soft and fluffy. The creature cheeped again. Then opened its mouth.

"You're probably hungry, aren't you?" Gridley didn't know much about birds, but it was evident that this one needed food. He looked around. There was nothing nearby. The corpse! It was on the other side of the tree.

He put the egg down and quickly dragged the remains of the body back to the nest. He could have carried it, it was only about a hundred pounds, but he didn't want to get blood all over himself.

Once he had moved it near the nest, he felt in his pocket. He always carried a folding tactical knife. Black-suit had wanted to make sure he had no weapons besides the revolver, but he had slipped his knife in anyways.

Using the knife, he sliced off a small sliver of flesh. The dead creature was probably the hatchling's mother. Or father, maybe. He didn't know, but right now it was waste-not, want-not. Regardless of the possible relationship, it was the only food he had.

Fortunately, the chick had no compunctions. It snapped the flesh when he dangled it close. It gulped a couple of times, then settled down on its haunches in an odd position to think about things.

Another egg was hatching. Gridley didn't wait for it. It took too long. He pulled the shell apart, exposing the baby. It cheeped weakly, then gaped at him.

Another slice of good ol' Mom, and that one was satisfied, too. Just in time. The third egg had cracked. Gridley paused. What in Hell was he doing? Hatching crazy-looking chicks in a place that he didn't know.

He shrugged. He'd always liked birds. Maybe these things weren't birds, but they were the only company he had at the moment. He had no additional drugs. The headset and tablet would run out of battery power before he could figure out how to use them without the attention focusing injection. It looked like he was here to stay. Might as well have some bird friends.

He fed the third chick, then picked them up and headed back up the ridge to a spot where there were some large rocks. He'd noticed the boulders on the way down but hadn't taken the time to investigate them. Now, he thought that they might offer some security, possibly a place of refuge. Whatever had killed the mother bird thing was too big to tackle with just a pocket knife.

He was in luck. The boulders leaned together in such a way as to form a man-sized, cave-like opening. There had been something living in the space, but it was empty now. Only some small bones and litter remained. He settled the chicks in the safety of the overhang and returned to bring the corpse up.

There were some smaller bird-like creatures pulling flesh off the corpse when he got there. They were about the size of turkeys. He threw a stone and knocked one down. It flopped about aimlessly until he broke its neck. It too had teeth.

Back at the boulders, he fed the chicks more flesh from the carcass of their parent. They cheeped at him and clustered near when he returned. He'd read somewhere about how birds imprint on the first moving thing they see after hatching. It looked like he'd inherited a family.

# Chapter Ten

# Plans

Kathleen was furious. Jones was an idiot. He thought he could play the game of changing time. Ha! If Cadeyrin were hurt, she'd go back and suffocate Jones in his cradle and the blazes with the repercussions. That set her thinking. Perhaps there was a way. She was, of course, restrained by the fact that she didn't want to meet herself. She couldn't risk losing her memory again. It had been hard enough to recover it the first time her energy field had gotten entangled with that of a previous version of herself.

The very fact that a Florida professor had disappeared when he touched two versions of the same object together simply showed that temporal paradoxes were incredibly dangerous and impossible to predict. Her formula didn't address such phenomena directly, but she thought that it was equivalent to suddenly getting an integer as an answer to division by zero.

⚬

The cab pulled up at Geoff's office. Since she'd only been gone a little over an hour, she hadn't bothered to call him. She went up the elevator and shortly was sitting with Geoff.

They discussed the situation. Geoff was all for attempting some legal action, but Kathleen had come to the conclusion that the people holding Cadeyrin considered themselves above the law. If that were the case, then they wouldn't hesitate to use force if they found themselves thwarted in any way. She felt that it would be best to try and outsmart them.

They decided that Geoff would use an investigator he knew to try and find where Cadeyrin was being held. If it were somewhere in the city, Kathleen would use her time-travel ability to jump back, enter the facility when it wasn't guarded, then jump forward and rescue Cadeyrin. It sounded simple, although Geoff apparently had a difficult time conceiving of the entire operation.

The part that bothered her the most was the possibility that she might somehow meet herself. She'd just have to be careful not to go near the place where he was being held before she did her time-travel rescue. That way, there would be no chance of a paradox. Still, the idea that she might exist simultaneously in the here and now made her worry. She hadn't solved that portion of the equation either. What she did know was that, when she extended the math to try and model the effect of simultaneous existence, there was no pure solution. Or rather, there were a lot of possible solutions. Anything might happen in that case, and there was no predicting it.

She'd told Agent Jones that she'd make up her mind in the morning. He'd agreed that they'd let her have the night to consider her options. She was to arrange a meeting through Geoff the next day.

Jones obviously felt he was in complete control of the situation and could let her run free. After all, he had the one thing that she'd do anything for: Cadeyrin. He knew she wouldn't risk him. He had a smug expression on his face when they parted.

———◦O◦———

Back at her house again, she wandered through the mostly vacant rooms thinking. She'd never furnished the place. There was a bed along with a small dining table with a couple of chairs. That was all. The refrigerator was stocked, as was the pantry. She only used the place when she needed to buy some provisions, things that weren't available in the Sangamon. She'd never brought Cadeyrin here either.

She'd jumped into the future with him without knowing what the effect would be. Jumping into a time where he'd never existed might have had some effect on him, but she'd had no choice. He needed medical care that she could not give. It apparently hadn't hurt him. He'd been recovering just fine when he was captured.

She sat at the table and drank a cup of instant coffee. It was horrible. Bitter, and it didn't even really smell like coffee, but it made her think.

She hadn't been near the hospital when Jones grabbed Cadeyrin. She'd been about a mile away at the veterinarian. That might be far enough away for her to avoid a paradox effect. Maybe she could jump back and hide near the hospital until the men brought Cadeyrin out and then trail them. That would be better than waiting for Geoff's investigator.

She'd have to be careful, though. She thought through the time sequence since she'd brought him here.

They'd driven to the fire station, then the hospital. She'd taken Ulfsa to the vet. She'd gone back to the hospital, then to see Geoff at Tate. Then she'd picked up Ulfsa, gone to Boom Park, and retreated to George's house in 1981. When she'd returned, she'd gone to Geoff's office, been picked up by Jones, and taken to St. Paul.

Who knew? Cadeyrin might be held in that same building. If so, she'd have to be extra careful. Once she was done with Jones, she'd gone back to Geoff's office and then home.

If she could just stay away from herself or even being anywhere near herself as she moved around, she might be able to avoid a paradox. She couldn't keep it up, though. The situation could easily get out of control if she moved around a lot on various time strands. It would be easy to lose track of where she'd been, and the consequences might prove disastrous.

She jumped up and went to the bedroom. The closet held some supplies that she had intended to take back to the Sangamon. Among them was a pair of binoculars. With them in hand, she got in the Land Rover and headed for the hospital again.

This time, she parked across the street from the hospital entrance. She hoped the agents wouldn't recognize her Land Rover.

From where she was parked, the binoculars gave her a good view of the Emergency Room. If anyone were coming out, she could see their faces. There was no one in sight at the moment, just light nighttime traffic. She closed her eyes and concentrated.

———◆———

To an observer, the SUV would have been there one moment and not the next, but no one saw it disappear in the darkness.

---

A man in a small car thought he saw a space in the next row in the parking lot. He accelerated, moving quickly between the parked cars, turned into the next row, and drove about halfway up. Suddenly he realized that the space he was heading for had been filled by a large SUV.

"Damn it!" he said. "I never get a break. Where did that S.O.B. come from anyway?"

He drove on by and found a spot about five rows over.

---

Kathleen slumped in the seat. According to her calculations, her prior self should be entering the vet's office about now. She raised the binoculars and scanned the hospital. Then she sat up. A black SUV with tinted windows had pulled in and taken up a station adjacent to the ER doors. Some men got out and went in. She wasn't able to see their faces, but the back of one of them looked like Agent Jones.

About ten minutes later, they came out, wheeling Cadeyrin towards the SUV. His hands were handcuffed, and he had a wild look on his face, but he also looked weak. Her heart almost broke.

"Don't worry, my darling. I'm going to get you out of this. Please have patience and don't try anything that will get you hurt," she whispered. She put the binoculars down and wiped her eyes.

The SUV was beginning to move. She started her vehicle and followed.

---

Thirty minutes later, the black SUV drove into a parking garage that served an office complex in Maple Grove. She'd been wrong in assuming that Cadeyrin might be held in St. Paul. This was even better since she'd never been here on this timeline. There was no chance of a conflict.

# Chapter Eleven

# Hostage

Cadeyrin was feeling very fuzzy when the men came into his room. The nurse had given him something through the tube that connected to his arm. Shortly after she'd put the liquid in the tube, all the pain faded, and most of his desire to think faded along with it.

He was awake, lying in a sort of bemused daze. The men came in, shoving a protesting nurse in front of them. Cadeyrin had no expectations of a hospital, and at first, it seemed like this might be normal behavior. He watched with his eyes partly open.

One of the men slapped the nurse, who dropped to the floor. That wasn't what he expected. He had thought such violence might not be present in Kathleen's time. He tried to sit up, but the effort was almost beyond his ability. He tried again, but one of the men shoved him flat with the palm of one hand. The man had the ill grace to laugh as he did.

That was too much! Cadeyrin caught the man's hand with his and twisted hard. There was a snap, and the man staggered towards the wall with a cry. Cadeyrin made a massive effort and sat up.

His eyes sought out the second man. That one was injecting something into the tube that went to Cadeyrin's arm. He grabbed the man's hand and yanked the needle out, but the room had already started to blur. He felt a wave of sleep approaching and fell back onto the bed, his eyes closed.

⸺◆⸺

The short man with the hypodermic dropped it on the floor and turned to his injured partner. "Shut up about your hand and help me get this guy transferred to the gurney in the hall."

The other man, his face white, came off the cabinet on which he'd been leaning and lunged for Cadeyrin with murder in his eye. "That son-of-a-bitch broke my wrist. When I get through with him, he won't need a gurney."

"Get the gurney, damn it! If you touch him, I'll make sure the boss knows, and you don't want to get on his bad side."

"You wouldn't! Just let me work him over a little. I still got one good hand." The injured man inadvertently moved his wrist and moaned.

"Aw, you're no good. I'll get the gurney myself. Just don't you touch him, and I mean it," the other man said.

The nurse had slid over to the side of the room and now made a dash for the door. The short man lunged and caught her arm as she plunged through the opening.

"That isn't going to help," he said, almost kindly. "We've got two other guys with guns holding everyone off in the hall. Now that you're up, get that gurney and wheel it in here."

She complied, her eyes wide.

—◆◇◆—

Cadeyrin wasn't sure where he was. He was moving a little. Rocking back and forth. Now there was acceleration. He was in the pickup. Kathleen had to be driving. He had something that he wanted to tell her, but he couldn't open his eyes at the moment. He tried to talk with no effect. His mouth didn't seem to want to work. The darkness rose up again, and he forgot what he was going to say.

—◆◇◆—

This time, when he became aware of himself, he could hear people speaking softly nearby. They were saying something about him, but he couldn't make any sense out of the words.

"Keep him healthy. Take care of him as if he were the most important patient you've ever treated. We need him in good shape, at least until we achieve our objective. What happens to him after that isn't important."

"I treat all my patients the same. They always are important. To somebody. Don't worry; I'll make sure he recovers. I just wish you hadn't given him ketamine on top of what he was already on. It's not a good combination, especially when the patient is recovering from major surgery."

"Just take care of him. Give him anything you want. We've got quite a few drugs here and can get anything. Just give the guard a list. They'll get everything on it. I just want him healthy."

None of this made much sense to Cadeyrin. He felt sick at his stomach, and his chest hurt. He couldn't breathe well and felt like he was drowning. He coughed, a deep hacking cough.

"He shouldn't be doing that. Get that oxygen going, stat. He'll rip something open and bleed to death before we can get him to the hospital."

"He isn't going to the hospital. I suggest you get the oxygen on him, yourself."

Hands moved his head and placed something under his nose. His breathing didn't hurt as much. He relaxed and faded into blackness again.

———◦—◦◦—◦———

Cadeyrin opened his eyes. He was in a windowless room. The light was bright, and he squinted as he looked around. It was somewhat like the hospital room, but not the same. It looked like someone had converted it from some other purpose.

There was an intake of breath, and he looked for the source of the sound. An attractive woman with dark skin was looking at him from a deep chair.

"So, you're awake?" She smiled, and her smile was radiant and friendly. Her dark skin made her teeth seem even whiter than they were.

He cleared his throat experimentally, then spoke, "I'm awake."

His voice wasn't very firm, and the quaver in it shocked him. Even speaking made him feel bad.

"I'm weak. I'm sick, I think. What happened to me?"

Then he remembered being struck by the stone.

"Oh, yes. I think my ribs are broken. I'll have to take care until they heal. You don't have to worry about me. I'll rest for a while, and then I'll be able to get up."

She looked startled, then said, "I think you believe you're getting up. Don't try it. You've had surgery; your lung was punctured and full of blood. Then you were given a drug that you shouldn't have had. It's going to be a few days before I'll let you move."

He'd become conscious of another urge while she was speaking.

"I'm full. I need to relieve myself," he said, looking away from the nurse. He didn't know how she'd take discussing bodily functions.

She bent near the foot of the bed, looked at something, and said, "No. You're passing urine with no problem. You don't need to go."

That was wrong. He had the feeling that his bladder was full. It was uncomfortable. "Yes, I do. I need to go, now let me up."

She laughed, then said, "You've got a catheter in place. It's draining the urine from your bladder. If it's uncomfortable, it's because it is pressing on the bottom of your bladder a little too strongly. That's where the signal to urinate originates. Don't worry about it."

He lay back, trying to ignore the pressing sensation of needing to go. "Where am I? Is this some part of the hospital?"

He abruptly remembered the man striking the nurse.

"No. Where am I? Who are you?" His tone changed and deepened with suspicion and anger.

The woman looked concerned and moved forward to place her hand on his forehead.

"Some people have arrested you. You're in a holding facility. It's my job to take care of you and make sure that you recover from your surgery. My name's Shaelle. I'm a nurse. A pretty good one, too, even if I say so myself, so you just need to relax. You're in no shape to do anything, and they aren't going to let you out of here at the moment. Please just relax and work on getting well."

He recognized that she was worried about him, and, in truth, he felt awful. He was terribly weak. He was no stranger to pain, but this was a different level of injury. He sighed and dropped his head to the pillow.

"I'm going to wait. Will you tell me what these men who have taken me prisoner want?" he asked.

She smiled a little sadly. "I don't know what you've done or why they want you, but they said they wanted you healthy." She shook her head affirmatively as if to convince him and herself.

He recalled the conversation that he'd overheard somewhere back in the blackness. What he could remember didn't have that meaning. They wanted him alive until they achieved some objective, but then his health wouldn't matter. Apparently, this woman was lying to an extent. She didn't want him to cause a problem. Maybe she really did want him better. She'd said that she treated all her patients the same.

He smiled and said, "I'll do what you want if it will help me get well. Right now I feel like I've been run over by a herd of bison."

Shaelle laughed. "Oh, I'm sure it's not that bad. I've never seen a herd of bison. There aren't any around here, that's for sure." She laughed at her attempted humor.

He smiled again. "Maybe there aren't any bison here now, but there were at one time. You just have to go to then, and you'll see."

She busied herself, taking his pulse and listening to his breathing with a cold, silver thing that had tubes going to her ears. When she finished, she said, "Lucky for us, we can't travel in time if there are such dangers."

She didn't know. Cadeyrin sighed and turned his head away. Kathleen had told him that some people in her own time wanted her secret of travel. Maybe that was what this was all about. When he turned back to her, she was looking at him with a different expression, one he'd seen before. She found him attractive; it was obvious in her eyes. She was good-looking and seemed exotic to him. Her dark skin looked warm. For a moment, he allowed himself to think about her, but his mind interjected a vision of his beautiful Kathleen. This nurse, attractive as she might be, was no competition for the woman he loved.

She moved tentatively toward him, but he turned his head away, rejecting both her and the circumstances of his captivity. He heard her sigh, then retreat towards the door. It opened and closed quietly.

He'd just have to wait until his ribs had healed. He had the patience of a hunter, one who could wait until the game became available.

Once he had his strength back, he'd set about getting free and locating Kathleen. How hard could it be? There were more people now than in his time. He knew that, but surely if he asked, someone could guide him to her. He'd wait, listen, and try to gain as much knowledge as he could. When he was better...well, they'd be well-advised not to oppose him.

# Chapter Twelve

# Scouting

Kathleen continued down the street. She didn't want to risk entering the parking garage. Her targets had given no sign that they realized she was tailing them, but her natural predilection was to be cautious.

She parked a couple of blocks away on a residential street near a large Englemann spruce. In a few minutes, she had walked back to the building they had entered. Now, how to do this?

She considered her options. If she entered the place, they'd know or would soon find out that she knew where they were holding Cadeyrin. They probably couldn't capture her, but she was still vulnerable to some things. Like a bullet in the brain, she thought. A slight tinge of fear washed over her. This situation wasn't like stalking a dangerous beast.

She'd done that. Beasts didn't plan much ahead. They had known means of doing harm to one, means that required physical contact. Why they could simply shoot her from an adjacent rooftop! She'd never know it was coming.

Cadeyrin's training kicked in. She took a deep breath and relaxed. As she did, she remembered that the enemy wanted her knowledge, her formula, and her cooperation in training people to use it. They wouldn't out and out kill her until maybe after she'd helped them. She cynically expected them to decide that she couldn't be trusted not to tell others about her method of time-travel. That decision would inevitably lead to her death.

No, she couldn't let them know she was close. She took note of the building's address and returned to her SUV. There was a business store a few blocks away. She entered and purchased a notebook computer. She didn't need much processing power, just internet access.

There was a coffee shop adjacent to the business store. They conveniently offered Wi-Fi access. She set up her computer pausing to sip coffee and nibble on a cinnamon roll. Once she was ready, she went over to the counter and asked for the Wi-Fi password. It was unoriginal: guest1.

That gave her the access she needed. She ordered another cup of coffee and began to research.

The county tax records showed that a corporation owned the building. The corporate officers' names weren't available. She scrolled down until she saw that it had been set up by a law firm, which acted as the controlling manager.

She went back to the tax record. There were some statistics about the building's size and so on, but no floor plans. Construction was completed in 2001. There was a builder's name mentioned.

The builder was a large company, and they had a website. Someone on their marketing staff had seen fit to include the building in the sales and past projects section. There were a series of color pictures of various features but no floor plan. The pictures helped a little but didn't offer the information she wanted.

She went back to the sales page and clicked on the building project page again. She took the time to read through the description and found the architect's name.

On to the architect's site. That got her most of what she wanted. The architect had provided a rendering of the building's floor plan in his completed projects sub-section. She captured the floor plan pages by printing them to files. Then she sat and drank a third cup of coffee while she studied the various parts of the drawings.

She was shaking from caffeine before she finished. She wasn't used to coffee. She'd lost the habit during her time in the past. Cadeyrin only drank cold water, and she'd picked up his habit. It was all her body needed, and she'd come to realize that she felt better as a result.

Now that she had a picture of the building, she knew where the services, HVAC, and so on were located. That would be an adequate spot to start. It would most likely be empty at night.

She paid and headed back to the building. This time, she parked several blocks away in a doctor's office parking lot. That was, she hoped, a good place. Her car would not attract any attention until maybe at night when the lot emptied. She didn't intend to be gone that long.

❖

A small hatchback had followed her into the lot. It pulled in beside the big SUV, and the driver got out. He glanced into the Land Rover and then looked around. Where had the driver gone? She'd been right in front of him, and there hadn't seemed like there had been enough time for her to go inside the building while he parked. He shrugged and turned towards the office. His appointment was only a few minutes from now. Couldn't be late.

❖

Kathleen looked around. The weather was clear, and it was now almost night. She set off briskly, heading towards where the completed building would stand in a few months.

It was under construction, and the skeleton stood empty at the moment. The floors were up as were some of the interior partitions. She ignored the no trespassing signs and moved into the shadows along the east side. From there, it was easy to climb onto the first floor. She looked around, trying to get oriented. The primary HVAC vent column went up the center of the building between two elevator shafts.

She moved cautiously over and looked up and down. It was black below, although some residual blue sky showed overhead. She waited until it was dark, then began a tour of the building.

She'd covered most of the space, moving carefully to avoid falling, when a car pulled up in front. The door slamming was what alerted her. Two men stood by the vehicle talking. They were too far away, so she couldn't make out what they were saying. The men had flashlights and waved the lights around randomly, so she didn't think she could safely approach.

That was bad. She retreated a little, hiding behind a steel column. When they started towards the building, she closed her eyes and disappeared.

She appeared exactly a day later in the same spot. There was no one in the parking lot at this time. Thinking that someone might come, she hurried and finalized her inspection.

It seemed to her that the logical place to hold Cadeyrin would be on the top floor. He was a valuable hostage, and the top floor seemed right. Of course, she was inexperienced in such things. Maybe they'd hold him in the basement. That might be better. They could have some kind of dungeon – no, that was silly. They couldn't have something like that, or the maintenance people would know about it. Best to try the top floor first.

She walked up and looked down the halls. The walls were missing at the moment, but the steel studs were in place so she could tell where the offices would eventually stand. She moved into one, did some quick calculations, and jumped forward to a day in 2002 in the middle of the night.

The building was now finished, and she was standing in someone's office.

She jumped back, moved to another office, and jumped forward again, taking care not to arrive at the same time that she'd been in the first office. She didn't want to make a mistake and be there simultaneously. No good could come from that.

Working in this fashion, she investigated twenty offices. She was tired and cranky as she popped into the twenty-first room. She looked around dejectedly, expecting another office, but this room was furnished differently. It had medical supplies and a table and chair bolted to the floor. She flashed back to her start time, moved one room over, and jumped ahead.

This room was set up like a hospital room. Perhaps they engaged in interrogation in the room next door, and this one was for recovery. Kathleen wasn't sure of the room's purpose, but this looked promising. If they were going to hold her man in here, they'd need a facility that would duplicate his hospital room. He was in no shape to simply throw in a cell.

She rubbed her forehead. She was making what was perhaps an unwarranted assumption, but it was all she had. They might not care if Cadeyrin lived long. They only needed him to get her cooperation. Once she gave them the information, both Cadeyrin and she were probably dead.

She just didn't know, but this spot seemed to have more promise than any other. Now she needed to prepare to rescue him. She'd need Geoff's help.

# Chapter Thirteen

# Cooperation

Geoff had set up a meeting. They were seated on opposite sides of the fifth-floor conference table just down the hall from Geoff's office. Jones had brought one other man with him, but his role wasn't clear. He kept quiet throughout the first part of their meeting.

Jones leaned back with an attitude of being in charge and said, "Okay, Ms. Whitby, or should I call you something else, Mrs. Caveman or what? Does that Neanderthal of yours even have a last name?"

Kathleen opened her mouth in outrage, but before she could speak, Geoff interjected, "Being antagonistic is usually a sign that one holds a weak position. If you were truly confident, you would probably be nicer."

Jones sat up straight and said, "Let's get one thing straight. I am in control here. We are holding her pet caveman to ensure that she makes the correct decision. He's in good health, or at least as good as one could expect him to be with a perforated lung and all. Of course, he could take a turn for the worse, and we might not be ready to provide appropriate care. You understand what I mean?" He looked at Kathleen.

This threat was too much. Kathleen's sense of humor had always been a little odd, and now she felt that Jones was so dramatic that his actions seemed a parody. She laughed out loud. Jones sat back with a puzzled expression.

"I don't see why you're laughing, young woman. This is a serious situation. We may not be able to hold you, but we do have your man, and we can keep him. He is hurt. He might not get better. We're doing the best we can but under difficult circumstances. Things happen. Besides, you owe your government your secret. We need to have complete control of time."

She'd regained control by now. Shaking her head negatively, Kathleen said, "My formula is my discovery. You know what I was working on, so just hire some other physicists to duplicate my research. The data I was using is freely available. I'm not stopping you.

Jones shook his head in turn. "Do you think that we haven't tried that? We've got several lines of research that we're following up on, but you seem to have somehow struck on the most accurate method. We've only had a partial success—"

She interrupted, "You mean you've sent someone through time?"

He shrugged. "Well, we used a soldier. Obviously, he wasn't trained in higher math like you. He was to carry out a specific mission so that we could observe the effect. He disappeared and has not returned. I'd count that as a proof of concept, except we haven't detected any result."

She sighed. They were probably going to duplicate her formula eventually. Maybe she'd be better off just giving it to them.

Jones continued. "We'd like to recover our man. We gave him a 97% chance of success, and he isn't known for failing his assignments. We'd like to know what happened."

She sighed again, then said, "You might not notice the effect. You see, it would change the timeline, and you wouldn't realize that history had changed for you."

He started to speak, but she held up her hand, interrupting him. "Now, before you start wondering why my actions haven't changed the present, they have, but only a minor amount. I've been careful not to meddle in ways that would have far-reaching repercussions. The timeline is robust and self-healing to a certain extent. You could change it by, say, killing someone who was destined to be famous or come up with a critical invention, but the very few things I've done so far have had little effect."

Jones tapped his fingers on the table as he said, "That sounds suspiciously like a veiled threat. Are you saying that you could attack us through time?"

Jones' compatriot leaned forward, intense interest on his narrow face.

So that was their real motivation. Kathleen had thought that it would be something like that. They wanted to change the world in ways that would favor them or whoever they were working for. The fools thought that they could control the effects.

Anger washed over her. Her voice rose, and her hands started to shake a little.

"You idiots think you can control timeline changes? You obviously haven't come close to the correct formula. I can move myself and a limited amount of mass precisely because I understand how to control the few variables that deal with temporal positioning. When you start to calculate repercussions of your actions, especially actions that deal with critical actors in time, the variables explode geometrically. The possibilities become almost infinite. Our government cannot even foresee the effects of daily actions it takes, despite having access to an unlimited amount of funding. There are so many unintentional results that cause problems now. Why would I want to give you the power to screw things up?"

Jones started to answer, but the silent man at his side placed his hand on Jones' arm. His jaw snapped shut.

The man turned to Kathleen and said, "We have resources that you could not imagine. With the computing power that we have assigned to this project, we can control all the critical variables. Some minor changes might escape us, but with time-travel, we have a real chance to make this world better. Do you understand? We will continue with our research until we've mastered time. You can shorten our quest and save the taxpayers a great deal of money, but you cannot stop us. Do you imagine that you're the only one who's traveled in time?"

She opened her mouth, then closed it. She looked at Geoff, but he only shrugged. He would do what he could to protect her, but time-theory wasn't law practice.

She turned back to the thin man. "No. I hadn't heard that anyone else had traveled temporally."

He smiled a little nastily. "When we found out about your discovery, we started researching. There are quite a lot of people who have moved in time, just in the past few years. You understand that records are more thorough these days, and we can run extensive searches on the data that we've collected. We've located several recent time-travelers. One, in particular, a young college student in Florida, managed to bring back a young woman who, we think, is a contemporary of your hunter. We'd like to question him and her, but they've disappeared, much like you disappeared. We assume they're elsewhen. The good thing is the young man in question agreed to work with Professor James Wolf, who has come up with the procedure we are experimenting with."

That was news. Kathleen had heard vaguely of Wolf. He was at some university in Florida. She'd read somewhere that he had some groundbreaking theory about time-related issues in quantum physics, similar to those findings on which she had been working.

She asked, "Did Wolf come up with just a formula or a process?"

"He came up with a formula. We think it's incomplete, but it does work. We're not convinced about its accuracy. Our research group came up with a clever way of electronically programming our traveler with the correct data to launch him to his destination. That allows us a degree of control. We thought it worked, but apparently, something has gone wrong."

Kathleen looked at Jones. He was looking at his hands. She wondered if this was something that she could cooperate with them on without giving away her secret.

"Look...I, uh, I mean I'm worried about your test subject. He might not have ended up where you intended. I haven't decided to give you my formula, but perhaps I could recover him."

She thought that her help would allow her to analyze their process. She could determine whether they were on the correct path. That would give her critical information. She was becoming more convinced that they'd misuse the ability. It would be best if she could see that they'd never gain the control they were seeking. There was surely something she could do to keep them from mastering time-travel, regardless of the consequences. She might locate the Florida student and make him understand that he couldn't work with Professor Wolf. Somehow she could interrupt the development. She had to. Her sense of duty to the world was too great for her to ignore the potential for harm."

Jones raised his face and said, "You'll give us your formula, or your friend will suffer."

The thin man said, "That's enough, Jones. We'll accept your assistance, young lady. Help us find our man, and then we'll talk about further cooperation. We really need your help, you know."

Jones made an exasperated noise, then said, "Okay. That's what we'll do. Why don't you come with me, and I'll see that you get the information you need to get started?"

Geoff interrupted at this point. "I don't think that would be a good idea. Have the information sent to this office, and she can go over it here."

The thin man agreed. "We can do that, but only if I remain present to monitor what she does."

Kathleen was okay with that. There was no way he could watch and tell what she was doing unless he was able to read her mind accurately. She'd gained more than what she'd hoped. Her goal for the meeting had simply been to distract them. If they thought that she was going to help them, they'd possibly be a little less cautious in guarding Cadeyrin.

She wanted to find out how he was, though.

"I'd need to speak to Cadeyrin. I want to make sure that he is actually alright. If you've harmed him, then all offers of assistance are off."

Jones didn't answer directly. He pulled out his cell phone and pressed a couple of buttons. She could hear the call connect faintly, then someone said, "This is blue. Go ahead."

Jones pressed the speaker button and said, "Red here. Put the patient on."

Blue answered, "He's nearby. Just a minute."

Jones looked at her and said, "No tricks, now. You can talk to him for thirty seconds just to assure yourself that he's healthy."

Kathleen waited, holding her breath.

Cadeyrin's voice came on. He sounded like they had drugged him.

"Kathleen?"

"Oh, Cadeyrin! Are you alright? Have they hurt you?"

He cleared his throat a little and then said, "I don't feel very well. I'm okay, I think, but they used some kind of stuff on me that makes me feel—"

He was interrupted by Blue. "You've heard him. He's okay. Put Red back on."

Jones clicked the speaker button off, held the phone to his ear, and said, "Red here."

He paused to listen, then answered, "Fine. Continue as you have been. We're making progress here."

He turned to look at Kathleen, then added, "I'm guaranteeing that he's well cared for, so continue to take care of him. I'll let you know if there's to be a change in his treatment."

His expression left her no doubt that his last statement was a threat. She answered him. "Don't you let anything happen to him, Jones. I'm not the helpless girl I was. If anything happens to him, I will take action, and you won't like it. I can guarantee that."

# Chapter Fourteen

# Temporal Trouble

The two of them didn't bother to stand when Jones left. He'd be back tomorrow in the morning with materials for her to study. Meanwhile, his leaving the room seemed to lighten the air as if some dark cloud had dissipated.

Kathleen started to speak to Goff, but he shook his head and raised his finger to cross his lips. Instead of speaking, he took a piece of paper, scribbled something on it, and pushed it over to her.

It said, "They may have bugged this room. Let's meet in the drugstore across the street on the corner in thirty minutes."

Kathleen stretched, sighed, and said, "Maybe their research has taken them on a different path from my equation. I'm not sure I can help, but I guess I'll try."

Geoff picked up where she left off. "Yes, it sounds as if they'll release Cadeyrin if you help them. If you can get their guy back, that would undoubtedly be of some assistance, even if only to him. I'm sure he doesn't want to be stuck somewhere back in time."

"I'll see you in the morning, then," she said. She stood and left.

<hr>

Twenty minutes later, Kathleen became aware of a presence standing near her as she looked at first-aid products. Geoff smiled when she turned around and said, "Thought they might have bugged my office. This mess has got me jumping at shadows everywhere. I'm not used to cloak and dagger-type stuff. My clients usually are more into securities and investments."

Kathleen looked over her shoulder. No one was nearby. She still kept her tone low as she said, "I just wanted you to know that I'm taking action. They've given me through tonight, and they expect me to help tomorrow. I'm pretty sure they won't be expecting any resistance from me."

Geoff frowned. "Don't underestimate these people. I suspect that they are far more experienced at this kind of thing than we are. Let's hope they aren't expecting anything, but still – " He paused to check their surroundings. "You'd better act with extreme caution. If you don't mind, would you give me an idea of what you intend?"

It couldn't hurt to tell him. Perhaps he'd have an idea that would help.

"It's simple. I'm going back before the building was built, then transfer forward into Cadeyrin's room. I've investigated, and I'm sure I know where it is."

"What if they're waiting for you and taser you, then keep you drugged so you can't transfer back out?"

She sighed. "They could do that, I guess, but I wouldn't be able to explain my method to them if they drugged me. Or, at least I don't think I could. If I'm sober enough to talk coherently, then I could transfer out."

He was still dubious. "They could threaten to kill Cadeyrin if you leave."

That would be bad. Kathleen was worried about that exact thing. So far, there was no readily apparent counter-move. She could feel her hands starting to shake as she said, "If they do, then I'll take extreme action. I could eliminate Jones before he was born, I guess. I've never tried to figure out if something like that would irrevocably damage our present time-stream."

Geoff said, "Promise me that you'll discuss anything like that with me. I'd hate to wake up some morning and find that I was married to someone else or wasn't a lawyer."

She laughed a little at his weak humor. "I promise."

There was no reason to wait for dark to get started. Kathleen could park far enough away from the building that Jones' men wouldn't know she was there unless they were following her, and as far as she was aware, they weren't trailing her yet, unless...Maybe they had a tracking device on her car. She'd have to take public transportation to her starting point. That would have to work.

She'd collected two pistols and some other gear from the gun safe at her house and was heading back towards Maple Grove. She didn't keep much in the house, just some extra clothes, first-aid supplies, and some extra firearms. She had come forward through time to the house maybe twice in the past six months of her personal time. She started to close the gun closet but then paused. It was heavy and bulky, but maybe...She made up her mind and stuffed the Kevlar bullet-resistant vest into her bag also. It might be heavy and slow down her movements, but she could always make up lost time. She laughed to herself. Time wasn't a problem. As long as she could keep from conflicting with her past or future self, she had all the time in the universe. She suspected that, even with her increasing familiarity with temporal travel, there were issues that she would never really grasp. Humans were just too tied to their linear existence to be able to understand without an intensive effort.

That led to another thought. Kathleen paused in the middle of the living room. What if there were creatures who were familiar with or even actually lived with free movement in time as one of their primary attributes? That would be interesting, but –. She gave up the thought as non-productive. It was an interesting speculation. She should think about it more when she had her current problem solved.

She parked the SUV at a convenient location near a downtown hotel, took the backpack into which she'd shoved her gear, and walked casually over to the entrance. Once there, she entered the lobby, sat down, and called a cab.

The driver thought her destination was a little strange but let her out on the side of the parkway about a half-mile from her destination. Shaking his head, he merged back into traffic. When he looked in his rear-view mirror, the young woman wasn't there. He looked again. She couldn't have hidden. There was nowhere she could be hiding. Maybe another car had picked her up. Maybe not. He met some strange ones in this job.

—◆—

Kathleen moved off the road into the adjacent field. There was a small clump of trees about fifty yards down the fence line. That would do. It looked as if it had been there for years. One of the trees was large and had to be much older than the enemy's building.

She threaded through the bushes and undergrowth. There was some litter in the middle of the grove, but nothing fresh. Nothing to indicate that anyone had been here recently.

She unpacked the bulky vest and put it on, covering it with her light jacket. It wasn't too unwieldy, although it made her look several sizes larger than she actually was. It was good that her life in the Sangamon was so active. The vest might once have seemed an intolerable burden to her, but now it was merely an inconvenience.

She checked the two nine-millimeter semi-automatics. Both were loaded and ready to go, as were the two extra magazines she'd brought. As an afterthought, she slipped a tactical folding knife into one of the pockets of the vest.

The two pistols went back into the bag with their holsters. Kathleen didn't intend for anyone to see her, but there were still laws about carrying handguns in the time before the building had been constructed. She didn't want to be seen walking into the construction site heavily armed. That would be sure to cause a stink.

She checked her surroundings once more. Nothing, no one nearby. She closed her eyes and vanished.

—◆—

It was night, just as she'd planned. The clump of trees was much smaller; now, just the two larger ones were present. She set off across the field, moving diagonally towards the construction site.

There were still some men present, poking around and moving some tools or something. She snorted in exasperation. She didn't have to wait for them to finish. She flickered forward an hour. The site was now completely vacant and dark.

Once in the building, she moved slowly, taking care not to trip over any debris or fall into an opening, of which there were many. She worked her way to the right room on the top floor. The drywall was absent, so she slid between two of the metal supporting studs, then moved over adjacent to the room's doorway.

She strapped the pistols on and looked around. Then she closed her eyes, visualized the correct values, and mentally plugged them into her equation. She vanished.

———⋘⊙⋙———

Something felt wrong. In response, Kathleen snapped her eyes open. There was a momentary feeling of triumph. She'd done it. Cadeyrin was lying in a hospital bed on the other side of the room, looking at her. She started to speak but was instantly overcome with intense nausea. Her stomach felt like it was about to be pulled out.

Cadeyrin's eyes opened wide, and he lifted his hand in a warding gesture. Kathleen felt as if something were ripping her apart. She dropped to her knees and bent to the floor, holding her stomach.

In a pained voice, Cadeyrin moaned, "No. Go now!"

Something inside her acted in self-preservation. The pain was intensifying so rapidly that she couldn't consciously plan. She moved in time to her most comfortable destination. One moment she was on the hard floor; the next, she collapsed on her side in some tall grass in the Sangamon.

———⋘⊙⋙———

After a time, she regained some strength. It was quiet and sunny. The sun was coming down from directly overhead, and its warmth helped her sore stomach. She gradually relaxed and straightened out. As she did, she became aware of some wetness between her legs.

The ground was dry, so that wasn't the source. Kathleen investigated, finally pulling her pants down to see what it was. There was blood staining her underpants. Not a huge amount, but enough to make a wet spot.

What could that mean? She'd felt like she'd been struck in the stomach and then her guts were practically wrenched out. Retreating to the Sangamon had immediately caused the pain to subside.

Now that she thought about it, she remembered that Cadeyrin had seemed to be in some pain also. He'd told her to go. What had happened?

Her train of thought was abruptly interrupted. There was a slight noise nearby. Something had brushed through some dried weeds, and the ensuing rustle alerted her. She pulled both pistols and thumbed the safety off each of them.

With considerable caution, she lifted her head to look. There was a startled pause, then a rush. Kathleen jumped up, shooting three rounds with her right-hand pistol at a snarling saber-toothed cat that was just yards away.

The loud noise of the shot seemed to frighten the creature more than the bullets that struck it. It stopped and turned, then staggered and coughed. Kathleen aimed carefully and fired one round at the area directly behind its ear. It slumped forward and dropped.

Looking around for more, she reloaded the pistol. The cat was a homotherium, a medium-sized saber-toothed cat with short rear legs that reminded one of a hyena. They often went about in pairs. This one's mate would surely attack in seconds. She readied herself.

There was nothing. Just some small birds singing off in the grass somewhere and a very slight breeze. The sun shone down with its bright light, and everything seemed cheerful, despite the violence.

She walked over to the cat. It was dead. There was so much blood coming out of some wounds on its chest that it would have died quickly from those had she not put a bullet in its brain. It was lucky that the creature had made an error. If it had come upon her lying down, without her guns ready, the outcome would have been different. It was more than able to take down prey larger than a mere human woman.

She sighed and mentally gave thanks for Cadeyrin. His training had molded her into a capable huntress, one capable of defending herself in the primitive wilderness.

She started. What was she doing? She shouldn't be back here in the interglacial period. She had intended to rescue Cadeyrin. She'd failed due to something she'd never encountered. The stomach pain was intense, and it had forced her to flee his presence.

She wasn't about to accept defeat. She rechecked her weapons, then closed her eyes and jumped forwards in time. She intended to arrive in his room a second after she'd left.

She snapped her eyes open in the same room a minute later. Cadeyrin was lying back, his arm over his eyes and his other arm across his lower stomach. She had a moment to observe the room was still unoccupied before the pain in her stomach returned harder than before. She didn't wait. She jumped immediately back to the past, this time under complete control.

She was back at the construction site at night. There was something that was keeping her from carrying out her plans. Perhaps the enemy, Jones, and his group had some kind of temporal shield. She didn't know.

She was still in pain. The abdominal pain had reactivated to a slight extent the psychological pain she'd felt from the scars that she'd born around her waist and thighs from birth. She limped slowly back to the grove of trees.

By the time she was back, the abdominal pain had eased a little. The pain from her scars was more mental than physical. Cadeyrin's treatment had his love had gone a long way towards removing that disability. She was now fully confident that she was a valuable woman, deserving of a handsome man's full love. She just had to find a way to free him.

From the trees, she jumped back to the future, called a cab, and returned to where she'd left her SUV.

Cadeyrin wouldn't have to wait long. As soon as she figured out what was causing this problem, she'd return to him a few seconds after she'd left. Meanwhile, she needed food and rest.

She drove to her house. It was mid-afternoon by the time she'd parked in the garage. She still had almost fifteen hours before she was to meet with Jones at Geoff's office tomorrow. There was still plenty of time to act.

# Chapter Fifteen

# Extorted Assistance

Kathleen sat in her kitchen, slowly eating a bowl of tomato soup and some crackers. She paused every few bites to sip some water and think.

Something had driven her away from Cadeyrin. She'd been careful to avoid any paradoxical contact with herself. As far as she now knew, she hadn't been anywhere near his location during the two brief times she was there. A temporal paradox couldn't be the reason she had to retreat. Besides, if it had, it would be doubtful that she'd even remember who he was now.

The last time she'd encountered herself, she'd almost lost the memories of the entire span of time that she had been in the past. She'd met herself just a fraction of a second before she'd jumped to the past to escape the attack of the man who'd murdered her beloved Professor. That brief overlap had caused her to temporarily forget the months she'd spent in the Pleistocene between jumping away from the attack and jumping back. She'd almost forgotten Cadeyrin, the most important part of her existence!

Temporal paradoxes were incredibly dangerous. Kathleen didn't exactly know what would happen if she were to be forced to remain in the same place as a prior or a later version of herself, but it most certainly wouldn't be anything good for either version. The math didn't seem to have a unique solution in such a circumstance, and the exact result was impossible to predict.

So that left other factors to consider. Perhaps Jones' group had some shielding. If they'd known that she'd try to rescue Cadeyrin, they might have planned to repel her in some way. She needed to find out more about their research.

How far had they gotten? She was unfamiliar with this Professor Wolf's activities. Apparently, he had some insight that he'd gained from a college student who had allegedly traveled in time. She didn't know about that either. Perhaps it would be better to appear to work with Jones for a while. That way, she could gain insight into their activities and capabilities.

She finished her soup. She was tired. Her stomach still tinged a little despite the interlude and the food. She'd showered and changed her clothes.

There was no more blood, and that was good. Kathleen couldn't quite figure that bit out. It didn't seem to fit into what she knew about the problems associated with a temporal conflict, but there was no single clear-cut single to the equation in the case of a paradox. Maybe physical symptoms were in the range of potential effects.

Meanwhile, she thought that she should rest. As much as she wanted Cadeyrin's arms around her again, she had to be prepared to give her best to break him free. Anyway, it wouldn't seem like she'd taken days to prepare from his perspective. She fully intended to get him moments after she'd seen him last. It was only in her time-stream, her personal, sequential lifetime, that it would take time, time together that she hated to lose.

⸺◦⸺

She was a little late getting to Geoff's office. The morning commuters seemed hell-bent on displaying the worst of Minneapolis' traffic. She was hung up on the freeway for almost an hour in stop-and-go mode.

Jones greeted her with a sneer when she walked in.

"Not too anxious to help, huh, Whitby? I'd think you'd want to get working to get your caveman released. Maybe he's not as exciting to you as I thought? Perhaps not enough upstairs in the intellectual department? It must be difficult to carry on a decent conversation with someone who hunts animals with flint arrows for a living."

She didn't dignify his remarks with an answer. It was evident that he hadn't conversed with Cadeyrin. She'd met only a few people who had the intellectual capacity her beloved had. It wasn't his fault that he was born in the Pleistocene. In the time they'd been together, he'd learned English, learned to read, and was engaged in absorbing books and ideas at a frightening rate. If he was a caveman, it wasn't because he couldn't think.

She said, "Hello, Geoff. Hi, Jones. I'm ready to get to work. Where is the material you brought? It may take a while before I can figure out what you've done to your experimental subject."

An old man moved forward. "I'm Professor Wolf. I understand that you're the young genius who has this time-travel thing fully figured out."

Kathleen smiled. He reminded her of her dead mentor, Professor Mackleroy, the first victim of the battle for control over her equation. Part of her animosity for Jones was that he and Reed were apparently the lead agents working for the government in the attempt to control time. It was evident to her that Jones would have killed Mackleroy if he'd thought it would help him get control of time. The fact that Drew had been a foreign agent and had killed the Professor only indicated to her how seriously these people took the issue of time-travel.

"I don't know about genius," she answered. "I was merely working on a question that seemed interesting and appropriate for my dissertation. It just happened to result in me stumbling on a way of understanding and controlling time."

Wolf was excited. It showed in his eyes and general animation.

"So, they tell me you went to the Pleistocene and met a man there? Is that right?"

Kathleen could feel her cheeks heating up. She knew she was blushing again. Some parts of her old personality were just too ingrained to fade away.

She answered, "A man was going to murder me, and I was trying to escape. Before I was quite aware of what was happening, I'd solved my equation with a random set of variables. I ended up a little over twelve thousand years ago. My studies have led me to place the time in the Younger Dryas period. Certainly, life was difficult for Cadeyrin. He's told me of events that sound like they confirm some of the theories about the St. Lawrence becoming a primary conduit of glacial melt that destroyed the North Atlantic Conveyor system. His people had major floods on the east coast. Extreme cold and dust storms followed on the heels of the floods."

Wolf nodded. "I'm not very knowledgeable about geology and climatology. I'm not qualified to argue with you over that. However, I'm most definitely interested in your equation."

Kathleen frowned and looked down. "Professor, I'd like nothing so much as to discuss it with you, but I haven't yet made the decision to give it to Jones' group. There's just too much power and too much danger to lightly give up control."

Wolf looked confused. "But, it's our government. They're the only group that has the funding to investigate time thoroughly. After all, we're talking about an inexhaustible resource. Even our government couldn't explore all of it in any reasonable time."

He just didn't see what worried her. That was apparent. Kathleen inspected his face. It was true. He was genuinely puzzled.

"It's a decision that I have to make when I'm ready. Meanwhile, I understand that you have an experimental subject lost somewhere in time."

Wolf sighed and said, "Yes. We sent him on a mission that would have made a slight change. One that we could easily see, but one that would have no long-term effect on history. He apparently failed in the mission by going to the wrong time. He hasn't returned. I'm afraid that my understanding of time isn't adequate to calculate where he went."

Kathleen interjected, "When. You mean 'When' he went."

Wolf said, "I can't change my language habits easily. Yes, that's precisely what I mean. I don't know when he is."

Jones had been listening and tapping his foot impatiently. He burst into the conversation. "Enough of that. Whitby. Wolf is going to lay out his entire thinking for you. I don't think I need to tell you that we view this as vital and confidential information. You will not repeat it to anyone. I expect you to study what we're doing and to make corrections. We need a completely reliable method of time-travel."

He apparently had forgotten her reluctance to disclose her formula. If she did what he wanted, it would amount to giving them her secret. She smiled innocently at Jones and answered.

"I'll help as much as I can. The first thing I need is a complete view of what you have at this time."

Jones nodded and motioned to Wolf. "That's your job, Professor. Get to it."

⎯⎯◆⎯⎯

Wolf paused for a drink. His voice had become hoarse after the first two hours of discussion. He was an incorrigible lecturer and had proceeded in exactly the manner he would have if he were teaching a class. Kathleen had relaxed and followed along. This was going to be easier than she'd thought.

At this point, it was apparent to her that Wolf had gone astray in some critical aspects of his understanding and most especially in his math. She said nothing, but she had an inward feeling of pride. She was a better mathematician than he was. Her results proved it.

There were two negative repercussions of his errors. The first, and to Kathleen's thinking, the least important, was that he couldn't guarantee that a time-traveler would arrive at the intended destination. The method that the government was using depended on mentally programming the traveler with environmental cues that were specific to the desired target time. They used a psychoactive concoction of drugs to facilitate the mental assimilation of the cues.

She'd tried to figure that one out, but it didn't seem to fit with her method at all. The best she could figure was that the government had used knowledge from drug experiments to tailor their approach. She'd heard somewhere that the CIA had tested giving LSD to unaware subjects for some reason. If they'd do that, there was no telling what kind of knowledge about drug effects they'd generated over the years.

The second and far more important issue was that Wolf had completely ignored possible long-term changes in the time-stream. Wolf's error arose, in part from his source. Logan Walker had apparently been a somewhat marginal personality, a computer gamer, a poor student, but quite intelligent, nonetheless. He'd made a drug-induced transition to the Pleistocene, fallen in love with a girl there, and become a changed man from that experience. Kathleen could fully sympathize with him. Her experiences were remarkably similar. The uncompromising realities imposed by primitive life and her reliance on Cadeyrin for survival had made a huge difference in her own outlook.

Walker had no thought of math during his transitions. They had been drug-induced. Instead, he'd apparently had a desire to escape an uncomfortable situation when he'd first transited to the past. When he came back, he had been under the influence of a mushroom-based hallucinogenic and had ended up in the present, a time that Walker was fully familiar with and for which he had an obvious affinity.

The idea that there would be no irreversible damage to the time stream was one that Kathleen found to be dangerously naive. She had always been careful to take no actions that would change her past. She could change things in her future By future, she meant the future that she would have if she had never traveled in time. That was the very definition of progress. One never knew what would happen in the future, and no line of research should be discarded solely for that reason alone.

She believed that one's personal past was and should remain unchanged. Her equation showed that it was possible, in fact probable, that changes in the past could result in long-term divergences in the time-stream. These would amount to differences in the experienced reality of the world for not just one or a few people, but for everyone. In short, if you weren't careful, you could change history and not even be aware of it. It would just be the way things had happened.

She didn't want that. The world was problematical enough without people poking around making random changes. Things might get better, but she doubted it. The overwhelming probability was that things would become incalculably worse.

The interesting thing was that the time-stream was self-healing as long as divergences weren't too large. Most people and most activities didn't create a huge splash in the world.

For example, you could stop someone from getting married and having children, as long as they weren't critical to history. On the other hand, you couldn't do something like stopping Thomas Alva Edison from becoming an inventor. His inventions were too important. A minor invention might be invented by someone else, but significant efforts wouldn't and couldn't be replaced or changed without creating long-term distortions of the temporal flow. The repercussions of that were nearly impossible to calculate.

Wolf's theory and his math seemed to show that the time-stream would always heal itself. If an event didn't happen in the way it historically had, it would occur in a similar and equally convenient time and manner. There would be no long-term uncontrolled changes. His math implied that changes could be made that would have positive results without leading to unanticipated adverse consequences.

This implication made her even more suspicious of Jones and company. With that basis for their thinking, they probably figured they could manipulate the time-stream to facilitate their group's power and positions.

She thought their motives would become clearer the longer she helped them. If they were the sort of people she thought they were, neither she, nor Cadeyrin, nor Wolf, nor Geoff was safe once they gained control of time.

———◆———

Meanwhile, she thought she could see a way to help locate their lost subject.

"You say that Logan ended up in the Pleistocene at about the same time that I did?" she asked.

Wolf cleared his throat, then said, "Yes. It seems like he met up with some Clovis people who had traveled south along the east coast to avoid the same climate problems that forced your man's people westward. I've thought about that, and I can't quite figure it out. Why would you both select the same time frame for what were essentially random jumps? Of course, with just two travelers that we have any real data from, it could be simple chance."

Kathleen said, "No. I believe that it's due to some odd across-time-attraction. Say an "affinity." I'm not sure about this, and I haven't the knowledge to model it mathematically, but I'm pretty confident that there was some intra-temporal attraction between Cadeyrin and me. He told me of having a vision of me arriving in his life before meeting me. He's uncannily spiritual in addition to being very intelligent. It wouldn't surprise me to find that Logan's girlfriend; what's her name again?"

Wolf answered, "Serensaa."

"Oh, yes. I'd forgotten. Well, Serensaa might have an affinity with Logan Walker. In fact, she probably does. You could say that they were somehow intended to be together."

Wolf paused, thinking. Then he said, "Logan did mention the surprising presence of a fox at the times he made temporal jumps. I discounted that. It seemed unrelated. Would foxes have anything to do with time?"

Kathleen laughed at the idea. "I don't think so, but maybe that one Fox was also interlinked in some fashion. I haven't looked into any aspect of time that is related to this idea. Now that I've had the thought, I believe it's probably worth more analysis. When I get time, I'll work on modeling it."

Wolf said, "I'd be interested in discussing it in greater detail."

"That would be great," she said. Then she remembered Jones and Reed. "If only the government wasn't so intent on grabbing all the knowledge."

Wolf shrugged. "You said you had an idea about finding our man. How do you want to proceed?"

"I will need to know the parameters of his mission and see the temporal cues that you programmed into him. I'll also need to see his return cues. Perhaps with those, I can locate him." She paused. "You understand that I absolutely refuse to allow any drug concoction to be injected into me."

Wolf smiled. "I imagine that would be counter-productive for you. With your complete control, you wouldn't need the drugs anyway."

Kathleen didn't mention that she had the ability to move into an altered mental state without drugs. Nor did she mention that changing her mental state was an absolute requirement for her time jumps.

# Chapter Sixteen

# Family Man

Gridley had moved his base of operations. It had been weeks since he'd ended up here. Maybe almost four months. He wasn't sure. He'd lost track of the days.

The thick overhang of vegetation along the edge of the clearing hid him almost entirely. He shifted his position a tiny bit, moving slowly, trying not to give himself away. The prey animals were approaching slowly, pausing to nibble on plants as they worked their way through the open area towards the water. It was time for their mid-afternoon drink.

The reptilian creatures weren't nearly as smart as his girls. They stuck to their habits, moving out to browse on the conifer-like trees in the morning, lying about and resting through the mid-day hours, then gradually moving towards the lake for a drink before heading back to cover for the night. This habit made them easy to ambush.

He'd killed one every couple of days since he'd first encountered them. It was an activity that had become as mundane as going to the grocery store, with the exception that his targets were dangerous. They were quadrupedal but often walked on their hind legs, particularly when browsing. That position allowed them to stretch their necks to reach branches that were nearly ten feet above the ground, and it also gave them a better view of any approaching danger.

They could repel an attacker with the sharp spikes that took the place of their thumbs. If several of the adults massed together, swinging their thumbs aggressively, even one of the big ugly predators would hesitate. Gridley always took care not to allow them to corner him. When he'd kill one with his improvised spear, the others would usually move off slowly and soon return to browsing. Sometimes, though, they would mass to attack.

After being treed for several hours by an enraged herd of them, he'd learned to back into the trees quickly so they couldn't see him. They'd mill about for maybe ten minutes, but then their constant hunger would drive them towards the trees where they could forage. He'd wait for another half an hour, by which time they were usually far away, before cutting up his prey.

Hunting was easier now that the girls were reaching adult size. They had become really helpful, sometimes bringing down the herbivore target themselves without his participation. Like any good father, though, he worried about them. He didn't want them to be hurt by those thumb spikes. He'd devoted too much effort to ensure their survival since they hatched.

They had repaid him. He'd read about birds imprinting on humans somewhere in his previous life. He could now say for certain that imprinting was real. The three girls were definitely his. There was no doubt about that.

He had gone through periods before without much human contact, and it didn't bother him much. He'd started talking to the chicks from the first day. They'd bonded with him and knew their names, and now, as they learned to hunt together, they often showed that they knew what he wanted before he had even communicated with them. They were smart, but how smart, he didn't know.

They were lucky that the area wasn't densely populated with animals, especially the big, ugly predators. Those were too dangerous to face. Lucky they were stupid and easily outwitted.

The landscape was mountainous, with high ridges sliding off to deep valleys that often held fast-running streams, some of which fed small lakes. The trees were mostly conifers of some kind that he didn't recognize; pines, though. Not spruces.

⚬

His reverie was interrupted. Directly across from him, he'd seen a tiny flash of red. He looked carefully. There! It was Lolita. She was backed in among some tall, dry weeds that provided a close match for most of her body colors.

He suddenly saw her staring at him. When he met her eyes, she bobbed her head in a way that he recognized as showing embarrassment. He nodded his head and slowly motioned towards a single animal that had strayed from the bulk of the herd.

This time, Lolita bobbed her head slowly up and down. She agreed. That cow was vulnerable. It was too far from the rest of its group to make use of their protection.

Lolita made a show of staring at a section of dense brush opposite the straying herbivore. He followed her stare. Belle appeared momentarily, then drew back into the overhanging trees. She was almost in position to drive the stray towards him. He glanced off to his left. Fancy was hovering nearby, trying to stay in concealment.

Of the three, she was the least adept at stalking. Fancy was a bit of a pantywaist. She was overly fastidious and also cautious about things. She'd hang back until she had satisfied herself about a situation, but when she made the decision to participate, she was all-in. This quirk was a liability in the hunt. She sometimes couldn't restrain herself from attacking too soon.

The stray would soon be in an ideal position. He scanned the area. In just a few minutes, it would be time for action. He was glad that his kids were large enough to help.

His "kids," he'd taken to calling them that, since "chicks" didn't seem to describe them accurately. Especially now. They were his family, his charges, and, lately, his staunch defenders.

They'd grown quickly. The biggest was about one hundred and forty pounds. Grid hadn't been able to determine their sexes. He suspected they were all female, but their anatomy was just too undifferentiated for him to be sure. Anyway, when he talked to them, he used feminine pronouns.

In light of that decision, he'd named them Belle, Fancy, and Lolita. The big one was Belle. She was a straightforward girl who liked to eat, and it showed in her size.

Lolita was an out-and-out flirt. She was the smallest, but quick and cunning. She was also affectionate and touchy-feely. She liked to be close to him. It was sometimes a hassle, for she would sometimes slip between his legs when he was walking. She'd tripped him more than once.

The kids had been a headache to raise. At times, he'd thought that he was totally crazy to try and keep them alive. More than once, he'd made the decision to walk off and leave them, but they always followed him, and their piteous cries touched a caring part of him that he'd thought was dead. They were exclusively carnivores, of course.

Finding them food involved locating dead animals or killing smaller ones. The small turkey-sized predators had provided enough food for a while. He'd gotten quite good at throwing stones at them. They were easy to kill. While cautious, they could be baited with rotting meat. They couldn't resist coming to see what smelled so good.

His kids were fastidious. They liked their meat fresh. That meant he had to hunt every other day. Their requirement for fresh meat had kept him busy and also helped keep his mind off of the question of where or when he was.

It hadn't taken him long to create a set of usable spears. He had found flint, and after some practice, he'd become moderately adept at knapping. His spear points would win no beauty contests, but they worked.

His primary targets were the odd, reptilian plant-eaters. The largest ones were maybe five hundred pounds in weight and stood around ten feet high. They were herd animals and instinctively banded together for protection.

They fed mostly on the conifers, with their tooth-filled mouths grinding sideways like those of a cow. They ate a lot and concentrated on that business almost exclusively. Their eyesight was good, and they could run at a fair rate. Although not as fast as his kids, they were still faster than a human.

⸻ ◆ ⸻

The kids loved the meat, and he'd gotten used to it too. It wasn't bad. Not like chicken or steak, but it was edible if you didn't mind the strong flavor. The turkey-sized creatures tasted better to him, but they were the second choice for his three charges.

They'd moved to a cave that he'd located. It was on a cliff face, high over a river. Access was via a ledge that ran down at an angle from the top of the cliff. It was wide enough that his family had no problem with it, but it wasn't wide enough for anything truly large to come down. This gave them a sanctuary of sorts. They needed it.

---

The big Uglies, as he called them, were huge. When he saw the first one, all he could think was T-Rex. That wasn't what it was, though. It had an irregular ridge along its back and a flattish head with a long jaw. Also, there were horn-like protrusions over its eyes. He didn't remember anything about T-Rex having horns.

He'd been stalking one of the plant-eaters when this massive beast popped out of the trees and waded into the herd, grabbed one, shook it to death, then grabbed another and killed it before the rest could flee.

The big creature had made short work of the quarter-ton animals, finishing them off in just a few snaps and gulps.

He'd watched, terrified, from behind a nearby tree. The big ugly could move quickly but wasn't terribly agile from what he'd seen. He didn't want it chasing him. It could run faster than he could. The thing that was terrifying about it was its coat was fluffy yellow feathers. It was a giant killer yellow ducky with massive jaws – a three-foot gape – and long pointed teeth.

It had big arms with large sickle-shaped claws. Altogether a fearsome beast until it called. Then it made a cheeping sound that was totally out of character for both its size and nature. He expected a monster-like roar, but it cheeped and rather cheerfully at that.

When he hunted, which was often, he kept close attention to any cheeping sounds. Fortunately, the big Uglies were scarce. His kids' species was rare also. He thought that they were more plains creatures. He'd not seen any adults, save the first corpse, the kids' deceased parent.

There were other creatures, of course. Some were bird-Like things that he recognized as pterodactyls. They came in various sizes but were mostly little scavengers or insect eaters. There were small, furry creatures that spent most of their time in holes, only popping up periodically to comment on the day with little chirps. Those were probably his remote ancestors, but they weren't nearly as interesting as his girls.

There were also armored tank-like things that reminded him of walking pine cones covered with spikes. They looked impregnable – armor and sharp prongs everywhere. He left them strictly alone. They were too big and looked too powerful. He'd chucked a stone at the first one he'd met. The sizable rock bounced off its forehead with a 'clonk' sound, but it hadn't even blinked. They were just too heavily armored to be targeted.

⸻ ⬩◦⬩ ⸻

He grasped his spear tightly. The plant-eater was now in an optimal position, far enough back from the leaders of the herd so that they would not return to defend it.

He looked at Fancy. She was practically dancing with excitement. He pointed in Belle's direction. She'd been watching for that signal and came bursting out of the undergrowth with a hissing shriek. The prey animal dropped to all fours and started towards the fleeing herd.

Lolita slipped out of the weeds and dashed silently towards the oncoming prey. It saw her and swerved towards his position. He waved at Fancy, and she went, moving from zero to full-out in two strides.

The prey animal turned back just in time for Lolita to jump high on its side, raking downward with her sharp claws. It made a bleating noise and started to turn back towards him.

Moving perhaps twice as fast as he could run, Fancy slammed into its neck as it turned. She missed her strike, except for one claw that hooked the spike-thumb's neck. Her weight yanked its head around, and it went down almost like a football player downed by a face-mask tackle.

Belle arrived at that moment and piled on top of the beast as it tried to rise. She caught its neck with both foreclaws and then raked her killing hind claws down its ribs, slicing between them and exposing pink lung tissue. Lolita had the creature by the throat with her claws dug into its neck by then.

Before it could gather its wits to struggle, Fancy grabbed its side with her front claws and then ripped across its exposed belly with her right foot. The huge killing claw cut deeply, and entrails spilled out.

The prey animal bleated again weakly. Lolita still had her grip on its throat.

Grid arrived at that moment and jammed his spear into one of the wounds Belle had made, searching for and finding the spike-thumb's heart. It convulsed then stopped moving immediately.

The four looked at each other for a moment. Then Grid held his arms wide. Without hesitation, the three creatures came to him for a group hug. Their bloody muzzles nuzzled his armpits and neck as he pulled them close. He didn't care. They were his family.

⸻◆⸻

When he talked to them, they responded by coming close and making pleased sounds. About a month ago, their vocalizations had started to sound odd. A week later, Lolita had floored him by saying, "Damn." She'd used the word appropriately also.

They'd been playing. Grid had made it a point to work with the girls at hunting, thinking that there might come a time when he couldn't provide. He was a little nervous about their teeth and claws, but they never once bit or scratched him or each other. What conflicts they had were resolved by mock fighting that involved standing tall and making attack-like gestures, but not touching.

That stood to reason. The claws, particularly, were so large and sharp that conflicts could cause serious injuries. Such creatures, if prone to fighting among themselves, would probably not survive.

Lolita was trying to sneak up on him from behind a screen of bushes, but he'd seen her. She immediately stood up, made her embarrassed head bob, and then acknowledged being caught with the expletive.

Astonished, Jason walked to meet her and asked, "What did you say?"

She bobbed her head in greeting, opened her mouth, and said, "Grid see me. Damn!"

In retrospect, the only thing that was odd about it was her lips didn't move. She somehow made the right sound with her mouth slightly open.

He had laughed in delight. His girls were way smarter than he'd thought. If they were, as he suspected, some kind of Raptors, he'd once read that they would be only a little smarter than a chicken. That supposition was totally wrong. They were, based on Lolita's actions, smarter than anyone had suspected.

Today, both Belle and Fancy had followed suit and started talking to him. Their vocabulary was well developed. They'd been learning from him all the while they were silent. Now, suddenly, he had company.

They were practical, only talking about actions and things. He guessed he couldn't expect any philosophy from them. Still, their companionship was wonderful, especially now that they had grown enough to help him hunt. Maybe philosophy would come later.

He optimistically calculated that his odds of survival had increased greatly. Adopting the kids had been an incredibly fortuitous act.

# Chapter Seventeen

# Tracking in Time

Kathleen's first reaction to finding out about the Reagan project was fury. She usually had a difficult time masking her feelings, and this was no exception. Wolf seemed startled at her initial vehemence about the concept.

Fortunately, Jones had left the room to make a phone call. He was obviously bored with the discussion, apparently being more interested in the actual results rather than how they were obtained. It wouldn't have been as easy to hide her feelings from him.

The fools! They actually thought that stopping Hinckley from shooting Reagan would have no effect. Had they completely forgotten Brady's terrible wound? If they somehow prevented the attempt, the Brady anti-gun initiative would never have a reason to exist. Regardless of her opinion that the effort was mistaken, its absence would certainly have a measurable impact on the many people who were involved. One of these people might eventually become historically significant, and the change could spiral out of control. Such things were impossible to predict.

Even the effect of keeping Reagan's near-death from being a reality would irretrievably change reality. From her perspective, anyone who wanted to experiment with such effects must have an almost insane self-image. They apparently thought they could keep everything under control and also apparently thought they knew how to create events that shaped the world. The government's current financial condition proved that was a mistaken notion.

Nevertheless, Kathleen proceeded to go through the contextual cues that the subject, one Jason Gridley, had been given. His drugged state would have made sure that he visualized them with sufficient intensity to move through time to the cue-programmed period.

That was the one part of their procedure that would probably work, she thought. They had carefully selected a subject who was both capable operationally and who had little desire or linkage to the modern world. Gridley's wife had been murdered under suspicious circumstances. She had been his only living relative. If there was ever any man who probably wanted to travel in time, it was Gridley. He surely must want to go back to save his wife.

Such an action might cause a temporal divergence and Kathleen couldn't decide if it was advisable or even possible. However, his lack of connection to the present time may have been instrumental in his failure to return.

She had developed an idea that people might be drawn across time to others with whom they had some undefined form of spiritual affinity. If Gridley hadn't come back to the present, having no anchor here so to speak, he might have gone anywhere.

Such a random jump would render him untraceable. Kathleen had decided that she needed to transport to the same time and place as he'd originally arrived. Once she had finished working through the contextual cues for 1981, she spent some minutes writing down her impressions.

Jones had been sitting nearby. The silence eventually got to him, and he interrupted her. "Well, what's the result? Would he have gone where we sent him?"

Kathleen continued to write, pointedly ignoring him until she finished transcribing her thoughts.

"It looks as if the cue-programming is correct. I think he would be more likely to end up at the desired time than not. It's just that the equation you're using is..." She paused, considering what words to use. "Not the same as mine."

Jones said, "Just make it easy for everyone. Give us your equation. You know we have your old laptop?"

Kathleen realized they probably had it, but it would be of no use to them. She'd used a state-of-the-art shredder program on the disk and wiped all of her data irretrievably.

"So what? If you managed to get anything off of it, you wouldn't need me, so why all the urgency to get me to give you my formula?"

He didn't answer but just sat staring at her, hostility apparent in his attitude.

Kathleen was putting on a bit of a show for them. The instant they'd told her when they were sending Gridley, she could have gone directly to that time within a second or so. She didn't want them to have any clues about her method, and that involved a certain amount of dissembling. She meant to make it look as complex as possible.

"Look, Mr. Jones. I can help you. You haven't yet convinced me that giving you my method would be useful. It seems to be more or less specific to me alone," she said, hoping that he didn't sense that she was lying. "Professor Wolf's method may well be more general and usable by anyone. In any event, I'm convinced that I can arrive at the time you sent Gridley. I'll just have to be in the same location."

Jones grinned nastily. "We'll have a private jet at the airport. We'll have to go to Washington. If you can get to him, just tell him the operation has been postponed and bring him directly back to this time. You can do that can't you?"

She nodded affirmatively.

<hr>

An hour later, they were well on the way to the east coast. The small jet had been warmed up and was waiting, engines running when they drove up. There was no sign of security, except for a couple of guys in black suits who looked like armed guards, although they were trying to act as if they were mere bystanders.

They'd hustled into the plane, and the pilot had wasted no time in taking off. He'd apparently had clearance from the tower in place, and they moved quickly past several large commercial jets to the head of the runway queue.

Once in Washington, the procedure was just as expeditious. They led her to a black SUV with darkly tinted windows, hustled her inside, and then drove out of the airport through a back gate. The traffic was dense, but in less than an hour, she was standing in a barren room across from the hotel where Reagan had been speaking before Hinckley shot him.

Jones said, "We've had this office for years. It was vacant in 1981, so there will be no furniture, no one there, except Gridley, assuming that you arrive at the same time." He paused to consider, then continued.

"Look, Kathleen, I'm not happy that you won't cooperate, but I only want the best for you. This Gridley guy, he's got a hair-trigger. He's an experienced combat vet, and he's armed. If you suddenly pop in near him, he might shoot you. I want you to bring him back if you can. I most definitely don't want him to kill you."

She interjected, "Yeah, that would make it hard for you to get my formula, wouldn't it?"

He nodded, slowly, "We intend to have that formula. I'm letting you help us on the chance that we can analyze your actions, and Wolf can use the data to help him fine-tune his approach, but you already knew that, didn't you? You're smart. You've already figured that out."

She nodded. "Yes. I assumed that was what you are hoping. I have no problems with you using any data that you can generate by watching me."

She was confident that they would be able to generate no additional data from her actions. Everything she did in preparation for time-travel was mental.

In a rather sarcastic tone, Jones said, "That's nice. By the way, Gridley has the same small twenty-two revolver that Hinckley used. It's easily concealable, so he may not appear to be armed. You tell him he's recalled and you bring him directly back."

He stopped for a moment, then added, "Or, just tell him to activate his recall device. Either one would be adequate. Here's a badge that identifies you. Show him this. He'll at least listen to you."

He handed her a small piece of plastic. She glanced down. Her picture was on the front. These people were efficient, if nothing else.

She said, "Okay. I'm going now. Turn on your recorder or video or whatever if you want to watch me."

There were no obvious clues to her travel. However, just to confuse them, she walked around the room, gradually spiraling in towards the center. Once at the center of the room, she turned around three times to the right and once to the left. She sat down cross-legged and checked the straps of her backpack. Then she rested her hands, palm upwards on her knees. She formed loops of her thumbs and index fingers, sighed deeply, and then shut her eyes, visualized the variables as usual, and moved into 1981.

Kathleen hadn't ignored Jones' warning. If this Gridley were dangerous, she'd best not surprise him. She carefully added some time to her arrival. She intended to arrive after the assassination attempt. That was at 2:26 PM.

She could check to see if Gridley was on the street at that point. If he were, she'd try to approach him, hoping that her appearance was non-threatening.

The first thing she noticed was that the room smelled of burned gunpowder. There was a bundled painter's drop cloth in the corner. She inspected it.

There under a fold was a series of slightly burned holes. Kathleen lifted the cloth, unfolding it. The holes went through several folds and then stopped. Gridley had shot all six of his bullets into the canvas.

She looked around for any other clues. There, over at the side of the room, was a small cylindrical object and a headset connected to a smartphone. She picked the cylinder up tentatively. It was an empty injector pen. Gridley had used the recall system. That should mean he was back in the present.

Kathleen considered. They didn't think he was back. They'd given no indication to her that Gridley had come back. Perhaps he hadn't. The return process might have been defective.

She picked up the headset. It should be set with cues for the modern world. A sudden suspicion prompted her to check it. She donned the headset and pressed the recall app on the phone. The visual cues began to flow over her in 3-D. The program ran for a couple of minutes. When it stopped, she removed the device and put it in her bag.

The bastards had sent Gridley back into time deliberately. Far back. The visual cues were so blurred and fast that she hadn't been able to place them at first, but now, after she'd had a moment to process them subconsciously, she was left with a solid impression of a specific geological period. If her impression was accurate enough, she could travel there.

She composed herself, plugged values into her variables, and blinked. The hotel room had disappeared.

She was surrounded by conifers and the air was dryer. She'd arrived. Now she had to find Gridley.

# Chapter Eighteen

# The Cretaceous

Kathleen knew that she'd jumped backward slightly over a hundred million years. The period would be highly dangerous.

She opened her pack and pulled out her only weapon, a nine-millimeter pistol. Jones knew she had it but hadn't said anything. Perhaps he assumed that she was too weak or inexperienced to use it on him. The very thought made her angry. She wished she had him in sight right now.

The nine wouldn't be much help against anything truly large and mean, but it might bail her out if she used it carefully.

She looked around. The trees were thick, clustering along a ridge. Perhaps she could see better from the top.

A few minutes later, she was at the crest of the ridge. There was a jumbled protrusion of rocks that towered over the thick trees on the far side. She clambered to the top of the pile and perched on a convenient boulder.

There was a stream on the other side of the ridge, buried deep in a valley. The terrain was mountainous and seemed to be mostly knife-edged ridges and valleys. The vegetation was almost exclusively conifers of some kind, but she didn't recognize the species. There weren't any flowering plants visible, although ferns were growing here and there under the trees.

Far in the distance, specks were moving in the air. As Kathleen watched, one of them came closer and closer. It flew like a gliding bird with only a few sporadic wing beats. As it neared, she could make out a large crest on its head. It must surely be some species of pterodactyl.

That conclusion was interrupted by a loud grunting sound coming up to her from the valley below. There was nothing there, but as she watched, a huge bulk shouldered through the trees far below near the stream. It was some kind of dinosaur.

She was used to the megafauna of the Pleistocene and the inter-glacial Sangamon. Dinosaurs were completely different. She had no knowledge of them and no expectations, other than the assumption they would be unreservedly fierce and aggressive.

This place was going to be a problem. Kathleen was sure she'd arrived at the period where Gridley had been dumped. However, she wasn't entirely certain of her accuracy. The visual cues didn't allow for that since one time in the Cretaceous would be more or less like another. A difference of a few days or weeks could make her mission impossible to achieve.

———◦———

She sighed. Might as well walk around and look for the man. Having come from the same starting location, she had arrived at the same physical spot that he had. However, she'd initially been so anxious to orient herself that she'd neglected to search the immediate area for clues. She moved back down the ridge to the spot where she'd first opened her eyes.

She slowly combed the area but found nothing. She extended her search and moved through the trees. Something had made a nest in the shelter of a fallen tree, but now only fragments were left. Some creature had apparently destroyed it. The ground was scuffed, though, and she couldn't make out any distinct tracks. Several smashed eggshells were the only clues as to the occupants.

———◦———

A sense of presence warned her. Kathleen turned slowly to see a big, ugly creature rising from where it had been resting in some thick bushes. It was covered with small, yellow, down-like feathers and looked like some monstrous baby duck, except its mouth was full of business-like teeth.

It gaped, showing jaws that she instantly equated with those of a T-Rex. An incongruous cheeping sound came out as it stepped one large step forward, its leg pushing through the bushes as if they weren't there.

The thing was too large for the nine-millimeter to make much of an impact, but perhaps the sound would discourage it. It had turned its head to look at her better from one side, reminding her of a chicken eyeing a bug that it was about to eat.

She aimed carefully and shot at the saucer-sized eye. The yellow dinosaur recoiled and made a nasty hissing scream, raising one of its arms and raking it against the damaged optic.

This creature was no T-Rex. Its arms were longer and apparently more capable. She backed up while it was distracted, then turned and dashed up the ridge towards the rocks.

The creature made another hissing scream and followed, its legs moving deceptively slowly. Its stride was so long that it quickly began to gain. Kathleen dodged through a thick stand of trees, hoping that would slow it down.

It followed her directly through the trees, easily pushing its way through the trunks and leaving two of them leaning sharply.

She continued up the slope. The rocks might be some shelter. They were piled high, and her pursuer didn't look particularly agile. Perhaps it couldn't climb very well.

She was panting as she reached the first of the stones. The yellow thing screamed again from close behind. She whirled and fired five shots into its opened mouth. That slowed it down.

It stopped and raked at its face. Blood was coming from the back of its throat and running between its teeth. The yellow feathers on its breast were rapidly becoming crimson-stained. At least the bullets had some effect, even though they would never be adequate to stop it permanently.

She used the brief respite to work her way up a crevice in the rocks, then quickly climbed beyond the creature's reach. She was safe unless it could climb.

Panting, she paused to regain her breath. As she rested, a thought struck her. She'd panicked like an idiot. It could never reach her as long as she saw it coming. She'd forgotten she could duck through time. If she moved an hour or even a few minutes, the creature couldn't possibly catch her unless it was incredibly lucky and happened to be in location when she re-appeared.

She was glad that Cadeyrin wasn't there to see how poorly she'd reacted, but perhaps he would have also been alarmed. He wasn't any more used to dinosaurs, even feathered ones, than she was. His experience was in hunting the megafauna of their adopted home period.

The creature had recovered and was scrabbling ineffectually at the crevice that she'd climbed. It was still interested in her, turning its head to the side to stare balefully up at her perch with its undamaged eye.

She didn't want to harm it irrevocably, but it seemed intent on hanging around until she came down. The next time it turned its head to look up at her, she fired a round into its eye. The 110-grain bullet hit with a splat, and the yellow creature squawked, then began to blunder around.

Her shots had either blinded it completely or damaged its vision enough to make it difficult to see. It crashed into some rocks, then knocked a small tree over. She stood, determined to escape while it was distracted.

Below the yellow creature moved into an open area. There was a flash of brightly colored feathers, and a much smaller bipedal dinosaur leaped up and clung to the yellow one's ribs. The smaller one made a convulsive movement with its feet, cutting long channels with its talons. Blood spurted and ran in rivulets down the yellow dinosaur's side.

Big Yellow hissed again and spun ineffectually. The brilliantly colored one dropped off and dodged, making a quick flash of green, blue, and red feathered motion. Kathleen noticed that there was a second feathered creature watching the battle from a vantage point on a low-lying, flat rock. She hadn't seen it arrive.

The two small dinosaurs reminded her of colorful birds of prey. Their eyes had the same distant, uncompromising gaze as that of an eagle. This second one was a little larger than the first. She judged that this new arrival probably weighed about as much as she did. It swayed back and forth, gauging the distance. When Big Yellow came close, it leaped, timing its jump to land along the big one's spine. It climbed quickly upward, digging in both foreclaws and the eagle-like hind talons as it climbed.

The big one screamed again as the smaller creature reached its neck. It tried to claw the rider off, but the smaller dinosaur was too quick to be caught by the big one's blunt claws.

The first two colorful dinosaurs were suddenly joined by a third, slightly smaller one. This one appeared out of some bushes at the side of the clearing.

Kathleen was fascinated, despite the danger. The small ones looked like some maniac's version of a Roadrunner combined with a threshing machine. Bright, almost iridescent red, blue, and green feathers made them look harmless. Their natural weapons marred their attractive appearance. Seriously deadly-looking claws tipped their extended fingers, and their feet had a giant, hooked claw that they kept raised until they flexed their toes to use it.

She could see the results of their kicks with that claw. Ribs showed through the gaps in the big yellow creature's side. The claw must be as sharp as a ceramic knife.

The smaller creatures also had teeth but didn't use them in their attack. Instead, they waited for openings, their brightly feathered bodies blending surprisingly well into the undergrowth. When the big creature turned, the two that remained on the ground would leap in, grab with their forelegs and kick hard with their hind claws.

The big animal's fluffy yellow coat was streaked with bright red blood. The damage was having a definite effect. Kathleen was impressed at how deadly their attack was. The smaller dinosaurs were about her size, seemingly too small to attack such a giant, but they were systematically cutting the huge one apart. The battle would have been less one-sided if the large one could see, but her shots had substantially increased its vulnerability.

Big Yellow must have outweighed them by thousands of pounds. She guessed it was nearly thirty feet in length. The battle was fascinating. She had a fleeting thought that a modern paleontologist would pay any amount to be able to see such an attack.

Kathleen's thought brought her back to her position, and she moved slightly. She'd been so impressed by the smaller animals that she'd neglected to think about how they might view her. She'd be far easier to kill than the big one. Of course, she could move in time, but these three displayed a level of intelligence that she found impressive. They were coordinating their attack in a way that made them seem almost human. She wanted to see the outcome, but prudence dictated that she'd better move now.

She drew up her feet and prepared to slip down the other side of the rocks.

As careful as her movement was, the smallest of the colorful creatures saw it.

It turned and looked directly at her. Its mouth opened, and to Kathleen's utter astonishment, it said, "Stop," in a tone that left no doubt that it meant what it said.

Paralyzed, she sat there wondering just what had happened. She must have heard wrongly. Dinosaurs didn't talk, even if they looked like colorful birds. They most definitely didn't speak English and use the words in a meaningful manner. What was this creature?

The battle below had paused for a moment. Big Yellow was breathing heavily and weaving unsteadily, suffering from blood loss. The small ones were now back in the trees, watching it expectantly, waiting for it to collapse. During the quiet, she heard a slight rustle as something pulled itself over a boulder.

She spun, aiming the pistol at a man who was working his way up the boulders behind her. He grinned and held up his free hand in a surrender motion.

"You're safe, Miss. I was just coming up to help you get down," he said.

Kathleen took a deep breath, then said with a degree of satisfaction, "Jason Gridley, I presume?"

He nodded. "They sent you after me? Are there any others searching?"

"No. I'm the only one that came."

"They must think highly of your survival skills, Lady. Did they send you back to kill me?"

Kathleen shook her head from side to side. "No. They told me to tell you to activate your return device. Obviously, you did. I don't think they wanted you to survive." She paused, then added, "I'm not on Jones' Christmas list either, so don't worry. I'm friendly."

Gridley moved up and sat beside her, looking down at the bloody climax of the battle. The three colorful attackers were approaching the failing yellow giant. They walked cautiously, moving this way and that, pausing to watch the big creature when it moved. They were obviously deciding exactly how best to finish the job.

The small one squawked, "Now!" and the three leaped onto the sides and back of the large carnivore. They clambered quickly up to its neck, clinging with their front claws. Once there, they simultaneously kicked downwards with their killing talons, cutting through layers of muscle to reach the large veins and arteries below the surface. Blood spurted in huge gouts, staining the ground a bright red.

The yellow creature hissed weakly, then its strength failed, and it collapsed on its chest. The smaller ones leaped off and dashed away as it rolled slowly on its side. They were instantly back, ripping at its exposed abdomen.

Gridley laughed and said, "I wasn't sure the girls were up to something as large as a Big Ugly. They are damned good, though, aren't they?"

She was astonished. "Those three are your 'girls'?"

"Yeah. They're my family now. All I've got. I saved them and kept them alive. Now they defend me. We hunt together, too. They are kind of like birds. I guess they imprinted on me. Anyway, they've lately begun to talk. They carry on a pretty good conversation, too." He shook his head affirmatively.

"You mean these things, I assume they are dinosaurs of some sort, are intelligent enough to talk in English?" she asked.

"Yes. The girls are very clever. They've always impressed me with their understanding. I started talking to them when they were little. Now they know enough words to communicate, although they don't actually converse in the way we do."

Kathleen shook her head in amazement. "This will really flip the lids of a bunch of stuffy paleontologists. A magazine article I read said that Raptors were the smartest dinosaur, but they were almost certainly less intelligent than a chicken."

Gridley smiled, "Well, meet Lolita. She's the smartest and deadliest chicken you ever saw."

Kathleen turned to follow his gaze. The smallest of the three creatures had silently climbed the stones behind her, holding a chunk of bloody meat in its mouth. It was now standing about five feet away, inspecting her. She froze. It was easily capable of leaping that far.

Gridley said, "Lolita. Friend. Friend. You understand?"

The creature abruptly tossed the meat in an arc that landed on Kathleen's lap. It bobbed its head several times in a kind of greeting, then repeated, "Friend. Grid, friend."

Gridley laughed and said, "You're supposed to eat the meat now. It's not bad. Just take a small bite and then give it to me."

Kathleen wasn't averse to raw meat. More than once, she and Cadeyrin had eaten fresh meat from their kills. She took the meat, smelled it, and then chewed off a large mouthful. She nodded her head at Lolita and handed the meat to Gridley.

His eyes had widened as she chewed. He'd obviously assumed that she would be grossed out by the concept. Now he nodded back with a degree of respect in his eyes that hadn't been there before.

Kathleen swallowed and said, "Not bad. Maybe I should introduce myself. I'm Kathleen Whitby. I'm a physicist. I discovered time-travel and traveled to the last ice age where I was stuck for a time, so eating raw meat is nothing to me. I've done it many times. You do what you have to to survive."

Gridley smiled. "I thought they'd sent some inexperienced office worker to try and bump me off. They must be mad that I didn't follow through on their plans."

She asked, "You mean saving Reagan from Hinckley?"

He looked disgusted. "Oh, no! That wasn't what they had in mind at all. They instructed me to shoot Reagan. Told me that the bullets in the revolver were frangible and would powder without hurting him. The secret service agents were supposed to grab Hinckley, and I was supposed to activate my return and disappear."

He shook his head disparagingly. "The bullets were real. I'd have killed Reagan. That's what they really wanted. Then the return cues sent me here. They don't want me back."

Kathleen sighed. "That's what I'd figured out. Those people have been trying to get my time-travel formula from me. If I give it up, they'll kill us for sure."

Gridley glanced at her, unsure who she meant. He passed it off and asked, "When you say your time-travel formula, are you implying that you have a different way to travel? One that doesn't rely on their device and drugs?"

"Yes. I can go any when I want, as long as I don't encounter myself. Paradoxes aren't ever a good thing."

"My God!," he exclaimed. "You're just what I need. If I could only save– "

She interrupted, "Annie. I know. Your wife who killed herself."

"How do you...Oh. They must have briefed you. Well, I'm sure she didn't kill herself. The circumstances were very suspicious, and she wouldn't have done that anyway. I know it."

Kathleen replied, "Even if she was murdered, saving her might not be possible. You see, you have to be very careful with modifications to the time-stream."

He looked hard at her. "You're saying you won't help me?

"No, I'm not saying that. I'm just cautioning you not to get your hopes up. I'll try to figure out whether or not it would be possible, but we'll have to handle Jones and his group first."

The other two feathered killers arrived at that moment, and Gridley introduced them to Kathleen. They were a little stand-offish about her. She wasn't really part of their group. She felt that they wouldn't attack, but she resolved to move carefully around them anyway.

After she'd met Fancy and Belle, the group climbed down from the rock pile. Gridley had invited her to come to their den where they could make plans.

# Chapter Nineteen

# Dinosaur Hunting

Gridley's base was indeed a den. He'd found a spot where two huge slabs of rock rested against each other. The overlying piece must have once been attached to the more massive one that reclined against a cliff. When it broke loose, the bottom somehow kicked out, leaving a large inverted triangular opening between the two. A boulder fall almost entirely blocked one side except for an opening near the top, about thirty feet up in the darkness. The other side of the slab provided a tall and narrow entrance opening into what was a surprisingly spacious cave with a mostly flat floor.

Gridley had constructed a fire pit at the back, using the opening above for a natural chimney. Smoke hung in wreaths and coils about the rock above but gradually worked its way out through the hole, leaving the living space below smoke-free. It was a good arrangement.

Kathleen was surprised to see that there was a single sleeping pad, covered with tanned hides for comfort. It was spacious and comfortable looking.

Catching her glancing curiously at the bed, Jason laughed and said, "I know what you're thinking, and you're right. We all sleep together. The girls are warm-blooded. Their body temperature is a little higher than mine, so they make for good sleeping companions."

"Aren't you worried that they might bite or claw – uhn, in their sleep?" She paused midway through the sentence to think of how to put it in a way that didn't directly question his sleeping partners' good intentions.

"They are good kids," he responded without offense. "They are smart enough to know that I take care of them. Now that they're mostly grown, they pull their own weight and more when we're hunting, but they still rely on me to make the fire and think up things that make our life easier."

Kathleen thought that over. From the evident pride in his speech and attitude, it was plain that he was deeply attached to his three charges.

Just then, Lolita came over to where he was sitting and snuggled her head up against his chest. She sighed and lay partially down, leaning against him. He absentmindedly fondled her neck, smoothing the fine feathers there, then scratching carefully along her back. In response, she made a pleased crooning sound.

Kathleen smiled at the picture, mentally subtitling it, "A Raptor and Her Man." She sat in silence for a bit, trying to frame what she wanted to say. She'd been formulating a plan of action but wanted to explore all of the ramifications first.

A warm, feathered body bumped against her, jostling her out of her reverie. Belle, the largest of the three, had apparently decided that she was an acceptable human and now wanted to snuggle. Kathleen cautiously lifted her arm and was rewarded by Belle moving closer against her chest.

Sitting on her deep pelvic bone, Belle was almost as high as Kathleen. Most of her twelve-foot length was in her feathered tail. Her pelvis protruded directly below and in front of her hips, keeping her from lying on her front. Instead, she sat in a more upright posture, unless she was lying on her side.

She opened her toothy muzzle and sighed. Kathleen experimentally tightened her arm around the feathered body. It felt soft and comfortable, despite the razor-sharp claws. Belle moved a little, trying to reach a maximally comfortable position, then relaxed.

Watching Jason work on Lolita's neck, Kathleen asked, "Will she mind if I scratch her like you're doing?"

Grid said, "Watch out if you do, or you'll end up being requested to do it all the time. She loves it. Just don't bend her feathers too far the wrong way."

She carefully began to lightly stroke Belle's neck, then worked her fingers between the feathers and made tiny scratching motions. This action elicited a huge sigh from the satisfied creature. Kathleen found herself smiling in return.

Fancy had been watching, uneasily shifting her weight from one foot to the other. Her personality made her nervous about Kathleen, but the sight of Belle getting attention finally became too much for her. She stepped across the cave with exaggerated care and thrust her face right up to Kathleen's.

Kathleen glanced at Gridley. He was watching carefully. He nodded approval, so she stopped scratching and moved her left arm out in a welcoming gesture. Fancy moved around and settled loosely against her left side.

The presence of both of the colorful creatures pressing warmly against her was comforting. She worked her hand around so she could scratch Fancy's neck a little. It was pleasantly warm between the two feathered furnaces, and she gradually became drowsy. She didn't feel like she was sitting with deadly predators. Instead, it felt like she was cuddling with some overgrown, fluffy stuffed toys.

Kathleen opened her eyes. Fancy had stirred and was now standing, looking at the cave mouth. Belle was still leaning against her but was watching the entrance also. After a moment, Kathleen heard a distant bellowing sound. That must have been what woke them.

Jason was stretched out full length on the pallet with Lolita lying on her side in a ridiculously relaxed pose. He lifted his head and said, "It sounds like lunch has arrived. All we've got to do is go and get it."

Despite her growing desire to be working to free Cadeyrin, Kathleen couldn't resist the urge to see the girls in action once more.

"Okay. Let's go," Kathleen said. "I haven't been hunting since the Pleistocene. I'd like to see how you do it in the Cretaceous."

Grid laughed. "That's great! You'd be a good member of our group."

She stiffened, having been reminded of her primary objective, then said, "Sorry, I'm already bespoken. My husband is an incredibly skilled hunter. We hunt with a wolf as our partner."

Gridley sobered. He could tell that she was upset. "Look, Kathleen, I didn't mean that the way it sounded. It's just that I'm happy to have another human around to talk to. The girls, as smart as they are, aren't quite up to extended discourse. At least not yet."

At this point, Fancy turned her head and said, "Stop talk. Go. Now."

Gridley shrugged his shoulders with a "see-what-I-mean" expression on his face.

"Okay, Fancy. We'll go now," he said.

She was already out the entrance followed closely by the other two.

⸻ ◆ ⸻

The group trotted down the hillside toward the stream and then spread out. Kathleen stayed close to Gridley. She had her pistol but only had a few shots left. He had an unlikely-looking spear. It was long and heavy with a sharp flint point. He'd tied a cross-piece about two feet behind the tip.

"It's a modified boar spear," he explained. "Our primary prey is not very aggressive, but they do have sharp spikes instead of thumbs. The cross-piece keeps them from sliding down the spear shaft and getting at me with their spikes."

"I see," she said.

He continued, talking as if they were on a walk in a park.

"The cross-piece might also come in handy if I run into anything more vicious than the herd animals. The big ugly yellow ones, for example, although I'd hate to irritate one of them by sticking it with a spear. It would likely just ignore the wound, and I'd get eaten. We stay away from those guys if we can. The one you shot was an exception. I'm pleased to see that the girls' technique works on them, too. They use their hind claws to wound their prey, then wait until it's dead before they start to eat. It's a pretty safe way of hunting."

Kathleen could barely get a word in; Gridley was talking so quickly. It was evident that he'd worked hard to survive and was proud of how well he'd done.

"Are there any more of that kind of dinosaur?" she asked. "I mean the girls' species. I'd think that they would be your worst opponent."

He shook his head. "You know, it was just a fluke that I found them. Their nest had been destroyed, and most of the eggs were either broken or eaten. Their mother, at least I think it was their mother, was dead nearby. I was looking at the eggs when they started to hatch. Something about the wee little dears touched me, and I decided to take them in. Been the best decision I've made since I got here, too. But, to answer your question, I haven't seen any more of them. They must be rare in this region, or maybe they prefer a different terrain, the plains maybe."

Kathleen thought this over. It was just as well that there weren't many of the colorful creatures in the area. They could easily ambush and kill an unsuspecting human. Their claws were capable of inflicting easily fatal wounds.

She asked, "What have you been doing for first-aid? Surely you must get cut or injured at times."

"Yeah. I've been hurt a few times. Been lucky, I guess. Nothing seems to infect the wounds. It's not like there aren't microorganisms either. I've seen a few of the herd animals with badly infected wounds. The big ugly yellow predators aren't very efficient hunters. They often wound animals that get away. Sometimes they just seem to forget they've bitten a creature and go after a different one. Maybe it smells better or something. I don't know."

Belle appeared in between some thin trees ahead and slightly upslope from where they were walking. She looked meaningfully at them and then turned her head to look forward.

"Okay. That's the signal. The prey is close. We'll go quietly from here. You just stay close to me and do what I say, no questions, no arguing. Understand?"

She nodded.

He turned and jogged off along the stream without a word.

Kathleen followed a few paces back. If this soldier thought this was hunting, she had a few surprises for him. The animals in her adopted time were far more suspicious, having been hunted by men and various kinds of really stealthy predators.

Jason reached a screen of brush and stopped. He worked his way diagonally through a thin area and disappeared. She followed and discovered him peering through some leaves at a group of creatures that she tentatively identified as Iguanodons.

They were dubious-looking beasts and not at all attractive the way Gridley's girls were. Their hides were feather-free and grayish slate-brown with yellow irregular blotches. They were mostly walking on their hind feet to better browse on some low-hanging branches.

Their heads reached maybe eight or nine feet in the air when they were standing upright. Their bodies were perhaps twenty feet in length from their nose to the tip of their tail, and Kathleen estimated that the bigger ones might weigh close to a ton.

She'd thought that Iguanodons were larger than these things, but then she didn't know if there were subspecies that might have been smaller. That appeared to be the case here.

Even from fifty yards away, she could hear the grinding of their teeth. Their mouths moved sideways like a cow's, grinding up the twigs and leaves they were stripping from the branches. Every so often, one would pause and swallow a mouthful, the lump moving visibly down its throat.

Jason looked at her and pointed. There was a group of three stragglers following the main herd. Kathleen understood. That was the target. They were far enough away that the herd members probably wouldn't come to their aid.

She nodded in agreement.

There was a brief movement, a flash of color on the far side of the stream from the stragglers. Fancy showed her head for a moment. When they noticed her, she bobbed her head up and down slowly.

Jason whispered, "She's ready. Lolita is following them, and Belle's somewhere back in the bushes behind us."

Without waiting, he jumped out of the bushes waving his arms and shouting, "Booga-Booga-Booga!"

Kathleen was startled, and it was a struggle to contain her laughter. The tactic was absurd, but it worked. The entire herd of the plant-eaters craned their necks to look at him.

Apparently, he didn't fit their image of a predator in any way. They were more curious than fearful.

The scene was frozen for a second, but then one of the three stragglers bleated. It had seen Fancy charging across the stream. The three started to run for the protection of the herd, but it was too late.

Lolita came sprinting alongside one and casually hooked its shoulder with her fore-claws, bounced off the ground, and turned in mid-air to deliver a double kick with both legs.

The knife-like killing claws caught and cut through the herbivore's abdominal wall, and it fell, spilling entrails in a steaming heap. It wasn't dead despite the horrific wound. It tried to stand but was unable to regain its feet. It made a pained bleating sound and collapsed again.

Lolita stood nearby, her head cocked, watching its struggles while Belle and Fancy caught up. The three turned as one and started towards the other two stragglers, but Gridley yelled, "No!"

They looked at him and stopped. Fancy made a hissing sound and stamped her feet, displaying her frustration.

Gridley said, "If they were by themselves, they'd try to kill more. They waste a lot of meat that way, but they probably never know when they're going to make another kill, so it makes a kind of sense. I've been trying to teach them to conserve the game and not to frighten it out of the territory. That's a hard lesson for them to understand, but I think I'm getting somewhere."

"How much meat is on that creature?" she asked as they walked up.

"I can usually get a couple of hundred pounds off one if the girls will let me cut it up decently. They tend to get over-eager and often start eating a chop that I've just cut off. I can't fault them, though. They're programmed to eat while they have food. A larger predator could show up at any time and take it away."

It was true. The three were already working at the liver.

---

Kathleen helped carry the meat back to the cave. Gridley had figured out how to smoke it and got a fire going to dry strips of meat on poles. The girls weren't interested in the operation. They were full and sleepy as a result.

Night fell, and the two humans moved into the cave to sit in the opening. Jason got up periodically to tend the fire. Kathleen felt strangely moved by the firelight. It was similar to sitting by Cadeyrin at night.

"Gridley, I've been thinking. I know you want to rescue your wife. I know the math for time-travel. I have lost people that I wanted to save, but I have never tried."

She was thinking of Professor Mackleroy. Of course, if she had kept him from being murdered by Drew, he would still have died from his cancer. But she needn't say that.

"Here's what I think we should do. Give me some time to investigate the circumstances of your wife's death. If she can be saved, we'll do it. I want you to agree to let me be the judge. If I think that we will create irreparable damage to the time-stream by saving her, you'll have to let her go. I know that's hard, but that's the way it has to be."

He didn't answer, staring instead into the fire for a long time. Finally, without turning his head, he said, "I don't like it, but I'll agree. You're the only chance I've got to get her back."

"Okay. Now that's going to take me some time. I'll have to track Annie down and maybe go to several different times around her to see what's going on. Do you want to return to the present?"

He snorted. "No. Those people tried to get rid of me. They wanted me to kill Reagan. What do you think my chances would be if I returned and they got hold of me?"

She nodded. "Yeah. That was a stupid question. You'd better stay right here for a while. I know where to find you, and I think you'll be quite safe in the girls' care."

He smiled grimly. "Safer here than there, that's for sure. I'll wait for you to come and get me."

Something struck him, and he paused, then continued. "I hate to leave the girls. I'm sure they'll be all right without me, but I…I guess I'm pretty attached to them. If I could have Annie and them, my life would be perfect. I don't even mind the lack of hot, running water."

She smiled. "It might be difficult for them to share you with Annie, don't you think? Besides, Annie might not share your enthusiasm for this type of life."

He shrugged but didn't say anything.

Kathleen was tired at this point. It had been a long day. If she went back now, Jones would undoubtedly want to debrief her, and she wasn't feeling up to fabricating a consistent story about not finding Gridley. She'd do better with some rest.

She stood and walked into the cave. Reflected firelight lit the large area with a flickering glow. She found a couple of free skins and stretched out on a sandy patch close to Gridley's sleeping pallet where the girls had disposed themselves.

She moved fretfully. It felt like she was wasting time here, but she needed rest, and Cadeyrin wouldn't suffer. She intended only to make him wait a few minutes in his personal time.

Lolita sniffed loudly, rolled over, and came over to her. She lifted the corner of her covers invitingly. The feathered dinosaur lay down beside her and allowed her to pull the hide cover over them both.

It was warm, and she went to sleep.

# Chapter Twenty

# Debriefing

Despite the warmth given off by her sleeping companion, Kathleen didn't sleep well. She was restless and kept waking up to thoughts of what she would tell Jones. It seemed like the best thing to say was that she didn't find Gridley. She'd tell about the events in the room but not about finding the return device and analyzing its treacherous programming.

She'd brought the phone and headset with her to the Cretaceous, so there was no chance they'd have a record of finding it in the safe room. A smartphone in 1981 would have attracted a lot of unwanted attention. They might have documented the mysterious bullet holes in the painter's drop cloth, but she'd only say that was what she'd found without speculating on why Gridley had discharged his revolver into the folded material.

Her overall report would be negative. She hadn't found Gridley, and there had only been the clue of the drop cloth. That was meaningless to her. Of course, Jones would question her closely about it. She intended to ask him if they were sure the return device's cues were programmed correctly.

She knew it wasn't correct, but it might be interesting to see if Jones could dissemble on an impromptu basis as well as he could tell a deceitful, pre-planned story.

⸻◆⸻

Morning came, complete with a series of deep bass hoots from the other side of the ridge. The girls jumped up and hastened to the entrance to look.

Gridley sat up and said, "That's just old whip-tail. He's a brontosaurus or something like that." He shrugged and added, "Well, that's what I think he looks like anyway. He travels around in this area and comes by every couple of weeks. The girls are interested in him, but he's too large to attack. I don't think they'd survive the encounter, so I've kept them away. Uh, when are you going to go look into Annie's situation?"

Kathleen frowned. "I've got to go debrief with Jones first. I should be able to get him to allow me a few hours to rest. I'll say that I followed several false leads searching for you and I'm too tired to do much else until I recover. Once I'm free of him, I'll start checking on your wife."

His expression displayed what she thought was extreme sadness.

"Don't worry, if I can save her, I will," Kathleen said. The only problem was she was not sure how to tell if keeping someone from death would be a major mistake. If the time-stream suddenly changed and her present changed as a result, would she know it?

She'd just have to do the best she could.

She gathered the colorful girls for a goodbye hug.

Fancy leaned on her harder than the other two. It appeared that she'd decided Kathleen was her special friend.

Kathleen said, "Goodbye." The three brightly feathered dinosaurs bobbed their heads and repeated the word. As if that wasn't enough, Lolita, the most talkative of the group, came over and leaned against her leg, then added, "Come back soon."

Kathleen smiled. They were unbelievably smart.

—◦—

She shut her eyes, visualized the variables, and found herself on the National Mall in the middle of a bunch of tourists. She'd traveled in the past of course, and she'd forgotten about that. It was wise to always return from the same point at which you'd departed. It was inconvenient to have to retrace her steps whenever she jumped in time.

Her appearance went mostly unnoticed, except for one obese woman who felt that Kathleen had invaded her personal space.

"Watch out! Don't you come pushing up on me like that! It's just like you people, always crowding somebody who's mindin' her own business."

Kathleen moved away quickly without responding. She filtered through the crowd and made her way to the street. She was about halfway back to the hotel when Jones showed up. He climbed out of a double-parked black SUV.

"Hey, Whitby! Pay attention to where you are. Get over here and get in."

She looked disdainfully at him without answering. He motioned to her again. She started to move towards him, but then two men grabbed her arms and hustled her towards the vehicle.

That didn't last long. The two stopped and looked foolishly at their empty hands. They'd held a woman's arms a second ago. Now they were empty.

A bitter voice spoke from behind them, "If you idiots will mind your manners, I'll get in the car by myself."

Kathleen had dropped back in time, stepped away from where they would be, then jumped back a millisecond after she'd left. This action was cutting it close, but she had timed it perfectly. At no point was she present at the same time as her previous self.

They spun around and reached for her again, but Jones snapped, "That's enough, guys. You can't hold her. She can vanish any time she wants."

The two stepped back and allowed her to climb in beside Jones.

"Well, Kathleen, you gave us a little scare. When you didn't come right back, I was sure that you'd decided to try and break your caveman out without helping us. I took action, of course, but now, here you are. Want to tell me what you've been doing?"

She hardly heard his question; her mind was fixated on the idea that he'd done something to Cadeyrin.

"What have you done? If you've hurt him, I'll — "

He interrupted her implicit threat. "Don't get your panties in an uproar, Whitby. He's fine. I just had him moved. That's all. I got to thinking that holding him in Minneapolis might not be such a great idea. I put him on a plane, and now he's here in DC."

She started to speak, and again he interrupted.

"Don't get your hopes up. I've got him in a secure facility that you're not going to find. Your best bet would be to give me the time-travel formula and quit wasting time. He's recovering well from his surgery so far, but you know people sometimes have relapses."

Kathleen was furious. Her face felt drained of blood, and her hands were shaking. She was barely able to control her voice.

"Jones, I swear that if you hurt him, you're going to regret ever thinking about time," she whispered.

He grinned a little. "And, I suppose you're going to be the one to make me regret it? What can an unwanted girl like you do? Even your own mother didn't want you."

When she started to speak, he said, "Yeah, we know about your birth. Pretty sad. You know it's highly unusual for an aborted late-term baby to be allowed to survive. You were lucky. Now be sensible, and you'll get to continue being lucky."

Somehow she recovered her wits. Perhaps it was the way he threw her mother at her. He expected it to hurt, but she'd left all of her anger about that in the Pleistocene. She'd finally found a way to rise above it and forgive her mother, thanks to Cadeyrin's love.

"Jones, let's just stick to business, huh?" she said.

He leaned back, his eyes narrowing, "Okay. If that's what you want, you go first."

She took a breath and said, "I went to the room at the exact time Gridley should have arrived using your device. He wasn't there, so you must have made a mistake in your programming. Your method might not be as accurate as you think it is."

He said, "Noted. Go on."

"He'd been there, I think. There was the smell of gunpowder in the air, and I found a painter's drop cloth that had six bullet holes in it. Someone had folded it so that the bullets were stopped. They must not be too powerful. Anyway, the bullets weren't there, so the person, Gridley or whomever, must have taken them out of the drop cloth. Gridley wasn't there either, so I tried to figure out where he might be."

She paused for breath. Jones looked at her with a slight sneer.

"Go on. Where did you think he went?"

"Well, if he activated the return system and your cues were accurate, you wouldn't be asking me that question. He'd be here, wouldn't he?" She waited, but he didn't say anything, so she asked, "Were the cues accurately programmed for the present?"

He moved his hands a little, and the corner of his mouth twitched. He glanced momentarily upwards and to the left before answering, "Of course, the cues were programmed to bring him back here, but maybe they weren't as accurate as we hoped. Did you find any trace of him?"

He was lying. She'd seen the movement of his eyes and knew it as an almost sure indication that at least part of what he said was false.

"I thought about that, and I've been looking for him in the room. I made several jumps back and forth in the past five years to check the place. That's what took me so long. The room was empty each time I appeared. The last jump was for about five years ago. I thought that the door was just closing as I appeared, so I left the room and looked outside. A man was walking away down the sidewalk. I don't know what Gridley looks like from the back; you remember you only showed me a picture of his face. Anyway, I followed the guy. He went to the National Mall and got lost in a bunch of tourists. I tried to track him but couldn't find him, so I jumped back to now. I was in a group of tourists also when I arrived. I walked over to the street, and there you were. That's all I have to say, except that I'm exhausted and need to rest, so would you take me to the hotel and get me a private room?"

She added with some sarcasm, "By private, I mean one that doesn't have any of your people in it and preferably no bugs or video cameras."

He snickered, "You don't need to be so suspicious. We have you on a short leash with your man held captive. I know I can't keep you prisoner, but you can't free him, so you'll be around when I need you. I suppose that I can arrange a room for you. Do you want room service also?"

She tried to relax and smile a little. It was a forced smile, but Jones seemed to think that he had allayed her suspicions.

She said, "I can order room service if I need it. Right now, all I want is a hot shower and several hours of sleep. Traveling in time is exhausting, you know."

She was lying. Her time jumps were instantaneous and effortless. They came with a momentary perceptual distortion, but she'd gotten so used to the effect that she no longer noticed it.

—◦—

In the hotel, she cleaned up. Her hair was smokey from Grid's fire. She was surprised that he hadn't noticed that. It would have been very suspicious in light of the story she'd given him. After showering, she dressed again and then climbed into the bed as if to rest. If they were watching, the only thing they would see was a large lump. She'd moved the pillows alongside her body, creating an ambiguous bundle under the covers.

Her plan was to jump backward, investigate the Annie situation, and then jump forwards, leaving the pillows supporting the covers for just a few seconds. With any luck, they wouldn't notice her absence.

# Chapter Twenty-One

# About Annie

Kathleen materialized in the bed in room 303 a year prior to when she lay down and arranged the pillows. There was no one present, so she straightened the covers and left, making sure the door was locked.

Downstairs, she checked in and requested room 303. It was vacant, and they gave her the key. She told them she'd be back with her luggage and left the hotel.

She needed a computer and Internet access. There was a coffee shop across the street. It would have Internet service. She'd try to borrow someone's computer.

She was in luck. A nerdy guy with greasy hair was drinking what was probably his only cup of coffee. He didn't look like he could have afforded a second one.

She smiled at him and asked, "Do you mind if I sit at your table?"

He stuttered, "N—no. Sit down."

She proceeded to weave a story about being new in town, and someone had stolen her laptop. She desperately needed to check her email. Would he let her use his machine?"

By that point, he was so enthralled that he would have probably given it to her. She turned the display so that he couldn't see it and began to research.

It didn't take long. Annie Gridley had committed suicide just three weeks ago in a park right in DC. She was an aide for Senator Rasmussen. He was the chairman of the Ways and Means Committee, a powerful man and one who had a taint of scandal that always followed him around despite no one ever being able to prove or find anything.

Her body had been discovered in a grassy area well screened from the street by trees. A man had been walking his dog and had called it in at about 5 in the morning. The newspaper article quoted her mother as saying that they had spoken at nine the night before, and Annie had been excited about the impending return of her husband who was due to finish his current tour of duty in the middle east.

That gave Kathleen eight hours to investigate. She'd start at nine and check Annie's apartment hourly. When she determined it was vacant, she'd go back and move through the hour incrementally until she saw something.

She closed the news site and opened Wikipedia. A little research and she had a picture of Deinonychus. The artist's rendering didn't look exactly like the girls, but the time frame and location were most likely correct according to the information on the page. There were no other similarly sized raptors in the area and time where Grid was. She mentally shrugged. It didn't really matter; she knew the girls better than any paleontologist. They had no interest in a name that some primate living a hundred million years later assigned to them.

She closed the browser and thanked the nerdy guy for his computer, then stood and prepared to leave.

He asked plaintively, "Will I see you again?"

Kathleen was amused. It was almost like he assumed this was a date. She shook her head gently, "No. I've got to leave town soon. The email I was waiting for came in, and the news was bad." She assumed a sad look but then mischievously bent and kissed him quickly on the cheek.

He instantly turned a bright red. When she glanced through the closing door, he was still red, although now he was holding his hand on his cheek as if to preserve her peck.

———◆———

She took a cab to Annie's apartment. It was on K Street and was in a renovated row house. The Gridleys had rented the top floor. There was no rear entrance, so Kathleen simply had to watch the front for Annie to leave.

Kathleen closed her eyes and opened them on the last day of Annie Gridley's life. She was in front of Annie's apartment. The problem was there was no convenient spot to sit and observe. It was now almost nine o'clock at night, and she had to keep watch for possibly eight hours. She also had to avoid being noticed, in case there was someone who cared to notice her.

She cast around. Parked cars lined the side of the street across from the apartment. Perhaps that was a solution. She walked up and down the block, watching.

Eventually, a car left. It was replaced almost instantly with a smaller SUV driven by a woman. The woman looked exhausted and in need of sleep. Surely she wouldn't check her vehicle until morning.

Kathleen walked over and examined the SUV. It was locked. That figured. Nothing was ever easy. She glanced at her cell phone. The woman had pulled in five minutes and twenty-five seconds ago. She blinked and moved backward a full day. The parking space happened to be empty. She stood approximately where the SUV would be and jumped forward a second after she'd left. When she opened her eyes, she was sitting inside the car, her molecules having adjusted themselves to fit the available space.

The doors were locked, so all she had to do was to sit and watch. She scrunched down into a comfortable position and resigned herself to wait.

At fifteen minutes after eleven, a black limo pulled up in front of Annie's apartment. She came out, walked down the steps waving, and got in.

Kathleen wrote down the license number as the vehicle drove away. Then she opened the door and climbed out. The SUV's alarm went off as she'd suspected it would. She blinked and moved to the middle of the previous afternoon. No sense in getting involved in explaining why the car alarm went off.

The time frame was after eleven. Kathleen hailed a cab and was shortly delivered at the park in question. It was large and offered many hiding places that overlooked the grassy area where Annie's body had been found.

The cab ride had taken her eighteen minutes. She counted the minutes mentally. Eleven fifteen plus eighteen and maybe two minutes to walk to the grassy area gave her eleven thirty-five. She blinked and was then.

There was no one in sight. Perhaps they hadn't come directly to the park. Maybe Annie had been killed elsewhere, or it was possible she had walked to the park from another location and not arrived in the limo at all. Kathleen sighed. This time detective stuff involved a lot of waiting, even if she could snap back and forth effortlessly.

She jumped forward to one in the morning. She looked around, then stiffened. There was a body in the clearing. So, it had happened before one.

She jumped backward to midnight. This time there were three people in the grassy area. One was a short and rather stout bald man, one was a young woman, and one was a taller and younger man. The older man and the woman were discussing something. She seemed to be pleading with him.

He shook his head, said something, and turned to walk away. She started after him, but the tall man grabbed her arm. She screamed, but he muffled it instantly with his other hand.

By this time, the stout man had disappeared. The tall man pushed the woman to the ground and placed his foot on her back, holding her down. He pulled out a pistol and aimed at her head, then paused to say, "You just couldn't leave it alone, could ya? The boss said I was to make it look like you shot yourself, so turn your head sideways. You won't feel a thing; it'll be over so suddenly."

He stopped, frozen by the feel of a gun barrel at his right temple.

Kathleen said, "That's right. It's a gun. Now drop that piece and let the lady up. Maybe I won't pull the trigger. There's a chance that I won't, but I can guarantee that if you try anything, I will shoot you. There's supposed to be a body here, and I don't much care if it's the wrong sex."

The gun dropped. The man lifted his leg, releasing Annie, and then suddenly tried to grab Kathleen's arm. He caught her wrist and laughed in triumph but then stopped, staring at his empty hand. He'd had her, but where was she now?

A solid blow hit the back of his head, making a loud clunk. He dropped like a stone, landing face-first in the grass. Kathleen grunted in pain and almost dropped the pistol. She'd struck him so hard that her hand was stinging. Lucky that her weapon weighed as much as it did. A lighter gun might not have brought him down so easily.

Annie was standing, her hand over her mouth. She was shaking in terror but managed to ask, "Who...who are you? You saved me. We've got to get out of here. The Senator has another man in the car."

Kathleen took her arm and said, "Don't worry. We're gone right now." She closed her eyes and moved her lips slightly.

---

It was bright daylight. Kathleen was still holding Annie's arm. She smiled and said, "We're in the same place, just a week ago. I trust you're nowhere near this park right now? Ever come here before?"

Annie began to gasp heavily, and her already wide eyes now seemed about to pop out of her head. Kathleen was afraid that the other woman was going to lose control and start screaming. It was a bit much. Jumping in time for the first time was always confusing.

She searched for the best way to explain, then said, "Listen, Annie. I know who you are. I'm friends with Jason, and he's asked me to look after you. Right now, there's no time to get hysterical. I've got to know what's going on. Why were you about to be killed?"

Annie made a convulsive effort to regain control. Kathleen patted her shoulder and said, "That's better. Let's walk. We don't need to stand here in the middle of this grass. Would you like to go for a coffee?"

"Y—yes, I believe that would be nice right now. Uh, when is now, again? Did you just somehow rip me out of there and into the daylight, or am I crazy?"

Kathleen laughed. "I ripped you through time. You're safe right now. We have to figure out how to keep you safe. Don't worry about how you got here. It's an ability I have that comes in handy at times, that's all."

The walking was helping. Annie was visibly calming down. She took several deep breaths, visibly regaining control, then she said, "Okay. I'll take that on faith for now. You say you know Jason? What does he like to be called?"

Kathleen said, "Well, I just met him, and we're not old friends, but from the way he talks about himself, I'd say he thinks of himself as 'Grid,' not as Gridley or Jason."

Annie sighed. "That's about as correct as it gets. He always calls himself 'Grid.' So what are you going to do with me?"

Kathleen said, "First, I'm going to buy you a coffee, then we're going to sit down and drink it, and while we are, you're going to tell me what you know that almost got you killed. After that, I'm going to have to do some serious calculating to figure out what to do next."

⸻◦⸻

After a few sips of coffee, Annie arranged her thinking and began to tell Kathleen her story.

She had been the Senator's aide for nearly a year. He'd come to depend on her for most things. A week ago, no, actually this week, maybe right about now... Annie looked over her shoulder at the front window of the coffee shop, then resumed.

She'd been putting some papers on the Senator's desk for his signature, and one of the desk drawers had been open slightly, exposing the corner of a document. She'd only meant to close the door, but the paper had something about time-travel on it.

Annie paused and then took a sip.

Kathleen's mind was racing. Time-travel... So, Annie wasn't entirely unfamiliar with the concept. Well, the government knew about her secret, so why shouldn't they have reports on the subject.

Annie had read the paper and the other two in the drawer. They spoke about a time-travel research project that was in progress. There had recently been a little success, and there was hope that more was to come.

Under the last document, there was a copy of an email. The information on it had startled her.

The Senator was corresponding with someone she didn't know. The email address was unfamiliar, and she couldn't remember it at the moment. Anyway, the ideas in the email were horrifying to her.

They were talking about changing things back in time, in history to make the population more compliant, more amenable to their plans. They intended to set things up so that they would rule perpetually. There would be no more elections. In short, they were going to take over the country.

They'd planned on killing President Reagan as their first step. With him gone, some elements of the economy would change, providing them with a reason to have their candidate declare war on Russia. That would allow for a military take-over of the country. They could simply go back and make deals or eliminate anyone they wanted until the country today fit their intended result. The steps necessarily were vague, but the email concluded, they could modify things at will until they'd reached the desired end state. It was awful.

Kathleen agreed. It was awful. So this was what Jones' group was working towards. She would never give up her formula now, even if it meant...she swallowed hard, then finished the thought. Even if it meant that she might not ever see Cadeyrin again. He'd surely understand if he knew.

It was up to her to make sure this didn't happen. If the enemy was willing to make such radical changes in time, then perhaps she shouldn't worry so much about the minor changes she might have made. Speaking of which, one was sitting right in front of her.

"Annie, this is going to be hard for you to understand, but before I rescued you, I started from a time where you were dead. The papers said you'd committed suicide. I had to investigate until I found the precise moment to intervene. Your Jason asked me to keep you from being killed. Now that I have, the time-stream will change a bit. I was worried about that, but I can see I'm going to have to change it more. Senator Rasmussen and his group have got to go. They can't be allowed to take over. I just hope my suspicion is correct."

Annie looked puzzled, and Kathleen added, "I suspect the time-stream is self-healing to an extent. Changes will gradually fade out as long as they aren't too extreme." She paused, thinking, then added, "I'm going to have to keep you safe, and the best place I can think of is to take you to where Grid is. Then I've got some additional preparations to make before we can take action. Are you ready to go? I warn you; it's going to be strange. Grid is living in a cave in the Cretaceous period with three dinosaurs."

Annie snickered, "If it involves that guy, I believe it. He's the most outrageous risk-taker ever. Let's go. I can't wait to see him."

They walked outside and headed for an alley where they would be unlikely to be observed. On the way, Annie, apparently having second thoughts, asked, "How long ago would that be, anyhow?"

Kathleen answered, "About one hundred and twelve million years ago. Don't worry. The dinosaurs aren't everywhere, and the cave is a secure location. He's adopted three small ones, and they think of him as their parent."

Annie's eyes grew large. She said, "I could see him doing that. He's always liked animals."

Kathleen added as an afterthought, "I believe they belong to the species known as Deinonychus. They're small raptors with big killing claws on one of their toes."

Annie's last words before they disappeared were, "I really hope they like me."

# Chapter Twenty-Two

# An Unexpected Delay

Kathleen watched as Annie ran to Gridley. The two embraced and kissed.

There was a soft sound beside her. She looked down at Lolita. The feathered creature turned her blue and green head to Kathleen, then asked, "Grid's mate? Is she Mother?"

Kathleen didn't know how Annie would take to being the mother of three killer raptors, but she nodded. "Yes. She's Grid's mate. That makes her your mother. Treat her well and take very good care of her. She's new here and doesn't know how to survive."

To her surprise, Lolita answered, "We will love her. She will be safe."

On her other side, Belle asked, "Can we be mother? I would like little ones."

Kathleen started to answer, but then it hit her. She'd been forced away from Cadeyrin almost the same way she'd been forced out of her own presence to avoid a paradox. Was it possible?

She ran over to Grid and Annie, caught her breath, and said, "You two be safe now. I'll be back. There's something that I most urgently have to do."

Then she was gone.

She walked into the lobby of her hotel, took the elevator, and entered room 303. Once inside, she climbed into the bed, arranged the pillows the way she remembered, and moved into the present, her present time.

She sat up, stretched, and climbed out of bed. The clock on the nightstand showed that she'd been lying down for only a minute or so. That wouldn't do. She couldn't appear to recover so quickly. She went to the bath, relieved herself, and returned to bed.

As she rested, her mind focused on her equation. It was inconvenient to have to change locations physically. She was tired of the delay involved. Despite her ability to jump in time, she still had to live her life sequentially a moment at a time, and travel ate that up. If she could travel through time, was there any way to simultaneously change her position on the globe? She resolved to work on that. There was a possible modification of her formula. One of the constants she used might not be a constant at all. It could relate to physical coordinates. She had ignored it, but now it might be useful. She'd need to be extremely careful, though. It wouldn't do to materialize in the vacuum of space or maybe underwater or something. After some thought, she discarded the idea for the time being and began to plan on how to deal with Jones.

She had to put on a good show in present time to keep Jones from harming Cadeyrin. Of course, when she figured out how to get him, she would go back and break him out within minutes of when they captured him. That was what Jones, with all his conniving, didn't understand. She didn't need to know where Cadeyrin was now. She already knew where he was then, and back then was when she was going to get him.

She grinned wryly. Her whole notion of preserving the time-stream was going to end up totally discarded. Once she got hold of her man again, she didn't care what happened. They'd be safe, and that was all that counted.

Meanwhile, she could use a nap. She relaxed and drifted. In her dream, she imagined a little voice saying, "I'm here now." It didn't have a source, and that bothered her, but the emotional overtones were those of a warm, happy dream. Her face relaxed, and a slight smile curled her lips.

She slept until morning.

One of the men who had tried to hustle her into Jones' SUV met her in the lobby.

"Good morning, Ms. Whitby. Did you sleep well?" He was making an effort to be pleasant, trying to make amends for grabbing her.

She was in a good mood and not inclined to hold grudges. "Yes, thank you. However, I need to visit the pharmacy down the street."

He looked as if he might object, so she added, "I need some essential feminine supplies."

His expression showed that he understood. He sighed and said, "I'm supposed to take you to meet Jones. I'll call and tell him you're going to be delayed a bit."

She smiled and said, "Thank you. I'll be right back."

He nodded, then pulled out his cell to report as she left the lobby. She turned right and headed towards the drug store. Once there, she hastily searched the isles, selected her merchandise, paid, then returned to the store restroom.

She locked herself in a stall and opened her package. Five minutes later, she was sure. Both tests had shown positive. She was pregnant.

She continued to sit, trying to think of what this meant and how best to deal with it. It was now obvious that she'd been forced from Cadeyrin's presence by the presence of her fetus. There had been enough temporal difference between his body and his DNA in her body to create a paradoxical effect. Her own body wasn't affected, but when half of her baby was being pushed away, it amounted to the same thing. There was no way she could approach Cadeyrin through time. She wasn't sure now that she'd be able to be near him even if Jones released him. She'd done too much jumping back and forth.

There was only one thing she could do if she wanted to free Cadeyrin. Well, there were actually two, but she'd never, never consider the alternative. It would be too devastating, considering her own tragic birth. No, she had to carry the baby to term and deliver it before she could rescue her husband.

She sighed in exasperation. Cadeyrin might not realize that it had taken her eight months or more to get around to rescuing him, but she certainly would. It wouldn't be fun, being without him for that long. And, where was she going to hide during those months? Jones would certainly try to figure out a way to use her child against her.

With both Cadeyrin and her baby to protect, things could easily become more complicated than she could handle. She didn't waste time wondering if she could simply give Jones the formula. She knew that neither she nor Cadeyrin would survive to see another day in that event.

Time was passing. They were probably already getting worried about her coming out of the drug store. Her mind raced. She felt trapped in a no-win scenario.

Like the coming together of roulette wheels, the situation clicked into place in her mind. She couldn't let them know she was pregnant. They could probably check her purchase, and they would know she'd bought the tests, even though she'd flushed the sticks down the toilet. The result of the tests was the first roulette wheel.

The things hadn't wanted to go down and might be stuck in the throat of the drain. Well, let them dive for them, she told herself.

The second wheel represented the time it would take for the baby to be born. It would be about eight months of her sequential life. There would be no jumping back and forth to reach the time that she'd delivered the full-term baby. She had to live the entire sequence.

A warm maternal emotion flooded through her. She found herself holding both hands on her abdomen and smiling. She'd live the entire time and enjoy it. She had to do everything she could to ensure her baby was nourished and safe.

That thought led to the third and final wheel clicking into place. Jackpot! She'd go and stay with George and Ulfsa. The old man had a second bedroom. As far as she was concerned, money was no object. She could afford excellent care, regardless of where she lived. She'd be with her wolf, and that was good. She could – why she could go this instant.

She closed her eyes and opened them in 1971. The store was an old one and had been there at that time. Nothing had changed except the product lines. She was amused to note the absence of all of the USB charging devices and cords that cluttered the check-outs in her time.

She walked out, summoned a passing cab, and headed to the airport.

Air travel was far more pleasant in 1971. She walked in, purchased a ticket with some of the old dated cash she carried, and then walked to the gate. No one questioned her lack of baggage, the one-way ticket, or her single status. No security. She could feel herself relaxing. This time might be a good one in which to raise a child also.

The Feds weren't aware of her presence here. In fact, she legally didn't exist. That might be a bit of a problem for health care and the hospital. She'd see about getting a social security card issued under another name. She'd read somewhere that it wasn't too difficult, at least before modern computers and tracking.

Three hours later, the plane landed in Minneapolis. It was snowing and cold. The wind whistled through the cracks in the Jetway, making her wish she had heavier clothing than the light garb she had on. Once inside the terminal, she stopped in confusion. There were no shops and only a couple of newsstands.

She regained herself and entered a cab. After a brief discussion with the driver, she had him take her to Macy's downtown. There she bought some heavy winter clothing, opting for a coat that was a couple of sizes larger than what she actually needed.

"I'll need this before too long," she whispered to herself with a feeling of satisfaction.

The street outside Macy's was deserted, and she had to walk a couple of blocks before she could catch a cab. This time she gave George Schwartz's address.

She knocked at the door as the cab drove off. There was a wild scrabbling from within paired with a whuffing sound. Ulfsa was trying to open the door.

She could hear George coming.

"Take it easy, wolf. I'm coming as fast as I can. Who could be coming over at this time of day and in a snowstorm too?"

The door creaked, and George peered out. "Why Kathleen! What are you doing here? You just left yesterday. I didn't expect you for maybe a week."

"It's a complicated story, George. I'm about to freeze to death right now. Do you think we could have some coffee and talk it over? I really need your help."

He hastened to usher her in. "Of course, you can have my help. I've been so excited about you and the financial thing that I could hardly sleep. It's given me a different perspective on my life. I'd about given up when we first met. You've given me a reason to continue. Of course, I'll help. What do you need?"

He looked like he thought he'd have to engage in some physical labor or perhaps fight to defend her. She laughed and said, "It won't be so difficult. I just need a place to stay."

He relaxed. "That's easy. You can have the spare bedroom. I'll have to clean the junk off the bed, but it should be fine."

She smiled and added, "I hope you won't get tired of me. I need to live with you for maybe eight months."

"That's fine. Uh, did you say eight months?" His eyes opened wide. "Don't tell me. I know. You're pregnant!"

She nodded affirmatively.

"What about that man of yours? Where's he going to be this whole time? He should be by your side," he said. His face showed that he disapproved of Cadeyrin's absence.

"That's the complicated part. He's captive, and I can't rescue him until I have the baby. But, you have to understand. He won't know I've been gone eight months. I'm going to get him just a few hours after he was taken hostage. I just need the eight months with you to bring the baby to term. Is that going to be okay?"

George looked a little dazed. "I suppose I'll understand it if you tell me often enough. This time business is sure confusing. Anyway, consider yourself at home here. It isn't very luxurious, but it's all I have."

Ulfsa interrupted by shoving his head under her arm, nearly knocking her down. She bent down and wrapped her arms around his thick coat. He whined a little and pressed closer.

George was as good as his word. The spare bedroom was packed full of his deceased Mary's possessions. He'd been trying to get up the courage to donate them but couldn't bring himself to take that final step. Now he packed them up and arranged for a charity organization to pick them up in the morning.

The bedroom was small but adequate. It had originally belonged to George's daughter. Now that she was in California, she never visited or called.

George had tried to notify her about Mary's illness and then about her death, but there had been no answer to the letters he sent, and he had no phone number to call. He didn't know if the letters had been delivered.

"You just use this room like it is your own. Do whatever you want. Paint or paper, I don't care. It'll be wonderful to have someone in the house again. I'm looking forward to this," he said, standing at the door.

"Thank you. I don't want you to worry about funds. I have plenty. We could even move to a different house if you want."

He said, "No. I'm used to this one. It's just nice to have someone here again. I hope you don't mind, but I'm already starting to feel like you're a daughter. One I've never met. It's going to be nice to get to know you."

She was relieved. The old man had initially been extremely depressed, and she'd had no assurance that he would take her in even though he'd agreed to watch Ulfsa for a week or so. He seemed like a different person now. His energy level was far higher than it had been, and he seemed happy. She was glad that simply being there made such a difference to him.

She'd eventually leave. She had her own life to live. But, why couldn't she stay in touch with him? The thought of taking him to the Sangamon passed through her mind. He might enjoy the wilderness. She'd have to discuss it with Cadeyrin, and they'd have to figure out something to do about those forest giants. They couldn't have some unknown primate hanging around, throwing stones whenever it got a chance. That would have to be solved. Perhaps they could go backward a millennium or so.

She said, "I have to buy some clothes and supplies tomorrow. Do you have a car?"

He did. It was in a free-standing garage at the back of the house. It was several years old, but she didn't care. Basic transportation was all she needed.

—◦—

That night she stretched out in the small bed and listened to the regular breathing of Ulfsa on the floor between her and the door. She felt totally safe for the first time in days. She'd noted the precise time she'd transited out of the restroom in the drug store. After she had her baby, she'd reappear just a few seconds later. Jones would never know she'd gone. He might be suspicious if he investigated her purchase, but there would be no evidence that she was pregnant. Unless…oh, of course, she'd probably look a little different. Her flat stomach would be fuller, as would her hips. Maybe her breasts would be larger? She didn't know. She hadn't thought about it, but now that she did, she fully intended to breastfeed. Her breasts would be different also. So what? Who cared what Jones thought? She didn't. She'd be able to jump through time to Cadeyrin then. She was looking forward to seeing the last of Jones.

# Chapter Twenty-Three

# 1971

It had been a few days. Kathleen had purchased some plain but warm clothes at an area thrift shop. They were slightly worn, and that made them a little more comfortable from the moment she put them on.

She'd gotten basic supplies at the drug store, groceries, and refueled George's car. It was an older Chevy, and the large doors and wide, comfortable seats promised to be easy to use once she had gained weight.

Ulfsa was content with her presence, although he did seem to miss hunting. The local parks were not a really good place to take a huge wolf. She kept him leashed at all times, even though there was no current leash law in the city.

They were on one of their frequent walks. The nearest park was about half a mile, and they'd just left the street. Ulfsa was sniffing at dog-sign on the base of a leafless oak tree while she was attempting to adjust her clothing to minimize the cutting edge of the bitter wind. It was cold. Almost as cold as during the ice age.

There was movement on the street, and she turned automatically to see. Her hunting responses had become blunted by the lack of necessity to be aware constantly. There were no predators in this modern time and this location.

No, that was wrong. Kathleen made a mental note to try and be more aware. Three scruffy men were heading directly toward her. Their attitude wasn't reassuring. One had dropped back to watch the street, and the other two were separating. They intended to come at her from different sides, not a friendly way to approach.

Ulfsa moved closer protectively, and a low rumble sounded from his throat. He wasn't in full attack mode, but he was warning the men to stay away.

They didn't seem to recognize the danger. They came on. The man directly in front of her tried to distract her, to keep her attention from his circling partner.

"Hey, what kinda dog is that?" he asked. He moved his hands, waving in Ulfsa's general direction.

Kathleen scoffed, turning slightly to keep an eye on the circling man.

"I've been attacked by a lot more dangerous things than you. You'd best go about your business somewhere else," she said. The wind was gusting, and he pretended he hadn't heard.

"What was that?" He held a hand cupped to his ear and started forward.

Ulfsa took two stiff-legged steps forward and growled a full-throated growl.

That got the man's attention. He stopped instantly, and a hint of concern passed over his face.

"Hey, lady. Hold onto your dog. I ain't gonna hurt you."

She heard a rush of footsteps between wind gusts and ducked under the arms of the circling man. As she ducked, she swung her leg, tripping him. He stumbled forward past Ulfsa.

The wolf turned in a lightning-fast move and slashed with his fangs. A bright splash of red instantly stained the guy's dirty jeans.

The man yelled and staggered back. Ulfsa jumped forward but stopped when he felt the leash tighten.

"Damn it!" the other man yelled. "I'm gonna kill that dog." He fumbled at his coat, finally exposing a small pistol stuck in the front of his waistband. He took his eyes off of her to pull it. The hammer had hooked into a belt loop, and the revolver was stuck in his pants.

He struggled with it for a moment, then raised his eyes again. The woman and big dog were gone. His buddy was sitting down, groaning, and trying to staunch the bleeding from his thigh.

"Where'd they go?" he yelled at the third man as he came running up.

"I don't know. They just kinda disappeared. I might have taken my eyes off them. I don't know. They aren't here now, though," he gasped, catching his wind.

A voice behind them said, "Wrong. I simply walked over here."

They snapped around. Kathleen was facing them, standing in the shadow of a small spruce tree. They started forward but then stopped as they saw she was holding a large, semi-automatic pistol pointed in their general direction. At that moment, Ulfsa came out from under the edge of the spruce branches and walked calmly up to her side.

The two men froze, their eyes wide. Then the one with the little revolver started to pull it again.

Kathleen said, "You really aren't that stupid, are you?"

He stopped and raised his hands.

"Just let us walk away, lady," he said, backing up. His friend took two sideways steps and grabbed at the wounded man's arm.

With a groan, the bleeding man hoisted himself to his feet, and the three moved away.

Kathleen watched, unsure whether she should try to hold them or let them go. She'd already snapped back in time to retrieve the pistol and move to the spruce tree's shelter. It had been a little too close to her presence in the here and now of the moment. She didn't like risking the possibility of overlaying her time-translated presence too closely on her sequential presence. The danger of an overlap causing a temporal paradox effect was constantly on her mind. It would be bad if she lost some element of her memory again. She had to keep everything working together, gears meshing like an intricate watch, to realize her goal to rescue Cadeyrin.

She could move through time again and try to send a police officer to the park. If he arrived in time to arrest the three, she'd still be holding a very illegal and as yet unmanufactured handgun. The serial number was one that Sig wouldn't reach until 2003. That would cause problems that she didn't need. She sighed, relaxed the tension in her shoulders, and watched the three move towards an automobile parked down the street.

The impact washed over her as she watched. Tears came to her eyes. She wasn't actually the tough woman who had confronted the attackers so competently. She really...she really...oh, she just wanted to be safe in the past with her man.

The incongruity of her thoughts caused her to laugh wryly through her tears. Most people would be terrified at finding themselves in the Younger Dryas period or the Sangamon. The beasts did pose a bit of a problem, but they weren't actively evil as those men had been. She felt more at ease facing a smilodon than her fellow humans.

Ulfsa whined to get her attention. She came back to the moment and saw that he had noted the automobile departing.

"Good wolf!" she said, fluffing his ruff around the base of his right ear. He leaned towards her with a brief show of affection and then pulled on the leash as he started towards a distant stand of trees. The threat had departed and, to his mind, no longer existed. He'd deal with it when and if it reappeared.

She shook her head, clearing her thoughts. Ulfsa was right. She had to live in the moment until she reached the end of her self-imposed confinement in this time. When the baby was born, she would be free to continue the rescue. She just had to make sure that her arrival in the future was closely contiguous with her departure. No one would even know she'd gone.

Together the two continued their walk. Ulfsa seemed to be completely relaxed, only focusing on his needs and the scent markers of other canines. Kathleen was unable to relax fully. She had allowed herself to slip into a lower level of alertness, but the men had shown her that was an error. Now she was always scanning the area, looking for things that were out of place and it was wearing on her. She'd much rather be in an environment that wasn't so densely populated.

Later, at the house, George was angry. "The neighborhood has gone downhill. There are a lot of newcomers, and some of them aren't desirable neighbors. We should call the police."

"No, George. I took care of it," she said. "I don't want them alerted to either my carrying a gun or Ulfsa. I'm sure that they'd cause some trouble if they were aware that we were harboring a wolf."

He laughed. "And the gun, young lady. I never thought I'd see a beautiful woman who was as ease with a big handgun as you are."

They both laughed a little uneasily.

George added, "If I could afford it, I would have moved long ago. Maybe we should take some of the money you've got invested and move to a safer place, especially considering your condition."

His eyes strayed to her midriff, now showing a gentle curve that it had never had before. His expression was warm and concerned.

It was moments like this that made her feel lucky. George wasn't just a lucky haven. He had taken her to his heart, and she now felt that he was very much like the father that she'd never known.

The move was out of the question since she didn't want to touch the funds. She hoped it would be the last time that the issue came up. She'd be more careful in the future. No one would have a chance to catch her unaware.

━━━◆◆◆━━━

The days passed slowly as winter ground on. Many times the weather was so cold that she let Ulfsa out in the small rear yard rather than walking him. He could easily have wandered away but was too smart to leave without her.

George proved to be a caring man. His age kept him from helping her as much as he would have liked, but she appreciated his well-intentioned attempts.

She was running short of funds by mid-March. Following her instructions, he had bet the original silver that she'd given him on the Super-bowl. They'd taken the winnings and invested them. They agreed that they didn't want to touch the funds until her fund-raising plan was complete. Meanwhile, George's small retirement had proven to be inadequate to cover the needs of two people and the appetite of a large wolf.

She needed to do something. The lottery hadn't been implemented yet, so it was out of the question. However, a little thought gave her a possible answer. The Kentucky Derby was coming up and was scheduled for May 1st. That was a potential source of funds. She'd need to do some research in the future, though. However, she could easily do that without returning to her home time. All she needed was to move forward to May 2nd.

⟡

George had taken to Ulfsa in a big way. The wolf was easy-going and accepted the old man to a degree that surprised Kathleen. While he still slept in her bedroom at night, Ulfsa sometimes went in and lay by George's bed, spending an hour or two in the man's company. At other times Ulfsa would sit, looking out the window with a faraway gaze.

Kathleen thought that he missed Cadeyrin and probably wanted to hunt. She kept him well fed in an effort to make sure that his predatory instincts remained in the background. Most of the time, he acted like an enormous but restrained dog, sniffing things politely and not responding with hostility, even when dogs barked or snarled at him.

He'd get an aloof expression on his furry face and stare right past any dog attempted to be overly familiar or aggressive. If the dog were big and acted hostile, he would stiffen and present his side in a manner that Kathleen knew indicated that he was prepared to react decisively should he be attacked.

She would make every effort to drag him away from the impending confrontation when she saw that behavior. That had always worked.

⟡

They were in the park, going for one of their twice-daily walks. They usually followed the perimeter, stopping to investigate interesting trees and bushes. Once they had walked halfway around, Ulfsa often led her towards a large grove of trees that fringed a small, reed-filled pond. The cattails were dry and sere at this time of year, and ice covered the water.

There was a family of muskrats that had somehow found the water and now made their living off of the cattails and other plants along the bank. They had constructed a modest house, mostly a pile of reeds mixed with mud, near the center of the pond. They both enjoyed watching the small mammals whenever they appeared through a hole in the ice.

Today, as they approached the pond, Ulfsa pricked his ears as a flurry of barking sounded from ahead. He pulled on the leash and made a short whine as if to say, "Hurry up," to Kathleen.

When they had gone far enough through the trees to see the pond, she saw a pack of three large mixed-breed dogs out on the ice, trying to tear into the muskrat den. They weren't having much success since the mud and reeds were mostly frozen. Despite the ice, the dogs had managed to rip a small hole through and were taking turns sticking their faces in and barking at the muskrats.

Kathleen knew the muskrats also had a muddy den in one of the banks of the pond. If the dogs became an actual threat, they would retreat under the ice and go into the den. In fact, they probably had already left the reed house since the dogs seemed to be losing interest.

One of the canines, a dubious-looking yellow and brindle beast, chanced to look around and saw the two. It immediately barked and started their way, slipping on the ice in its haste.

The other two dogs followed, snarling. Kathleen feared that the pack, frustrated by their lack of success with the muskrats, would press home an attack. She moved up beside Ulfsa and unclipped the leash. He would need the freedom to maneuver. She wasn't worried about him running away.

She dug under her thick coat, trying to reach the pistol that she had carried on every walk since the episode with the three men. Her swelling abdomen now made it uncomfortable to carry, so she'd started placing the holster in the middle of her back. This was more comfortable, but it also made the gun difficult to reach, especially when wearing heavy clothes.

The lead dog reached the shore before she could retrieve the weapon. It didn't wait for the other two in its haste to close. It rushed directly at Ulfsa. The wolf dodged sideways, slashed with his jaws, and then lunged directly at the dog's bleeding side. Before the yellow and brindle mutt quite knew what was happening, Ulfsa had ripped his throat with a single slashing bite.

The dog turned, trying to close with its larger foe, but it was rapidly losing strength. The other two animals, slow to follow up, now paused. Ulfsa was facing them, his head held high and his body at an angle. He made no noise, and that lack seemed to disconcert the two.

Kathleen's efforts finally paid off, and she drew the forty-five but did not shoot. It wouldn't be necessary.

Ulfsa took a lordly step forward, and the two dogs backed up. Their pack-leader was now lying on his side, breathing his last, and without him, their courage seemed to evaporate. Ulfsa took another step towards them, and that did it. They turned and fled.

Kathleen stooped to look at the lying dog. It was dead, a pool of blood spreading out from its ruined neck. She straightened and shoved the pistol in her pocket as two men came through the trees.

"Bull! Here, Bull!" one called.

Then they saw her standing by the dead dog.

"God-dammit! That's my dog. You killed my dog," he shouted.

The other man grabbed his shoulder as he moved forward.

"Watch it, Louis, that's a wolf there!"

Louis was too enraged to listen. He shrugged off his friend's grasp and rushed forward; his fist raised to strike at Kathleen. Ulfsa interposed himself with a leap between the two, catching the man's wrist in his jaws.

The guy howled and pulled back. Fortunately, Ulfsa's fighting philosophy involved the minimal amount of force necessary to achieve his goals. He let go the instant the man began to move away.

Louis held his wrist with his other hand. A little blood was leaking through his fingers.

"Your dog just bit me!" he screamed, retreating. "I'm gonna call the cops!"

The other man looked embarrassed as he glanced at Kathleen.

"You better leave," he said, waving her away.

Saying nothing, Kathleen moved back into the trees. Ulfsa stood for a moment and then followed. She could hear the first man cursing as he inspected the yellow dog.

The two walked to the edge of the park, then crossed the street. Once back in the house, she didn't mention the incident to George. She didn't want him to worry.

It was becoming more and more evident that they needed to move. Despite the fact that Ulfsa was well-behaved, he did not fit into a city. If the police received a complaint, they could complicate her life incredibly. Between the undesirable new people in the neighborhood and the possibility of the police, she was rapidly losing her confidence in this place as a real sanctuary. She would have to take action. It worried her. She had become far more competent through her experiences, but she still found traces of the scarred, small, frightened, and insecure girl inside herself.

Now, if Cadeyrin were with her, things would be different. She felt a flush as her heart expanded. There was a corresponding pulse of warmth from below. She missed him incredibly. She placed her hand protectively on her stomach, bending her head down to look at her developing baby.

She whispered, "Don't worry, little one. I'll never leave you. You're loved and wanted."

There seemed to be a tiny answer in her mind: a contented sigh.

With new resolve, she decided that the Derby was their best chance of moving. Her other money was not yet ready to touch. She didn't feel that this was an emergency—yet. She could probably wait until after the horse race.

The last week in April, she borrowed George's old car, packed it, and set out alone. George had wanted to go with her, but she insisted that he stay and keep the wolf. Traveling to another state with a huge wolf who undoubtedly wouldn't be welcomed at any motel just wasn't in the cards.

She drove steadily southward in the spring sunshine, finally stopping at a roadside motel for supper and rest. She'd reach Louisville the next day.

Once in Louisville, she found an inexpensive motel close to Central Avenue in the south part of town. It was, in fact, a little sleazy with people coming and going at odd hours. She soon came to the conclusion that some of the rooms were being rented on an hourly basis. As long as no one bothered her, she didn't care what was going on in the other rooms.

She settled into a daily routine. Breakfast was at a diner down the street, as was lunch. For supper, she usually picked up some fast food from a fried-chicken place. Evenings she watched the TV and tried to ignore the sounds from the adjacent rooms. When she was tired of TV, she spent a little time studying pari-mutual betting. She'd never bet on a horse race before, and the very language seemed exotic.

◦

The day of the race dawned, bright and clear. She had purchased a general admission ticket the day she'd arrived and duly presented it at the gate. There were throngs of men and gaily-dressed women inside. She felt drab and unattractive in her plain dress and sweater. Her stomach protruded and made her feel like she was maneuvering a huge load as she threaded through the crowd and approached the betting windows.

Once in line, she saw a few men glance at her as if they suspected that she was lost. There were far more men than women lined up to place bets, and as far as she had noticed, she was the only visible pregnant woman.

The men in her line obligingly made room for her. The guy directly behind her attempted to strike up a conversation.

"Are you here by yourself?" he asked.

Kathleen looked back at him, evaluating. He appeared safe. Middle-aged and non-threatening.

"Yes. I've always wanted to see the Derby," she answered.

"It's an experience," he replied. "There is a tremendous amount of tradition here. The first Derby was run in 1875. Even the building is old. The two spires on the grandstands were built in 1895. You're participating in an annual rite," he said.

"I know," she answered, although she had not known of the history that he quoted. "It's nothing like what I'd expected. Some of the dresses are amazing."

He laughed. "I'd expect a woman to notice that. I'm more interested in the odds, myself." He nodded at the board with the horses' names.

"Well," she said. "I don't know much about it. I'm going to place a bet just for the fun of it."

"Not many ladies would do that by themselves," he said.

"Maybe not, but I'm going to do it anyway."

"Do you want me to help you? I'd suggest Bold Reason. He looks strong to me," he said.

Kathleen smiled. "I'll take that into consideration. I think he'll place at least."

"Oh, you know horses?" He looked moderately interested but also a little skeptical.

"No, not really. But, I just have a feeling," she said.

"Oh, a hunch. Well, sometimes that's the best way to bet. In your honor, I'll place some money on him also." He paused, then asked, "Where's your husband?"

The question took Kathleen by surprise, but she quickly recovered, "He's...ahh...he's overseas right now."

"In the army?" he asked.

"Yes. He's halfway through his tour. I can't wait for him to get back," she said, trying to play the part of a young army wife, worried about her husband.

"I hope he comes back to you soon," he said with a sad sigh. Then he added, "My son was at Hamburger Hill. He didn't come back to us."

"Oh," she gasped. She could feel her eyes tearing up in sympathy. She placed her hand on her cheek and said, "I'm sorry for you. So sorry."

He recovered himself and said, "I'm sorry too. I shouldn't have said anything. Now I don't want you to worry about your husband. He'll come back to you soon." He looked away, embarrassed.

She arrived at the window and quickly arranged her bet. The man behind her was openly disapproving.

"Young woman, you're risking a very large amount of money. Are you sure your husband would approve?" her acquaintance said.

Meanwhile, the clerk looked somewhat like a sly dog, licking his chops at the prospect.

She placed ten thousand dollars on a trifecta with Canonero II first, followed by Jim French and Bold Reason. The clerk counted her money and issued her bet while her self-appointed adviser watched.

As she turned to leave, he cautioned her. "Don't lose that slip. Should you be lucky enough to win, you'll need it. They won't honor any bets without it. I still can't believe that you're risking so much on such a low probability. A trifecta, no less. The odds are over forty to one against you."

She just smiled and said, "Good luck to you."

Her stomach was acting up. She'd missed out on morning sickness in the first trimester, but either the baby was unhappy, or something she ate was disagreeing with her. She felt distinctly nauseous.

She looked around with a little desperation. The lady's room was convenient, and she hastened over. Once in a stall, she sat and waited until the feeling subsided.

Perhaps it was simply due to her nerves. Despite the fact that she knew the results of the race in advance, she couldn't help feeling nervous. What if they thought she was cheating somehow. She'd prepared a story about seeing the three horses in a dream, in case anyone asked, but it now seemed silly and unbelievable.

She washed her face, reapplied what little makeup she wore, and found her way to the grandstands. As long as she was here, she wanted to enjoy the experience.

---

It was a long time until the race started. Kathleen was hot and wished she had an umbrella or one of the broad-brimmed hats some of the ladies wore. The race itself took only a couple of minutes, and the excitement of the crowd was intense. Kathleen had started for the betting window before the race was over. She didn't want to be caught in the crowd.

---

The actual payout was mostly routine. The clerk did ask her about her choice in a mostly conversational way, but she suspected that he was wondering about her bet. The payout was a little over four hundred thousand dollars. She had to take a check for the amount.

That had been something that had caused her some worry. She couldn't see carrying a large sum of money. The check folded away in her purse, and she walked away, trying to look as inconspicuous as possible. She saw her acquaintance a considerable distance away through the crowd. He was looking around as if searching for her. He'd definitely have a story to tell his friends. She ducked a little as she walked out. She didn't want him to find her.

Outside, she headed for her car and immediately headed for the highway. Outside of town, she filled the tank at a convenient gas station and headed north.

---

Two days later, she parked the car in the garage. She'd stopped at the bank and deposited the check. The pari-mutuel operation had taken the taxes out in advance. The final sum was a little over two-hundred and twenty-five thousand.

Ulfsa was the first to greet her as she entered the small house. George came stumping in from the kitchen shortly after.

"It's about time. I was getting really worried," he said.

She laughed. "Well, it's not like there is any cell coverage. I didn't want to take the time to stop and call. Sorry."

"Cell coverage? Kind of sounds like clothing to me? Is that something from the future?" he asked plaintively.

"I'm sorry, George. I should have called you. Everything went well. Here's a deposit slip showing the proceeds."

He glanced at the piece of paper; then, his eyes widened as he took in the amount.

"That's a lot. Did you have any trouble collecting?" He seemed worried.

"No, they were very polite. They did withhold some money for IRS. I gave them your social security number for it. I have one, but since mine wasn't issued until 1998, I didn't think it would be a good idea to submit it. It is income that came to you since I deposited it in your account, so there shouldn't be any problem," she said.

"Well," he said, then paused and cleared his throat in a way he had when he needed to say something unpleasant. "Probably not, but there's been an increase in police patrols around the neighborhood. I've started taking Ulfsa out in the backyard, trying to keep him out of sight. I think he misses his long walks."

Kathleen sighed. "That's what I was afraid of. The city is not a good place for a wolf, even a very nice wolf, like this one."

She bent, mindful of her swelling belly, and fluffed Ulfsa's ruff, scratching behind his ears. He whined and shoved his head against her leg in return.

She looked up at George and said, "We need to move to a more remote area. I hope that's alright with you?"

He nodded slowly. "I've been thinking about that idea. I'd like to check out the lake area up around Brainerd. It's kind of touristy, but there's a lot of wild lands there also. If we could get several acres, I think it'd be safe, although the people around there might be tempted to shoot at a wolf. We could let it be known that he's a pet. I don't think they'd have any objections the way people here in the city would."

That sounded good to her. They made plans to drive up the next day and investigate the area.

# Chapter Twenty-Four

# Trees and Lakes

The weather started out sunny and warm, but by the time they'd reached the St. Cloud area, it was overcast, with a cold northwest wind blowing.

"Looks like it might be thinking about snow," George said. They'd stopped to fill up. He didn't like to let the car get below half-full, especially if the weather seemed like it might turn.

Kathleen faced the wind, holding Ulfsa's leash. It was true. There was a hint of snow in the air. She walked forward, allowing the wolf to lead her until they reached a grassy strip where he sniffed around preparatory to relieving himself. The traffic was light, and no one seemed to notice the huge wolf along the margin of the road.

The wind grew worse as they moved north on Highway 10. The gusts shook the old car and caused George to have to correct constantly. By the time they reached Brainerd, they were both exhausted, George from the driving and Kathleen from flinching. Only Ulfsa seemed to be fully rested.

They drove through Brainerd and went up the road about fifteen miles to Nisswa. It was a small town directly in the heart of the Lake area, surrounded by summer cabins and resorts. The downtown motel had a vacancy.

The rooms exited directly to the outside of the building, and they were able to select a room that faced away from the office. Kathleen hoped this would mean that they could smuggle Ulfsa in and out with no problem.

As they left the office, the proprietor looked up and said, "You can walk the big dog out along the road. Just keep him on a leash. The locals have gotten a little more cautious lately. Last summer, two tourists were bitten by a stray dog, and the police now have orders to make sure that all dogs are leashed in the city limits."

Taking up her courage in both hands, Kathleen said, "So, you saw Ulfsa. You don't mind if we have him in the room?"

"No, Sweetie. I've got a weakness for big, furry dogs. I've had malamutes all of my life. Don't have any now. Barker died a couple of years ago, and I just haven't in my heart to suffer the loss of another pet. Anyways, I like the looks of your dog. He's big and looks like a wolf. What breed is he?"

George and Kathleen exchanged glances, then she said, "I'm not sure. He's very well-behaved, though."

The woman replied, "Looks like he might have some wolf in him. Maybe wolf and shepherd or something. Well, no problem as long as you don't let him run and also be sure to clean up after him. Can't have the tourists stepping in doggy doo-doo, you know."

Something else occurred to Kathleen. "By the way, do you know a good real estate agent? We're thinking about buying something around here."

"Well, there's Joe, uh...no. I think he moved somewhere. Oh, I know, you should call Clint Nelson. He's with Home Realty. I think they're located in Baxter or somewhere nearby. He's good."

◆

They arranged to see some properties with Clint the next day, then spent the remaining minutes of daylight driving around, looking at the numerous lakes in the area.

The drive gave them some ideas about what they might want. Kathleen decided that a lakefront property would be ideal if she could afford one. She'd always liked the water, and the area had some breathtakingly beautiful vistas. Beautiful, tall pines with a sprinkling of birch and other deciduous trees surrounded the lakes.

The next day, they met the agent, Clint, in downtown Nisswa, at a store with a totem pole that featured an elongated carving of Paul Bunyan near the bottom.

Clint proved to be a competent agent who had already lined up a series of homes for them to see. He'd selected these based on her stated price range and her casual mention of how beautiful the lakes were.

The agent was momentarily taken aback by the size of Ulfsa.

"Ah, are we going to take him with us?" he asked in an awe-struck tone.

Kathleen realized that the wolf's presence could be a problem, but he really couldn't be left cooped up in the room for the day.

"He'll be good. I promise," she said as prettily as she could.

Clint grinned and said, "I don't mind, although we won't be able to take him into any of the houses."

George chose that moment to walk around the car.

"That's no problem. I'll stay outside with Ulfsa while he sniffs around. Kathleen is the real buyer here. It's her choice."

Clint's eyes strayed to the gentle swelling under her coat. "I see. We'll try to find a nice place with an extra bedroom. I'd suggest that we restrict ourselves to looking at three and four-bedroom properties. We'll put the two-bedroom ones that I've selected on the back burner. If we can't find anything else that works, we can maybe look at some of the larger two-bedroom homes."

⋅⋅⋅◆⋅⋅⋅

Clint was entertaining and funny. He told them about the area and included some of its history. By the time they'd reached the first house, Kathleen was almost completely convinced that buying a property here was the correct decision.

They pulled into a pine-needle-covered driveway on a flat, heavily treed piece of land. The place they were going to view was set well back from the road near a small lake. It was surrounded by pine and spruce trees that made a soft susurration in the light breeze. Kathleen climbed out of the car, noticing that it seemed a little difficult. Her growing waist made such things harder.

The house was vacant. Clint said that the owners were part-timers who lived in the twin cities.

"They were last here about a month ago to check on the place. That's when they listed it for sale. I guess they got tired of driving back and forth," he explained.

Ulfsa was let out and immediately busied himself sniffing around the trees by the house. Kathleen caught his attention and said, "Stay." He looked around, gauging the extent of the yard, and then went back to his sniffing.

Clint looked impressed. "Will he actually stay here?" he asked.

Kathleen decided to open up to the man a little.

"Yes. He's very well trained. He views us as his pack. I'm the female alpha, and he'll do what I say. I don't mean to say that he understands everything, but he is remarkably intelligent."

The Realtor's eyes widened in interest. "So the two of you are his pack?"

Kathleen was reminded of Cadeyrin in his hospital bed. "Well, George here is a pack member too as far as Ulfsa is concerned. My husband is the alpha male, but he's...uh, he's not able to be here right at the moment."

"Oh. I was wondering what the story was, but I didn't want to ask," Clint said.

Kathleen remembered that this wasn't her own time. It was probably far less likely that a single, pregnant woman would be buying a home by herself in 1971 than it was decades into the future.

"He trusts me explicitly. We have the same tastes, and I'm confident that if I like the house, he'll be happy with it. In fact, he has never bought a house himself," she said with a smile.

They walked past a small guest house that stood about thirty feet away from the main building. The porch door was unlocked, and Clint held it for her and George.

Inside, there were three steps up to a raised stoop, making it apparent that the porch was an addition. The stoop had been the original entrance to the house.

Clint fiddled with a combination lockbox on the door and eventually held up a key that he used to open the door. They entered into a foyer with a laundry room/coat closet on the right side. There was a bathroom on the left. Straight ahead was the kitchen.

"This place has central heat. It's natural gas, so you basically won't have to cut wood or worry too much about the power going out," Clint said. He added, "Of course, if the power is out, the blower won't run, but there is a gas fireplace, and that is good enough to keep the place livable.

Kathleen walked through the kitchen. It had plenty of storage with cabinets on three walls. The fourth wall opened to a light and airy breakfast area with windows that overlooked a large patio shaded by several large pine trees. It looked very attractive, and she could see herself sitting there, having a cup of coffee in the morning.

The main living room was large and seemed even larger since almost the entire west wall opened to a sun porch overlooking the lake. There were two bedrooms downstairs and one upstairs.

George waved her up the stairs. "I'll stay down here, if you don't mind, Kathleen. My knees are bothering me, and that front bedroom looks just fine for me.

Upstairs she found two bedrooms. A small one that was more of an office than a bedroom, and the master bedroom. The master had a large, multi-pane window in the west wall that provided lots of sunlight and a spectacular view of the lake. There was a small bath with a claw-foot tub and a shower. A closet had been added to the north part of the room. Altogether it was very attractive, despite the light layer of dust.

She walked around the bed and looked out of the window. The sun reflecting off the lake picked out a loon and a small group of Canadian geese out on the water. It seemed irresponsible somehow, but she'd made up her mind. This house met all of her criteria. It wasn't necessary to look any further.

There was a clumping on the steps, and Clint entered the room.

"What do you think?" he asked. "It's a pretty view, isn't it? There is a drop-off down to the lake, but there are steps down to it. The owner has a dock stored down there. It's out of the water right now. The lake is still partially frozen. The dock will have to be put in after it melts."

Kathleen turned to him, her eyes sparkling to match the open water in the center of the lake. "I don't want you to think that I'm impulsive, but this is the house I'd like to buy. I want to make an offer on it. We won't need to look at any others today."

Clint looked at her face, then said, "I could tell that you liked it. Are you sure you don't want to look at anything else? I've got some others for you to see that are just about as nice."

"No. This house is the one I want. What will it take to make an offer?" she asked.

"I've got a blank contract form in the car. Give me a few minutes to fill it out; then you sign it. I'll call the owners when I get back to my office, and we'll see if they'll accept the offer. The place is listed for $109,900. What would you like to offer?"

She paused. Money wasn't really a problem. Diffidently, she asked, "Would it be okay if I offered $105,000?"

Clint smiled with the attitude of Ulfsa licking his lips before eating. "I'd say that would be hard for them to refuse. They're pretty motivated to sell. Want to rethink that number? Maybe offer less?"

She smiled back. "No. That's good enough for me. I don't want to overwork you."

That got a guffaw out of him. "Lady, if you only knew what I have to go through with some people. I'm used to a lot more back and forth than this is going to take," he said, laughing as he spoke.

Kathleen grinned and said, "Well, what are you waiting for? I'm ready to sign. I've got the cash, and I want the house as soon as possible. Can you make it happen?"

⁘

A few minutes later, they'd completed the paperwork and were headed back to the motel. Clint thought that he could call from their room and get an answer quickly.

⁘

It proved to be just as he'd said. He talked to the owners for a few minutes, then hung up and said, "I'll mail the contract to them for their signature. They've agreed to sell it and close as quickly as you want, provided they have a chance to remove their furniture."

She asked, "Would they sell the furniture?"

He turned and redialed the phone. "Hiya, it's me again. The buyer is interested in buying the place furnished. Would you consider that?"

It turned out that they would. They apparently weren't interested in any of the furnishings and were willing to let them go with the house if she'd pay full list price.

Kathleen didn't hesitate. Even though she thought she was probably paying too much for the used stuff, it was a big saving in effort. She wouldn't have to spend days trying to find new furnishings. The sellers were even going to leave the dishes, pans, and silverware. It was a move-in-ready package.

They modified the contract then Clint gave her instructions for the next step. A local attorney would handle the closing, and she'd need to place her funds on deposit in his escrow account. She agreed to do this the next day.

⁘

After the Realtor had left, George shook his head and said, "I'm not used to buying houses. Only had the one my entire married life, but it seems to me that you're somewhat fast. Are you sure about the place?"

She smiled, "It looks great to me. I think it would be a perfect place for me to spend time with you. Ulfsa will be happy there, and the hospital in Brainerd isn't too far away. I'm sure I can find a good doctor there who can take care of me."

George smiled, "No doubt. Don't worry about me. The downstairs bedroom right next to the kitchen is fine for me. I can lie in bed and look at the lake or get up and sneak a snack in the middle of the night without bothering you. It's fine."

They closed on the property three days later. The attorney had complained that it was too fast, but she'd pushed to get it done quickly, and he'd acquiesced.

They were settled in before another week had passed. The closing had gone smoothly, although the attorney was a little surprised at the fact that Kathleen was the buyer. He was, apparently, not used to the idea that a woman would buy a home by herself, especially since she paid in cash.

She shrugged it off. It was a little surprising to her that attitudes had changed so much in the relatively few years between the 1970s and her own time. There was a distinct difference in attitude. Men in the not-so-distant past were more likely to exhibit some level of chauvinism. They expected women to behave not exactly as second-class citizens per se but in a more deferential manner than she usually used.

George didn't have this attitude, but he said that was because his wife had always told him what to do. On the other hand, she did appreciate the fact that men went out of their way to hold doors open for her. The men at the local hardware store were also very helpful, although they did make some cracks about her needing a man around the house to handle repairs.

She'd laugh and mention George, referring to him as her father. That usually made them a little more respectful. About the third time she referred to him that way, she realized that he'd somehow moved into the void in her heart left by the murder of Professor Mackleroy.

She enjoyed the old man's presence. He was unfailingly cheerful and also good about household chores.

"Never liked anything but a tight ship," he'd say as he washed the dishes or swept the wooden floors.

The neighbors to the south had not been home when she had moved in. They'd been off in Duluth visiting one of their children. They showed up a few days later and proved to be friendly and a wealth of information about local life. They seemingly knew everyone in the small town and also knew what restaurants were good and which were only indifferent. They were also unobtrusive; she only saw them as they went back and forth from their garage or when they let their golden retriever out.

Ulfsa was immediately fascinated by the dog. She was named Jackie, and she showed a lot of interest in him also, even though she was intimidated at first by his size. He was twice her eighty-pound weight and towered over her.

Kathleen had no premonition of trouble. Ulfsa wasn't aggressive towards her. The two played chase, and she even taught him to fetch tennis balls.

She had gotten used to letting Ulfsa out without a leash. He had submitted to wearing a collar, and all of the people on the street knew about him. None of them seemed too worried about him. She suspected that most of them just thought he was a large Husky or something, even though they usually called him a "wolf."

So, when she needed to empty the kitchen trash, she allowed him to squeeze through the door before her. He ran off around the guest house and disappeared.

"Probably sniffing something in the front," Kathleen told herself. Then she heard the distinct sounds of a dogfight. She ran around the building to see Ulfsa standing over a large hound. It was bleeding from a slash along its ribs. Jackie was standing nearby, looking on with interest.

Kathleen cried out, "Ulfsa, let him go!"

The wolf glanced at her, then stepped off of the hound and sidled up to Jackie. Kathleen watched the defeated dog run down the drive, then glanced back to realize that Jackie must be in heat and Ulfsa was taking advantage of her. The two animals ignored Kathleen's commands to stop. She didn't want to grab Ulfsa; he was too large for her to manhandle and was intent on finishing what he'd started. She crossed her arms and looked away, waiting until they had finished.

The neighbor, Tom, came up. When he saw what was happening, he shook his head a little ruefully.

"I thought that she was due to go in heat. I was going to try and keep her in. We were hoping for some pure-blood golden puppies. Got a guy on the other side of Crosslake that has a registered male I was gonna use. Now it looks like we're going to have some golden wolves." He laughed.

Kathleen said, "I'm sorry. There was a hound that Ulfsa chased off, and before I realized what they were doing, they'd gotten going."

Tom said, "Oh, don't worry about it. It's my fault. I should have kept closer track of her. I know that hound. It belongs to Rich down the street. It's a pest. I'd sooner have her have Ulfsa's pups than half hound puppies."

Kathleen replied, "I don't think the hound had a chance at her. Ulfsa had him pinned down when I got here."

Tom replied, "Well, the two of them have gotten to be pretty close. They play all of the time. I expect that she's quite happy with him servicing her." He paused, then said with a worried tone, "I wonder if the puppies will be too large for her. He's huge. If the pups are too big for her to carry or birth, it could be a problem."

Kathleen hadn't thought of that. "Is there a good vet around? I'll pay for you to have her checked periodically. After all, he's my responsibility, and that makes me partially responsible for him getting her pregnant."

Tom replied, "I think the local guy is good. He's had to pull some porcupine quills out of her already. I'll give him a call and ask him if it's likely to be a problem. It's not like she's a really small dog. She's probably big enough to handle some large pups. Assuming that they come out alright, I'll give you your choice of the litter."

When she told him she couldn't take one, he assured her that it was customary for the dog's owner to have their choice. Thinking of George, she agreed. When she rescued Cadeyrin, she planned to move them back to the Sangamon immediately. George might not want to go. He was too old to hunt and might not want to be left alone with the possibilities of wild beasts. On the other hand, it might be nice if he was around to help care for her own baby if she and Cadeyrin were hunting.

She paused and placed a hand on her abdomen.

It seemed for a moment as if there was a little voice saying, "I'm here, Mommy."

She smiled, and then the idea of having one of Ulfsa's pups for George made sense. The pup wouldn't be as large as Ulfsa, but it was still company for the old man, whether he went with them or stayed here in Nisswa. She didn't intend to leave him alone. She'd come and visit often, but he would still be lonely. A puppy seemed like it would be good company.

"Okay. It's settled," she said. "I'll take one of the pups. But, you decide which one you want me to have. You can probably sell the others. They'll be impressive dogs, and people should be eager to get them."

Tom laughed. "They'll be impressive for sure. Even if they're only two-thirds his size, they'll outweigh any other dog in the area,"

⚫

The weeks crept by slowly. Kathleen was getting larger. She'd found an obstetrician she liked in Brainerd, and he'd recommended a pediatrician. George went with her on her periodic visits to the doctor. He was solicitous and had insisted on going. He made sure she took her vitamins in the morning and also cooked breakfast, an activity that she was pleased to have him do. She'd started lying in bed a little longer. Her back was sore, and she wasn't feeling as active or as capable as she had been.

She spent a lot of time sitting by the lake as the weather warmed up. It was now late spring, and it was often quite nice down by the lake in the afternoon. The western sun provided a lot of heat, and she would alternate between reading and napping. Ulfsa stayed close, except when Jackie came out.

Jackie was now quite large and not feeling comfortable at all. She was cranky with the additional weight and discomfort and often nipped at Ulfsa. His thick fur usually deflected her teeth, but he was more careful around her and seemed to be aware that she was expecting.

Altogether the move to Nisswa was proving to be a wonderful thing. They'd gotten out of the declining neighborhood in Minneapolis. She was happy with her doctor, and George seemed to be very pleased with the move also. He enjoyed fishing in the lake, although he never caught much, and he was apparently happy with her company. Only a few times had he expressed any sorrow that his late wife wasn't able to enjoy the view or the sunset.

It seemed almost too perfect a hideaway.

# Chapter Twenty-Five

# Travel and Danger

Kathleen was sitting on an Adirondack chair overlooking the lake. The wind was nearly still, and the sun shone through the crystal air heating her skin. She'd been there for a little over an hour, drowsing, and sipping water from a glass she had placed near the chair.

Ulfsa and Jackie were lying nearby. The two had become so close that Kathleen worried that she'd have difficulty separating them when it came time to return to the past. Jackie was getting quite large, and the vet had told Tom that she'd probably have her litter within a few days. It looked like she was more than ready. Her stomach was swollen as taught as a drum. An occasional movement could be seen despite her thick coat.

George had gotten hot and had retreated to his bed for a nap inside, leaving her to build up vitamin D in her skin and think.

Her plan was working. She had maybe three and a half months to go before she was due. Then she'd have to wait until she had recovered and was fit enough to engage in whatever action would be required to free Cadeyrin. She wasn't going to be gone long, so the baby probably wouldn't even notice that she wasn't there.

She snickered a little. It was very convenient to be able to move in time with the precision that her formula allowed. As far as the agents in the future knew, she was still in the drugstore restroom. She'd return to the closed stall a couple of seconds after she had left. Unless there was a camera watching, no one would ever know that she'd been gone.

Ulfsa suddenly sat up to watch some Canadian geese as they glided down to land in a shallow spot in the lake. The ice was mostly melted off, and the geese were returning north. The lake was smaller than many of the others in the area and didn't attract many fishermen. She thought that the geese appreciated the lack of boats as they splashed down and began to feed.

Something was bothering her, far in the back of her mind. She'd intended to check on Grid and Annie and the girls. Kathleen sat up in turn and looked around. There was no one nearby. Both neighbors were at work, and George was probably asleep. She shifted slightly in her seat so she could uncover the rifle that she kept wrapped in the edge of her blanket.

George was disapproving of her penchant to be armed at all times, but she didn't let that stop her. She'd been through too many tight situations in the last year to be at ease without a weapon.

Ulfsa cocked his head at her with an inquiring look on his face.

"No, you big furball," she said with affection. "We're not going hunting. You stay right here with Jackie. I'll be back in a bit."

He glanced at the sleeping golden retriever and then sighed. Kathleen grinned. He often seemed to understand more than a canine should. She wondered just how smart he was.

Kathleen paused, calculating. She had modified her formula during the past few months. Moving in time was only a single aspect of the relationship with the Quantum Plenum. Her first formula had only had a single temporal variable. A few days ago, she'd worked out the spatial component that she'd thought was in the relationship.

It had frightened her at first. She realized that she'd been very lucky to have always come back to the exact spatial location that she'd left. Now, with her enhanced comprehension of the relationship, she could move both in time and space. Thus it was nothing for her to jump back to the Cretaceous and end up near Gridley's base. Before, she would have had to take an airplane to Washington, then jump back. Now she could translate both her time and location, moving from Nisswa in 1971 to the Washington DC area over a hundred million years ago.

Taking a firm grip on her rifle, she stood up and disappeared from the wolf's sight. He flopped back in disgust. Jackie raised her head and looked at him but then closed her eyes again. The sun was warm, and it was a good day for a nap.

———◆———

Kathleen was standing on a hillside, and a stiff, warm wind was blowing through the nearby conifer-like trees. There was no grass, only coarse weeds that were dry and rustled in the gusts. There was a scuffling sound behind her, and she turned to see some of the turkey-sized mini-predators peering at her from the scrub.

She bent, grabbed a convenient stone, and hurled it at them. They squeaked and backed into deeper cover.

Kathleen wasn't quite sure where she was in relation to the cave's location. She needed to be a little higher to see the terrain better, so she started up the hill. It was rough going. The last time she'd been here, she wasn't nearly six months pregnant.

She shook her head disparagingly, then reminded herself to be careful. It wouldn't help Cadeyrin if she carelessly walked into some carnivore's ambush.

She labored up the hillside, and as she reached the top, she heard a faint cry. Turning to face downwind, she saw a brightly colored raptor running rapidly towards her up a ridge.

It cried again, and this time she could make out: "Kathleen!"

It was Lolita, intensely excited and happy to see her.

The small raptor pulled up in front of her and said, "I glad to see you."

Kathleen knelt and opened her arms in greeting. Lolita started forward, then stopped and looked at her carefully.

"You pregnant!" Lolita said. "I happy for you. We should go to the cave. There are some new bad ones around. You be safer there."

Kathleen replied, "Okay, but let me hug you first. I missed you, too."

They came together for a short snuggle, then Lolita looked around and said, "We'd better go now. Something is coming."

Kathleen was impressed. She hadn't sensed anything, but this wasn't her home territory, so that she might have easily missed it.

They went down the north side of the hill and traversed a ridge. Lolita led her around a steeper hill, keeping just inside the forest edge.

A short time later, they approached the base camp. Grid was seated on a rock near the entrance, working on a spear.

"Hey, Kathleen's here!" he shouted into the dark opening. Annie came out, now visibly pregnant. She appeared to be about as far along as Kathleen.

Annie pointed at Kathleen's stomach and laughed while Kathleen simply stared. She hadn't thought that she'd catch up with Grid's wife. Now it looked like they were probably going to have their babies at about the same time.

Lolita interrupted, "Go in cave now. We were tracked. GO, GO!"

Kathleen didn't waste time looking around. She jumped to the sheltering opening, following Annie inside. Then she turned and readied her weapon. It was her camp rifle and not as powerful as one of the heavier pieces, but she kept a thirty-round magazine in it.

Grid moved in beside her.

"There are some new bad guys in town," he said. "They are smaller than the big ugly yellow ones but still large. They are probably thirty feet in length and ten feet tall, although they are a lot lighter than the big yellow creatures. I don't know what they are. They showed up a couple of days ago, and we've had to be very careful hunting. They chased us off of a kill yesterday. I think they've got the idea that we're a good source of meat."

Kathleen glanced back. Annie was standing behind them, holding a spear. Lolita was walking back and forth just inside the cave opening, but the other two girls were missing.

"Where are Fancy and Belle?" she asked, dreading the answer.

Annie answered as if she'd read her mind. "Don't worry. They're Okay, or they were the last time we saw them. A couple of males of their species showed up, and they picked themselves a mate. Poor Lolita was left to stay with us."

Lolita, hearing her name, turned and said, "They gone to have babies. Like you two. Maybe I find a male sometime soon and do the same."

Kathleen laid a hand on the small raptor's head and said, "I hope he shows up soon. He's missing out on a beautiful and talented wife."

Lolita rubbed against her leg in appreciation.

———◆◇◆———

There was a hissing scream from the trees. They looked out to see two thinly feathered dinosaurs stalk into the open before the cave. The two newcomers were just as Gridley had described them. They looked like they were probably ten times as heavy as Lolita. Their movements were lithe, smooth, and far faster than the rather cumbrous ugly yellow carnivore.

The two stopped and looked the cave opening over cautiously, trying to determine if it were worth attacking.

Kathleen quietly said, "They look similar to Lolita's kind but bigger. Much bigger."

Grid whispered back, "I think they're related somehow. If that's so, then they'll be very cunning. They've just been in the area a short time, though, so they might not be as bad as I fear. I just don't know."

Outside, the two creatures had decided to investigate more closely. One moved off to the left and disappeared around the rock while the other headed directly towards the cave opening.

Grid said, "That tears it! The other one is checking to see if we have a rear exit. We don't. It will come back in a few seconds. It'll slide along the rocks, staying in cover until the last few feet, then attack. The one in front is supposed to keep us distracted."

That was precisely Kathleen's opinion also. She stepped forward towards the cave mouth and said, "Cover your ears."

Without waiting, she raised the rifle and fired three shots directly into the breast of the approaching creature. It dropped with a thud, then jumped back up, but immediately collapsed. This time, it stayed down and thrashed its tail while making vague clawing motions with its arms and feet.

Its companion shrieked, making a thin whistling sound, then came bounding around the nearby rocks. Kathleen had already turned to aim in that direction, and she fired five quick shots.

The dinosaur flopped on the ground, then clambered back to its feet, swaying a little. It seemed dazed for a moment, then it focused on the cave mouth and jumped forward quickly.

Kathleen shot three more times. The attacker turned and began to bound away. She raised the rifle, aimed carefully, and let off a single shot that struck the back of the dinosaur's bobbing neck. It went down in a tumble and lay still.

Lolita came forward, bumped on Kathleen's hip, and said loudly, "Ears hurt. Kathleen kill them. Good."

The small raptor walked cautiously out to check on the carcasses.

Annie said, "Good shooting, Kathleen. I'm glad you came along. Those guys were going to be trouble sooner or later. Now they're settled. Thanks."

Grid added, "Yeah, but now we've got a problem. There's a lot of meat there that will be smelling pretty high by tomorrow morning. It'll attract any meat-eaters in the area. We're going to have to cut them up and get rid of them if we can. They're heavy too, so it isn't going to be easy."

Out in the open area, Lolita paused, then raised her head from where she'd been checking the first dinosaur's chest wounds. She turned and came back towards the cave, stopping about ten feet away from the entrance to turn and stand, waiting.

There was some movement in the trees. Kathleen readied her rifle, mentally reprimanding herself for not bringing any additional ammunition. She'd shot nearly half the magazine.

She raised the weapon but then lowered it again. The motion in the trees had resolved itself into two brightly colored small raptors; one was slightly thin, and one more robust. It was Fancy and Belle.

The two saw Kathleen and sprinted towards her. Belle apparently didn't notice the carcasses of the two attackers until she almost tripped over one. She leaped into the air at the last minute, cleared the body, then screeched to a stop. She checked the closest body for movement, then looked speculatively at Kathleen.

Fancy came up and leaned against Kathleen's chest, then backed up to look closely at her swollen abdomen.

"Belle!", she called. "Kathleen having babies like Annie! Come quick!"

Belle came up, looked, and then cuddled up for her own hug.

She said softly, "We have a big pack with Annie and Kathleen's babies and ours too,"

Grid had come out of the cave and was waiting for his own share of the girls' attention. He said, "What? You have babies?"

For an answer, Fancy gave a loud cooing call that echoed off the rocks.

There was more movement in the trees as seven more raptors approached. Two large and five small, colorful creatures moved towards them through the undergrowth. When they emerged, the five chicks dashed to the two adult females. Two sheltered close to Fancy's legs, and the other three hid shyly behind Belle.

The two males stopped just outside the treeline, watching carefully, apparently reluctant to approach. Kathleen thought that was just as well. They were obviously unused to the idea of humans, and it was easy to visualize an accident being caused by an incautious movement.

Belle moved close to Gridley and leaned against him as he scratched her neck, hitting the spot that he knew she loved. She sighed loudly in satisfaction, then turned to nudge her largest chick close to him. He cautiously stroked its head and neck. The other chicks looked on with close attention.

The stroking seemed to impress them and alleviate any fear they might have felt. One of Fancy's two walked boldly up to Kathleen and chirped for attention. Kathleen bent and tickled the small creature's neck. It must have felt surprisingly wonderful because the little one lay down across her feet and wriggled in ecstasy.

The other chick careened around Fancy and bumped her head into Kathleen's hand, demanding its share of rubbing. Kathleen looked up and saw that Belle's chicks were clustered around Grid and Annie while Lolita and Fancy greeted each other formally with a sort of head-bobbing and weaving movement.

When she turned back to check on the two males, they had approached to about ten feet away. At her glance, one of them hissed and opened its mouth. The other flexed the claws on its fingers.

Both Belle and Fancy immediately moved between their mates and the humans, making throaty crooning sounds. The incipient threat display faded as the two males faced the females.

It was Belle who took the initiative. She bumped her head into her mate's side, making him stagger a little. He somehow managed to look embarrassed, a hard thing to do without movable facial muscles.

Belle looked over her shoulder at Gridley and said, "Grid, come meet my mate."

Gridley ambled forward until he was standing beside Belle and then held out his hand, palm down and fingers curled underneath. In a quiet tone, he said, "Keep your hands like mine. That's as close to looking non-aggressive as we can be. Extending your fingers is sort of like them extending their claws."

The male bobbed his head and watched as Grid bobbed his in return. The outstretched hand was sniffed, and that seemed to be adequate. The male relaxed.

Fancy's mate had watched the process and obviously knew it was his turn. Without waiting for his mate to press him on the matter, he bobbed his head at Kathleen, then moved closer with two slow strides.

She bobbed back in turn and extended her hand as had Gridley. The male sniffed it and then moved closer to inspect her stomach. Fancy moved a little closer and pressed her head against Kathleen's hidden baby. The male's pupils opened wide, then contracted a little as he processed how much his mate trusted Kathleen.

He moved closer and lifted his head, stretching his neck. Kathleen carefully scratched through the green feathers along the back of his neck, taking care not to bend them backward. He quivered a little but then relaxed.

Annie had come up beside her husband, and the two were now tickling Belle's chicks. Fancy's two had come over to join in the fun, and the two humans stood surrounded by colorful fluffy little raptors, each demanding to be scratched. Belle and her mate looked on, standing side by side.

Kathleen said, "This went much easier than I expected. The males are obviously as smart as the girls even if they don't talk."

Belle looked at her and said, "Our mates are very clever, and they are very good hunters. We chose well."

Annie responded, "Yes, you did, Belle. You chose very well. We're so happy that you've come back and brought your families."

Fancy's male walked over to the two bodies of the attackers. He sniffed their wounds carefully, then without wasted motion, he ripped into the stomach of one, using his large toe claw. He ripped out a chunk of liver and swallowed it with a gulp.

Fancy was hungry also and joined him. Belle paused to say, "We need to eat. No hunt for two days. More of these big ones coming. They keep us from hunting. Too dangerous." Then she followed her mate over to the second body. The chicks joined them as did Lolita.

Gridley laughed, then said, "That's handy. Here I was worried about getting rid of some potentially stinky carrion, and now the problem looks like it's going to be solved."

Annie answered, "I don't see how even ten raptors can eat that much. Those things are probably six or seven times as large as they are."

That reminded Kathleen of something. She said, "I had an opportunity to look up dinosaurs on the Internet before I came back. I'm not sure, of course, but I think the girls are what we named Deinonychus. The two big ones might be Utah Raptors. They're probably distantly related to the girls' species, and that would mean that the large ones are equally smart and cunning. They're likely to become a real problem if they're moving into this area."

Belle lifted her head, swallowed a bloody hunk of entrails, and said, "They are problem. They want to eat us."

Gridley shook his head negatively. "We can't let that happen. We'll have to move somewhere."

That initially seemed to be a problem, but Kathleen had a solution.

"These big ones are new in the area?" she asked.

Lolita answered, "Yes. We never see them before."

Kathleen asked Gridley, "You've been here how long?"

He thought a moment, counting up, then said, "I reckon it to be a little over two years at this point."

That seemed like it might be about right, Kathleen thought. She didn't know how long a Deinonychus would live but assuming that they lived about as long as humans seemed a safe bet. She couldn't expose the girls to a potential temporal paradox by accidentally meeting their parents. That was a given.

"Look, I can solve the problem. We'll move everyone backward in time five hundred years. That will leave the big raptor invasion safely in the future, and the local animals won't have changed much in that short time. The cave will still be here, and you might even find that the local herbivores will be less alert. They won't be used to you hunting them, anyway."

Grid cocked his head, then said, "That should be an acceptable solution, but can you move the whole group at once, or will you have to make more than one trip?"

She laughed. "No, one trip will work. I've moved a pickup and camper, so I don't think a few hundred pounds of human and dinosaurs will be too much."

The Deinonychus pack was still feeding, so the humans walked into the cave and gathered up their possessions.

"Load everything up. I have to be touching stuff to bring it along. Indirectly is fine. You'll have to hold it and clump together so that we're all touching, then I can manage," Kathleen instructed.

They gathered together, Deinonychus adults, chicks, humans, and their possessions. Kathleen spread her arms around as much of the group as she could, checked to ensure that they were all touching, then closed her eyes. There was a flicker, and then they were standing in front of the cave in the same location. The carcasses were gone. The treeline was different also. The weather was cooler than a moment before, and the wind had stopped.

The two males hissed involuntarily. Kathleen didn't blame them. It was pretty startling to travel in time for the first time. She almost didn't remember it, herself. She'd escaped Drew's attempt at raping her and found herself in shock, lying on a forest floor. She'd gone to sleep without moving and without knowing how dangerous such an action could be with predators roaming the area.

They checked the cave. It was much as it had been except there was a pile of leaves and litter that had blown into the entrance. It wasn't long before they had recreated the camp.

Kathleen handed her rifle to Grid. "It's only got seven or eight shots left. I'll bring more ammo to you shortly, but you should keep this. It might come in handy. I've got to go back and finish rescuing my husband."

Then she looked at Annie. "Grid, Annie, I think you're about as far along as I am. It would be best if you had your baby in a hospital. Will you come back with me? I'm staying in 1971 temporarily. You can stay with me until you have the baby. Grid, you can come, but I don't think the girls should. They'd be too noticeable in the future."

Grid answered, "Yes, Annie, you go. I'll stay here with the girls. I can come for the baby's birth. I feel a sense of responsibility to my pack. I wouldn't feel right, just leaving them here alone."

Annie responded, "No. I'll stay here with you. Kathleen, would you mind making some trips back and forth with me. If I could see an obstetrician to make sure I'm progressing correctly, and then come back to go to the hospital to give birth, that would be enough. I can't leave my husband here. Nor the girls."

—•—

It was decided then. Kathleen promised to be back soon. She'd speak to her doctor about Annie and then return when it was time for Annie's appointment. As the group watched, she closed her eyes and disappeared.

# Chapter Twenty-Six

# Found!

She was standing beside her lounge chair facing the lake. She paused, taking in the peaceful scene. A bark sounded behind her, and she turned to see Jackie looking at the sun porch. Ulfsa was on the verge of disappearing, running around the house towards the front. She wondered what was going on. Then she saw some movement through the windows.

A black-clad man was standing inside, poised over George as he slept on the couch. It wasn't the neighbor. Tom never wore anything black. She moved her hands to her chest, instinctively feeling for the rifle sling. It wasn't there. She'd left it with Gridley.

The man inside hadn't seen her as yet. She looked to the left, evaluating whether she could reach the shelter of the trees at the corner of the house without attracting attention. One deep breath, then two, then her mind started to work. She closed her eyes and jumped backward a full year.

The house was vacant when she looked at the windows. The weather was overcast, and a light drizzle made the day miserable. She walked around the house to the front, entered the unlocked porch, and used her key to open the front door. She gave mental thanks that she'd failed to re-key the place when she bought it.

She walked quickly through the kitchen and up the stairs to the master bedroom. Her timing would have to be precise. She couldn't afford to return too soon. Creating a paradox at this point could be fatal.

She opened the empty closet, then closed her eyes and jumped forward to a single second after she'd left. Anyone watching who had seen her disappear from the yard and reappear a moment later upstairs would have thought that she had some way of teleporting herself.

The closet was open in front of her. She gathered up her pistol, checked the breech to make sure it was loaded, then jumped backward in time again. She walked down the stairs, arranged herself where she had a clear shot into the sunroom, and jumped forward a second time.

The black-clad man saw her instantly and straightened. He was holding a knife in his left hand. Kathleen raised the pistol and said, "Drop it."

He laughed. "What ya' gonna do? Shoot me?"

She calmly replied, "If you don't drop it and move away from George. Yes, that's what I'm going to do."

She could see the guy tensing as if he were going to try something. There was a ripping sound from the kitchen area at that moment. Both of them looked toward the dining room door as Ulfsa came flying through, every hair on his body standing out and his lips drawn back in a fearsome snarl.

The wolf bounded once and jumped on the man before he could prepare. Kathleen dashed around the couch to see the guy down with Ulfsa's jaws on his throat. George had been awakened sometime in the last few seconds and was now holding the knife hand with all of his strength. The man was trying to stab Ulfsa, but couldn't get his wrist free, although it looked like George's strength was quickly fading.

Kathleen snapped, "Ulfsa, no!" Then she stomped on the man's forearm. The knife went flying.

Ulfsa released the man's throat and backed up a foot, still snarling silently.

She gestured with her pistol, and the man slid across the floor and sat in the corner.

"That's fine. Don't try to stand up. If I don't shoot you, Ulfsa will get you, and this time, I'll let him," she said. She looked at George. He had sat up and was rubbing his wrist.

She asked, "You okay?"

He nodded but didn't say anything. Then he bent and picked up the knife from where it had slid partway under the couch.

Kathleen turned her attention back to the man. "Who are you?"

He started to talk, then cleared his throat. His voice was harsh from the pressure Ulfsa had applied.

"It doesn't matter who I am. You want to know when I'm from," he said.

"Okay. When?" she asked.

"I was sent here by Jones. His people have been researching history for unusual financial activity. Did you really think winning such a large amount at the Derby would go unnoticed?"

Kathleen paused. The implication was that Jones had sent agents out all over time investigating financial windfalls.

"How did you find me?" she asked.

"It's taken me days, but it wasn't so hard once I found the motel where you stayed. You had to leave your license plate number at the front desk. A few dollars was enough to give me access to the register. From that point, all I had to do was follow the trail," he said.

"Why are you here?" she asked.

He rubbed his throat, then said, "We're checking a few of the more unusual financial transactions. Don't have the staff to do more. Jones told us that you were to be watched. We thought you were in the future. No one has reported you gone, but here you are, so I guess he was right."

She scoffed. "Huh. I'm still in the future. You're not really seeing me here now."

He answered, "You've been here a long time. You look like you're about ready to pop out a kid."

She smiled and patted her stomach with her free hand. "So what if I am? That's my business only. Now, give me the return device."

She waved her gun.

He reluctantly took the device out of a zipped pouch and slid it across the floor. She picked it up and then said, "George, come over here."

She handed George the pistol and said, "Shoot him if he moves." Then she glanced at the agitated wolf. "Ulfsa."

He looked at her.

"Hold him, Ulfsa," she ordered. The wolf returned his glare to the man.

"If George doesn't get you, Ulfsa will. Don't move," she said.

She stepped back and began to check the device. It was better than the one they'd given Gridley. It used VR to quickly move the subject's mind into a state where the time formula would be effective. Instead of thrusting the user into the remote past, though, this one was programmed to return the user to the future.

Kathleen thought for a minute, then made a couple of small adjustments to the setting. She gave the man a wicked grin. "I'm going to let you go. You can put this on and return to where you started. Tell Jones anything you like." She slid the unit back to him.

Thirty seconds later, he was gone.

George handed her the pistol. "Why'd you let him go? Won't that cause a problem for you?" he asked.

She grinned tightly and without humor. "Not really, he's going to arrive just before he leaves. The presence of his other self will be a paradox. Time doesn't allow that, so one or the other of them will be kicked back in the time-stream somewhen. My math hasn't been up to the task of analyzing precisely how it works, but he will end up sometime when he has never existed. Oh, and the memory of both of him will be affected, too. Chances are, he won't be any good to Jones for days. Jones won't have any idea what happened."

That night she lay in bed listening to loons calling on the lake. She couldn't generate funds again by any extraordinary means. Her stock market play with George was a slow method. They would be unable to follow that, at least until she cashed in, but that would be in the future, and she'd be prepared for them.

Right now, she had some weeks to go in the here and now. She'd have to arrange to bring Annie in for check-ups and also make sure they were both in the hospital when their time came.

Ulfsa gave a long sigh from his position at the side of the bed. He wasn't worried. There was nothing around to disturb his keen senses.

She closed her eyes and let the loons sing her to sleep.

# Chapter Twenty-Seven

# Puppies and Worries

The days gradually blended into summer. It wasn't actually hot, but Kathleen often felt like the temperature was boiling. She wasn't sure how she'd manage to make it through the next two months.

She had arranged with her obstetrician for Annie's care. As far as he knew, Grid's wife was Kathleen's cousin, living with her. They'd both been in for check-ups. It wasn't inconvenient for Kathleen. She'd been able to jump to the past, collect Annie, and jump back to the present with no trouble. They'd drive down for a joint appointment, catching up with each other on the way.

Kathleen had quickly grown to like, no, love Annie. Grid's wife was just about her age, and the two got along so well they might have been sisters. This relationship was something that Kathleen had never expected. Naturally, by both circumstances and acquired preference, a loner, she hadn't thought that she could come to appreciate another woman or that they could have so much in common. The main topic of conversation was their husbands and their hopes for their unborn children. It was fun and very nice to have another person to provide support. They both agreed that having a baby was wonderful, even if, at times, they felt like they were sitting on a potential keg of dynamite.

Another topic of discussion involved selecting and trying out names for the babies. In the time that they found themselves, there was no easy way to determine a baby's sex, so they worked on both boy and girl names.

Annie's pregnancy was almost textbook-like in its progress, but the obstetrician worried about Kathleen. The extensive scarring around her pelvis, thighs, and lower abdomen, although more flexible than it had ever been, made him nervous.

Her active lifestyle and the continued application of a poultice that Cadeyrin prepared had loosened the tight scars so that they weren't as much of a problem as they had been for the majority of her life. She had learned to live with the slight restriction on movement caused by the damaged skin. Now, her swollen abdomen began to cause pulling and stretching as she grew larger. Fortunately, the scars were mostly superficial. The saline had burned her skin but hadn't yet reached the underlying muscles before her mother had gone into labor and expelled her.

Kathleen was sitting in her favorite location: a lounge chair overlooking the lake. The house was on a bluff with a forty-foot drop-off to the water below. This bluff her an ideal viewpoint and also provided a wonderful, cooling breeze. She spent hours there on good days, reading and sometimes taking notes or doing calculations. She hadn't ceased her studying. Physics was something that she'd adopted as her intellectual persona, and she wasn't about to give it up.

She saw Tom heading her way from the house next door, so she marked her place and closed the book as he arrived.

"Hi, Tom! Beautiful day, isn't it?" she said in greeting.

He looked a little worried. "It's a nice day at that. You want to come over and look at Jackie? She's gone into labor, and I think she's having a hard time of it."

Kathleen laboriously climbed to her feet. Tom reached out to steady her at the last minute. She took his hand for a moment, then started towards his house.

Inside the laundry room, Jackie lay on a bed of old towels. The golden bitch was alternately panting, then straining, but not having any luck in moving the puppies.

Kathleen looked at her with concern. The puppies were naturally going to be large. Ulfsa was over twice as big as Jackie.

She turned to Tom and said, "Maybe you'd better call the Vet. She's struggling here. Doing a C-section might be necessary. I don't think she's big enough to get them through her pelvis."

"I've already called him. He's attending to a horse up at Breezy Point. Says he'll get here as quickly as he can. I'm just afraid it won't be soon enough."

As they spoke, Jackie gave a yip of pain, then moaned. She strained once again, and suddenly a wet and bloody bundle was delivered onto the towels. Jackie weakly turned to lick at the puppy.

Once she got it cleaned up a bit, it was obvious that it was Ulfsa's. It had wolf-like features that reminded Kathleen of Ulfsa when she first found him. He'd been so cute then; she'd never dreamed that he would mature into such a huge and handsome animal.

The puppy looked like him, but with one major difference. Its fur was a bright golden color.

Kathleen squatted carefully and picked up the wiggling bundle. It squeaked, and Jackie looked worried. Kathleen straightened, her heart filled with maternal emotion. It was such a tiny baby. Her baby would be even more helpless. Tears came to her eyes. The majority of her life had been loveless. She'd always felt like no one cared for her. How could that be? How could someone reject a baby?

She turned to Tom, her cheeks glistening, and handed the puppy to him.

"He's beautiful and perfect!" she said.

Tom nodded his head and lowered the puppy back to Jackie. It struggled to get at her nipples as she gave another great straining push. A second puppy popped out.

There was a pause in the action. Jackie nursed the two and tried to recover. She was exhausted. It had been difficult getting the pups out. Kathleen tried to feel her stomach to see if she could find how many other puppies were in there, but she was unable to tell.

Eventually, Jackie started straining again. Her panting was shorter now than before. She hadn't had enough time to recover from the first two deliveries.

There was a bang at the door, and the Vet came in.

"Hi, Tom! Young lady," he said. "What do we have going on here?"

Without waiting for an answer, he dropped to his knees and felt Jackie's stomach. Then he looked up.

"There's at least two more in there. From the way she's laboring, she's going to be lucky to get them both out and survive it. I can do an emergency c-section here, but it's dangerous. She might not survive that either. What do you want, Tom?"

Tom said, "I wish my wife were here. Jackie is really hers. I don't like to make decisions without her. I guess... I think maybe we should wait and see if she can get them out naturally. Is that okay?"

The Vet thoughtfully nodded. "We can wait. While we do, I'm going to set up an I-V for her. I can give her some pain medication, too. That might ease things a bit. She's probably in so much pain that she's fighting her natural urges to push."

Tom nodded. Kathleen had retreated to the laundry room door where she could watch without being in the way. The Vet fumbled at his bag, extracting the required equipment, then started the I-V drip and injected some medication into the tube. Jackie sighed in relief, then immediately gave a yip and pushed with a massive contraction. Another puppy slid out.

This time it was followed by a considerable amount of blood. The blood flowed freely for a moment but then ceased.

The Vet said, "She's torn herself with that one. At least it's stopped on its own. She's still doing alright. Now, if she can get the last one out with no more bleeding."

They watched and fidgeted for a short time. Jackie panted and tried to lick the puppies. They squirmed around, squeaking and trying to nurse.

Finally, the last puppy came out. Everyone gave a sigh of relief. Kathleen was happy, but now she was more worried than ever. What if her baby was as difficult to deliver? How could she ever stretch large enough to get a baby, even a little baby, out? The concept was frightening. It had been wonderful getting the baby in, but now she was by herself, and Cadeyrin wasn't there to help. It was up to her to get it out.

Tom handed her another puppy to hold, and her worry faded in the joy of holding the little bundle of life. This one was a darker gold, almost brown. The other two were gray and looked quite wolf-like.

———◆◇◆———

That night Kathleen didn't sleep well. Jackie had recovered enough to begin taking care of her pups, but Kathleen was still worried. What if her baby was so large that her scars tore? They already felt tight. What would they feel like in two more months? If her scars were worse, would Cadeyrin still love her? And, would he love the baby? He didn't even know she was pregnant. She couldn't get close to him to tell him, and it wasn't like she was going to ask Jones to give him the message. Her whole life seemed like a disaster. There was nowhere that she could escape to; the baby was inside her and had to come out. She was alone and had to deal with everything by herself.

———◆◇◆———

She lay there, watching the moonlight shining through the trees outside, and suddenly found herself sobbing quietly.

Ulfsa stood, looked over the edge of the bed, then jumped up beside her. He shoved his face into her neck and exhaled. It tickled, and she suddenly found her mood had broken. The depression and fear had evaporated.

She fondled the wolf's ears and stroked his neck. He carefully lay down on the bed beside her. At that precise moment, her stomach bumped with a series of little pushes and flutters. She gasped and put her hand on the spot. The baby pushed against her hand, and she was overcome with a feeling of tender warmth.

"Don't worry, little one. I'm here. Everything is fine. I'll be here for you, and I'll never leave you. I love you," Kathleen whispered.

Ulfsa's ears perked a bit, and he looked at her moving stomach. She couldn't tell if he understood, but his eyes glowed softly in the moonlight, giving him the appearance of wisdom beyond that which was usually expected of a wolf.

The baby moved again, then quieted. Kathleen let out a long sigh, moved to a slightly more comfortable position, and gradually relaxed into sleep.

In her dreams, she saw Cadeyrin. He was coming towards her, walking through a forest glade lighted with golden rays of sun slanting through the leaves. He held the hand of a small boy. Both of their faces glowed as they looked at her. Cadeyrin's eyes shone with love for both her and the boy. She sighed in her sleep.

Ulfsa looked at the sleeping woman. She had been the center of his life since he was a pup. He couldn't remember a time when she had not been there. He placed his head on his paws, keeping watch in the night.

Nothing would come on them without his knowing. He was prepared to fight to the death to protect her.

# Chapter Twenty-Eight

# Pain and Joy

Kathleen lay awake, unable to sleep. The wind was gusting fitfully, and a flash of lightning showed towards the southwest followed by the sound of thunder rolling over the lake.

Annie was sleeping in the bed beside her. They'd decided that they both should be in present time. Their babies were due, and Kathleen had been worried that she'd go into labor and be unable to jump back to get Annie as a result. It wouldn't do to leave Annie to have her baby in a cave, even a comfortable one.

Gridley was sleeping on the couch downstairs. The girls and their pack hadn't wanted him to leave, but they understood that Annie was going to have a baby and that it was important to him. Lolita had promised that they'd be careful, for what that was worth, coming from a deinonychus living in the Cretaceous.

Beside her, Annie moved restlessly, then groaned. Kathleen wondered if they'd eaten something that disagreed with them. Her stomach had been hurting on and off since about an hour after they'd gone to bed. It felt like she had some kind of virus that was making her cramp at intervals.

Here was another cramp. It was—Kathleen opened her eyes wide. She was in labor! The cramps weren't from a stomach virus; her baby was coming. She nudged Annie.

Annie moved fitfully, then made some semi-incoherent sounds. "Uhm, ugh. Huh? What time is it? What's going on?"

She rolled so that she could see Kathleen. "What's going on?" she asked again.

Kathleen had been panting through a particularly forceful contraction. When it relaxed a bit, she said, "I'm in labor."

Annie's eyes opened wide. "Oh. Now? I mean right now?"

Kathleen nodded with a forced smile.

Annie kicked off her coverlet and sat up.

"I'll get Grid. I– " She stopped suddenly, then said in a strange tone of voice, "I can't believe this."

"What do you mean?" Kathleen asked. "We're both almost due. Why shouldn't I go into labor?"

Annie made a frustrated sound. "Uhn, no. It's just that something happened when I sat up. I'm sopping wet. I think my water just broke."

Kathleen felt a wave of powerful emotion. Her eyes teared up, and she threw her arms around Annie.

"Oh, Annie! You too? This is too much for me. I never never thought that anyone would love me. I couldn't even entertain the thought of having a baby, and now you. I've never had a friend like you and, and, and we're going to have our babies together!" She started to sob.

Annie patted her hand. "Oh, sweetie! You saved my life. You took me back to Jase. I'd be dead without you. Of course, I'm your friend. I love you, and I'm so glad that we're together."

Kathleen responded by placing her head on Annie's back while she cried. She broke off with a gasp as another cramp struck.

"These are close together!" she said. "We'd better get to the hospital. It's about twenty miles, and I'm not sure I'm going to make it. Get Grid."

Grid's tousled head looked around the door jamb as if the mention of his name had magically summoned him. "What's going on up here?"

Annie said, "Get the car. We're both in labor."

"Good grief!" he responded. "Both of you?" Then, as if it might make a difference, he asked, "Do you know it's raining cats and dogs outside?"

Kathleen groaned and then sighed as her contraction faded, then said, "I'm really close. We've got to go now!"

He helped them down the stairs one at a time, then went to pull the car around.

Annie watched as he disappeared around the garage.

"My goodness, it's really storming out there," she said.

Kathleen was breathing heavily, recovering from another contraction as George hovered beside her, wringing his hands.

"George, you have to stay here with Ulfsa. There's nothing you can do at the hospital, and he'll need to go out as soon as it gets light. Don't worry about us. We'll be fine," Kathleen said.

The three of them glanced at Ulfsa. He was looking at the slightly open kitchen window. Then they heard it. A low moan gradually rose to become the sound of the town storm-warning siren. They glanced at each other in speculation.

The wind picked up, and there was a bang on the roof, followed closely by a large thumping sound on the south side of the house.

Annie asked, "What was that?"

Grid came in, shaking off the rain as she spoke.

"Something just happened out there," he said. "The top blew off the big tree by the house. It landed on the south side, between the neighbors and us. Missed the roof entirely, thank God. It would have collapsed the place. It's huge."

Kathleen groaned. What next? It wasn't enough that they were both in labor, but now they had a storm complicating matters. Another contraction started, and she groaned again. "Look, you guys, I've got to get to the hospital, storm or not."

Grid looked concerned. "We'd better get going. The only problem is there may be some trees down. That was a tornado or something similar. I don't know where its path went. C'mon, let's get in the car."

—◈—

The road did have trees and limbs down, but Grid was able to maneuver around them. Once out on the main highway, he turned south and accelerated through the rain. It wasn't falling as heavily now and was just more of a nuisance.

After three miles, a flashing light showed ahead of them. It was a Highway Patrol car. The officer came over to them, shining a flashlight through their window.

Grid rolled down his window. "What's the problem, Officer?"

The man turned his light towards the ground. "There's some trees down across the road ahead. You folks shouldn't be out here right now. There's been a lot of damage down toward Brainerd. Big tornado come through, and the weather isn't getting any better. Could be another one out there somewhere."

He looked speculatively at the barely visible, rolling clouds.

Grid said, "We've got to get to the hospital. Both of these ladies are in labor and Kathleen in the back is pretty far along."

The patrolman shone his flash through the window at the back seat. His voice changed, "That's a problem. Let me think." He paused, then quickly said, "Look, the highway is impassable. There are too many trees down and no way around until the road crews get them cleared. That's going to take at least till daylight. Uh, if you backtrack a couple of miles and then go off to the west, the road winds around the backside of Gull Lake and ends up just north of Brainerd. That's probably your best bet. I don't think the tornado came through over there."

Grid said, "Okay. I'm gonna turn around and give it a try. Thanks, Officer."

The man said, "Just be careful. There are trees and limbs down everywhere, along with some electric lines, so don't take any chances."

———— ◦◦◦ ————

They accelerated back northward and shortly turned off on the back road. It was gravel and rough. Kathleen bounced back and forth helplessly on the back seat. She gritted her teeth and tried to hold on.

The car came to a sudden stop. Grid cursed, then said, "It's no use going this way. The storm must have come right through here. The whole road's blocked."

Annie exclaimed, "Oh, Jase, what are we going to do now?"

They both turned to look at Kathleen.

She was between contractions and managed a sweaty grin. "Look, you two, let's go back to the highway. I might be able to do something about this, but it may be dangerous. Just get us back on the main road and let me concentrate."

Grid backed the car around in a neat three-point turn, then headed back the way they'd come.

Once they were back on the highway, Kathleen said, "Grid, stop the car right here."

"In the middle of the road?" he asked, surprised.

"Yes. We won't be here for long, I just...oh, oh, here comes another one!" She grabbed Annie's outstretched hand and squeezed, then made a sound that was partway between a groan and a scream. "Ow! That hurts!"

She panted and then gathered herself to say, "I just need a second. I'm going to move us back in time to just before the tornado. The roads will be clear then, but we've got to get through before the storm hits. I hope there won't be any paradoxical effects. We're pretty close to the house, but maybe we're far enough away from our previous selves to avoid any serious effects."

Annie looked fearfully at her. "What kind of effects, Kathleen?"

"I met myself once. Time doesn't like that very much. It instantly forced the two versions of me apart in time. I...I mean the present me, suffered partial amnesia for a while. I don't think that's going to happen to us. We're too far from the house. Don't worry."

Annie grimaced as Kathleen paused and added, "I hope."

Kathleen closed her eyes and concentrated. If only she didn't hurt so, it would be easier. She started again, trying to visualize the equation's variables. It would have to be precise. She wanted to move them back just an hour. She looked at the other two, then closed her eyes again and activated the transition.

Grid swore, "Damn! You did it. It's clear now. No rain or anything, but the clouds look bad."

Kathleen opened her eyes and said, "Drive fast. I don't have much time."

⸻◆⸻

The hospital staff was helpful and efficient. Kathleen was almost fully dilated by the time she got there. Her obstetrician was called and was on his way. It helped that he lived just a few blocks from the hospital.

She thought to ask the nurse about Annie. "Is my friend okay? Where is she?"

The nurse, an older woman who looked like she'd seen it all, said, "She's fine. If it's any consolation to you, she's having an easier time than you are. She'll be fine. Now you just concentrate on not pushing. I don't want those scars to tear...ah, here's the doctor."

She conferred with Dr. James, and then he moved beside Kathleen's gurney and said, "Breathe deeply, Kathleen. You're almost ready. Let me look."

He bent to look at her nether region, then raised his head with a smile, "The baby's crowning. It doesn't look like your scars are going to be a problem. I was fearful that your lower abdominal muscles wouldn't be strong enough to hold up, but you're progressing fine. Now, push!" he said as she suffered another strong contraction.

Kathleen strained, then screamed, although it didn't seem like she heard anything. She took a deep breath and pushed again. This time there was the feeling of movement and sharper pain as if something was tearing.

Dr. James was busy with the nurse between her legs. He lifted a blood-covered object and slapped it. There was a thin wail, then a more robust crying. He turned to Kathleen with a big smile and placed her wet, screaming baby boy on her chest.

Her arms came up and cuddled the noisy mite. The little one suddenly stopped screaming and turned his head towards Kathleen's breast. He nuzzled at her and then latched on. She laughed through the tears that were sliding down her cheeks.

"He knows what to do. Just let him teach you," Dr. James said. Then he added, "I'm going to give you an injection down there. Normally I do that first, but you delivered so quickly that there was no time. I'm going to have to stitch up some tearing, but don't worry. You'll heal up just fine."

Kathleen didn't notice. She was staring at her baby, taking in every feature of his little face. Her arms tightened protectively. There was no way she was going to let him go. She couldn't believe the immense joy and love she was feeling. How was this possible?

She'd imagined nothing like this. Somewhere deep in her psyche, a deeply held hurt was released, and she somehow felt whole. She had thought that having a baby was a mere biological function and that the product of labor would be just something she'd done. She had not expected to find instant maternal love. She'd had maternal feelings before, but this was different by an entire order of magnitude.

She had a sudden insight. She'd always thought that her mother had been heartless and cruel. Now she realized that her mother had, perhaps, suffered terribly by having elected to have Kathleen aborted.

What must have she thought when her baby was suddenly ejected alive and screaming with the pain of saline burns? Had she wanted to hold and comfort her?

From what Kathleen had been able to discover, the attending nurse had been a new employee at the clinic and hadn't realized what she was getting into.

Faced with her first abortion procedure, she had a personal moral crisis that resulted in her snatching the screaming infant and dashing out of the room.

Kathleen had survived because of the nurse's care. The woman had quit her job, taken care of the infant, and later arranged for her to be placed with her foster parents, the couple she'd known as Mom and Dad.

Kathleen had always felt hated and rejected by her birth mother. That feeling had poisoned her life, making her fearful and reclusive. It had taken Cadeyrin's love to begin to heal her wounds. Now, this little one, her baby, had brought her full circle. She suddenly found it in her heart to forgive her mother.

What had caused her mother to decide to have a late-term abortion? Kathleen didn't know, but she now felt a pang of sympathy. It must have been something awful. She only knew that nothing could have convinced her to abort this armful of joy that was trying to extract nourishment from her still unproductive nipple.

With a mental shift that almost felt like the click of a long stuck lock, Kathleen's long-held hurt and fear disappeared.

She looked up as the doctor said, "We need to clean him up and weigh him."

He gently took the infant and handed him to the nurse, who turned away to begin cleaning off the blood.

Kathleen suddenly had another strong contraction. There was another, lesser sensation of movement as the afterbirth slid out.

Dr. James examined it and said, "Kathleen, I've got to confess that I was really worried about you. Your scarring is alarming, but you've had an almost perfect birth. The baby's Apgar score is high; he's big and healthy. You've done a great job. Congratulations. By the way, what do you want to name him? I've got to fill out his birth certificate."

She paused, thinking about Cadeyrin. He would certainly want to have something to say about his son's name. He'd explained to her that names were very important to his people. However, he'd also said that some names had to be earned. She was momentarily at a loss, but then it came to her. She'd name the baby Cole. That was a strong, masculine name that had sounds that would easily fit into Cadeyrin's native tongue. If he objected, they could always give the boy a name from his culture.

She asked, "Do I have to give him a middle name right now? His father isn't here, and he'll want to have something to say about it."

Dr. James said, "Well, it's customary, but you don't have to give him a formal middle name. You can always have the certificate amended later."

"Good. I want to name him Cole," she said.

The doctor wrote it down, then said, "That's an unusual name. Can't say I've had too many Coles." He filled out the rest of the form and then said, "There. My job here is done. You'll be moved into a room, and they'll bring your baby in shortly."

Kathleen said, "I don't want to take my eyes off of him."

Dr. James said, "I understand. Well, we don't have to be quite so formal. I think you can hold him as they move you to your room."

She eagerly took the bundled baby from the nurse and then gasped, "Oh. I forgot. How is Annie? Is she okay?"

Dr. James said, "They haven't come for me yet, so she's still some time from delivering. Don't worry about her. I'm going to take good care of her too." He walked towards the door, shaking his head.

As he walked out the door, Kathleen heard him say, "This is as exciting a night as I've had for years. Two friends, two babies at almost the same time. This really is one to remember."

⸎

Kathleen hadn't been in her room for an hour when they wheeled Annie in.

"Annie! Good! We're going to be sharing a room," she said quietly so as not to startle Cole, who was asleep in her arms.

Annie looked at her rather blearily. "Hi, Kathleen. It kind of takes it out of you, doesn't it?"

Their conversation was interrupted by Grid as he walked into the room carrying their baby. He looked funny. He was trying to be overly careful and was walking as if he were on slippery ice. The expression on his face was a priceless combination of alarm, love, and extreme pride.

"Oh, Annie! She's perfect! She's beautiful. I've never seen such a baby. I'm so lucky. I love you, Annie," he said.

Annie laughed, "You'd better, you big lunk. Just wait until the girls see her. I hope they approve as much as you do."

He smiled, "I'm sure they will. They're her sisters. They'll love her."

# Chapter Twenty-Nine

# Plans

The house by the lake seemed full. Who had ever thought that babies would take so much work? Well, George probably knew about it, but he hadn't warned her. Kathleen was busy with a diaper. Cole seemed to go through the things at eighty miles an hour. She could hear Annie singing to Rowena in the other room. The brown-headed woman was a natural mother and had taken easily to things that Kathleen was still trying to figure out.

"It's because I had three younger siblings. My mother made me learn how to help," Annie said.

Kathleen smiled wistfully. "I didn't have any siblings, at least none that I know. I guess I was an only child. My foster parents seemed to know what to do, but I'm afraid that I didn't pay much attention. I always liked math more than housework, anyway."

Annie laughed. "That's going to change, my girl. You're going to be busy with that little guy for quite some time."

Kathleen's bad mood evaporated. She looked at the baby, and her face softened into a maternal glow. "I may not know how to care for a baby, but if I can master physics, I can learn to take care of a baby. How complicated can it be — " She stopped suddenly, made a surprised noise, then hastily flipped the diaper over the yellow stream that had shot up from the uncovered baby boy.

Annie laughed hysterically in response. Kathleen was irritated at her. "Why didn't you warn me?" she asked.

Annie conquered her laughter, then said, "Honestly, I forgot. Little girls aren't quite so, so...squirty." She dissolved into laughter again.

Kathleen snorted, then replaced the soaked diaper with a dry one. This time, she was careful to cover up the offending organ quickly, just in case Cole had an afterthought about the issue.

Annie watched and then said, "That's the way to do it. They'll surprise you sometimes, so it's always best to get them covered up quickly.

Grid called from the kitchen, interrupting them. "Hey, you two, food is ready. Get in here before it gets cold or Ulfsa eats it. He's turning into a terrible beggar."

Kathleen called back, "Well, if you-know-who wouldn't keep giving him table scraps, he wouldn't act that way."

Grid laughed as they walked into the room. "Yeah. I know, but he's so good at making a pitiful face that I just can't resist. I didn't know a wolf would act this way."

Kathleen replied, "Neither did I, but Ulfsa has been with me since he was just a day or two old. He's fully adapted to human ways, and he's really smart, so...well, that's what you get."

⚫

After breakfast, Kathleen carried Cole outside and sat in the shade of a pine tree near the lake. She nursed the baby and looked off over the water. Her eyes gradually took on a calculating look, although there was no one there to notice. The others were still inside.

Ulfsa came trotting up and threw himself down on the grass beside her with a deep sigh. She looked down at him and poked his furry side with a finger.

"You're in danger of getting fat, you big furball."

He raised his head and looked at her, then whined and looked around, checking to see if she was speaking to him.

He looked back at her, meeting her eyes expressively.

"Yes. I know. You miss Cadeyrin. I miss him too. I've been planning on how to get him back. I don't think I'll need your help, though. It would probably be too dangerous for you. Those people up there in the future seem to like shooting dogs. They'd be frightened of you, and rightly so. They'd probably go out of their way to shoot at you."

Grid and Annie came out, carrying Rowena.

"Hey, what's going on out here?" Grid asked.

Kathleen sighed and then replied. "I'm planning on getting Cadeyrin back. I know neither of you knows my husband, but you'd like him. I'm just lost without him, and he's in danger too. The problem is those people are maybe getting better at time-travel. They could find us here, and you and the babies could be in jeopardy. I...uh. I don't know what would be safest."

Grid said, "They're not good people, that's for sure. They could easily send someone back here to kill you."

She replied, "Not me. They want my formula too badly to risk me. They've got me on a long leash, though. Jones has intimated that he'll hurt Cadeyrin if I don't cooperate."

Annie interjected a question. "I don't understand how you came here to have Cole. Won't they miss you? How can your husband even still be alive if they're that bad?"

Kathleen said, "That's what time-travel can do. If you think about it, none of that has happened yet. They don't know I've even left. When I return to the future, I'll come back within a second of when I left. It's just that I'll be physically older since I lived nine months or so here in 1971."

Gridley nodded his head, then turned to Annie. "Mrs. Gridley, just let her deal with the timing issue. I've got some knowledge of time-travel, but she's the master."

Kathleen continued almost as if he hadn't spoken. "So. Here's what I'm thinking. I'd like to move you all back to the Cretaceous, provided you think that the babies would be safe there, Grid."

He nodded slowly. "Yes. We could take supplies back. You can do that, can't you, Kathleen?"

She nodded. "No problem. I can transport anything that I can touch."

He continued, "We'll make the cave more comfortable. I'm sure the girls will like the babies. They've expressed considerable interest in Annie's pregnancy. I think they can control their chicks and their mates, so it shouldn't be a problem. You are sure that Jones' agents can come here?"

Kathleen explained. "One was here. I made a mistake. I needed money, so I won a trifecta at the Kentucky Derby. They've apparently been watching for such unusual events in history. The guy tracked us here to the house and threatened us. I handled the situation and sent him off somewhere."

Her eyes wide, Annie asked, "Won't he come back?"

Gridley watched Kathleen carefully as she said, "No. I changed the setting on his return device. He won't have an easy time of it."

Grid said, "Ok. We won't worry about him, but there could be others. They know they sent him here, and he didn't come back. That's a red flag, don't you think?"

Kathleen answered, "Maybe, but I believe they're short-handed. There must be thousands of events in history they could construe as possible evidence of my presence. Anyway, they have no idea when you are in the Cretaceous. There are no clues for them, so I'm sure everyone will be safe in that period. While you're there, I can go and get Cadeyrin and come back. It won't take long since I can time things to be fast. You'll hardly know I've been gone. Cole won't even have time to get his diaper wet."

Annie laughed and said, "He might surprise you on that."

Gridley interrupted, "I hate to throw cold water on this idea, but what if you're captured or killed? I wouldn't mind spending the rest of my life with the girls, but our daughter needs to have access to humans. She might need medical treatment, and when she reaches adulthood, she will want social interaction. I think that you'd better get Cadeyrin first, then we'll all go to the cave, stay there for a time, and decide what to do after we're sure we're safe."

Kathleen considered that idea, then continued. "You're right. You can stay here while I get him, but we should collect the supplies we'll need for a stay in the cave. After I've got Cadeyrin, we can decide on a more modern time. Maybe not here, but somewhere when there are people."

Gridley said, "I'm not so sure about that either. I get the distinct impression that Jones' group is working towards world domination. They intend to kill historically significant figures and change the evolution of the country. If they can make changes in time that will lead to their domination of the world, they'll inevitably do it. Power always tries to increase and centralize itself. Their time-travel method will also become more accurate. They had no problem placing me at the right time in the past to make sure that Reagan died and Hinckley would be blamed. It's just their system is dependent on the mental state of the travelers. They sent me off to the dinosaurs just to get rid of me. Thought I'd spill the beans somehow. I'm sure they thought that it would be easier to get rid of me. They've got plenty of capable men they can use." He finished with a shrug, then added, "Also, I guess I love the girls. I'd miss them, and it's for sure they can't exist in any modern time. Scientists would go crazy wanting to dissect them. They're too dangerous, too. Maybe we'd better stay there."

Kathleen nodded slowly. "Maybe you're right, Grid, but I feel like the Cretaceous is just too dangerous to be home to our children. I think I have a solution, though. Cadeyrin and I chose the Sangamon as a time when there was plenty of game in North America. The climate is good, and the living is easy. The only problem was that we didn't realize there were hominins on this continent at that time. The way Cadeyrin described them, and from what I saw, they might still be here. The one I saw looked for all the world like a composite of the descriptions of Bigfoot that people give. I've been thinking, though, that we could go back another few thousand years. The climate would still be good, the animals would be there, and maybe the, whatever, let's call them Bigfoot, wouldn't be. Or maybe they wouldn't be hostile. We'd just have to be a little more careful, that's all."

Grid looked at Annie. "Mrs. Gridley, would that work for you?"

She said, "We could maybe travel back for supplies? Right? That wouldn't be a problem. I think I'm game for an extended time in my own private world. There's something addictive about not having to worry about keeping up with the neighbors. Oh, could the girls and their families come?"

Kathleen said, "Maybe. They could take care of themselves with the animals, I think. The only issue might be if one of them died, we couldn't return their body to the Cretaceous, and someone found their skeleton. That would upset science. I'm not sure I'd want to have that happen. It could change the world, and I don't know what would happen to us as a result. Don't forget, we're still a product of our time, even though we end up in the past."

The other two nodded. "I can see how that would be a problem," Grid said. Then he asked, "But, wouldn't that be the inevitable result of Jones' group messing with history? Wouldn't they run the risk of changing time so that they didn't exist?"

Kathleen said, "They'd exist in the old timeline, but maybe not in the new branch that their actions created. That's one of the main reasons I won't give them my formula. I'd also like to make sure they don't get their hands on the research they're using for their method of time-travel. The ability to travel in time is just too dangerous to trust in the hands of people who want personal power. I don't understand all of the ramifications and potential paradoxes, so I have grave doubts that they do. I'm afraid that they haven't even thought about it much."

Kathleen straightened. Cole had fallen asleep. She turned modestly away, rearranged her blouse, and then said, "Annie, would you take him for a few minutes? I'm going to go get Cadeyrin."

Annie started to shift Rowena so she could hold two, but Grid reached out for the sleeping baby, and Kathleen carefully handed him over.

Grid looked at her and said, "You're going now?"

"Yes," she answered. "I'm going to get my pistol, change my clothes so that I'll look about the same and go. Regardless of how long it takes me, I'll be back in a few minutes, your time. If...if I don't come back..." She swallowed hard. "If I don't come back, raise him for me, please. George has control of an investment that we've made. It will amount to millions of dollars eventually. You won't lack. Besides, you already know what's coming, so you can do well for yourselves."

Annie choked back a sob. "Kathleen, that's not something that will happen. You're going to be fine. I just know it."

Rowena, sensing something of her mother's upset, moved fitfully and started to cry. Annie busied herself calming her daughter.

Ulfsa had stood up when Kathleen did and followed her as she headed for the back porch. She let him come inside. George was standing there. He'd been watching them through the window.

"Looks like you've come to the decision to take action, then," he observed.

Kathleen hugged the old man. "George, you're like a father to me. I'm so thankful that I met you that I don't know how to express myself."

He hugged her back. "It's me who is the thankful one. I was ready to jump in the river, and you gave me a reason to live. I'm excited to see your baby grow and Grid and Annie's too. Besides I'd like to see some dinosaurs. Always was curious about those things."

She squeezed him tightly. "I love you, George. You know that, don't you?"

He said, "I suppose I should confess that I love you like a daughter. Have ever since I realized that you were in trouble. You've given me an amazing life since that time. Now, you be careful."

She walked up the stairs to change.

# Chapter Thirty

# Positive Action

This was the moment toward which she'd been working. She wasn't in as good a condition as she'd been before the birth, but she felt that it was a trade-off between time and her fitness for the job. At any rate, she didn't want to wait any longer to rescue Cadeyrin. He wouldn't recognize it as much of a delay since she'd appear in his time reference quickly. She could wait, but she had a vision of her waiting until she was sure the moment was right. What if she ended up staying with Cole until he was grown before she skewed her courage up. She'd then be many years older, and appearing in front of Cadeyrin as an older woman wasn't something she wanted to consider. Now was the time. Definitely.

She walked out the back door, waved at the Gridleys and Cole, then closed her eyes.

When she opened them, she was in the bathroom stall in the pharmacy. She felt the seat. It was still warm from her sitting on it. Her timing was perfect.

She exited the stall and looked around the small room. There was a wall-mounted trash bin for paper towels. She opened the lid and saw that it was partly full. She looked at her watch, noting the exact time, then shoved her pistol down to the bottom, making sure to cover it carefully, then left the bathroom and walked to the front of the store. The man detailed to watch her was just coming in as she passed the check-out desk.

"There you are," he said. A flicker of what must have been relief passed over his face. "I know we can't hold you anywhere, but I'm not used to this kind of situation. I was worried that I just let you walk off, even though I knew you'd come back."

Kathleen said, "You're holding my husband prisoner and hostage to my behavior. What am I supposed to do?"

The man held the door open for her and said, "This isn't something that I enjoy. I can't convince myself that you're some kind of national enemy."

She asked, "Is that what they're saying I am?"

He strode beside her as they moved towards the car, which was sitting in front of the hotel. "Jones didn't say that in so many words, but he implied that you had the potential to do something that would harm the country. That's why..." He trailed off, observing her angry look.

"It's my country, too. Harming it is the last thing I'd do. I'm trying to find a way to keep it safe," she said.

He moved in front of her to open the car door without a word.

She got in, and the car pulled out, taking her to wherever Jones was. She hoped that it was where they were holding Cadeyrin. That would be convenient. She sighed. Nothing in her life was ever convenient. Somehow things always seemed to require a tremendous amount of effort. She hung her head, looking at her hands clasped in her lap.

After a moment, Kathleen took a deep breath. She wasn't the old Kathleen. She'd had some amazing things happen in her life, and they had conditioned her to expect that positive action would eventually yield a solution. She'd initially felt that she was the victim of circumstance, washed back and forth like an empty bottle in the sea. Cadeyrin had taught her that she was desirable and effective. She'd learned that she could control her world.

Her entire path in rescuing him had been based on her deep feeling that she would somehow be equal to the task. She couldn't bring herself to doubt her abilities. Perhaps she couldn't see the entire path from the beginning to the end, but the next step or two was always clear. She wouldn't stop until she was successful.

No, she wouldn't stop. She looked at the back of her guard's head. If he only knew how truly deadly she could be when someone got in between her and those she loved, he'd never turn his back on her. Of course, that wouldn't make any difference considering her time-travel ability, but still...She smiled a small smile, just for herself. Jones and those who were behind him should be very worried. They should never have attacked Cadeyrin, and God help them if they continued.

She was amazed at herself. Kathleen, the unwanted, aborted child. She'd truly changed. She looked at her reflection in the rearview mirror. She still looked the same externally. The change was completely internal. It was only reflected in a small way by the enhanced confidence in her eyes.

The vehicle slowed, made a right turn, and pulled up in front of an official-looking building. This was where she was to meet Jones. She wondered if Cadeyrin was being held in this place. He wouldn't comprehend the structure of a modern building. Despite his competence, in many ways, he was terribly uninformed.

Once inside, they ushered her into a small conference room. Jones and another man came in just as she was sitting down. Kathleen looked up and frowned. The second man was Agent Reed. Her experience with him didn't lead her to have any warm and friendly feelings.

Trying to overcome her antipathy, she said, "Jones." Then turned to Reed. "Reed, I see you're still involved in this. Mind telling me what you're doing here?"

Reed responded, "I've always been involved. Jones works for me. He's been tasked with getting you to tell us what you know."

Kathleen said, "You're too busy? Or, is it just that you don't want to get your hands dirty?"

Jones interjected, "Hey! You'd better show some respect, you b–" He snapped his jaw shut, cutting off what he intended to say. There was a short pause before he added, "...beautiful young woman."

Reed laughed. "Ha, ha. Good one, Jones. She's more than stubborn. For some reason, she has decided not to be patriotic and help her country out. She doesn't realize that her bargaining chips are rapidly losing their value.

Our time-travel method is becoming better with every test. Professor Wolf's method might not be as easy as hers, but it has the potential to be every bit as accurate."

Jones said, "Listen, Whitby, you still have time to help us. We think that you can assist Professor Wolf in his work. That would make this whole process go much faster. You'd have a chance to become a national hero. Just think, part of the team that developed time-travel and allowed the country to become completely secure."

Kathleen said, "I'm sure Professor Wolf is quite capable of doing his own math. From what I've seen, your method is getting better, but it's still unreliable."

Jones blinked, then said, "That reminds me. We sent out a group of fourteen agents to investigate financial events in the recent past. Thirteen of them returned, but the fourteenth had some sort of accident. He was ready to jump, but then our observer saw a curious thing. He appeared right beside himself. It wasn't as if he was doubled. The two copies looked different. There was a soundless flash, and one of them disappeared. The other, who was the one we were about to send off, based on his clothing, seemingly lost his mind. He's being held in a safe place now, but he doesn't remember anything. Not even his name. Professor Wolf said it was some kind of paradox. Do you know anything about it?"

She smiled. It had worked. They wouldn't be able to trace the disappeared man. It would be almost impossible for her with her advanced ability. He could be in the 1970s or almost any when else, for that matter.

"No, I can't help you with that. It seems like a paradox to me. He must have returned before he left. The time-stream won't allow that situation to exist. The one who disappeared was probably snapped back to when he came from, but I can't guarantee that."

Jones frowned and asked, "Did you have anything to do with it? The others all returned with the information that the financial situations they were investigating were just chance happenings. He was to look into a very unusual trifecta win at the Kentucky Derby. Suppose you knew the first three horses in advance. You could have gone back and won that."

He looked accusingly at her.

"Yes. I suppose I could have done that, but why go to all that trouble and when would I have done it? You know where I've been every second since you put me in that hotel room," she said. Then she added, "All I want is Cadeyrin. I'm not interested in fame or money."

Jones and Reed both snickered. Then Reed said, "I've never met someone who didn't want money. If that's true, you'll be happy to help us just to free your man, even if patriotism isn't enough for you. You know, if we could master time-travel, we could save many, many lives. We could prevent terrorist attacks and even move people out of the way of natural disasters. You really need to reconsider helping us."

Kathleen heard the words but read the deeper, unsaid meaning. She shook her head back and forth slightly, then said, "What about Cadeyrin? Is he here in this building?"

Jones' fingers twitched, and his eyes flicked to the upper left, then he said, "Ah, no. We've placed him in a farmhouse somewhere near. You wouldn't be able to find it easily. The best part of the location is that there are no close neighbors. Sounds, such as cries of pain, won't attract attention." He smiled a tight smile.

Kathleen had noticed his fingers and eyes. He was lying again. It wasn't very noticeable, but her attention had been sharpened by her hunting experiences with Cadeyrin, where even a tiny clue could mean the difference between success and failure. Jones' involuntary movements were relatively easy to spot. It might mean that Cadeyrin was here. Maybe in an adjacent room.

Reed seemed to think that he could tempt her into cooperating. "Help Wolf with his math, and when we get the system working correctly, we'll let your husband go. I'll even see that you get paid for your time. You could write your own ticket in the academic world with that sort of accomplishment to your credit. Think of the publications you can write."

She largely ignored his nonsensical statements. They'd kill her and Cadeyrin, probably even kill Professor Wolf, once they had the secret. It wouldn't do to let it out. How naive did Reed think she was?

Then the mention of Professor Wolf tickled her memory. She thought quickly, straining her mind to remember something that she and Professor

Wolf had discussed in the brief time they'd spoken.

Ah. That was it. The two of them had been discussing a possible affinity between people separated by time. She'd meant to spend time thinking about that, but it had slipped into the back of her mind. Now, it might make all of the difference. She closed her eyes, preparing to jump in time.

Reed snapped, "Wait! Before you go back in time to get out of here, there's something you should see first."

She opened her eyes and looked at him with her brows pulled into a frown.

He handed her his phone. She looked down at the screen to see a short video clip of Cadeyrin. He was lying in a hospital bed. There was a handcuff linking him to the rail. In the background, there was a big man, an obvious guard. The man had a pistol strapped to his waist.

She raised her eyes to Reeds. "So, I already knew you had him locked up. When was this made?" she asked.

He said, "Just this morning as a matter of fact. I thought you'd like to see that he's recovering nicely."

Kathleen said, "I hope he is. You wouldn't want to harm him, you know."

Reed said, "No. We don't want to harm him, but we will if you don't help us. I don't know how many times I've got to tell you, Kathleen. You don't have any choice in the matter."

An idea had formed in her mind as he spoke. She was sure that Professor Wolf's life was in danger also. She didn't like that. The old man reminded her of her deceased mentor. Perhaps if she played along and helped or pretended to help them, she'd have enough time to figure out how to rescue both Cadeyrin and Professor Wolf.

She made up her mind. "Okay, Reed. I can see that I'm going to have to help. You promise that you'll let us go afterward?"

He placed his hand on his heart and said, "I swear that I won't hold you."

Out of the corner of her eye, she saw the shadow of a sardonic grin pass over Jones' face. It simply confirmed her suspicions. They wouldn't be held; they'd be killed.

----

They took her to meet with Professor Wolf. He had been provided with a workspace on another floor of the same building. Kathleen instantly felt at home there. The walls were covered with whiteboards, which were, in turn, covered with Wolf's thin, spidery scrawling. Equations marched in disordered groups across the white space.

Wolf used several colors of markers, and the overall effect was almost like some modern art project. He'd filled nearly every space on the walls and then gone back and made changes in different colors.

The old man was excited to see Kathleen.

"Ms. Whitby! It's so good to see you. I want to show you what I've been thinking. Let's start over here. The third temporal variable, here." He stopped talking to wave vaguely at a section of equations, then continued, "I've represented it with a theta symbol. Uh..Oh, wait a moment." He moved over to another wall and made some hasty scribbles.

"It looks like I forgot to account for minor quantum fluctuations. If I carry this factor forward, then..." He stopped talking again while he rapidly scribbled, changing equations and values across the intervening whiteboards.

Jones snorted, then said, "He's always like this. I don't know how he comes up enough even to eat."

Wolf wasn't as deeply absorbed as Jones had thought. He stopped mid-equation and said, "Eating has nothing to do with it. Solving this problem is quite enough for me." Then he continued writing.

Kathleen looked at Jones. "You might as well leave us alone. I've got to check through his work. He doesn't use the same notation I do, so we're going to have a bit of a problem getting on the same page."

Jones snorted, "You mean the same board?" He waved his hand at the walls. "Smitty over there will watch you. If you need anything, let him know."

Then he left.

Kathleen looked at Smitty. He smiled at her with a slightly embarrassed expression. She sniffed. Maybe he'd be sympathetic to her, but most likely, he wouldn't be any help. She turned to the Professor.

Wolf had paused and was now following his logic, his lips slightly moving as he went over the equations.

Kathleen settled down in a chair, then said, "Professor Wolf, perhaps you could take me through your work, starting at the beginning."

He jerked, then looked at her. "It might help if you showed me your equations. That way I could see where I'm going wrong," he said.

Kathleen smiled, then said, "No, I think you're onto a more general solution than mine. I don't want to influence your thinking until I understand what you're doing. Once I understand your logic, I can either contribute to it or provide my own solutions that we can then use to cross-check yours with."

Wolf nodded, then moved rapidly across to the board by the door. Pointing at the first line of scribbles, he said, "This represents what I call the general temporal flux. Follow my thinking, please."

He started off on a long-winded lecture that involved what he'd learned from working with the time-traveling Logan Walker. Over in the corner, Smitty's eyes fluttered, then gradually closed. He looked like he was planning on taking a nap. Perhaps he'd heard this all before, or perhaps he wasn't intellectually interested. Kathleen didn't know which, but she was pleased that he wasn't going to ask questions.

She glanced around the room as Wolf spoke. There were cameras on the ceiling. They were probably monitoring every inch of the space. She'd have to be circumspect in her dealings with Wolf.

Right now, she wanted to understand where he was going with his logic. She was determined to find some way to sidetrack it so that Reed and company could never figure it out.

Her awareness of the outside world faded as she immersed herself in Wolf's math.

# Chapter Thirty-One

# Physical Action

Wolf gradually led Kathleen through his convoluted logic. She noticed several points that she could have simplified. Some of his logic wasn't parsed exactly the way she thought it should be. In addition, some of his math used an older approach that Kathleen recognized as one that wouldn't arrive at a correct solution. Nevertheless, the overall idea was close to hers. It was enough to provide a reasonable degree of accuracy. She'd have to do something to keep Reed from this knowledge.

Meanwhile, she needed a moment of privacy so that she could locate Cadeyrin. She thought she'd have to jump into the night and carefully try to scope out all of the building. They were undoubtedly guarding Cadeyrin's room closely. If there was only a way to go directly to him…

Wolf was still talking, absorbed in his thought process. She'd lost track of Wolf's math, relegating his exposition to the level of background noise, but that didn't matter to her at the moment.

She focused on reviewing her own formula. The spatial variable, the one that she'd initially treated as a constant, would allow her to move in space as well as time. The only problem was she wasn't sure where she should go in the building. It would be a matter of changing the variable by a tiny amount. She'd have to keep very close control over the decimal places.

She considered her formula again. Wolf, looking over his shoulder at her, saw that she was involved in thought. He assumed that she was attempting to understand his work, and a smile flickered over his face, then he turned to continue.

Kathleen checked her logic. There was something she was missing somewhere. It was, uh, right there. She'd made a natural assumption. She'd ignored a critical aspect of the quantum plenum. If Bohm was correct, then everything, even a single electron, had some level of consciousness.

In her original work, she had ignored that concept. She'd made the assumption that consciousness didn't count. Her equation was adequate to move her precisely in time and now in space, but something was missing. She mentally added another set of variables. If she solved for them using an approach that was somewhat like the solution for a strange attractor pattern...She concentrated, mentally moving variables, then felt a wave of satisfaction. The order was hidden in what initially looked to be a chaotic system, but now she saw that it was a function of the awareness of the time-traveler.

Somehow she'd been amazingly lucky in her initial jump through time to the Pleistocene. Her transition had been driven by her overwhelming need to escape Drew's violent attack, and at the time, she had only the barest understanding of how her formula worked. Her personal awareness factor was a close match to that of Cadeyrin. That had been why she'd arrived at the precise time and location so that they would meet.

She remembered that he'd told her about his vision of her coming to him, coming into his life. She had always recognized that he was somehow connected in a very spiritual way to the overall consciousness of the Universe. She had thought that she didn't have such ability, but now she wasn't so sure.

When she'd been forced to make her first time jump to avoid the assault, she hadn't specified the consciousness coefficient. It had been left to vary randomly. Her personal pattern had somehow set it in a way she didn't totally understand, but one which resulted in the two of them meeting.

She made some minor changes in the equation. Even without activating the solution, she could feel a resonance in her mind. It was almost as if her thoughts were echoing in a larger chamber than her skull. The changed variables intensified the net effect, and it seemed as if there were a masculine overtone to her thinking. She gasped and clenched her hands. That must be Cadeyrin.

She could jump directly to his location!

Professor Wolf cleared his throat and asked, "Well, what do you think about the logic so far?"

She jerked, then said, "I got lost a little before you changed boards. I started thinking about the way you solve for the temporal offset. I believe that you could do that more efficiently.

His eyes gleamed. "Oh? Tell me what you were thinking." Then as an aside, he muttered, "This is so exciting."

Over in the corner, Smitty made a snoring noise out of his slightly drooping mouth.

Kathleen asked, "Don't you think we should take a bit of a break?"

Wolf started to turn back to the board but then, apparently remembering that maybe she was only human, said, "Yes. Well, maybe that would be a good thing. I could stand to stretch my legs. Smitty?"

Smitty snorted, then woke up. "What do you want now?"

Wolf said, "The young lady and I would like to use the restrooms. Are you going to insist on following us there, or are we adult enough to go by ourselves?"

Smitty yawned and said, "No. Jones said you could be trusted not to run out. Especially Ms. Whitby. Go ahead. I'll wait here."

Wolf held the door for her and then led the way down the hall. As they walked, he asked, "What did he mean by that? About you not running away, I mean?"

Kathleen said, "They're holding my husband hostage to make me help."

Professor Wolf looked bleak. "I've been concerned about the overall use of this. I didn't know about your husband, but it doesn't surprise me."

He nodded towards a camera set in the ceiling at the corner of the hallway and then whispered, "We can't talk here. Perhaps the bathrooms. I don't think the walls have any insulation. I've heard women in the ladies' room, and their voices have come through into the men's room fairly clearly. There's no camera system in there."

Kathleen smiled at him as she opened the ladies' room door. "We'll see if you can hear me then," she said in an almost inaudible tone.

As soon as she entered the vacant room, she listened at the wall. She could hear Wolf's footsteps, then the sound of him relieving himself. She grinned.

It took him a while, but when she thought he had finished, she knocked on the wall. After a moment, there was a cautious knock in return. Then she heard him ask, "Can you hear me?"

She answered, "Yes, and you?"

His voice came back, a little muffled but clear enough. "You'll have to speak up a bit. I'm afraid my hearing isn't what it once was."

She quickly walked to the door, cracked it open, and listened. No footsteps in the hall. This would be chancy. She returned to the wall and said loudly, "They're going to use time-travel to change history so that they end up ruling the world."

Wolf exclaimed, "Ahh! I was afraid it was something like that. What can we do?"

Kathleen answered, "There's plenty I can do. I'd like you to go back to the room and start writing on the board. If Smitty asks, tell him I'm still in the ladies' room. I'll be along very shortly after you, so you won't have to stall for long."

He murmured assent, and she heard the other door open and close as she moved into a stall and locked it.

The formula was ready. All she had to do was activate it. She did. She was back in the drugstore bathroom stall. There were a couple of women who were apparently washing their hands, having just finished their business. Kathleen listened to them talk, mentally urging them just to shut up and leave. It seemed to take forever before they were done refreshing their make-up, but they eventually left.

Kathleen popped out of the stall and opened the trash container. The women's discarded towels were wet, and she fastidiously pushed them aside, then retrieved her pistol. It went under her hoodie.

The door was just starting to open as another woman came in. Kathleen closed her eyes and transferred in time and space. She was back in the bathroom of the office building. She instantly closed her eyes again and reworked her equation, this time filling in the attractor variables with values she hoped would get her to Cadeyrin. Just before activating the jump, she pulled her pistol out and cocked the hammer.

⸺◆⸺

Cadeyrin was handcuffed to a bed directly in front of her, and a large man was standing right beside him. There was another man in the room, standing near a curtained window. He started to pull a pistol from a shoulder holster.

Kathleen raised her weapon and snapped, "Don't do that."

The man hesitated, then dropped his hand.

There was a scuffling sound from the bed, and she glanced back. The large man had started to draw his weapon, but Cadeyrin had caught his wrist. The big man's eyes were wide, and his mouth was distorted with pain.

Kathleen grinned mirthlessly. They had no idea how physically strong her husband was. Even injured as he still must be, his natural strength was easily more than any modern human. There was a crunch as the bones in the man's wrist gave way.

The big man groaned and fell to his knees, grabbing his wrist with his other hand.

She moved over to the kneeling guy and slammed her pistol against his temple. He dropped to the floor, unmoving.

The other man took the opportunity to grab at his gun. Kathleen spun, side-stepped, and fired just as he pulled his weapon free and shot at her. He hadn't expected her sideways move. His bullet slapped the metal door behind her.

He wasn't so lucky. Her shot struck his upper right chest. His right arm drooped. He slumped against the wall and released his pistol. It clattered across the tile floor and skidded under the bed.

Kathleen was angry. The shots would raise a hornet's nest in a few seconds.

Cadeyrin climbed out of the hospital bed and grabbed the railing, wrenching at it. It creaked, then broke, releasing the handcuff which slid off the end of the broken metal.

Kathleen jumped at him, and his arms came around her. She instantly transferred them back to the workroom.

Professor Wolf was looking at Smitty, who was trying to stand up, an alarmed look on his face as he reached for his holstered weapon.

Kathleen shoved her pistol in the surprised man's face and said, "Take it easy. I don't want to hurt you."

He raised his arms carefully. Cadeyrin reached around her and tugged the pistol out of Smitty's holster.

Professor Wolf finally recovered enough to say, "What – "

Before he could get any more out, Kathleen grabbed his hand and wrapped her gun arm around Cadeyrin. There was a moment of darkness, and the three of them were standing in the backyard, looking at the lake.

Professor Wolf staggered, then sat down quickly on the chaise lounge, holding his head as if to steady it.

Kathleen felt two strong hands on her shoulders. She was gently turned around and enveloped in her husband's embrace. She hugged him back and then quickly released him as he groaned in pain. She'd forgotten about his punctured lung and broken ribs. It had been almost a year for her, but only a couple of days for him.

She looked up at his face. It was pale, and some beads of sweat were forming along his hairline.

Despite how he must feel, he pulled her close again and then kissed her. They were almost instantly interrupted by a sharp bark, and then Ulfsa came dashing up.

The wolf reared and put his fore-paws on Cadeyrin's shoulders to lick his face. Cadeyrin laughed weakly, then pushed the big animal off. He said, "As glad as I am to see you, I've got to sit down."

Kathleen grabbed his arm and pulled him to the other chaise. Ulfsa came close and shoved his head under Cadeyrin's arm as he sat down. The wolf's wildly waving tail whacked the professor's face causing him to jerk his head back.

Kathleen smiled at the old man. His eyes were still confused, but it looked like he was recovering. She said, "Welcome to 1971, Professor. Don't worry about the wolf; he's ours. You're safe here."

Professor Wolf looked back and forth at the three of them, then he said, "I – uh, I assume this is your husband?"

Kathleen said, "Yes. Professor Wolf, meet Cadeyrin."

Cadeyrin smiled.

Kathleen's heart jumped in her chest. She had been so caught up in her vision of their problems that she had almost forgotten how she loved that kindly smile.

Cadeyrin said, "This is funny. Professor Wolf, meet Ulfsa. He's a gray wolf, and in my language, Ulfsa means small wolf."

The Professor said weakly, "He doesn't seem very small to me."

Kathleen added, "Well, he was small when I got him. We've had him since he was very young."

There was a loud bang from inside the house.

Cadeyrin jerked his head around and said, "That was a shot! What's going on?" He and the Professor both stood.

Kathleen said, "Get down over the embankment. There's an old concrete boathouse on the neighbor's property that will provide shelter. I'm going to check."

Cadeyrin shook his head negatively and said, "I'll do it." Then he groaned and held his side. "Maybe not. We'll go down to the lakeshore. You be careful," he admonished her.

She said, "Ulfsa! Come!"

The wolf glanced at her and then ran over to the house to stand pressed against the siding beside the door.

Kathleen had only taken a few steps towards the house when Annie, her face pale, came through the door.

"Kathleen! My God, I'm glad you're back. Help us! A man appeared out of nowhere and grabbed Cole out of my arms. He shot Jason, then disappeared. Oh, come quickly!" She popped back into the house.

Kathleen followed, glancing over her shoulder to see the two men climb back up the slope and head towards the house.

Jason was upstairs, holding his hand over a spot on the side of his stomach. He didn't look particularly distressed.

Annie was now holding Rowena, trying to get the frightened baby silenced.

Jason said, "Kathleen! He got away. I tried to stop him, but it was too quick."

She bent over, looking at his hand; there was only a little blood leaking through his fingers.

"Are you badly hurt?" she asked.

He shook his head negatively. "Not too bad. I'm going to have to get to a hospital, though. I'll probably lose some intestine from this. The bullet went right through. It missed my kidney, but I may have a perforated gut."

Kathleen drew in her breath. "That's bad enough." She looked around, "Where's George?"

Annie said, "He went for a walk down the road before this happened. He should be back any minute."

"He can take you guys to the hospital. I've got to get Cole back," Kathleen replied.

Annie looked frightened. "Do you know where they took him?" she asked.

Kathleen said, "I've got a really good idea where. The quicker I go, the better it will be. Annie, the tall man, coming in is my husband, Cadeyrin. He's injured, but he knows wounds, so let him look at Jason." Then she turned, ran down the hall and downstairs.

Wolf and Cadeyrin were in the dining room, looking around, having just come inside. She grabbed Cadeyrin, dragging him to the base of the stairs.

"They've shot Jason and taken Cole! I've got to go get him back!" she said. Then she stopped and wiped at the tears that had unexpectedly flooded her eyes. "Oh, my baby!"

Cadeyrin's face showed concern and surprise. "Your baby? Jason, Cole?" he asked.

Kathleen pulled him close. She was trembling with a combination of white-hot anger and fear. What if they hurt Cole? She couldn't think until Cadeyrin's arms went around her.

She found her presence of mind in his embrace. He was the same person, a solid, calm rock around which she had oriented her universe. She took a deep breath and then another, beginning to think clearly at last.

Cadeyrin loosened his arms and looked down at her face. "Who is Cole?" he asked, concern and interest showing in his ice-blue eyes. There was a note of tension and some other emotion that she didn't quite recognize in his voice.

She took a breath and said, "My dearest, I don't know how else to tell you, but you're a father. While you've been captured, I had to take months back here to have our baby. I couldn't rescue you while he was inside me. The laws of time wouldn't allow me to get close to you until he was born. You'll love him! I named him 'Cole, ' and he's the most beautiful boy in the world, I – I've got to get him back!"

Cadeyrin's arms tightened around her. He still looked confused and tense, but then he said, "Your baby – you mean my son?"

She nodded with her head held against his shoulder.

He placed his hand against her cheek and turned her face up to his.

She sniffled, trying to control her tears.

He said with determination, "Go now. Get my child. I'll take care of things here."

Kathleen was familiar with him. When he spoke with that tone of voice, he was absolutely serious. If she couldn't get Cole, Cadeyrin would next demand that she take him to the child so that he could free the baby. Only he wasn't strong enough.

She drew away and turned just as George charged into the room. The old man was holding a kitchen knife, waving it in the air.

"If you've hurt Kath – " He stopped, looking confused.

Kathleen said, "You missed the danger, George. This is my husband, Cadeyrin. Jason's upstairs. He's been shot, and they took Cole. I've got to get him. You take Jason and Annie to the hospital. Cadeyrin needs a gun. Get him one. He can stay here with Professor Wolf. I'll be back as soon as I can."

George shook his head dazedly, then said, "The guns are in the coat closet." He motioned to Cadeyrin. "I'll show you where they are. You get what you want."

Then he turned to Kathleen to ask, "Where's Jason?"

She waved at the stairway where Jason's feet were appearing. He was gingerly coming down the stairs, helped by Annie.

George's eyes grew large at the bloody stain on Jason's shirt.

Seeing George, Jason said, "It's nothing, Old Boy. I've been shot before. Just get me to the hospital, throw a few stitches in, and I'll be fine."

George said, "I'll bring the car around. Can you make it that far?"

Jason waved his hand in confirmation.

George grabbed Cadeyrin's wrist and pulled. "Guns in here. Come on."

They went into the kitchen, heading for the coatroom, followed by Jason and Annie with Rowena in the crook of her arm.

Kathleen squeezed past the group, then slipped past George and Cadeyrin to grab a box of ammo from the coat closet shelf. There was a nylon magazine pouch with two fully loaded magazines there also. She dropped this into her pocket, then paused by the kitchen island to open the ammo box.

She reloaded her pistol, dumped some loose cartridges in her pockets, and then looked up as Cadeyrin came back, carrying a short-barrelled shotgun.

"This will be what I need if anyone comes back here," he said, breathing in short, pained breaths. "Now, you go, but be careful. I want you back." His eyes shone as he added, "And, my son."

Kathleen took a deep breath. She was still furious. Jones shouldn't have taken her baby. The thought made her almost unable to use her formula. She made a massive effort to calm herself.

She disappeared.

One second, the room holding Cadeyrin's damaged hospital bed was empty. Then there was a slight whish of displaced air. Kathleen stood there, her pistol out.

She scanned the room. There was nothing. She was so angry that she hadn't planned well. She should have jumped to where or whenever Cole was. She thought quickly.

There was another problem that she needed to solve. Getting Cole back was critical, but the second problem was just as important, but in another way.

She had to do something to stop the group's development of time-travel. If she didn't, they'd keep bothering her and those she loved. If they eventually reached the point that they didn't need her, she suspected that they wouldn't want her alive to work against their plans. They'd kill her family and her; then they'd go on to change history, killing all who got in their way.

They'd selectively work through events a step at a time. Killing when necessary until the result was that they completely controlled the modern world. The fools didn't realize that they'd do irreparable damage to the world. They might even ensure their own annihilation. They could accidentally do something that would keep their ancestors from having children.

That was a good thought. Maybe she could do that. She mulled it over and rejected the notion. She was as susceptible as they were to changes in the time-stream. It wouldn't make it any more acceptable if she were to change time, rather than them. The ripples of a past event could be far-reaching, and she had no clear-cut way to calculate the potential damage. She could be responsible for placing humanity's existence in jeopardy.

She'd have to come up with another approach. Meanwhile, Cole was in danger. Perhaps she'd have more luck in the conference room where she and Wolf had worked on his math. She jumped.

---

Jones was sitting in the chair that Smitty had occupied. Kathleen covered him with her pistol and glanced around. There was no one else in the room.

She practically spat, "Jones, where is my baby? I want him back now!"

He jerked, his eyes widening.

"You have a baby?" he asked in astonishment. "Uh. Which Kathleen are you? I, uh, I mean, when did you come from? The Kathleen I know never had time to be pregnant."

She laughed bitterly. "That's what you think. You don't understand the first thing about time. When I was in the drugstore—surely your guard told you about that?"

Jones nodded cautiously. He was careful to keep his hands on his lap.

She continued, "When I was in the drugstore, I used a pregnancy test. I was suspicious because I couldn't jump into Cadeyrin's presence – "

Jones interrupted, "You were trying to rescue him? When was that?"

Kathleen stamped her foot in frustration and anger. "If I hadn't been pregnant, I'd have had him out of your control almost instantly, but I was expecting. That kept me out of his presence. It would have been a paradox due to the timing involved. Oh, I don't expect you to understand. Now, where's my baby?"

Jones shook his head negatively. "How did you have a baby?" he asked, still unconvinced.

She scoffed. "The usual way. It took a full nine months. I was in 1971. I was the one who won the trifecta."

His eyes widened in understanding.

She continued, "I had my baby, and then one of your men shot Jason and took Cole. Where is he? I want him now, or your life isn't going to last any longer."

Jones asked, "Jason Gridley? You rescued him?"

She raised her pistol in response and said, "In about two seconds, I'm going to shoot your knee. You'll never walk normally again. Now, where is Cole?"

In answer, Jones smiled a triumphant grin. Kathleen's finger started to tighten, but before she could fire, there was a footstep from behind her followed by a pop paired with a crackling sound. Her muscles cramped in an agonizing spasm. The pistol went sliding across the floor as she dropped.

She tried to use her formula, but the pain was so intense that she couldn't take the first step of moving her mind into the correct state.

A figure loomed over her. Someone jabbed a needle in her neck, and the pain faded, but so did the room.

It was hazy. That was the correct word: hazy. Things weren't in clear focus, and her mind didn't seem to be working correctly.

Kathleen gradually became aware that she was in a hospital bed. What had happened? Why was she here?

She raised her hand to wipe across her eyes, hoping to clear her vision, but her wrist stopped with a clink.

She slowly looked at her arm. They had handcuffed her to the rail. It came into her head in a piecemeal way. She wasn't Cadeyrin, and she wasn't nearly strong enough to rip the rail off the bed. Why...she was a captive.

She moved her head in the other direction. Someone was there.

It was Agent Reed.

"So, you're back with us now?" he asked. Then he added, "Don't bother trying to jump out of here. You're drugged. We don't think you will be able to make a successful jump, but just in case you do, we've rigged you with a fail-safe."

She must have looked puzzled.

Reed smiled slowly. "Technology has a far faster response than you do. You weren't immune to a taser. Now you're drugged with a compound that inhibits the mental state needed to jump. You probably wouldn't know its name. If it fails, though..." He grinned again, sadistically, then continued speaking.

"If it fails and you manage to jump, You've got an explosive charge taped to your back. We rigged it with a switch that requires a constant short-range signal to keep it from closing. Were you to jump out of this room, the signal wouldn't be present, and kaboom!"

She groaned. Her muscles were painful. The cramps had been intense.

She moved her lips, then tried again, "Wha...What do you want?"

Reed said, "Now, that's more like it. We gave you a lot of freedom. We thought that you'd see the light and offer to help your country, but you wanted to play hardball. If you want to play that way, you'd better be ready for the big leagues. This game isn't girls' softball. We want you to give us your formula. We'll test it, and if it works, we'll let you go. Your baby also."

Kathleen came back into herself a little more despite the drug. It seemed to have more of an effect on her emotions than her rationality. Everything felt flat and two-dimensional with no emotional charge.

"My baby? Cole? Where is he?" she whispered with an effort.

Reed said, "We just got a phone call from our agent in Minnesota. He's back in the present with a blond baby boy. Says that he shot Gridley and took the kid. He didn't know it was yours, but he figured that you'd want to rescue it anyway. Looks like he was right."

She repeated, "My baby?"

He continued as if she hadn't spoken. "He's bringing the kid here. They're on a chartered plane right now. I don't want to be cruel, so if you promise to cooperate, we'll give the baby – Cole, is it? – to you when he gets here. On the other hand, no cooperation, remember the bomb? Well, I can activate it at any time with this remote."

He displayed a small box.

Kathleen moved her hips a little. There was something under her low back. It wasn't very thick, but it was large enough to contain explosives and circuitry. She tentatively slid her back sideways, trying to see if the object would come loose. It pulled where it was taped to her sides but didn't move otherwise.

She vaguely wondered if she could jump through time, would she be able to rip the thing off her back before it exploded? No, that wasn't right. She'd have to be more creative than that, but her mind didn't want to work correctly.

She was distracted for a moment. There was a large clock on the wall. Its second hand moved in a series of small jerks, jumping from second to second. There was something about that image...That was it! A paradox! But was she strong enough to withstand the effect? The last time she'd become amnesiac for over a day. That couldn't happen. It would be a disaster.

She thought slowly. The her that had landed in the past hadn't lost her memory-only the her that had jumped from the past forward. Perhaps that meant it could work. This jump would be a tiny one. There would be very little difference between her two selves. Likely not enough to have much of an effect.

She closed her eyes as if she was exhausted.

Reed said, "That's right. Don't struggle. It won't help. Just lie there until you realize that you can't escape. Your only option is to – "

He stopped in shock as her figure blurred. The handcuffs clanked loosely on the bed.

The remote control disappeared from his lap into a slim hand that almost came out of nowhere. Then something slapped him on the neck, pulling at the lower edge of his hair. His hand went up, reaching.

He paused, his eyes opened wide. The girl was no longer on the bed. That was impossible! He reached for the back of his neck again, his face distorted in fear, but it was too late.

There was a loud explosion. Reed's headless body flew forward from the chair and landed on the floor.

— ◆ —

Kathleen was standing in an open space in July of 1400. She'd randomly selected a time when there would be little likelihood of encountering any humans or fierce beasts. She sat down shakily, discarding the remote control as she did.

Her memory was a little blurry, but that could have been the drug. On the other hand, it might be a residual effect of her brief time jump. Her past and present self had been present in the room for perhaps a second or maybe two.

The rational apparatus of her mind was clear. The drug had indeed had more impact on her emotions. A sudden realization struck her. They would have tested it on their own time-travelers. She knew from her experience that an altered mental state was necessary. She somehow was able to generate that state without the assistance of the VR glasses that Jones' people had to use.

A drug that inhibited that mental state wouldn't really have to affect the recipient's rational acuity. She'd come up with the thought that the paradoxical effect was more intense, the longer the time-jump.

That was so obvious to her now that she couldn't see why she hadn't thought of it before.

The first time she'd lost her memory for many hours, but the jump had been nearly eleven thousand years. She'd gone from the Pleistocene back to her apartment the instant before she left. That had forced her prior self to jump, and it had also partly disabled her memory. That amnesia arose from the energy pattern of her pre-jump self interfering with the pattern of her post-jump self. Pre-jump, she had no knowledge of Cadeyrin, and that circumstance had suppressed her memory of him. This time, the effect was minimal because the jump had been tiny.

She surveyed her surroundings. She was in a grassy field, entirely alone as far as she could see. She lay back into the grass and began to pull herself together.

Reed hadn't known that when she jumped through time, she had the option of not carrying things with her. He'd only known that she was always clothed and could carry guns and people.

It had been simple to jump backward a fraction of a second as she moved her arm, detaching the handcuffs by leaving them in the present, still locked, but now off her wrist.

Her doubled presence wasn't as disrupting as she had feared it would be. Her math had worked. The fraction of a second displacement hadn't bothered her. The human mind wasn't capable of responding to such a brief temporal paradox. Her memory was intact.

She'd next jumped back to the present, but changing in location, leaving the handcuffs on the bed. The bomb's circuitry hadn't realized that it had moved through time, and the continued presence of Reed's remote control kept it from exploding.

This time jump had been paired with a spatial move, placing her directly behind the seated man. She grabbed the remote control out of his lap and simultaneously jumped backward twelve hours into the small hours of the night.

The room was empty.

She ripped the bomb loose, wincing as the tape pulled the small hairs on her lower back. Holding it in her hand, she looked at the clock. There was time to rest for a bit.

Kathleen sat down in the single chair, where Reed would be in due time. Her head was still spinning from the drug. She rested, watching the clock.

After an hour of sitting, things began to clear up. She was somewhat amazed at her ability to think so quickly under pressure. The drug hadn't been as disabling as Reed had told her. Things were a little fuzzy still, but it was more an emotional fuzziness than an intellectual one. Her rationality was sharp.

She had been restraining herself for the past fifteen minutes. Her desire for Cole wouldn't wait, even though she could slide through time and collapse intervals, it didn't make it easier, knowing her baby was in someone else's hands.

She stood up, moved behind the chair, and positioned the bomb in her hands, straightening out the tape. She blinked out of that moment and found herself holding the bomb directly behind Reed.

She slapped it against his neck, pressing the tape along his jaw, then instantly jumped back to 1400, carrying the remote control. If Reed had been telling the truth about the deadman circuit, he had just become the actual dead man.

Now it was time for Cole, but she'd need a weapon first.

# Chapter Thirty-Two

# More Physical Action

Kathleen popped into her original base of operations, the house southwest of the twin cities. The place was still. She didn't know if Reed and Jones' group had ever found it, but as long as it had not been disturbed, there were more weapons in the gun safe in the hall closet.

She ran upstairs to her bedroom. Pausing at the door to glance at the bed. She had never slept here with Cadeyrin. He had always stayed in the past until he'd been injured. She wished for a moment that she'd realized the forest giants were present and hostile but then discarded the thought as non-productive. The image of the two of them in the bed was harder to dismiss.

She had not expected to find love in her life. Her sole ambition had been to show the world that she was valuable because of her research. She had buried that thought while simultaneously going through her daily ritual of looking at the extensive scars around her hips while trying to understand how her mother could have wanted her pregnancy terminated. That habit had added to her self-imposed sense of worthlessness and that, in turn, had ensured that she held herself aloof, sure that people would only see value in her as a direct result of her work.

Cadeyrin had changed all of that. When she'd found herself in the Pleistocene, her research was suddenly rendered moot. It had absolutely no survival value that she could see. His knowledge, the knowledge of what she'd initially thought of as a primitive hunter, was directly related to survival. She'd been extremely lucky to encounter him before a beast had finished her sad life. But then maybe she'd somehow pulled herself close to him. Based on her current understanding, that was more likely. The two of them were meant to be together. She sighed and ran her hand through her hair, then shook her head decisively.

The quicker she got her baby back, the quicker she'd be back in his arms. That was the important point. The two individuals she loved most in all the moments in time were waiting for her.

She dressed quickly, shedding the flimsy hospital garb they'd had on her. The open back gown had been handy. She'd been able to rip the bomb off easily.

Once dressed and back downstairs, she spun the dial on the safe, opened the door, and took out a slim nine-millimeter pistol. This one was easily concealable yet still held plenty of rounds. Tucking the firearm into her waistband, she closed her eyes, trying to generate the most intense feeling of Cole's presence she could. There would be little room for error.

For a moment, she feared that she was too upset to pull the time jump off correctly, but then she remembered the incredible sweetness of Cole's little face as he rolled his head in her arms to latch onto her breast. That was the connection she needed and also the motivation that jolted her into a pure action mode.

She took a deep breath and disappeared.

— ◆ —

There were two adult passengers in the business jet, not counting the pilot and co-pilot. They were currently approaching Chicago, and the flight had gone smoothly.

A man dressed in clothing reminiscent of military battle dress sat in one of the seats, drinking a cocktail and watching a woman trying to calm a screaming baby.

The woman abruptly looked up, and her eyes widened. The cocktail went flying as the agent jumped to his feet and spun around, but it was too late. There was a sharp crack, and he dropped into the aisle.

Kathleen waved the smoking pistol and said, "That's my baby, and I'm taking him now. You put him down on the seat, carefully, and then back up towards the cockpit. If you're cooperative, there will be no need for more violence. If you try something…Well, you just saw what happens when someone threatens my child. Now, move."

She waved the pistol peremptorily.

The woman started to do as she'd been told.

She stood and placed Cole on the seat.

As she backed up, the curtain that divided the cockpit from the cabin moved, and the co-pilot leaned around the corner with a pistol.

Kathleen shot him instantly. His body spasmed, setting his pistol off, firing three shots. One struck the other woman in the back, and the other two smashed through a window in the cabin.

The cabin pressure dropped like a stone, and the vacuum lifted Cole off the seat. Kathleen, already lunging forward, just managed to catch his left foot as he flew past her.

The plane nosed over and began a steep dive. Either the pilot had lost control, or he was heading for the deck to regain cabin pressure. Kathleen didn't wait to find out. She jumped through time as quickly as she could, holding tight to his foot.

⸺ ⸱◦⸱ ⸺

She dropped her pistol on the dining room table in Nisswa and gathered the screaming Cole into her arms, crooning to him. He hiccupped, then burped. His foot was red from the strength of her desperate grip.

His eyes opened wide in surprise, looking over her shoulder, then two strong arms encircled both her and the baby as Cadeyrin met his son for the first time.

She turned slowly within his arms. His face was shining as he looked at her, then looked down at the baby boy.

Cadeyrin said, "Before I met you, I'd given up on my life. I was wandering in the forest, just living from day to day. I'd lost my wife, my father, and my tribe. Somehow the spirits saw fit to give me another chance. I fell in love with you the moment I saw you in the tree with the Sabertooth below. It took me so long to win you that I almost gave up a second time. Then you began to love me back. My life since then has been a thing of wonder, a thing none of my people would be able to understand, let alone believe. Now, you've given me the most wonderful present you could. I – " His breath caught for a moment, then with an effort, he gasped out, "I have a son." A tear trickled down his left cheek.

Kathleen's eyes teared up in response, and she pushed herself against his muscular body. She was so lucky in this man. He was intensely masculine but still able to express his emotions. Warmth suffused her lower abdomen at the thought.

He added, "My life has been so much more than I ever dreamed it could be. Even journeying to the spirit world didn't predict this."

He tightened his arms around her, then looked deeply into her eyes. "Kathleen, you're my miracle, my wife, and my spirit mate."

He looked down at Cole. "This boy is perfect. Such a strong young one. He will be a mighty hunter."

There was an interruption of claws scrabbling on the tile floor in the kitchen, then Ulfsa came careening around the corner, his tail waving in wild circles of joy. He started to leap on Kathleen but then stopped and raised his head carefully to lick Cole's bare toes.

Cadeyrin laughed in joy. "Even the wolf greets the boy with respect. He will be a great man. It's up to us to train him properly. I want him to have the knowledge that you can give him. For my part, I will teach him about the beasts and the ways of the wild."

Kathleen laughed in happiness but then stopped short.

Cadeyrin, always sensitive to her thoughts, asked, "Something is bothering you. What?"

She answered, "I haven't finished my job in the future. I got rid of one of the conspirators, but the entire group will have to be stopped somehow."

He asked, "Which one did you kill?"

"Reed," she answered. "He won't bother us no again."

"Jones was the one that is more evil," he said. "He enjoys pain. I can see that he'll never leave us alone as long as he's alive."

Cadeyrin's eyes took on a clear, far look, like those of an eagle contemplating its next kill. He said, "He must be dealt with, but I'm not in fighting condition yet. My ribs need many days, perhaps two moons to heal properly."

Kathleen replied, "There's more. Jones and Reed worked for someone. I'm not sure that the higher-ups in the government know what they have been plotting. However, the man that wanted Annie dead is almost certainly involved somehow. I need to investigate him. Find out where he gets his orders and who pays the bills.

Cadeyrin nodded. He gently took Cole from her arms, raised the baby to his face, and inhaled the little one's scent. Then he smiled at her.

"He smells like you, and me also. I know your sense of smell isn't as keen as mine. Now I know Cole's scent. I'll be able to recognize him in pitch blackness. That's sometimes useful."

George banged in through the kitchen door carrying Rowena. Annie came after, helping a bandaged Jason.

Kathleen asked, "How is he?"

Annie said, "The doctor told us he was lucky. The bullet went into his abdominal cavity, but it somehow pushed a lobe of his liver to the side slightly. It passed directly through and out his back without hitting anything vital. We're lucky."

Jason grinned painfully and added, "Somehow, I don't feel very lucky. It still hurts like blazes, even though I know it'll be better in a few days."

Annie suddenly realized that Cadeyrin was holding Cole.

"Oh, my God, Kathleen!" she exclaimed. "You got him back. How did you do it?" She moved forward to caress her friend's child.

Kathleen said, "It was complicated, but never, ever get between this mama bear and her baby."

The men all laughed, Jason a little gingerly. George added, "That's the ticket, young lady. Us guys haven't a chance when a mama is defending her young."

# Chapter Thirty-Three

# Planning and S'Mores

That evening, they built a fire in the middle of a grove of old pines. Cadeyrin kept it small and in control, carefully arranging the wood, so there were few sparks. Some wooden Adirondack chairs provided comfortable seating. The two babies were content to lie on a blanket spread strategically between Kathleen and Annie. They discussed the situation as they watched the flames.

Gridley and Annie were unanticipated resources. His knowledge of the military somehow encompassed more about Reed's operation than she knew. Annie, having worked for Senator Rasmussen, knew that he provided oversight and somehow channeled funding for the operation. She had a suspicion that he was either working with or for someone else, a shadowy figure who was behind the initiative.

"I need to know who's ultimately behind the time-travel operation," Kathleen said.

Professor Wolf swallowed the last piece of the S'more he was eating, then wiped his lips with his sleeve. "Kathleen, maybe I can add a little. When Logan Walker's actions forced me to understand that time-travel was possible, I began to work with him. He was invaluable in the development of my thinking. He wasn't good with math at the start, but that young man had so much motivation, he applied himself. I know now that he wanted his Pleistocene girlfriend back in the worst way. He thought that he could kill two birds with one stone. Helping me allowed him to generate the needed credits to graduate on time, and also might have led to the knowledge to get Serenesa back. Uh...I believe I'd like another one of those S'more, please."

Annie laughed and fitted another marshmallow on an empty stick, then handed it to Wolf. He leaned forward to hold it over the embers, then continued.

"We published an article about the concept. It wasn't long before some group contacted me about time-travel. I was uneasy about the contact. It was…" He paused to place the toasted marshmallow on a chocolate bar sandwiched between two graham crackers.

"Hmmph. Well, err, as I was saying. It was somehow suspicious. The way it happened, I received a phone call from someone asking about the feasibility of time jumps. The individual refused to identify himself and had blocked caller-id. He said someone would contact me." He looked at Kathleen.

"When that someone contacted me, it was a man that I've never seen since. He had a distinct accent. Probably Eastern European, but I don't know. I'm not a linguist," he said. "Anyway, they wanted me to develop time-travel for them. They'd pay for it, and I was to have a private lab set up somewhere. When I explained that I had all that I needed and my students would suffer by my absence, the response was disconcerting, if you know what I mean?" He looked around the circle to make sure that everyone was paying attention.

"I was told that I'd work for them in one form or another. I said that I didn't need money and a lab, while nice, wasn't necessary. All I wanted was a chalkboard. I like to do my calculations the old-fashioned way. In chalk. Later that same day, I was called by Senator Rasmussen. He said that I was onto something that would significantly enhance national security. Well, I could understand that, but I could also see by that point that there was tremendous potential for abuse. Time-travel is probably the most dangerous idea that man has ever come up with, notwithstanding nuclear bombs."

He paused, then looked at Kathleen bemusedly, then said, "Uh, I meant man, in the generic sense of humans. It should really be 'woman.' Kathleen, your research is ahead of mine, and from your results, you have a far better understanding than I."

Kathleen shook her head impatiently. "That's not essential to this conversation. I can give you my formula. It's not as complicated as your approach. You have an archaic way of dealing with some of the calculations that seems to lead you off on a tangent."

He looked hurt but continued. "Err. That may well be. You have to remember that I'm an old man. I learned my math a long time ago. It's been adequate till now. So...Well, let me finish. Rasmussen made it clear that I had no choice in the matter. He said that once I demonstrated my theory would work, that I could go back to teaching. I was a little unhappy that I wouldn't be allowed to publish, but he promised to see that the University Physics Department got some significant federal grant money. Since I had no choice, I went to work for Reed's group. Rasmussen would sometimes come by, but he never spoke directly to me in person."

He paused to take a bite of the now cold S'more. "Cold, but it's still good," he said. "There was one thing, however. I was working on the chalkboard with the door open. Rasmussen had just looked in at me. He and Jones were talking in the hallway. I don't believe they thought I could hear them. For a fact, I couldn't hear very well. Old man and all that. However, I did hear Rasmussen say something about they should try to make me hurry; he was getting impatient. Then he said, and this I heard clearly, 'You know what that means. Someone is going to be sanctioned if results aren't forthcoming quickly.' That's about the extent of it. As a result, they tried to push me to work faster. I was almost ready for testing at that point. Logan had made his trips under the influence of psychedelic drugs, and I'd come up with the idea of the VR headset to substitute for that. It wouldn't be useful to have our time-traveler have to wait hours to metabolize a mind-altering drug out of his system. He might get killed before he could respond sensibly. Uh, I'm digressing, aren't I?"

Grid said, "I don't think you can help it, Professor. You just like to lecture."

Wolf looked at the group, frowned, then smiled. "I do like the sound of my own voice too much. I'll finish quickly. We had some successes, but we lost Jason here. I don't know what happened to him, but apparently, Kathleen was able to get him back. You already know most of the rest."

Gridley swore under his breath. "Your time-travel system worked. The problem was not in your calculations. It was because they wanted me to assassinate Ronald Reagan, and they didn't want me coming back to haunt them when I understood the result."

Wolf grew pale. "Why in Heaven's name did they want to do that?"

Grid said, "Their end goal is to change history so that they control the world in the present time. They think they can manipulate themselves into power if they make enough small changes. Killing Reagan was just a test case. Hinckley was almost successful. Reagan nearly died, so it wouldn't have been a big change to have him die as a result of the shooting. I don't know what the outcome of the change would have been, err...or what they thought it was going to do. Probably something that would help them. Anyway, when I tried to return, the VR program was set so that I ended in the Cretaceous."

He paused and grasped Annie's hand. "They'd already killed Annie. She knew too much. I'll never be able to pay Kathleen back for getting my wife back to me, and Rowena, too, of course."

Annie said, "I can't add much, save that one of the emails I saw was from a non-profit organization. It was something like Humanity for the World or maybe for the Future. I can't remember too clearly."

Kathleen repeated, "Humanity for the Future. I can get Geoff to fund an investigation of any group with a similar name. Maybe we'll find out something that way."

Wolf raised his head and asked, "Did you say Humanity for the Future?"

Kathleen said, "Yes, why?"

He licked a bit of chocolate off a finger and said, "I got the impression that they were somehow related to the first people to approach me about time-travel."

Kathleen asked, "So Humanity for the Future is a legitimate group, then? That's the correct name?"

He said, "Yes. I'm sure of it."

Kathleen said, "So, I'll get an investigation started into them. That's our first step. Now, what's next?"

Annie asked, "Are we safe here? Won't the government people just come after us? They know where and when we are."

Kathleen nodded slowly. They do. We should jump out of here, but I'm a little reluctant to go to our home in the Sangamon. There are hostile hominins there. They broke Cadeyrin's ribs. Taking the babies to the Cretaceous might be a possibility, but it's not a long-term solution. We can't stay in the past forever. We'll need things that we can only get here or, uh, maybe in our home time."

Grid said, "The Cretaceous would be good. I'm worried about the girls and their families. I'd like to check on them."

"Okay, then that's settled. I'll get Geoff to start researching this non-profit, and we'll wait in the Cretaceous, just to be safe," Kathleen summarized.

Cadeyrin stretched, yawned, and then said, "We could spend one night in this house. The bed looked very comfortable." He looked at Kathleen out of the side of his eye.

Flustered, she stuttered, "We...we could go first thing in the morning. That should be okay. We'll just keep our weapons handy."

The fire was mostly burned out, with just a few embers glowing in the darkness. Gridley dragged a garden hose over and put it out, carefully soaking the entire bed of coals.

They went inside. By the time she and Cadeyrin had gotten Cole arranged on a makeshift pad on the floor, where he was watched closely by Ulfsa, Kathleen's breath had become more rapid. She felt a warmth in her body that needed cooling. Cadeyrin turned out the lights, leaving the moonlight shining off the lake as the only illumination in the room.

They intended to be quiet so as not to wake Cole, but Kathleen forgot where she was in the joy of the moment. They stopped as the baby cried out. Ulfsa shoved his nose against Cole's back, and the child was still again. After a moment, Kathleen cried out once more. Cadeyrin silenced her with a kiss.

# Chapter Thirty-Four

# Things That Go Bump

Ulfsa whined softly. Cadeyrin's muscles tightened, and Kathleen raised her head sleepily as the pillow of his shoulder became rock hard.

He said, "There's something wrong." He moved quietly to the edge of the bed, then opened the closet with the firearms.

Kathleen paused, then looked around in alarm. He was right; something was wrong. She didn't know what she sensed, but there was a feeling of wrongness. There was something outside in the dense evergreens, something dangerous. Ulfsa was now standing in the doorway, his ears flat and his back fur ridged. His lips were drawn back in a silent snarl.

She whispered, "Get the guns. I'm going to take Cole to the basement. I'll wake Grid, and Annie can bring Rowena down. Get a pistol for George. He can use one. I don't know about the professor."

Cadeyrin made no response, but she could hear the muffled click of weapons striking together as he gathered what he needed.

She picked up Cole and started for the stairs, but Cadeyrin forestalled her.

"Wait. They might be in the house. Let me go first." He moved toward the door, pushing the semi-automatic camp rifle into her free hand as he passed.

He whispered over his shoulder, "It's got a thirty-round mag, and the safety is off. Get Cole safe before you start shooting, and be sure to move after you shoot. They'll shoot back at the flash. You go to the basement. I'll get Grid."

He was off down the stairs.

Kathleen followed, moving quietly. There was no sound in the house save the hum of the refrigerator. She passed through the kitchen and turned into the laundry. As she did, she saw a motion through the glass of the porch door. Two men were coming around the screen porch, heading for the side door.

Her breathing increased, and she practically leaped down the stairs. The basement had several smaller, enclosed areas. She carefully laid Cole on his blanket beside the sand-point well-head. The water softener and water heater provided partial shelter for him.

He sighed, then stretched his arms before dropping back to sleep. The move hadn't fully awakened him.

Kathleen slipped back to the stairwell and carefully peeked around the wall. Nothing. There was no sound from above.

A sudden movement caused her heart to skip a beat, and she raised the rifle part-way before she realized it was Annie carrying Rowena.

"Annie, get down here quickly. Put her by the water heater with Cole. That's probably the safest place in the house if the shooting is all upstairs. I need to get up there now."

Annie's eyes were wide with terror. She whispered, "I don't have a gun."

Kathleen answered, "There's a hammer on the wall by the workbench. Grab it and wait by the door. If anyone comes down without warning, hit them and do it hard."

Annie moved to the workbench and made a little noise as she fumbled for the improvised weapon.

Kathleen kept in a crouching position and crept up the stairs. She moved through the door and into the kitchen area. As she passed the door leading to the bathroom, Gridley grabbed her and pulled her into the darker space.

"Stay here in case anyone comes in from the porch. Stay down. Less likely to catch a stray round that way," he whispered.

She was quivering as she waited in the dark. Where was Cadeyrin? He might have slipped outside somehow. She knew him. It wasn't his way to let the enemy bring the battle to him. He understood the value of attack as a strategy. It would force the enemy to respond and disrupt their plan.

There was a shot from above her, followed by two more. Cadeyrin had apparently gone back upstairs and had climbed out onto the roof. There was plentiful cover there in the form of dormers and gables.

There was return fire from out in the yard. Kathleen started to move but then held still. She should get where she could shoot. There was nothing to see from the bathroom door but the other side of the hall. No one had tried to come through the outside door.

She raised her rifle and waited for a moment, then lowered the weapon. She wasn't used to this kind of thing. She should have thought of this before. She closed her eyes.

The bathroom was now empty. Kathleen had gone.

—◦—

The Deinonychus pack had grown. There were five adults and five chicks and there promised to be one more adult soon. Lolita had finally located a suitable male. The two were in the preliminary stages of courtship but had yet to commit to each other fully.

Lolita was watching the male move. He was engaged in a stylized courtship routine that could be compared to an elaborate dance. He had performed the first part without flaw and now poised on one foot, his muzzle held high in the air.

Kathleen suddenly appeared beside the balancing male. He yeeped in surprise and jumped away awkwardly, then spun, his arms opened wide, and his killer toe-claws extended in a full threat display.

Lolita leaped forward and shoved herself in front of Kathleen. The startled male looked as surprised as he could, considering that he had few facial muscles. Facial expressions were not part of the Deinonychus' repertoire.

Lolita hissed at him.

He lowered his head in submission while moving his arms indecisively. This wasn't the way courtship rituals were supposed to go. He'd tried unsuccessfully to impress a mate last year, but he'd been too immature. Now he was ready, and he liked the look of his intended, except she was doing something strange.

She had turned and was cooing and nuzzling the strange creature, giving every evidence of affection.

Now the strange one had stooped and was stroking his female's head. It suddenly hit him. The two were acting as if they were almost sisters. Part of the same pack! This was unexpected. He backed up and watched; his head cocked to one side.

Lolita said, "I have a boyfriend. A boyfriend. I wants babies. Kathleen, where your baby? Where Grid and Annie and their baby? I have a boyfriend." She made an excited squawking sound.

Before she could answer, the other two adult females and their chicks surrounded Kathleen. Belle and Fancy were equally glad to see her. Their mates were more reserved and stood back a little, but they'd reached the point where humans were an accepted part of their life.

Kathleen didn't waste any time. "Girls, listen to me. Grid and Annie and our babies are in danger. Bad humans want to kill them. I need your help. I want you to cluster together, and I'm going to move us in time. There are three other good humans besides Grid and Annie and our babies. They are two old males and one young, powerful male. He's mine. He and Grid are fighting the bad ones. They're shooting, so you have to be careful. I don't want you to be hurt. Okay?"

Lolita said, "My boyfriend come. He help."

Kathleen looked at the confused male. He was staring at the group as if he couldn't believe his eyes. She doubted that he'd be helpful. He was as likely to attack George as the bad guys.

"He might not recognize the good people. I only want the bad ones killed," she said.

Lolita cawed, then said, "He only attack ones I attack. We make no mistake."

She moved over to the male, making an exaggerated head movement, bobbing her head repeatedly and then shoving it against his neck. He looked stunned. She'd accepted his courtship, and he hadn't even finished the dance.

After a moment, he bobbed his head in response. He wasn't going to waste time. If she was happy with him, that was all that counted.

Lolita immediately nudged him close to Kathleen. He moved closer hesitantly.

Kathleen held her hand out to him. He sniffed at it. She nodded her head in greeting and received a nod back.

"Alright. I guess he will do. Lolita, you keep him under control. I'm going to move us into some trees behind the bad humans. You can spread out and jump them. Watch for guns!"

The feathered predators moved close together until they were all touching. Kathleen couldn't wrap her arms around the entire group. A touch would do, though.

She closed her eyes.

----•----

They were in a pine forest. The small, colorful killers huddled for a moment, inhaling deeply.

Kathleen had placed them on the northern neighbor's front lot. The gunfire was originating between them and the house. She hoped no one had been hit.

She caught the girls' attention and waved them out to form a flanking action. They were past masters of this kind of hunting and were also used to taking orders from Gridley. They vanished in the darkness, the chicks following silently.

----•----

The squad leader was furious. The guy on the roof had shot one of his men, and a shot from the back downstairs bedroom had wounded another. How had they known his group was about to attack? His planned operation was in ribbons. They'd have to improvise.

He clicked his com unit and said, "L3 and L4, work around to the south side of the garage. You might have a better vantage there. L5 and 6, form up with me, and we'll move out into the yard to the north. L7 and L8, hold position and wait for anyone to break out of the back of the house. We can't let them reach the lake. There's a boat down there."

He moved along the log he was hiding behind, then looked up as something moved quickly around a tree. It was too low to be a man. It was – he screamed in mortal pain.

◆

Kathleen heard two screams from the south side of the front lot. All of a sudden, two men broke from behind trees to the north and started running towards the house as if devils were pursuing them.

Cadeyrin fired twice. Kathleen saw him move, changing position as soon as he'd shot. She smiled. The attackers weren't going to reach the house while he was on the roof.

There were more shots from the lakeside. She momentarily saw Cadeyrin run across a roof valley, keeping low and staying in the shadow. There were no more shots. Kathleen looked around as Lolita approached. Blood had splashed across her breast, and her head hung low. Kathleen turned in shock. Had she been shot?

The little raptor came up to Kathleen and said, "All dead. Dead. Dead. No more shooting. Lolita have no more boyfriend. Dead. I sad." Her voice, usually smooth, now had a quaver that seemed to betray her emotion.

Kathleen opened her arms to the disconsolate Deinonychus and hugged her tightly. The fluffy creature pushed her head under Kathleen's arm.

She said, "Oh, Lolita. I'm so sorry. He was very brave."

Lolita said, "No. No. Not brave. Just too slow. He not know about guns."

Kathleen said, "You will find someone else. I'll make sure you do."

She suddenly remembered that Cadeyrin didn't know about the Raptors. He might shoot at them. Kathleen yelled, "Stop shooting. They're all dead."

She jumped up and trotted towards the house, followed by Lolita. She could see Cadeyrin poised on the roof, aiming at one of the pack. His target was walking towards the house. Cadeyrin hesitated, then looked at her, then looked back again at the approaching raptor.

She went forward to meet Fancy, who was followed by her chicks. The rest of the pack came up. The only one who had been hurt was Lolita's prospective mate.

Cadeyrin went to the lowest part of the roof and swung down, then came slowly over to her.

He looked carefully at the Deinonychus pack, then asked, "What are these things? Where did they come from?" He looked sternly at her. "And, why are you out here? I wanted you safe in the house."

Grid came out of the house before she could answer. The girls greeted him with excited chirps and clustered around his legs, vying for his attention. The chicks made yeeping sounds and pushed close. Only the two adult males hung back. Finally, one of them came over to Kathleen and tentatively bobbed his head in greeting. She bobbed back.

Cadeyrin watched their greeting and immediately copied her movements. The male hesitated, and Cadeyrin bobbed again. This time, the male bobbed back.

Kathleen smiled. Her husband might be uneducated by modern standards, but he was very quick to understand. Knowing animals as he did, he instantly recognized the greeting and emulated it.

She got Gridley's attention and asked, "Is everyone else okay?"

He nodded, his arms full of feathered dinosaurs. "All fine, but the babies are screaming their heads off down in the basement. Ulfsa and Annie are down there with them."

She could hear a police siren in the distance. The situation was a mess. Dead men all over the place. The whole street had to be awake, and people were probably huddling in their basements in terror. It would undoubtedly make the news in the Twin Cities. That record would be instantly available to Jones. He'd know his attack had failed.

She said, "Let's go. Everyone inside. I've got to get Cole, and we need to gather supplies. We're going to the Gridley's cave for now, maybe to the Sangamon later. Come on, hurry. The police will be here in a few minutes, and there's no way we can explain what happened. They can't see the pack, either. Hurry!"

⸺◆⸺

They entered the house in a loose group. Kathleen grabbed at Ulfsa as he charged out of the laundry room door, heading for Belle. The Deinonychus backed against the wall, holding her clawed arms outspread in a defensive posture.

Kathleen said, "No! Ulfsa. Friends."

He looked at her in confusion. The feathered creatures smelled of blood. They'd been fighting.

Kathleen held onto his furry ruff and pulled Lolita close with her free hand. The small raptor leaned against her knee as Kathleen stroked her neck. Ulfsa relaxed slightly, then cautiously sniffed at the stranger's feathered coat.

He sneezed, then sniffed again.

Lolita extended her head and sniffed at his side, then buried her muzzle in his fur. She pulled back quickly. "He have thick feathers."

Ulfsa wagged slightly, and Lolita sniffed at his back leg. She raised her head and said, "He boy. Hi, boy, You like Lolita?"

The wolf responded by sniffing her again.

Lolita asked, "Why he no talk?"

Kathleen was worried. They were running out of time. She said, "He can't talk, Lolita. I'll tell you about him later."

Lolita watched Ulfsa intently. The wolf had his eyes on Kathleen, seeking cues about the situation.

Lolita said, "Look! He think you his Mama. Hey, boy. Annie is Mama, too. Lolita want be a mama. Maybe we be friends. Okay?"

Kathleen laughed in spite of her worry. "Lolita, he isn't as smart as you. He knows 'pack' though. He thinks we are all in the same pack. Now go on and follow Grid."

———————◇———————

There was space in the living room for everyone to gather close, even though the old men and Ulfsa kept as far from the blood-covered raptors as possible. Everyone was carrying something; even the chicks held some folded blankets.

Kathleen said, "Okay. Get ready. There may be some creature nearby when we get there. Keep the guns ready in case it isn't friendly."

Gridley had opened his mouth but shut it when she spoke and reinforced her statement by nodding.

The sirens had stopped when the police arrived at the garage. There was a pounding at the front door, and Kathleen took that as a signal. She shut her eyes and transported the entire group into the distant past.

———————◇———————

Geoff was sitting in a coffee shop, trying to read something on his phone while drinking a latte. He was due in court in an hour, so he needed to get back to his office to gather his materials. He started to rise but then set back down as Kathleen walked through the door and came over to sit with him.

"Hi, Kathleen. I'm glad you're here. We have a problem. Unfortunately, I don't have much time. Got to be in district court shortly," he said.

She smiled tiredly. "That's okay. I'm only here for a few minutes. Let me tell you why and then you can tell me about the problem." Without waiting for him to answer, she continued, "I need you to hire the necessary people to do a thorough investigation of Humanity for the Future. I want to know everything about it, especially where their money comes from and who is behind the group."

He paused, his coffee cup lifted part-way.

"That's a non-profit, isn't it?" he asked.

"Yes. I've got a reason to think they're behind the government time-travel initiative. In fact, I'm suspicious that the government doesn't officially know about time-travel. It's what might be called a black op, or maybe even it's totally private. I want to know, anyway," she said.

He considered. "That might be expensive. Good investigators don't come cheap, and this could involve work all over the world. I don't know how much it would cost. Are you sure you want to do this?"

Kathleen said, "Geoff, I'm dead serious about this. If you have to spend every cent I have, I want to know all about this group, so please just get it done."

"I can see you're serious. So, that brings me to the problem. The IRS has finally frozen all of your accounts. Now, they say there are taxes owed." He frowned as he dropped this bomb.

She moved restlessly in response, then said, "Is there enough free cash or stocks to sell so that we could get this investigation moving?"

He said, "No. They've been thorough. Everything is under their control. We're trying to get answers, but they aren't being responsive."

Kathleen said, "I don't have time for this right now. Look, Geoff. Your firm has administrative control of an old trust. It's the George Schwartz "K" trust. Do you know about it?"

He laughed. "How did you find out about that thing? It's been in the partnership for nearly fifty years. Every new partner is told about it. The beneficiary, George Schultz, died a few years ago, but we're prohibited from doing anything with the trust by its wording. There's a mysterious sealed envelope that is part of the thing. It apparently contains additional instructions, but it's not to be opened – "

She interrupted him. "Until someone shows up who can correctly quote the cover of the envelope. It says, 'Further instructions for disposition of trust assets in the event of the apparent death of George P. Schwartz.' The word 'apparent' was inserted deliberately."

His jaw dropped. "You...you had something to do with this, didn't you?"

She nodded. "The letter contains instructions that specify me as the beneficiary of the trust. By now, the value will be several million dollars, depending on the current stock market, of course. I want you to sell the stock and use that to pay for this investigation."

He said, "I'll get it started. There will be a little legal work involved, but I should have the money free by next week. Takes three days to settle the brokerage account after a sale, you know."

She nodded silently.

He asked, "Did you know you'd need the trust money? How did you decide to set that up?"

She said, "Didn't know I'd need it. I spent time in 1971, and I was initially trying to set up money that was usable during that period. You just can't withdraw bills from now and then expect to spend them in the past. That wouldn't work well. So, I started a fundraising operation with old silver dollars. Then I got the idea to bet on a sporting event. I won the trifecta at the 1971 Kentucky Derby."

He laughed out loud. "That's incredible. You cheated, though, didn't you? Won't that make a difference in the world somehow?"

"Not that I can see. The only people who were out of anything were the bookmakers. History says there was a certain amount of money bet at the race. It apparently didn't make much difference that I took some and bought a house, rather than it remaining the property of some bookmaker somewhere. I've been as careful as I can be not to make any irrevocable changes in our world."

He asked, "Are you sure your interfering in the past won't make a difference?"

"I'm relatively confident it won't, but there's no guarantee. My math only goes so far. There are things I'm still discovering about time, but I haven't observed any changes so far. That's not the way it will be if the government has its way. They intend to interfere with history and change the modern world," she said, frowning.

He shuddered at the thought, then asked, "How will I contact you about the investigation results or if there is any problem?"

She said, "I'll contact you in four days and then weekly after that. This is urgent. These people are dangerous, so you be careful. I don't want you hurt. I've set them back, but their organization still has plenty of resources. By the way, they're probably the ones that sicced the IRS on me. They're trying to make things difficult unless I cooperate."

Geoff shook his head negatively and said, "Wow. What do you think they are doing? What's their long-term plan? It could help me direct the investigators."

She said, "In brief, they're trying to own the world. Their current time-travel method is too cumbersome to be effective in all situations. They want my formula. It will give them immense power. They have no qualms about killing to achieve their goals, so you watch out."

The two stood and walked towards the door in silence. They headed down the street towards Geoff's office, but Kathleen made a quick turn into an alley. Geoff watched her from the street.

She turned and waved at him, then disappeared. He leaned forward in surprise, looking at the suddenly empty alley, then smiled and hurried towards his office.

# Chapter Thirty-Five

# Investigation and a Mate

Kathleen was waiting in Geoff's office when he entered in the morning. He jumped in surprise, then said, "You're going to give me a heart attack sometime if you keep this kind of thing up."

She shrugged and said, "It's been four days. I said I'd check in now. How's the work going?"

Geoff placed his briefcase on the floor beside his desk, opened it, and pulled out a couple of sheets of paper. He had covered them with handwritten notes.

"This is what I've been told so far," he said. "I hired an investigation firm I've used before. They haven't had any trouble with the research. The public record for Humanity for the Future is easily available. It was formed as a non-profit in Maryland and has been operating as a charity, soliciting donations and handing out grants to academic researchers. The research they are sponsoring is supposed to be social in nature. They seem to have an interest in how to shape public opinion using social media. Oh, and they're also interested in developing progressive curricula, stuff that ultimately ensures that students don't learn much about history, civics, and economics. If I were going to judge, it looks like they'd like to make sure that the populace is uneducated and compliant."

"Okay. But what about the people behind this group?" she asked.

"I was getting to that. Senator Rasmussen is involved peripherally. He apparently arranged a grant for physics research. I'm presuming that's the time-travel initiative. They've spent some big money on that," he said.

He scanned the second page quickly. "There isn't any clear lead on a backing group, but the initial information points towards Kenally Mondassin. You know who he is?"

"Sort of. Isn't he from some European country, maybe Austria or somewhere nearby? I read somewhere that he's worth billions. He supports a lot of socially disruptive political movements, I think."

"Yes, that's mostly correct. Here's his bio." He pulled a printed sheet out of his briefcase and handed it to her.

She glanced at it. "I'll read it later. Right now, I've got enough. I'll check back in next week. You be safe. I can't emphasize too much how bad these people are. Don't let them find out that you're investigating them. Uh, any news about the IRS freeze?"

He shook his head. "No, they still haven't responded. We may have to appeal to an elected representative to get any movement out of them."

"Keep trying. I might eventually need that money," she said with a smile.

Geoff remembered something that had piqued his curiosity. "Why does the envelope mention the 'apparent' death of George Schmitz? Our records show that he died in Nisswa in 2001."

Kathleen looked past him. Her eyes were far away as she answered. "I just left him in the Cretaceous a few minutes ago, so he's not dead to me."

Geoff looked confused. He opened and closed his mouth, at a loss for words.

Kathleen continued, now looking directly at him, "Let me ask you something: Is anyone ever really dead? Especially if I can visit them whenever I want in the past?"

He started to say something in response, but before he could, she blinked and disappeared.

⸺◈⸺

They had concluded that Lolita was depressed. She wasn't acting in her usual fashion but was spending a lot of time by herself, sitting on a rock ledge that overhung the cave entrance. She wasn't interested in eating and didn't even show much interest in the two human children or her nieces and nephews. That last was unusual for her.

It was depressing for the rest of the group. Everyone recognized that she was sad, but no one knew what to do about it. Finally, Grid asked Kathleen if she could help.

Kathleen had spoken to Geoff about the investigation and was now waiting for the requisite four days. Forced to abide by the odd laws of the time-stream, she couldn't simply jump away from Geoff into his future four days later. She had to wait through the entire four-day period. There was an odd restriction that prevented her from jumping into her own future more than a few seconds. She still hadn't figured that out.

She was working on her theory. This prohibition had something to do with the indestructibility of information. If she moved into her future, she would inevitably gather information that was not present in the past. It couldn't be forgotten or erased, and the result of a successful future jump would be to create a serious disruption of the time-stream.

She'd been extremely puzzled by the fact that she had no difficulty taking Cadeyrin into what was, for all intents and purposes, the future for him. She'd finally decided that the individual executing the jump was the determining factor. He had no ability to transfer through time, and that somehow made the difference. Her thinking hadn't gotten beyond this point, although she was working on it in her spare time.

Gridley caught her coming out of the cave, carrying Cole. Cadeyrin was sitting at the fire pit in the common space, waiting for the baby.

"Kathleen, is there anything you can do for Lolita? She's breaking my heart," Gridley said.

She handed Cole to Cadeyrin and smiled maternally as her husband's face lit up with pride.

"I've been thinking about that. There aren't many of her species in this area. For the most part, they don't do well in mountainous terrain. I talked to Fancy and Belle. They found their mates down on the plains. I think we could jump back through time a couple of years while moving down there. Maybe that would allow her to find someone."

He nodded. "That could work. Will you take Cadeyrin with you? What about Cole?"

She said, "It might be dangerous. I'll just take Lolita. If it's just the two of us, I can keep close to her and yank her out of trouble, if need be."

Gridley looked up and waved at the small raptor. She was staring out over the tops of the trees and didn't notice him until he whistled.

He motioned for her to come down, and she slowly stood and threaded her way down the steep path.

When she came within speaking range, he said, "Lolita, Kathleen is going to take you to the plains to find a mate. It might be dangerous down there, so you stay close to her. She can jump you both back here quickly."

Lolita made a small grunt of surprise, then said, "No one for me. I want babies, but no mate here. Maybe down on plains?" She looked up at Kathleen questioningly.

Kathleen stroked the colorful feathers of the raptor's neck in a way that she knew Lolita liked.

"I think we can find someone for you down there. We'll keep looking until we're successful. I'd like you to have babies, too."

Lolita looked more animated than before. "When can we go? I wants now."

For an answer, Kathleen walked back into the cave and came out with her rifle.

Cadeyrin stood, carrying Cole, and came over to her.

"I heard what you were discussing. She needs a mate, or she's going to lose all interest in living. I think it's a good idea for you to go, but this is an unknown land to me. There are dangerous animals, more down there than up here. Will you be careful? Jump out if there is any trouble?" he asked.

Kathleen kissed him without speaking, then reached down to take Lolita's clawed fingers.

The two disappeared.

---

The humidity in the air was higher than up in the hills. The terrain was Savannah-like. Kathleen could see some large dinosaurs moving in the mid-distance. There was a waterhole near where they'd arrived.

Lolita immediately pulled on Kathleen's fingers, leading her into a thicket. The two threaded through the thorny bushes until they found an opening to peer through.

Lolita extended her feathered arm and pointed. There were some odd-shaped dinosaurs near the water. These were a type that Kathleen didn't know, but they looked like plant-eaters. They were low to the ground and heavily armored with bony plates and spikes along the sides of their bodies.

The creatures were a family grouping. The young were in the middle of the group as they moved away from the water.

The two continued to watch the action. Some of the small meat-eaters dashed out and drank. Kathleen thought these were Troodons. They were active creatures, dashing back and forth. When they reached the water, there was a bit of alarm as a small crocodile lunged out, trying to reach one.

The Troodons jumped straight in the air, then dashed away. The Croc backed into the water, hoping they'd come back, but by then, they'd moved around the edge and were already drinking. By the time the crocodile could reach their new location, they were moving away, nipping at each other in play.

Lolita said, "We waits here. Everybody got to drink, huh? Good place to see who lives here."

Kathleen started to answer, but Lolita had stiffened, watching intently as something larger pushed through the undergrowth on the far side of the pool.

The newcomers proved to be a species of plant-eating dinosaurs that Kathleen thought might be astrodons. Her lack of specific knowledge was bothersome. She'd have to become more adept at recognizing the life of this time if they were to stay here for any lengthy period.

The astrodons waded into the pool, causing water to slop over the edges. Their presence was apparently a signal that there was no danger nearby because, in less than five minutes, a group of iguanodon-like creatures interspersed with several smaller ostrich-like dinos showed up.

It looked like the smaller creatures were accustomed to relying on the Astrodons for lookouts. The big Astros' necks were at least twenty feet long, and their eyes were huge, despite the relative smallness of their blunt heads. There was at least one of them watching the area at all times, even when the rest of the herd dipped down to drink.

Lolita had frozen.

Kathleen tried to follow her sight. There. Across the waterhole in some thicker plants. A colorful, feathered head popped up for a moment.

It was a Deinonychus. Lolita said softly, "Nice. Nice boy. Any girls?"

She answered her own question almost immediately.

"No girls. There another boy down there. They hunts as a pair. Not mated yet or girls be here."

She backed past Kathleen. "You stays here. I join hunt. You be quiet."

She was gone out the back of the thicket in a few seconds.

Kathleen watched, unmoving. The two males were stalking the ostrich dinos. Of the animals at the water, those were the smallest and least well-armed.

One of the males was now looking directly across the water to an area off to Kathleen's left. He bobbed his head a bit, careful not to attract the ostrich dino's attention.

It was a tiny movement, yet one of the Astros immediately turned to look. The Deinonychus was too small to threaten the big animals, and the curious Astro, now satisfied that there was no immediate threat, dipped his head to pull some weeds out of the water. He munched the soggy mass of vegetation contentedly.

The ostrich dinosaurs had sensed something, though. They were nervously looking around, seeking some clue as to what was happening. The other male Deinonychus came charging out of a small patch of weeds. Kathleen couldn't figure how he'd managed to get in there without being seen.

The ostrich dinos leaped for the firm bank and accelerated, running directly in front of the second male Deinonychus. He jumped out and ran forward, but his timing was too slow. The ostrich dinosaurs' long legs had come up to speed, and they were running away at a much faster pace than the Deinonychus could muster.

As the ostrich dinos slowed for a moment to funnel between two nearby stands of trees, Lolita popped out from behind a tree trunk and jumped onto one of the smaller ostrich dinosaurs. She had her hand claws dug into its side the instant she struck, and her weight unbalanced it. It ran several paces in an increasing sideways mode, then fell in a thrashing mess of dust and feathers.

Kathleen watched intently. Here came the two males, looking confused if their hesitant advance was any indication.

The dust settled, and there was Lolita, standing proudly on the corpse of the ostrich dino. The first male Deinonychus stopped and hissed threateningly, but the second bobbed his head tentatively.

Lolita bobbed back. The male approached, bobbing.

In a few minutes, both males were eating while Lolita looked on. She'd taken a few bites, but Kathleen knew she wasn't hungry.

After the two had satisfied their initial hunger, the one that had responded to Lolita approached her, holding a dripping piece of the prey's thigh in his mouth.

Lolita bobbed a little bob of assent, and the male went into a courtship dance. He moved back and forth, displaying his flexibility, then posed sideways to Lolita as if to say, "Just look at how muscular I am."

This show continued for several minutes. The other dinosaurs had left the water hole, disturbed by the hunt, so Kathleen focused on the dance.

The climax was apparent. The male moved close, bobbing, then stooped low, his wing-arms held back and down in a non-threatening position, as he presented the meat to Lolita.

She took it from him daintily and gulped it without chewing.

The other male had been watching, but at the climax, he went back to eating.

Lolita moved around the waterhole towards Kathleen, her new mate following in some puzzlement. He obviously thought she would join up with him and his brother and wasn't sure why she was leading him off in the other direction.

Kathleen moved carefully out of the thicket and came into view. Both male Deinonychus froze, staring at the strange animal. They were trying to determine if she was predator or prey.

Lolita's mate, being closest, made an aborted threat display. He instantly ceased when Lolita turned to him and made a loud squawk.

The small raptor turned back to Kathleen and approached, making a cooing noise. Her mate watched, frozen in surprise.

Kathleen knelt as Lolita came up to her and the two cuddled together, Lolita making exaggerated sounds of happiness.

Kathleen said, "Don't overdo it. I don't want him to think I'm your mate."

Lolita snorted, and said, "No. He know we mated. He not know you. He watch and see what I do. Not worry, Kathleen."

When she raised her eyes from Lolita, the male had approached to within ten feet.

Kathleen extended her hand to him, trusting that Lolita would be quick enough to prevent any mishaps.

He sniffed it carefully, smelling Lolita's scent on her fingers. He abruptly made a decision. Apparently, this new creature was not harmful. He moved closer.

Lolita showed her appreciation by nuzzling his neck and cooing loudly. Kathleen was about to reach for him, but a crashing in the scrub on the far side of the pond disrupted the introduction.

A large, ugly, yellow dinosaur stalked out, pausing as it cleared the saplings to look around.

She knew what this thing was. After the first one she'd seen, she wasn't willing to wait around. It was an Acrocanthosaur, thirty feet long and maybe six or seven thousand pounds of aggression.

The other Deinonychus male had silently disappeared from the far side of the pond at its appearance.

The Acro, seeing the three of them clustered together on the far side of the pond, made a cheeping noise and then started directly for them. The pond wasn't very deep, and it waded straight through, slowing as it slogged through the muddy bottom.

Lolita's new mate dashed away but then stopped and yeeped when he realized that Lolita was remaining with Kathleen. He ran around in a worried circle but then came back and tugged at Lolita with his hand.

That was the moment Kathleen needed. Her hand was on Lolita's neck, and she instantly transferred the three of them back to the area in front of the cave.

◄O►

The new male made a surprised squawk and flopped on his side. Lolita rubbed reassuringly against him when he stood up, looking wildly around. Then she led him away from the camp towards the trees.

As they walked into the edge of the grove, Lolita said, "We be back. You waits."

# Chapter Thirty-Six

# Responsibility Means You Pay

Cadeyrin was angry with her. She had made the determination that she was going to see Rasmussen by herself. Kathleen was nervous about her plan and wished he could come, but she also wanted to make sure that Cole had at least one parent left, should anything happen to her.

That wasn't what Cadeyrin wanted to hear.

"I'm stronger than you. If there's any fighting to be done, I should be there," he said softly.

That was one of the things Kathleen loved about him. He didn't shout. The only clue that he was angry was the tightness at the corners of his mouth. She pulled him close and kissed his cheek.

He resisted a little but then gave in and turned to kiss her back.

"You know I can't remain angry when you are near," he said.

She sensed that he was about to give in.

"Yes, but I can't stay away from you. You know that. I want to take you, but you can't travel in time. I can, and I can jump out instantly. I'm not going to let anyone near enough to aim a weapon at me. Don't worry. I'll be back."

He sighed and said, "I understand. I know that I don't have enough knowledge of the future to be very helpful. I'd probably kill the wrong man or get lost." His eyes and the hard set of his mouth softened.

She looked at him with a strange feeling. She'd loved him from almost the very moment she'd seen him, even though it had taken her a long time to admit it. Her reluctance was because her self-image was one of an unlovely, unlovable, despised, scarred child. That had been so deeply ingrained in her persona that it was almost impossible to discard. If circumstances and the harsh realities of the uncompromising ice-age world hadn't forced her to abandon that image, she would have never changed.

Now his trust in her abilities healed the last, lingering part. She not only was deserving of love, but she was also someone of value. Her opinions, her judgments, her actions were important. He trusted her to take care of herself and to make the correct decisions for both of them and their child.

She leaned forward to kiss his cheek again.

This time, he moved quickly to nibble with his lips on the side of her neck, just below her earlobe. It was the exact spot that drove her wild when they were making love.

She giggled in response. She'd won the argument.

"When I get back, I'm going to teach you how to jump in time. That way, you can go wherever you want. It comes in very handy for getting away from enemies, you know."

He said, "I know. I want you back, so you have to be careful."

For an answer, she kissed him again with more intensity.

It was night, and they were sitting by the fire in front of the cave. The Deinonychus pack members were all sleeping, as were the two old men. Jason and Annie were holding Rowena on the other side of the fire. The couple was talking quietly about someone they had known in the past.

Kathleen had a moment's embarrassment but then remembered that she wasn't the old Kathleen. She was different and more assertive.

She asked, "Will you two watch Cole for a while? We're going over behind those boulders."

Annie giggled, holding her hand over her mouth, but Gridley said, "Of course. Just leave him where he's sleeping. We'll get him if he wakes up."

Kathleen stood and pulled on Cadeyrin's hand. He came to his feet quickly, and the two walked hand-in-hand to the sheltered location.

Grid and Annie watch, smiles on their faces, as the two disappeared behind a boulder.

A movement in the darkness caught Gridley's attention. Lolita came into the ring of firelight and walked up to him. Her mate remained just within the outermost flickering light of the fire, standing in the sheltering edge of the darkness.

Lolita cleared her throat and said, "I tells you I be back. He not like fire, but he learning. I teach him talk pretty soon, you'll see."

Gridley and Annie both reached out to hug the little female. She snuggled in the warmth of their embrace and then added, "I maybe lay eggses. Babies, huh?"

Annie laughed joyfully and said, "Babies for everyone."

Gridley added, "That's what we want. Babies for everyone."

———◦———

Senator Rasmussen had been having a bad day. That stupid Reed had gotten himself killed somehow, and now Jones was on the point of rebellion. Jones had sent a squad off to try to get that troublesome woman, and they hadn't come back. In fact, they'd been wiped out to a man.

He couldn't quite figure out why they hadn't noticed the articles about the "Nisswa Massacre" in the papers from 1971. It was a big enough thing that it had received extensive coverage. Jones must have missed it somehow.

He looked at the man on the other side of his desk, dropping the report he'd been reading. "Jones, why in the hell didn't you see that your team had failed before you sent them off?" His voice was querulous. He didn't like that. He didn't like showing his anger, but this was incompetence of the worst sort.

Jones sneered as he answered. "I've already told you, Rasmussen. We didn't fail until the men got back there. There was nothing in the historical record until they failed. We couldn't have known the outcome until too late. It's not that hard to understand."

Rasmussen started to reply but waited as Jones added, "For someone of normal intelligence anyway."

"That's enough out of you. I'm not putting up with impudence. I'm the Senator here, not you. You're only a hired hand," he snapped.

They both turned as the office door opened.

————— ◆ —————

Kathleen walked into the Senator's office, locking the heavy wooden door behind her.

She waved her pistol at Jones and said, "Don't try to draw it. Lift it out with two fingers and kick it over here."

"How did you get in here?" Rasmussen asked, ignoring her gun.

She said, "It's easy when you can move through time. I've locked the door. Jones kick that over here. Easy!"

The pistol slid a few feet away from Jones' chair.

Kathleen said, "That was a little too easy. You just sit there, Jones, and don't try anything. I'm here to talk to the Senator, and I'll be gone before anyone knows the door's locked.

Rasmussen had recovered enough to bark, "Now see here, young woman, I'm a US Senator. You don't have the right to bring a gun in my office and threaten me."

She interrupted before he could draw a breath and continue.

"It's too bad, too. A senator who has sold his country down the river; a man whose ambition is to destroy the country and control the remaining ruins. I have nothing but contempt for you, Senator," she said.

Her expression reinforced the words. She looked as if she'd just turned over a rock and uncovered some filth that was too nasty to contemplate.

Rasmussen leaned back from her disgusted visage and said, "I, uh, we thought you'd be patriotic enough to see that we have only the best motives in mind. Why we're going to remake the United States in the way it should have been made from the beginning. We can direct the economy, education for all, and make sure that everyone lives a productive life – "

Kathleen slammed her pistol against his desk, making a loud crack. He shut his mouth with a snap and drew back farther.

"Look here, you pompous ass. You think you can implement a Marxist centrally controlled state that will benefit everyone? It doesn't work that way. In every single attempt to create such a form of government, the only ones who end up benefiting are those at the top. Our country has already gone far down that path. Tell me, why is the middle class disappearing? Why does the top one-tenth of a percent make almost all of the money? Why is the single largest employer in the country the government? Why is the dollar almost worthless now?"

He started to reply but then drew a deep breath. It helped him regain a degree of self-control.

"Listen here, yourself, you little bitch. We're going to master time-travel with you or without you. We've already got it under nearly perfect control. Wolf has – "

Kathleen laughed in his face. "Wolf is with me. He won't be helping you any further."

Jones had been moving his feet under him as the two yelled at each other. Now they were below him, and he was ready to take action. Without warning, he launched himself out of his chair and dove for his pistol, forgotten on the carpet where his weak kick had left it.

Kathleen saw the motion and disappeared.

Jones ended up on his knees, pointing the gun at the space where she'd been.

Rasmussen stood and snarled, "Too little, too late. I don't know why I've kept you around, you worthless piece of crap."

Jones swung the gun towards the Senator. Rasmussen's eyes focused on a sudden flicker of movement. Was the woman returning? His mouth flew open, and he made an incoherent cry.

It was answered by an inhuman screech. Something with red, blue, and green colors leaped off the floor and clung to Jones' back. The man spun around with an agonized cry. The thing flew off of Jones' back as he turned and landed on the carpet to the side of the desk.

Rasmussen saw blood suddenly gush out of gashes in Jones' coat. It shot out in strong spurts, spraying the surface of the Senator's desk.

Jones started to aim his pistol at the colorful thing, but there was a gunshot from the corner behind the Senator. The bullet splatted home in Jones' side. In response, Jones swung his gun toward the corner and fired as he started to fall. His pistol fell out of his hand, the barrel still pointed in the general direction of the Senator.

Kathleen walked to the edge of the desk, a tiny thread of smoke drifting from her weapon's barrel. Rasmussen looked silently at her for a moment and then looked down at his chest, befuddled. There was a rapidly growing red stain on his shirt where Jones' bullet had entered.

The colorful creature suddenly leaped to the top of the desk, spread bloody talon-tipped arms, leaned forward, and shrieked, displaying an alarming set of pointed teeth. Rasmussen fell backward into his chair, his face pale.

He coughed, and blood trickled down his jowls.

Kathleen said, "There's only one thing I want from you, Rasmussen. That's the name of the one behind this plot."

He shook his head weakly, denying the answer.

She leaned closer, then said, "Tell me, or I'll let her have you."

He gasped, "Wh...what is she?"

Kathleen grinned a mirthless grin and said, "She's a Deinonychus. A killer dinosaur. You won't like what she'll do to you."

He laughed weakly. "Dinosaurs are big and slow. Everybody knows that."

The colorful creature snarled and spoke. "That's what you think! Stupid man. I eat you liver." It jumped forward to the edge of the desk.

He gasped again, more weakly. His breathing was shallow and sporadic. Kathleen's face showed alarm. She leaned over him and said, "I'll guess. The man behind this is Kenally Mondassin."

Rasmussen murmured, "I can't...He'll kill me if I..."

His voice faded, and his eyes closed. There was one last rattling breath, and he went limp.

Lolita watched him for a second and then calmly said, "He dead. No talk anymore. Dead."

Kathleen put her hand on the small dinosaur, and the two disappeared just as someone began hammering loudly on the solid office door.

# Epilogue 1: Feathered Death

It hadn't been a good day. Of course, he expected that sometimes. With a business empire spreading across the developed world, there were always problems. There were always solutions, also. Sometimes they cost more than other times.

Kenally Mondassin had shouted at his valet, and the man had run out of the suite in fear. His trepidation was rational. Mondassin had been known to fire his staff at a moment's notice, and sometimes, if the offense were serious enough, or if Mondassin was in bad humor for some reason, the offending servant would turn up dead in an apparent accident or suicide.

The phone call that had upset the wealthy man had come from an employee in Washington DC. The valet had overheard Mondassin swearing about an agent Reed, who was apparently incompetent. The servant had tried to maintain a low profile, cautiously arranging his employer's evening wear on the bed and pretending that he hadn't overheard the conversation.

When the call was over, Mondassin began to dress, a task in which the valet was expected to assist. Midway in the process, there was an item on the news that caught Mondassin's attention on the big television screen that hung on the wall.

A United States Senator, one Richard Rasmussen had been murdered in his office. He'd apparently been killed by an obscure member of some government agency, a Stephen Jones. Jones had also been shot. The crime scene people were having a difficult time determining what had happened. Jones' gun had fired the bullet that killed the Senator, but Jones had been shot by another gun that was not to be found. In addition, someone had tortured him. They seemed to have taken a knife to his kidneys before they shot him. There was blood everywhere.

Mondassin stood completely still during the report, then began to swear again, finally ending with cursing at the valet. That might have been bearable, but the wealthy man swung his flabby arm and clouted the valet on the neck. That was the point at which the poor man broke and ran.

He was far across town from the villa. The Mediterranean Sea shone in the late evening sun to his right. If he could catch a bus to Rome, he would do his best to lose himself in the depths of the city. He fervently prayed that Mondassin was too busy to send someone after him.

He need not have worried. At least not yet. Mondassin was angry and wanted nothing so much as to calm himself enough to plan what to do next. He pulled on his tux jacket and walked out on the veranda, then down into the several acres of garden that graced the centuries-old estate.

The plantings were lush and immaculately tended. They were laid out in a beautiful formal layout that included a three-meter tall yew maze.

The maze had numerous stone benches for resting or trysts. Mondassin enjoyed following young women into the winding paths, giving them a few minutes' start.

He always promised to set them free if they could find the exit before he found them. They never did. He made use of a camera system that overlooked the maze to locate them. Viewing the broadcast on his cell phone allowed him to track his prey down quickly.

When he caught them, they had to pay, an activity that often took place on one of the convenient stone benches. The maze was an environment that he knew well. He had engraved every turn and cul-de-sac in his memory long ago.

Midway through the passage, he stopped and sat on a bench. It was quiet here, and he felt that he was now calm enough to begin to formulate an alternate plan. There were surely pieces of the time-travel initiative to gather. He was unwilling to declare it a failure.

He gradually became aware that something was looking at him from down the way. It was hidden in shadows, low, perhaps three feet off the ground. When he focused on the object, it apparently sensed that he had seen it. It slowly walked out of the shadow into full view.

It looked like a colorful bird, but too large, and definitely odd-shaped. It came closer and then leaned forward, spreading its wings. Mondassin watched with fascination. The wings were more like arms than flight appendages.

It suddenly opened its mouth and hissed, simultaneously flexing its fingers into an open position. With horror, the billionaire saw that it had teeth and long claws. He stood and trotted laboriously towards the other end of the maze.

At the corner, he looked back. The little monster was following slowly. He turned to round the corner. There were two more of the creatures in front of him.

They sprinted forward as the one behind him screeched. He cried out, bellowing for help. In response, a flock of pigeons flew up from the fountain in the garden.

Blood sprayed over the uncaring yew hedge. The smell was metal-like, mixed with the odor of feces.

# Epilogue 2: Feathered Fun

The evening was just about ideal. The wind was from the south, blowing in gentle gusts, and the nearby trees moved in response. The view down the hill was beautiful. The wind made wave-like patterns gliding across the dry late-summer grasses. In the common area between the two houses, a group of three children played an impromptu tag game with a flock of red, blue, and green raptor chicks. The adult humans sat on the porch of Cadeyrin and Kathleen's home and watched the young ones playing in the sunset.

A blotch of color was moving far down the hill, heading towards the houses. It was the adult Deinonychus. They'd been hunting bison somewhere out on the plains.

Kathleen stood and waved. The Raptors responded with a honking sound that carried up to the homes in the wind.

Professor Wolf, who was sipping on a Mojito, paused to comment, "I can't see that they're bringing anything back. Maybe they didn't find any game."

Cadeyrin answered. "No. They have something, but they can't carry much. They are not built for it. They have a hard time bringing things back for their chicks."

Gridley came walking up with Logan Walker. The youngest couple, Logan and his Clovis culture bride, Serensaa, had been more than happy to join the group in the early Sangamon.

The climate was ideal, there was grass for their horses, and the hominins that had originally driven Cadeyrin and Kathleen out of their home had not yet appeared on the continent. Wild game was plentiful, and Kathleen had transported machinery and supplies so that their homestead was self-sufficient.

Annie stood up and walked out to separate Rowena and Ashlyn, Logan and Serensaa's daughter. The two girls were always squabbling over Lolita's baby. The chick was smaller than normal and somehow aroused maternal instincts in the two little girls.

George came out of the house followed by Ulfsa. He sat on the porch swing by Wolf. The two old men had become good friends, even though there was little commonality in their interests.

Kathleen leaned back, relaxing against Cadeyrin's chest. She held his hand and watched the waves of grass and the yellow sun as it illuminated some puffy little clouds.

All of the moments of the future stretched before her like golden pearls on a string awaiting her presence. Life was good and she was prepared to fight to keep it that way.

**The End**

# Story Notes in Alphabetical Order

I did a considerable amount of research while writing this novel. While details and actions of the dinosaurs in the story are fiction, the animals are known to science. I took the liberty of adding attributes to them in order to make the story interesting.

## ACROCANTHOSAURUS – THE DEADLY FUZZY YELLOW DUCK

Acrocanthosaurus was a theropod dinosaur from what is now North America. It was similar to an Allosaurus in that its skull was long, narrow, and relatively flat. The Acrocanthosaurus was one of the largest theropods, measuring up to 11.5 meters from snout to tail tip and weighing up to 6.2 tons. Its skull was about 1.3 meters in length, only slightly shorter than that of the largest known Tyrannosaurus Rex, although the Acro's total size and weight were less.

The distinctive feature of this creature was a rather high ridge along its spine caused by extensions that were more than 2.5 times the height of the vertebrae from which they extended. The creature was bipedal with a long heavy tail. Its legs suggested that it was not a particularly fast runner, despite being the apex predator of its time and location.

My description of the creature as being covered with yellow down and making a cheeping noise was prompted by my sense of the absurd and is almost certainly not accurate.

## ASTRODON

Astrodon was a genus of large herbivorous sauropod dinosaur, related to Brachiosaurus, that lived in what is now the eastern United States during the Early Cretaceous period. Paleontologists have estimated adult astrodons to have been more than 9 m (30 ft) high and 15 to 18 m (50 to 60 ft) long. The creatures most likely inhabited broad, flat plains with rivers, similar to coastal regions of southern North America. Astrodon lived in the same locations as the dromaeosaurid Deinonychus and the carnosaur Acrocanthosaurus. It was most likely a primary prey source for both predators.

## CRETACEOUS PERIOD

During the Late Cretaceous, starting about 106 million years ago (mya) and lasting to 66 mya, the climate was warmer than it is today. The long-term trend for the period resulted in gradually cooling temperatures that restricted the tropics to equatorial regions. Northern latitudes experienced markedly more seasonal climate.

Dinosaurs reached their apex during this period and there were many species. In this story, I've limited the fauna to some of the more common (by the fossil record) types that would have been found in what is now North America. Both primitive birds and pterosaurs could be found in the skies during this period, although they did not seem to overlap ecologically. The birds became increasingly common and diverse, diversifying in a variety of forms.

The fauna was made more diverse by the presence of cimolodonts and multituberculates which were the two most common ancestral mammals in North America. Flowering plants began to appear during this time.

The Cretaceous ended with the K-T extinction event that occurred about 66 mya. Before that time, the fossil record shows dinosaurs. After that time, it shows mammals, birds, fish, and reptiles, but no dinosaurs.

## DEINONYCHUS

Evidence suggests that the dromaeosaurid Deinonychus inhabited a floodplain or swamp-like habitat by preference. The land was covered by tropical or subtropical forests, deltas, and lagoons, not unlike Louisiana. Other animals Deinonychus shared its world with include various herbivorous dinosaurs and the large theropod Acrocanthosaurus.

The Deinonychus had an adult mass of 70 to 140 kilograms which places them roughly in the human spectrum of weight. They ranged to about 3.4 meters in length and normally carried themselves in a posture that was approximately waist-high to a human, although, in a fully upright position, they probably could look a human directly in the eye. Its skeleton suggests that it was an active and nimble predator, capable of outrunning a human. It most likely hunted as an ambush predator, lying in wait and dashing out when a prey animal came near. There is good evidence that the Dromaeosauridae family had feathers. Multiple fossils of Microraptor have been found with feathers and that animal is in the same family, although more primitive than Deinonychus.

Eggs from the Deinonychus species are estimated to have a diameter of 7 centimeters (2.7 inches). Skeletons of various sizes have been found together, indicating that the creature cared for its young and possibly hunted in packs. Its primary prey seems to have been the ornithopod dinosaur Tenotosaurus, although it was possibly capable of bringing down larger animals. The tenotosaurs were larger animals, ranging between 1 to 4 tons and most likely unkillable by a single Deinonychus, thus the supposition that they hunted in packs.

The most noticeable aspect of the Deinonychus was its large, sickle-shaped talon on the second toe of each hindfoot. This talon has been reconstructed as being nearly five inches in length (120 mm). This fearsome talon has been hypothesized to be the creature's main weapon.

It has been estimated that the related creature, Velociraptor, was approximately as intelligent as a rather dull chicken. In order to add interest to this story, I made an artistic decision that the Deinonychus was more intelligent than a modern African Grey Parrot. African Grey's have been shown to be able to learn vocabularies of more than 1,000 human words and can use the words correctly and even creatively to express thoughts, including humor. If the Deinonychus was on that level of intelligence, then my Deinonychus characters become more believable. Regardless of the realism or lack thereof, I had a lot of fun writing about them.

## GASTONIA

Gastonia is an herbivorous ankylosaurian dinosaur from the Early Cretaceous of North America. Low and flat, it had heavy armor in the form of a bony shield across the lower back and large shoulder spikes. It was medium-sized in terms of its relatives, with a length of about five meters and a weight of approximately two tons. It probably was more or less indifferent to attacks from all but the largest predators. Its armor and spike weaponry would have been sufficient to discourage any but the hungriest carnosaur. The tail was moderately long and lacked the tail club that similar species displayed.

## HOMO HEIDELBERGENSIS - THE FOREST GIANTS

Homo heidelbergensis is an extinct species of the genus Homo that lived in Africa, Europe, and Asia up until about 600,000 years ago.

The skulls of this homonin indicate that its brain was nearly as large as that of Homo sapiens. Homo heidelbergensis appears to have been the ancestor of Neanderthals, Denisovans, and modern humans (which arose around 130,000 years ago). Homo heidelbergensis appears to have migrated into Europe and Asia somewhere around 125,000 years ago. It is not known to have found its way to North America.

Males of the species averaged about 1.75 m (5 ft 9 in) tall and possibly weighed a light 62 kg (136 lb). Females averaged 1.57 m (5 ft 2 in) and 51 kg (112 lb). This is based on a reconstruction of limb bones. However, according to Lee R. Berger of the University of the Witwatersrand, significant fossil findings show that the species had some populations that averaged over 2.13 m (7 ft) tall. If these taller individuals' weight was proportionate to their height, they would have been as large and possibly heavier than the largest modern humans.

My Forest Giants are the result of my speculation that a population of such creatures somehow survived the advent of modern humans by retiring into wilderness areas where humans seldom came. They could have migrated to the new world earlier than humans. If they survived, using the same reclusive strategy, they could have been present at the time this story begins. Tails of their presence along with modern humans could have been handed down verbally from generation to generation, resulting in the ongoing belief in Sasquatch/Bigfoot.

If these creatures were few in number and extremely reclusive, they might have found areas of wilderness in North America where they could survive relatively unnoticed.

## IGUANODONS AND HADROSAURS

Iguanodontoids are often included in the Hadrosauroieda superfamily. The Iguanodons were large herbivores that could stand upright but probably preferred to walk in a quadrupedal mode. They have been estimated to weigh 3.5 tons and to be about 10 meters (33 feet) in length.

My usage of them in this story is problematic. The characters could have mistaken one of the various hadrosaurs for iguanodons, although the observation of a thumb spike would be a good indication that the animal was actually an iguanodont.

## MICRORAPTOR

Microraptor was one of the smallest non-avian dinosaurs. Adult specimens can be up to 83 centimeters long (2.72 ft) and possibly weighed 1 kilogram (2.2 lb). They were also among the first non-avian dinosaurs discovered with evidence of feathers and wings. Their feathers included long flight feathers on their legs as well as on their wings and their bodies were thickly covered with long plumes on their head.

Careful analysis of their remains indicates that they displayed a black, glossy coloration similar to many modern birds. Their feathers may also have shown iridescence. Microraptors may have been nocturnal predators and the dark coloring might have helped them ambush prey. They were an ancestral species to the Deinonychosaurs although the two may have overlapped and been present at the same time.

## SANGAMON PERIOD

The Sangamonian Interglacial Stage is the term used to designate the last interglacial period in North America. It ranged from 75,000 to about 125,000 years ago. It was a period of diverse mammalian species in North America, where the large animals roamed freely prior to the arrival of human populations. The climate was favorable and winters were generally mild in lower latitudes.

## TENONTOSAURUS

Tenontosaurus was a medium-to-large-sized herbivorous ornithopod dinosaur. It was about 6.5 to 8 meters (21 to 26 ft) long and 3 meters (9.8 ft) high in a bipedal stance, with a mass of somewhere between 1 to 2 tons. It had an unusually long, broad tail, which was stiffened with a network of bony tendons.

## TROODON

Troodon were smaller dinosaurs. When standing upright, they were possibly waist-high to a human. They were up to eight feet in length, a good part of which was neck and tail. They may have weighed up to around 100 pounds and the largest specimens are similar to Deinonychus in size, although they probably averaged smaller. Their limbs suggest that they were quick and agile. The retractable curved claw on their foot reinforces the idea that they may have been predators. Their eyes were large enough to allow them to hunt at night and they also had some amount of depth perception. Troodon had a large brain relative to their body size. They were probably a match in intelligence to some modern birds. They seem to have matured into their full size by 3 to 5 years of age.

# About the Author

Eric S. Martell set out to become a scientist when he was five. He has a PhD. in experimental psychology. When personal computers came along (way back in prehistory), he became adept with them and spent years in software design, working on projects that ranged from early childhood learning software to military training. He has been trained in various types of energy healing, is an expert in real estate investing and sales, and holds a black belt in Tae-Kwon-Do. He is also a pilot, scuba diver, guitar player, outdoorsman, and is addicted to both science and science fiction.

Eric's science fiction books offer both believable science and compelling characters set against realistic action. They are carefully researched, and, while his fictional science sometimes strains against the bounds of current knowledge, it is always plausible. His stories cover alien invasion in an apocalyptic setting, political structure, space travel, advanced weapons, quantum physics, hunting, war, romance, time travel, and alien worlds.

He's been published in a series of anthologies and has published many full-length science fiction novels. His writing goal is to provide his readers with stories they cannot put down and he takes readers' suggestions seriously.

Notices about new books, free short stories, opinion posts, and preview pages for many of his books can be found on his author blog at
**EricMartellAuthor.com**

***

**<u>A request for you:</u>**

I make every effort to ensure your reading experience is enjoyable. This involves multiple editing steps, interior book layout, design, and using a professional cover artist/designer. Even so, it is becoming more difficult to find readers. If you liked this book, please leave a review and tell your friends.

Reviews may be left on the platform of your choice or emailed directly to me through my blog.

**Thank you,**

**Eric Martell**

Venice, 2021

# Also By Eric S. Martell

**<u>The Time Equation Series</u>**

Heart of Fire Time of Ice

Paradox: On the Sharp Edge of the Blade

All the Moments in Forever

Time Enough to Live

All Things in Time

**<u>The Belter Series</u>**

The Pirates of the Asteroids

The Belter Revolution

**<u>Cyber-Magic Series</u>**

CyberWitch

Nano-Magic

**<u>The Gaia Ascendant Trilogy</u>**

The Time of The Cat

Second Wave

Confederation

**<u>Other Books</u>**

Dustfall

Asterats and Other Stories